This book is dedicated to all the friends and fam... ... ... storm. Who stood by me when all the chips were down and my life seemed over. Particularly my mother Debra and my sister Denae, who were the lighthouses who guided my mind back to the shores of health and happiness. I will forever be eternally grateful for everything you all did to save me.

Grandma Louella,

You are my enduring example of class, intelligence, and womanhood. I love you with all of my heart. Thank you for raising me into the man I am today.

David Chappell

Age of the Great Prophets

David Chappell

Copyright 2016

ISBN-13:

978-0692812785 (Createspace)

ISBN-10:

0692812784

Chapter 1

Since the beginning of time, man has tried to find God, and many found the Lord through organized religion. With each new religion and each new adaptation, we are always reaching to be closer to Him. The pursuit of God was purely spiritual for the majority of our human history, until the introduction of science to human society. With the onset of science, man felt he could surpass the limitations of faith by uncovering the real truth behind the natural circumstances of this world. As time has passed on, science has become bolder and bolder in its attempt to usurp the knowledge of the world from the Lord. Through trial and error, man has come closer and closer to uncovering the physical secrets of the world and creation.

In 1952, a provisional research organization was founded in Europe. This organization was founded with a mandate of creating a world class physics research organization. In 1954, the organization we know today as the European Organization for Nuclear Research (CERN) was founded. Its core mission was purely physics research, focusing on understanding the atom. CERN's main area of research is particle physics, the study of the essential constituents of matter and the forces acting between them. It was truly an international research effort, with twenty European member states such as Great Britain, France, Germany, Italy and Switzerland. In addition, there are six countries, Israel, the United States, Japan, India, Turkey, and Russia with observer status. With its goal of understanding the essence of matter and the universe, CERN began building Colliders in Europe. The first, built in 1971, was the Intersecting Storage Rings (ISR). The ISR and its subsequent seven Colliders were built to create atomic collisions in order to examine the reaction. These collisions were designed to recreate the events of the Big Bang when atomic particles crashed into each other at high levels of speed leading to the creation of new and diverse particles. As the Colliders that CERN built became progressively stronger, they were better able to recreate the original conditions of the Big Bang.

Most Colliders were only able to observe the particles that make up most of the physical world but the newest Collider, called the Large Hadron Collider (LHC), was designed to uncover the deeper secrets of the universe by uncovering the mystery of dark matter. Dark matter is a substance of the universe that we have never been able to see. We can detect the presence of dark matter in the universe by examining its gravitational pull on foreign objects. Dark matter is everywhere but its detection has eluded physicists for decades. The LHC was designed to uncover the secrets of dark matter and dark energy, and perhaps possibly utilize these secrets for the benefit of mankind. However, humans have not considered the resulting effects of uncovering such an elusive natural phenomenon.

The 30th Congressional District of Texas was created in 1993. Since its creation, there has been one congressional representative, Eloise Myers, to be elected out of this district. Myers has a strong tradition of politics in her family. Her uncle was a Texas state senator and her cousin is a city council member in Dallas. With such a long tenure serving the city of Dallas and with such a strong political network surrounding her, it is hard to imagine that anyone could knock her off her post.

The district is mostly made up of Blacks and Hispanics. With Congresswoman Myers securing the majority of the black vote just by the nature of her race, it would be difficult for the opposing Republican Party to find someone who could create enough of a spark among Hispanics, Whites, and Independents to win the ballot. The current Democratic administration is struggling to keep its message afloat amid a miserable global economy. The United States is recovering from a recession that impacted the economy and society on all levels. Despite continuous efforts to reverse the economic conditions, the President was just unable to make a noticeable impact.

Several candidates came forward for the Republican primary. One was a retired school teacher who did work as a community organizer for the Dallas metro area. Another was a local businessman who had 30 years of experience in the private sector. Although these candidates were somewhat viable for the election, it was a young upstart state senator named Jose Valdez who really caught the public's attention.

Jose had been waiting for a chance to run for Congress for the last few years. He was a first-term state senator, and at 27, he was young, fresh, radical, and new on the national stage. At 6'4, he stood taller than most politicians. He was bilingual and multi-ethnic. His mother legally arrived from Guatemala when her parents moved to Texas in 1965. His father was a Mexican car technician who had dated Jose's mother for two years before attempting to leave town shortly after she got pregnant. On his flight away from town, Jose's mother said the man got in a car accident and lost his life. He had no family in the United States but Jose's mother never bothered searching Mexico for his name, Francisco Basurto. Jose's mother said that in order to get across the border he became a drug mule. This was something that always shamed Jose. His mother was a hotel maid and a school janitor who worked 14-hour days just to make sure Jose had clothes for school and food on the table. Her parents passed away in 1980 and 1983, leaving her alone to raise Jose, born in 1989.

Although it was a tough life, Jose was able to succeed in school due to his unnatural intelligence. Jose was gifted from a young age in all subjects, and was also a very social child. He ran for student body president and won every year in elementary school. With his height, he was also a naturally gifted basketball player, and from middle school onward, was the star point guard on his team. When he wasn't studying he was always on the local basketball court working on his game. Being a Hispanic ball player growing up in urban Dallas did not deter him; it only motivated him. He balanced playing basketball with his other extracurricular activities which mostly revolved around school organizations: school president, head of the audio-visual club, and also a member of the theatre club.

His mother recognized his early interest in politics and pushed him toward it. She would take him on visits to the state capital and the Mayor's office when she had time off during the weekend. He loved being the center of social attention, being in charge, and making decisions. He managed to stay active in and out of school all while keeping his grades at the top of his class. His efforts on the basketball court and in school gave him the opportunity to choose several schools for both athletic and academic scholarships. He was ranked the third best point guard high school prospect in Texas after leading his team to the state championship game in his senior season. He eventually chose the University of Texas at Austin for a full ride scholarship. His mother was both proud of and grateful for his hard work.

Keeping in tradition with his love of leadership, he also got involved in college politics. He ran for one of the university-wide representative positions his freshman year and won, providing him opportunities to network with fellow students. Over the years he acquired a large task-force of friends whom he could leverage in future years. He also took part in a paid internship during the summer after his freshman year with the Congressional Hispanic Caucus. This internship placed him at the nation's capital, where he worked in the office of a Hispanic representative. This internship was perfect for him. He relished in the experience, soaking in as much information and making as many contacts on Capitol Hill as he possibly could.

He was completely hooked on politics. He declared his major as pre-law and political science, but he also took many philosophy and theology classes. Jose was growing up to become quite a force in the community. His service was a testament to his commitment to the under-served. He worked tirelessly on the weekends as a mentor for under-privileged youth and volunteered at a homeless center, where he spent a lot of time trying to uplift others in need. As he grew more into a man, he began to have a clear focus on his goal. He wanted to be great! Sure he wanted to help people and make a positive impact in people's lives, but he wanted to be in the best position possible to do that. He wanted to be on the city council, he wanted to be in the state senate, he wanted to be in Congress, and Lord willing, he would one day be the President.

Although his basketball career was flowering, he devoted all his free time to reading political theory and staying involved in the community however he could. With his hard studying he was targeted to graduate early. He interned for the Dallas City Council after his sophomore year and interned in the State Senate. His sophomore year he ran for Vice President of Internal Affairs and won with 59% of the vote. His junior year he ran and won the position of President. He was on the fast track to political power in the community. He was growing so influential and powerful on campus that his Dean took note of it and decided to invite him to a fundraising dinner for the university. This was his big opportunity to meet big players in the Texas financial and political world and he would make the most of it. He ended up meeting Ron L. Boone, an oil tycoon and a major player in Texas circles. Boone is a major Republican donor and his grandmother was also Guatemalan, so when Jose introduced himself and had a chance to talk with him for a short time, they immediately hit it off. You see, Jose is a Republican to the bone. He was always neutral growing up as a political lover, but after 9-11 his sentiments suddenly changed. He felt that Democrats had the wrong strategy with the war on terror and he was a major Bush supporter during his presidency. As a young Republican attending a donor's dinner hosted by a liberal college, it became a match made in heaven when he and Boone hooked up. It seemed like they talked for the entire engagement and by the end of the night Boone had found himself a fresh new face of the Republican Party.

At the end of his three years at UT Austin, Jose had a choice: a career in politics or a shot at a basketball career. With his extensive political experience, he was able to secure a job as an aide for the mayor of Houston. On the basketball floor his skills were improving. He was starting and gaining more attention around the league. His team had made the NCAA tournament for two years in a row now. Though the lure of a basketball career was strong, he felt dedicated to his pursuit of public life. He had put in so much work for what seemed like his entire life. So now that he had a foot in the door he was going to take it.

He accepted the position as Assistant to the Mayor of Houston and applied to attend the University of Houston, College of Law. It was a three-year program and the night classes were perfect for his schedule in the Mayor's office. So Jose worked hard at school and worked hard as the mayor's assistant. He was responsible for everything involving the mayor. He edited his speeches, kept him on schedule, drove him around, and did basically anything the mayor needed. Being at the mayor's side at all times, except during school, gave him much recognition in the community. He was tall, good looking, well spoken, and hard working. He was also bilingual which helped in a community with a large amount of Hispanics.

At the end of his second year at school and his second year in the Mayor's office, the chief of staff left for another job leaving the position vacant. After holding many interviews with several viable candidates, the Mayor decided to stay in the office and promote Jose to the position. It felt like all his hard work was paying off and he was turning himself into an accomplished and promising young politician. However, he wanted much more than what he had and he wanted it soon. He felt like he had the skills to do so much more than he was doing. He was ready to take it to the next level. So he started voicing his opinion to his friend Boone.

Boone had always thought Jose would be a great candidate for public office. And with his background, his work experience, and his J.D., he felt like he could position him to make a run for something. They thought about City Council and they thought about Mayor, but no, Jose didn't want that. He wanted to be a Congressman, so he wanted his next step to only propel him to that level. He was motivated by his love of people and his compassion for the underserved, but he had an itch in him that just had to be scratched. He wanted to be the best and he did not care how he had to do it.

The incumbent Republican in the Texas Senate District 23 was retiring, leaving an opening for a run on the Republican ticket for Jose. Though lacking real life experience, Jose was more than prepared to run for this position based on his political skill and good looks. Boone and his close friends were his main backers, but Jose was able to make a tremendous impact on the campaign fundraising trail himself. He raised good money, produced a good primary campaign, and managed to defeat his Republican rivals. Now with the ticket in his control, he focused his energy on his Democratic opponent. There were radio ads, television ads, and bus stop photos. No expense was spared for this election bid. Jose's name rose like a phoenix in the mouths of local Dallas constituents. He had a unique flare about him that brought attention to his message and his goals. He wanted to increase border security to prevent illegal immigration, reduce the spending in the Texas government, improve the poor education rates in Texas, and most importantly, combat the threat of terrorism in Dallas by shoring up the borders and increasing the security forces around key locations in the state. Jose was a young Republican but he was up-to-date on his talking points and had developed a nice reputation as the tough but smooth politician.

After a tough race Jose ended up winning the Texas Senate seat for District 23 in the heart of Dallas. He was moving up and moving fast in the world of politics. His term as state senator was marked by several successful bill sponsorships involving immigration, education, counter terrorism, and most importantly, border security. He was quickly making a name for himself as the premier young Hispanic Republican. He was the perfect prototype for the future of the Republican Party in a country with a growing number of Hispanic voters.

As the end of his term was fast approaching he had to make a decision on the next step to take. He was young, dynamic, and passionate. The voters connected to his promise for a different approach to politics. He was popular in Dallas and he was ready to take his newfound popularity to the next level. He decided to put his name in the hat for the upcoming Republican primary for the 30th Congressional seat of Texas.

This is where our story begins for Jose. It was election night, November 8, 2016. He had battled and won against his Republican primary running mates months prior, and after a hard fought battle against incumbent Eloise Meyers, he was anxious to hear the results which may or may not propel him into the national spotlight as the newest Congressman to come out of Texas.

James hadn't gotten that much sleep the night before. He had a deadline for eight that morning for a piece about UN sanctions on Iran. He grumbled as he rolled over away from the light sliding through the blinds in the window. It was just another day to him. Nothing felt exciting about his job right now. He was stuck behind a desk doing articles on international news. Although it was a great job out of college, James still expected much more from his job. He wanted to travel the world and report in the first person instead of from behind his desk. Unfortunately, there wasn't much of a demand for another international traveling reporter, so James had to just wait.

He enjoyed his job, he truly did. He worked hard his entire life to get to where he was. He had worked on the school newspaper since the fifth grade and never stopped all the way through college. He wrote about everything from sports to school affairs to politics. At 23, he had a lot of room to grow professionally.

Unfortunately, the most affordable and work accessible apartment complex in the area had its only unit left with a bedroom window facing the sunrise. It was only worth the pain on the mornings that he had to wake up early. He sat up and poured his legs off the side of the bed. He rose up from the bed and walked into the kitchen to make a cup of coffee. After he poured the water and replaced the grounds, he plopped onto a chair at the table and put his face into his cupped hands. Life was great in college. He had pretty women, fun friends, and a full ride scholarship. When he got out of school and got this job it just sucked the life out of him. He lost passion in his life because he lost passion in his work. James was determined and desperate for change in his professional life.

He finished making his coffee and turned on his laptop to re-read through his article to make some finishing touches. He spent the next 20 minutes or so reading through it. He liked what he saw and he sent it off. James had an ongoing assignment with Iran and the Middle East. Iran was going through demonstrations against their Theocratic Democracy. The rich in Iran were growing in prosperity ever since the international community ended sanctions. To regain some trust of the international community, Iran ended its self-constructed nuclear program for an internationally built and monitored nuclear energy program. It was the crowning achievement of United Nations' Secretary-General Lenz Krause.

After he sent in his assignment he got up and took a shower and got ready to head in to work. Dress code was fairly loose at his department but he always tried to wear a collared shirt and some nice dress shoes. He grabbed his laptop bag and his wallet and left the house. It was a chilly but sunny fall day in southern California. It was November and a cold front had just moved through so the weather was chilly but the sun was out and the sky was a shimmering blue. He got into his car and turned the ignition. James listened to all kinds of music but mostly hip hop. He flipped through his favorite stations as he started his car and took off down the street. The job was in a downtown office complex. The Los Angeles Galley was a small-time newspaper compared to the other big market papers in town. It was still a great job for James to have gotten out of college.

There were twenty-five other people on staff at the newspaper. The editor of the paper was named Kenneth Cruise. He was a real hard ass for quick deadlines and perfection in the staff's writing. All he cared about in the end was a greater audience for his paper. The newsprint market was drying up faster than a drop of sweat in an Arizona August, and as a result the paper was trying to branch out to reach a younger and more diverse demographic. Cruise made blog entries mandatory and required each member of the staff to have a public social media account. While he was a hard ass, he was reasonable and willing to take a chance on a good idea. James just had to find a way to utilize it.

He got to work about ten minutes early. "Hello, Melinda, how is your morning going?" Melinda was the front desk assistant. She was a red head with striking emerald eyes. "Hi, James, I think Charlie left a message for you." Charlie was the sports writer. He had taken James under his shoulder because they had gone to the same school. James said, "thank you" to Melinda and walked on past to his desk. James did not have an office yet but one day he hoped he would. He walked past the maze of about a dozen cubicles to his in the back corner. As James got to his cubicle and put down his laptop bag, Charlie came up to him from around the corner.

"Hey my brotha, how was getting in your article last night?" Charlie asked him.

"It went fine," James said. "I was ahead of schedule so I didn't have to stay up late. I just woke up as normal and sent it in the morning."

Charlie had an approving smirk on his face and shook his head. "Good to hear," he said. "I've got a load of work to do here. The second half of the college football season has been crazy. The Pac 12 has so many good teams, and USC is definitely hanging right in there. There has been a high demand on a lot of Trojans articles but their new coach is a real son of a bitch. He has closed practices and hates answering questions from the media. It's making it real hard to do my job under so much pressure."

James looked at him with an evil smirk on his face, "Couldn't happen to a nicer guy," and then he lightly punched Charlie on the shoulder.

"Thanks for the support there, buddy," Charlie sarcastically responded. James started to unpack his laptop and plugs and get ready to start researching for his next article. The Middle East was on fire. Lebanon,

Turkey, and Iran were having massive protests in the street over wages and jobs.

Charlie stayed around chatting with James for a few more minutes before he had to go back to his desk to start making phone calls. James settled into his desk and started researching. Just as he was getting into a good groove, a man poked his head around the corner. "James, are you busy?"

The tall white man with the black business suit and screaming gray tie barged into his cubicle without waiting for the proper invite. "I read your article James, and I must say I was very impressed. Your work has been coming along quite nicely here in your first few months. Keep up the good work and maybe you can move up the chain on the stories we got coming in here. Susan and Daniel get the majority of the international news assignments but I can see that you will be competing with them soon enough."

James looked up from his work and acknowledged the man and his seemingly sincere compliments. The man was Kenneth Cruise. "Thank you very much. I am just trying to do my best," James replied with a forced smile.

As much as James appreciated Cruise's work and the opportunity to succeed here, he was still eager to get more hands-on assignments. Susan was currently in Israel covering the rash of suicide bombers attacking Jerusalem. Daniel was in China covering the rising tensions in the South China Sea and he also had been on assignment in South Korea covering North Korean war games.

James was patient though. He knew if he continued producing high quality work that Cruise would eventually give him more intense and hands-on assignments. "Keep up the good work," Cruise said, as he left.

James felt good about his place in the company for being so young, but James did not want his youth to be a reason for Cruise to hold him back.

James knew that all he needed was one break to make a splash. He knew his reporting and writing skills were top notch, and that if he just had the one story to break him through he knew he could make it to the big time. But for now James just got settled in his seat and got back to researching the Middle East. James didn't know exactly what was coming but he could feel there was something big about to change that would give him his opportunity.

Chapter 2

The streets were lined with vehicles as Jose pulled up in his limo. His campaign manager, Bill, pulled around back of the civic center to get exclusive parking for the hopeful young Texas state senator. "You never want to be late to your own party," Jose said with a cautious smile. It's not that Jose was pessimistic; he just knew that the chances of him pulling this out were slim with such a strong opponent. What Jose needed was faith that God would place him exactly where he needed to be. He had faith in himself and faith in his efforts, but his faith in the Lord had all but waned away in the past few years. "The polls close in an hour, so that gives you plenty of time to relax and talk with your staff, volunteers, and constituents before the final tally comes in."

The town car had a television in the back seat that Bill and Jose were watching intently. All the major political networks were hinting victory for the male Republican businessman from Boston. "I can't believe Mark Knight is going to pull this out," exclaimed Jose. "It bodes well for me if he keeps hanging in there in the polls."

His communications director was waving them into the opening in the back of the building. She waved him right up into the parking spot waiting for them. She seemed anxious as she leaned in to open the car door. Exit polls had undoubtedly been out for the last few hours but Jose had not taken a look at any of them. Sharon opened the door with a smile of relief. "We all have been waiting for you."

Jose knew he had been a little late but it was important for him to take some time to himself before he showed up at the election party. Maybe it would be easier on him if the results were clear-cut but the polls had the vote pretty much split for basically the entire election season.

Jose pulled himself out of the car and proceeded behind Sharon as she walked into the corridor that led to the back door of the complex. He turned around to face Bill as he walked up behind him. "Does everything look good?" Jose asked as he was adjusting his tie.

"You look fine, Jose," Sharon assured him. "This is your big moment, kid. The stars have aligned for your success tonight, and I can feel it."

Jose took these words to heart and turned back toward Sharon who was waiting at the door holding it open for him to get there. "Channel 4 and 12 reporters are here and they want a chance to talk to you to get some statements about your feelings on the exit polls. Right now they are slightly in your favor for most of the major polling companies at around 52% to 48%," Sharon said as she guided him through the door with her hand on his back.

As Jose stepped through the door, the crowd seemed to turn and face him all at once and began clapping. It was a tender and heartfelt moment for all of those involved in the campaign. They all had worked so hard to get to this moment: countless hours of phone calls, canvassing the district, letter stuffing for each and every young volunteer and staff member. Jose walked forward to greet his supports and raised his hands to his chest in thanks for their hard work and determination.

Jose did not consider himself an overly emotional person. He was focused and determined in situations like these, not emotional about the care and admiration he had for his supporters. Jose knew he had a destiny to fulfill to be great and that he needed dedicated people like this in order to make that happen. As the clapping subdued Jose made his way over to the reporters for a statement on camera. They were huddled in the corner of the room talking amongst themselves about the election and how it was coming to a close after months of campaigning. Sharon walked up first and announced that everyone would need to make a semi-circle in order for everyone to get a good shot of the budding young state senator.

A seasoned reporter named Cain Dillenger was the first to have his question in once the cameras and the lights were set up on Jose. "Early results are showing a tight race between you and the Congresswoman. How is your confidence right now, Jose?"

Turning on that surefire charm, Jose put on a half-smile and responded with a chest full of confidence. "I feel great about the vote tonight. I can't rely on fate to determine my success. I feel as though my staff, the volunteers, and I put in the work necessary to pull out a close victory tonight."

The crowd pushed and shoved each other vocally to get in their next question. Sly Douglas, a reporter from Channel 4, was up to the task. "The minority vote was important in this race being that you are Hispanic and the member is African-American. Do you feel you were better able to appeal to constituents outside of the race and even into your opponent's pool of voters?"

Jose calmly responded, "I feel this race was one that stretched beyond the limitations of ethnicity or gender. This was a race about policy, and who was better able to relay their message to the problems of Dallas residents, both black and brown."

Jose felt confident with these questions but his mind was floating off elsewhere. The polls were almost closed and Jose was ready to see what the results would be as they came in over the next hour or so. The questions were over quickly and Jose thanked the reporters for all of their hard work during the election.

Bill, seeing that they were finished, came up to him and said that maybe it was best for him to go around and meet with his supporters in the hour leading up to his celebration or concession speech. Jose walked around the civic center for the next hour shaking hands and talking with supporters and volunteers.

The polls were now closed and the precincts began reporting. With 5% in, Congresswoman Meyers only led by 123 votes. Jose knew it was going to be tight the entire night. Everyone did. So the entire building was in for the long haul. Another few minutes passed by and more precincts were reporting that it was still a virtual tie. Jose continued to make small talk with his friends and family while the precincts came slowly trickling in. His mother came up to him amid the tension of the polls coming in. "Jose, how are you feeling my dear?" she said with a concerned look on her face. Jose was seemingly keeping it cool for everyone else, but his mother could always tell when he was truly bothered.

Jose leaned in to speak to his comparatively short mother, "For the first time since the fourth grade I feel nervous about an election. I am trying to hold it together, but I really want this."

She looked at him with warm, loving eyes and said, "My dear if the good Lord wills it, then it shall be so. Always believe in Him and He will never let you down, even when things seem impossible."

Religion did not play first on the team of his life. It came off the bench in the second quarter. With his career as a politician, religion was only important for votes. "You are right, Mother," he responded earnestly with a renewed sense of optimism in his voice. "I must have faith in myself that I did all I could to pull this through."

Jose's mother looked at him somewhat disappointed and puzzled. "No, it is never about yourself, son. You must remember that. I know you have had plenty of success in your life and hard work has brought that to you, but always remember that it is God who truly allows your life to take shape into what it will become. Never forget that, no matter what success comes your way."

Jose loved his mother very much and appreciated her kind words. It's not so much that he took heart in her spiritual words of faith; he took heart in her honest belief that God would look out for him. That was all he needed to take a moment and pull himself together as he prepared to make more rounds.

"Thank you, Mother, I love you. I hope one day I can have as much faith as you do."

Carmela moved to him and kissed him on the cheek. "God will undoubtedly test your faith one day and I know you will be ready to face the challenge."

He gave his mother a grateful smile and turned to find Sharon, who instantly appeared next to him. "Fifty percent of the polls are now in," she said. "The vote is still within 100 votes."

"Thanks for the update," Jose said, giving Sharon a tight smile. All indications were that it would be a close race but no one expected it to be this much of a nail biter. Jose was pacing through the room trying to keep a positive mood in everyone's hearts and minds as well as keep his own composure as the votes kept coming in. "It looks like Mark Knight is going to be elected President by a wide margin," said Bill. Great news for Jose because no one saw it coming.

"Good for me, great for the party," Jose said to Bill.

Eighty percent of the vote was in, and Jose had gone up a few hundred votes. The night was wearing on and the crowd was beginning to grow more optimistic with Jose pulling ahead as of late. Eighty-five percent was in and Jose was growing in his lead. These late precincts were all showing favor to the young state senator. If it kept going along these lines he could shore up his victory soon.

Jose looked up from a conversation and saw Sharon approaching. He excused himself and turned to her.

"We have ninety-percent of the vote in," she said. "You're up by 600 or so votes."

Jose walked over to the television. Though it may not seem like a lot, because the vote had been close all night it seemed like this vote lead would put Jose over the top. Everyone was glued to the television to see if the national news stations would finally call their hotly contested battle. Gerald Eagle, the host of one of the hour long daily shows on the liberal leaning political network, came on the screen with a special announcement. "Out of the District 30 in Texas it has been a close race all night between incumbent Democrat Eloise Myers and Republican Jose Valdez, but we can finally call a winner."

The crowd all came quiet at once. You could almost hear the heart beats in unison as the cautiously optimistic crowd leaned to hear what they had been waiting all night to hear. "With 95% of the precincts reporting, the young state senator pulled ahead of the incumbent and we feel comfortable enough to call Jose Valdez your next Congressmen representing District 30 of Texas."

The crowd erupted into a frenzy of cheers, clapping, and shouts of joy. All the work they had done had not been in vain. Carmela, Jose's mother, raised her hands in the air and shouted, "Thank the Lord! All praise be to Him!"

Just as the other cable news networks were reporting the victory, Bill got a call on his cell phone from Eloise Meyers. Bill walked over to Jose and handed him the phone, "Representative Meyers is on the phone for you," said Bill with an accomplished wide grin on his face.

"Hello, Eloise, it is nice to hear from you," Jose said into the phone.

"Yeah, I bet it is with the news you must have heard," Eloise said.

Jose smiled and relished in the joy of the moment. It had been a tough campaign between these two warriors. Now it was finally over. Eloise continued, "I am calling to congratulate you on your victory. I concede my seat to you." There was a small pause as she gathered herself. "I know you will be great. You have so much potential, young man."

Jose really appreciated these words. The campaign had crossed the line of civility several times, and it meant a lot to him that she would compliment him in such a way. "Just remember to use your newfound success for the good of the people, not just for the good of yourself. The bright lights can change people. I see it every year with freshman members. Just remember to stay true to yourself and you just might stand a chance to save your soul in that city."

Jose chuckled lightly at the last part of her remark. "Thank you, Eloise, but I am confident that nothing can shake me from my commitment to being a good person."

Eloise openly laughed but quickly subdued herself to respond. "Son, you have no idea what you are in for." She sounded grave and somber with this remark. Jose wondered to himself how she could be so negative after spending so much time on the Hill in her own career. "Good luck, Jose."

"Thank you."

Jose said goodbye to the former Congresswoman and handed the phone back to Bill. "Do you have your victory speech ready, Jose?"

Jose thought for a second and patted his hands against his pants pockets. He didn't find it there. Then he reached inside his suit jacket and found it in the inside pocket folded up. "Here it is. Are we ready for it now?" It was just then that Jose saw him enter the civic center. In the mass of people, he did not know why he stood out so much, but because he came in so late it brought something to Jose's attention. He was tall, with a strong build, in a long black trench coat. His bald head shined in the lights from above. Jose went back to the task at hand, thinking that the man was just a strange aberration in the crowd of excited supporters.

Everyone was coming up to Jose wishing him congratulations as he was preparing for his victory speech. It was hard for him to get a clear mind with so many people vying for his attention. "Are you ready for the speech?" Bill asked.

"Yes I am ready," Jose said as he made his way to the podium.

"Remember to take your time. This is your big moment."

Jose took a moment to scan over his prepared speech to get comfortable with the tone and pace.

When Jose got his composure together he stepped up to the podium and calmed the crowd. "Thank you everyone, thank you." He raised his hand to quiet the crowd as he began his speech. "We are here today because we are hopeful for something new to change this country. We are all here because we believed, against all odds, that America has a better vision for prosperity and success."

Jose was really in a groove with his speech. As he continued, his eyes scanned the crowd and he noticed the tall white man in the trench coat he had seen enter earlier. It was so strange to Jose. It looked like he was looking at two different places at once, like a chameleon. Jose stumbled in his speech slightly to catch his breath and blink his eyes to take a second look. Upon the second look the strange, tall man looked normal. Jose continued with his victory speech, taking his glance from the strange man. "We need less government control in our lives. We do not need people in D.C. trying to tell us what to do here in Dallas. We are here because we believe in individual success. We believe in hard work, in each other, and America should be for Americans." Jose was really revving up the crowd, compelling them into cheers of "Jose! Jose!"

As the speech came to a close, Jose scanned the crowd and he noticed a glimmering sparkle in the light reflecting from the overhead fixtures in the crowd. As his eyes adjusted to where the source of the metal was, he saw it was shining from the man in the trench coat. Jose looked even closer, and he noticed a silver chromed pistol. The man and Jose made eye contact as Jose stopped mid-sentence. Jose did not know how to react and he waited to see what the man was planning on doing. Bill looked over to see what Jose was staring at, and saw the gun.

The man turned away from Jose on the platform and pointed the gun toward the crowd. The gun went off! One shot! Two shots! The crowd began screaming and running toward the exits. Bill ran up toward the new Congressman to try and get him off the stage. This only drew the attention of the lone gunman. A blast went out and Bill hit the floor. Jose was kneeling down behind the podium. He looked around to see the shooter turn his attention away from him temporarily and back toward the crowd. Jose took this brief opportunity of chaos and made a run and jumped headfirst toward the gunman. The man saw Jose with what seemed like one eye, and turned quickly to take aim at the Congressman-to-be.

Blast!

Yet another shot rang out from the extended clipped pistol as Jose dove toward the pale, white gunman. The bullet tore through Jose's shoulder as he landed on the gunman. He knocked the gun from his hand and a struggle ensued. The man and Jose wrestled and threw punches, fighting to get back toward the gun. Jose ignored the tremendous pain in his shoulder as he fought for his life. Jose punched the shooter square in the nose, breaking it. The man fell back on his back and covered his nose. This was Jose's chance. With his good hand he reached out for the gun and grabbed it. Before the assailant could recover from the blow Jose turned the gun on him.

Jose pointed the gun at him and looked him in the eyes as he gathered himself. Jose saw the man's eyes, which grew in size and turned canary yellow with thin black lines sporadically jetting out from the black center. Jose thought he was seeing things, but recomposed himself.

"Stop!" shouted.

But the assailant, with a devilish expression on his face, made a leap at Jose. Jose pulled the trigger, aiming right at his chest. The bullet ripped into his body and the man screamed and fell back on the floor, stopping his assault on the new Congressman and his supporters. Jose, bleeding profusely and in pain from the shoulder, slumped against the wall and passed out waiting for the cops and the ambulance to arrive.

Renowned American scientist and Professor Frederick Slater was one of the best the world had to offer. He had the smarts, the charisma, and the work ethic. Frederick, or Freddy, mumbled to himself as he ate his bagel. He stayed in a rental studio on the outskirts of Geneva, Switzerland, about thirty minutes from the main laboratory. Freddy was an excellent astrophysicist. At the age of thirty-one he was still young in the field. Despite his age, he had already published four books on his scientific theories on dark matter. Freddy grabbed the flash drive with his presentation on it as he was throwing on his jacket. All he needed was his phone and his wallet and he was set to ride on one of the most important days in his career. The phone rang on his way out of the door.

"I'm in a hurry, Lawrence, I have my presentation in an hour and fifteen minutes and it takes an hour to get there." Lawrence was Freddy's childhood friend from Greeley, Colorado, where they both grew up together. They both attended the University of Colorado in Boulder.

"Is this really going to change the world, Freddy?"

"I hope so, Lawrence. This is my life's work. I think I finally figured out why we haven't been able to recreate the Big Bang."

"I know you tell me that. I wish I understood more about the science behind it."

Freddy closed the door, locked it, and then hurried down the stairs, breathing in short bursts as he ran to his car. "Well the science behind it is complicated, but essentially I think I have figured out how the universe was created. I have unlocked the secrets behind dark matter. I really do not have time to explain it all to you. I have tried to explain it to you several times but you always check out half way through."

Lawrence knew he was right, but he wanted to care because he knew it was important to his friend. "Well I know you say it will create a new power source and you have all the materials to detect it and use it, but you said you need a sample first, right?"

Freddy jumped into his rental car and started driving out of town. Geneva was truly a beautiful city, one of the most beautiful in the world. Even though the snow-capped sparkling mountains of Colorado were breathtaking to Freddy, the mountains and landscape of Switzerland had no rival. "Yes, you are right Lawrence, we need a sample."

He paused and took in the smell of the air. "I love it out here, Lawrence. Being brought on the staff was one of the best things to ever happen to me."

"I thought you missed being home; you were just complaining about missing the Buffs' football games the other day."

"Yeah I miss being home. I miss CU games, I miss the Broncos games, and I miss my family and my students, but the air is so sweet out here and the people are so friendly. I was spoiled growing up in Greeley but I am being spoiled out here right now."

Lawrence grumbled at the thought of his friend not coming home anytime soon. "Who the hell am I going to get to come listen to my music if you don't come home?"

"Ah yes, I forgot I was one of your only fans."

"Shut up, asshole," Lawrence said sternly. "Just because you think you are going to change the world doesn't mean you have the right to talk about my music. All we need is one big break and we can make it big. Maybe when you get famous we can be your official band and get some publicity."

Freddy laughed inside at this ridiculous statement. Think of a scientist with a theme song. "Sure whatever you say, Lawrence." He was focused on weaving down the highway as he was talking to his friend.

"So this thing is really going to change the world huh, buddy?"

"Only if it works my friend, only if it works. If it all goes as planned I want it to end hunger and poverty."

"Whoa dude that is quite a lofty goal."

"That is what I want, Lawrence. That is what this is all for." Freddy paused as he passed a big semi on 3 lane highway.

"Well I called to wish you good luck. I know today is your big day, buddy."

"Thanks, friend. I am going to need it. Now I need to get off the phone before I crash."

They said good bye to each other and Freddy went speeding down the highway toward the laboratory. He got there with some time to spare.

"It is a big day today, Frederick." It was Henry Hangruler, one of his colleagues. "Everyone has been talking about this presentation that is going to reveal the way to discover dark matter. I sincerely have my doubts."

Henry was not what you would call a rival because everyone there was working toward a common goal, but Freddy and Henry did not have the greatest working relationship.

"Well it excited you enough to be waiting in the parking lot for me to get here," Freddy shot back as he slammed the car door and walked toward the building.

Henry had a wrinkled look on his face at this smart remark. "I was merely here to wish you good luck, comrade." Henry spoke English fluently but he had a heavy German accent. Freddy actually thought they might be good friends because his grandfather had been from Germany, but alas, Americans are not quick to make friends when visiting Europe. Especially Americans who think they have all the answers. Being a hotshot young scientist had it setbacks for Freddy. "If the rumors are true, and you really did find a way to find dark matter, then not only me, but the entire world, will be in gratitude."

"Well I only have a theory right now. Let's wait and see if they even approve my testing before we move any further."

"Well you are the great American, brought here to save us paltry Europeans just like you have done several times before. Whatever would we do without our great American saviors?" Freddy could tell Henry was being facetious now and he quickly dismissed him as they walked together toward the entrance.

"Just wait and see if I am right," Freddy said. "I am claiming to be no one's savior."

"I will definitely be waiting to see."

Freddy walked into the board room. Everyone was standing around chatting. The air was abuzz with excitement. When the board elected to bring in the young American scientist, they never thought he would be producing the answers to their questions so quickly. He had only been on staff here for three months, and he was far exceeding their expectations with his research and theories. The lead scientist, Alfred Linchkin, greeted him and placed a hand on his back in warm welcome.

"We have all been patiently waiting, Professor Slater. Please come to the front; everything is set up and ready for you."

All eyes were on Freddy as he walked through the board room to the middle of the table where the screen had been set up. He put the flash drive into the computer, opened his briefcase with the supporting documents, and then handed them out around the board room table.

After everyone had taken a seat the young professor uploaded his power point and prepared to begin his presentation. "Now as we know, the Large Hadron Collider can operate at up to 7 teraelectronvolts, or TeV, per beam. The current record for a collision is between two 3.5 TeV beams. Now, what many of us think is that we will uncover the secrets behind the Big Bang, dark energy, and dark matter, by increasing the energy per beam."

Freddy gathered his thoughts. "I am here to tell you that I came up with a theory as to why that is not how to solve the problem. You see, we have all been under the assumption that there was one big bang that flung particles at each other at a high rate of speed, which created one large collision. I am here to tell you that there were two big bangs, in rapid succession of one another, and that is why we have been unable to recreate the conditions of the big bang. If we create two successive atomic collisions at a TeV rate which I have calculated to be within our current range of operations, then we will be able to recreate the origin of existence and create dark matter.

"I have created two devices which will help with the uncovering and collection of dark matter. The first of which are special gravitational distortion goggles. When they are charged, it can give a read out of the unseen gravitational pull in the air. If there is a substance distorting the natural pull of earth's gravity, then the goggles will be able to pick that up. The second device is a special Dark Matter Magnet Vacuum, or DMMV, designed to extract and hold dark matter. In order to attract the dark matter out of physical objects, we must use a small sample of dark matter in the combustion magnet that will draw other samples of dark matter into the machine slowly. You will be able to increase and decrease the rate of suction by increasing the energy output of the combustion magnet."

The crowd gasped at these revelations. How in the world could this man have found a way to discover dark matter and a way to utilize dark energy all on his own? "I can tell by your reaction that you are highly skeptical of my findings but rest assured, I have tested and retested my theories. By my calculations on gravitational pull on the earth's surface, there is dark matter located somewhere on this planet. I have calculated that there are two places on Earth that are distorting the earth's gravitational pull. All I need is a sample of dark matter to test my goggles and suction machine, and we will be able to detect it and collect it. Dark energy is everywhere in the universe as well. If we can harness the power of one sample of dark matter, we will be able to mine the universe of its natural occurrences."

The crowd was in a quiet murmur. This was groundbreaking news coming from the scientist. "I have calculated that with the use of my dark matter generator, we would be able to create power at a rate surpassing oil, coal, and natural gas combined. Its EROEI (energy returned on energy invested) is tremendously high. By my estimation, we should be able to find dark matter in the earth through detection. We should be able to find it in the dirt, in rocks, in trees, everywhere as long as there is a source. A source is a spot where dark matter has been absorbed into the environment. This can be found naturally occurring in outer space, but like I said, by my calculations we should be able to find it on Earth."

The young professor moved on to his final point. "I hope one day we will be able to create enough dark matter in this and other laboratories to fuel the world, but until then, we must make do with our hopeful sample and find it naturally occurring in the earth. If we can, we change the world. We can have a low-cost, highly efficient fuel source that will be able to power cars 100 times stronger and faster than they are today. Planes will fly faster, space shuttles will fly further and faster. With this energy we will change the world."

Alfred Linchkin, chairman and head scientist of the European Organization for Nuclear Research (CERN) staff at the Large Hadron Collider, was the first to step in and quiet the crowd after the end of the speech. "What a fantastic theory on dark matter and the Big Bang, Professor Slater. However, you must know that two successive blasts from our atomic cores will almost undoubtedly cause a meltdown of some sort. Do you really expect us to risk weeks, months, and maybe years of repair for your grand experiment?"

The professor, knowing this question would come, calmly addressed the clamoring crowd. "I know that my theory is correct. It is based on years of my research. There were in fact two big bangs in rapid succession. If we continue with research as is, we will be wasting all of our time and millions of publicly funded dollars."

The crowd began yelling at him, "This is crazy!" "How can we afford the risk?" "Is it really possible that there were two big bangs? How come no one has come up with this theory before?"

Amid all of the questions, Professor Slater calmly raised his hand to quiet the crowd. "If this experiment does not go as I foresee it to go, then I will calmly gather my supplies and move back to America, never to bother any of you ever again. I will even help pay for any damage my experiment may cause."

With that Henry chimed in, "Give him what he wants. What is the worst that could happen? If he succeeds then we change the world. If he fails, we lose time on repairs but we can focus our energy back on our original theories. I say give him a chance."

Freddy knew that this veiled endorsement was just a way for Henry to gain more control over the study if a failed experiment led to his departure.

"Well, as chairman and lead scientist of this operation, I say that based on the information I am reading it would be worth a try," Alfred said as he scanned the pages. "No one has ever theorized a second bang, and if it is correct, it could answer why we have yet to have any kind of breakthrough. Prepare the machine for testing tomorrow."

Freddy was elated that all his hard work, and his kind relationship with Alfred, had finally paid off. Freddy announced, "I promise none of you will be let down."

Freddy went to his office and did more sample tests for the rest of the day, in preparation for the test tomorrow. He got home at around 3:30 a.m. Geneva time, which was early evening in Colorado. He called his girlfriend. "Hey honey, how are you doing?" he said casually, as if nothing big was going on.

"I was waiting for your call all day. How was your presentation?"

"It was great. They accepted that my ideas were a possibility and they are setting up the corridor for two successive beams tomorrow."

"That's great news darling! How are you not excited? If you are right it could change the world."

Freddy was happy but he knew what the stakes were. He staked his entire reputation in the academic community on a hunch he had. "I said if the experiment failed I would leave and come back home. I feel like if it fails I would have to come back in shame. Shame for myself, shame for my country, and shame for my university, so I guess you could say that I am a bit nervous over this situation."

Jennifer Inna, the cheerleader, choir girl, and pastor's daughter, who was always positive, would have something to say that would cheer him up, Freddy thought to himself. She was always there by his side, ever since they met in college. "If what you say dark matter will do for the world is true, then it is worth a bad mark on your career. You can't be thinking about yourself right now. Think about progress. Think about our future with cheap, affordable energy for all men and women."

She was always a good person to talk to when he got down on himself. Freddy took her words to heart. "Thank you, dear. I appreciate the words. I just want everything to work out as I planned."

"It will, dear, it will."

Freddy had to go to sleep to get up for the test tomorrow so the couple said their goodbyes until they could talk the next day.

Freddy was up early from excitement for work that day. He got his things together and sped off for the laboratory. The air was crisp that morning as he cruised down the highway. It was as if the world was standing still in preparation of his impending discovery. Or maybe it was all just in his head and things would not be successful? Nevertheless, Freddy shook off his pessimistic thoughts and got his mind focused on the task at hand. He pulled up to his parking spot and got out into the laboratory to begin setting up.

Alfred came into Freddy's office as he was getting ready for the test. "We have set up the atomic shaft for two rapid successive shots. All preliminary tests show that it will undoubtedly disrupt the shaft and damage many super conducting magnets. However, the test should run successfully so let's hope your theory is correct."

Freddy looked up from his desk and said quite confidently, "It will work. I have no doubts."

"How can you be so sure of your success?"

"Because I just know it. Call it intuition, call it confidence, hell you can even call it faith if you believe in that sort of nonsense, but I know it will work."

Freddy stood up and approached the older scientist. "God has been keeping the universe a secret from us for far too long. It is time for humans to move beyond the limitations of faith and take the universe under our control. In order to do that we must figure out how it all started. I have dedicated my life to this goal and I am sure that we are on the precipice of historic success."

Alfred put his arm around Freddy's shoulder, bringing him for a close embrace. "I remember when I was a strong Christian once."

Freddy was shocked. "You? A devout Christian? How could you be with all the knowledge you have of the universe?"

"I know it is hard to comprehend how such an ardent scientist could still have had such a devotion to an unseen and unknown being, but it is true. I was God fearing and God loving in my youth. As I have grown older I have come to realize that God is only within ourselves. The universe is so vast and undiscovered that there could be anything out there, but I believe God has given us the power to determine and shape our own destiny."

Freddy walked back to his desk to show Alfred his prototype goggles. "Are those the gravitational distortion goggles?"

"Yes, they are," Freddy replied cautiously.

He had yet to really have a chance to test his goggles in the field but everything on his readouts showed they should work. "Here take your pair. I only have ten here, but I have forty more in the cabinet."

Alfred took the pair of goggles and tried them on. "Not exactly made for their looks," Alfred said as he put the hulking battery charged goggles onto his face.

"I used to be a Christian too," Freddy said as he kept unpacking his goggles and testing the battery power on each one.

"Oh yeah? What happened?" Alfred asked.

"I watched my grandmother go to church her entire life. She was healthy, devout, and always so positive about God and heaven and Jesus. Then she was diagnosed with Alzheimer's and it wiped it all away. I saw her become a shell of her former self. She had no personality, no life in her soul. How could a loving God do that to one of His subjects? I just never understood how she could be a good Christian and go to heaven when she couldn't even remember her own name."

Alfred put the goggles in his pocket on his long white lab coat. "Well what you are about to do is prove that God did not exist. At the very least you are about to prove that what God did to create the universe can be replicated. I think it is safe to assume that whatever ounce of faith you may have had stored in your body will be gone after you make your discovery today," said Alfred.

Freddy replied, "I can see how you think that but there is still always a part of me that wants to be faithful to something. My girlfriend is just so devout. She was raised in the church, her father is a pastor. I see how happy and fulfilling it makes her life and I want that for myself sometimes. The only thing that fulfills me is my work and pushing myself and humanity to its limits."

"Never give up on yourself, Professor Slater, but beware. If there is a god, and you are uncovering his secrets, I am sure he will not be too happy with you."

"Yeah but if there is a god and I am uncovering something wrong, then wouldn't he, with all his power, come down here and stop me from doing it?"

"Not if you were supposed to find it. Remember that we have God inside of ourselves not hovering from above. God is working through you to complete a task. Maybe instead of thinking about the fact you are uncovering His secrets, you are instead revealing His greatness to the world and for humanity to share. You could be saving the world from itself," said Alfred.

Freddy finished all his prep work and was ready for the test which was scheduled to begin in 20 minutes. "I can only hope that what I am doing will save the world and not destroy it. If there is a god, he knows I do this only for the furtherance of humanity and human existence."

"Well only time will tell what your future holds, Freddy. Now let's go run this test and change the world," Alfred said as he pulled Freddy up from his chair and wrapped his arm around his back again. "I know this will work. It has to work. The world has been waiting for the next great discovery for years now. This will change everything."

Freddy brought the box of goggles to the examination room with Alfred by his side. Where the examination room was stationed in the corridor was where the collision should take place. There was a large glass two-paned window that covered one side of the wall in the room. There were two large tables that hung below large square ceiling lights. Several computers were lining the tables, beaming with live statistics from the corridor's receptors. Five scientists including Freddy, Alfred, and Henry were in the examination room. The other scientists were Colleen Embers, from England, and Francis Monreaux, from France. They were both senior scientists and eagerly ready to support the young Freddy, should his experiment be a success.

A large countdown clock was fixated on the thin strip of wall above the large glass windows. It was locked on 5 minutes, awaiting word from the team of scientists that they were ready. Freddy went over and checked the computers one last time, and then signaled Colleen to begin the countdown. Colleen pressed the button on the control panel and the machines began warming up. "What do you expect us to see if it is a successful test, Professor Slater?" asked Professor Monreaux as he was fixating his goggles onto his face.

"I don't exactly know. I don't know how the impact will show up on the goggles, especially if dark matter is formed. Just be prepared to see a distortion in the air. It could show up as a solid matter in the goggles but be invisible to the naked eye without. Since it is all based on calculations I am not entirely sure."

The clock ran down to ten seconds and all of the scientists in the room huddled around the center window. "Here it comes," yelled Freddy tensely. The magnetic cannons that shoot the atoms made no noise as they shot off their payloads toward each other. Freddy calculated that the collision would take 3.23 seconds to happen, and then .32 seconds for the second collision to occur. Freddy counted out loud, "One! Two! Three!" At first there was nothing for a brief moment, but then there was a bright light that was emitted seemingly from nowhere.

It blinded the scientists, causing them to cover their eyes and look away. In a few seconds the light faded away and what was left was a glowing black object. It was a floating black sphere that distorted the air around it into waves like the kind you see in a heat wave. The scientists gasped at this discovery. Freddy had done it! He had discovered how to create dark matter. Freddy knew that this was only one half of a successful test. He would have to test his engine prototype.

"Congratulations, Professor!" exclaimed Colleen as she hugged the excited young scientist. "We need to find a way to extract it. I propose using a syringe with a tiny needle and sucking the dark matter out of the air."

Freddy was sure this would work because the dark matter was still a solid matter although it floated and was transparent to the naked eye. Freddy went to the door that led to the corridor and hurriedly walked through as the other four scientists waited on the other side of the glass. Freddy stepped carefully toward the dark matter, careful not to disrupt it. He gathered up the sample of dark matter successfully and walked backed to the testing room. There he had set up his small engine. He put some of the dark matter into two small vials, one to be tested by the staff, and another for the DMMV (Dark Matter Magnet Vacuum). The rest of the dark matter he planned on using for the dark energy engine.

Freddy walked up to his engine. He hands were sweating with the anticipation of what was going to come. If he had calculated his theory correctly, the engine should power on once the dark matter was introduced to the energy core and he flipped the switch. Freddy walked up to the engine and placed the needle in the opening to the energy core tank and he pressed in on the syringe to the release the dark matter. He flipped the switch to the machine and much to the pleasure of the young professor, the engine came on.

"You did it, Professor Slater, you did it!" yelled Alfred.

The room erupted into applause and everyone, even the skeptical Henry, gave Freddy a handshake and a hug. "We must begin the tests to see how powerful this matter is," said Henry, who seemed to have become Freddy's biggest fan.

"We must search the world to find the two sources you say you calculated to be on the planet. It may take a long time but that must be our priority," Alfred said over the excited mumblings of his colleagues.

"Yes, finding dark matter in large quantities is what will truly change the world. We only have the discovery right now. We must find the substance in order to make this a great thing for all of us."

"We will set up a press conference for later today," stated Henry. "Your announcement will change the world!"

Chapter 3

James settled in to his research as the day crawled forward. He was reading about the new success in post-war Iraq when the news flashed across the wire. Social media was blowing up minute by minute that there had been a major scientific discovery in Europe. Details were hazy at the moment for James but from what he could gather there had been a discovery of a new resource and that man had recreated creation. James was eager to hear the real news behind this discovery. He called the office of the European Organization for Nuclear Research and all they could tell him was that there would be a press conference at 8 p.m. Geneva time, which was 11 a.m. Pacific that day.

"A new energy resource discovered out of thin air," James pondered. "I wonder what this will do to the Middle East and oil prices."

James continued trying to gather as much information as he could, but he had to wait until the press conference to see what the official announcement would be. James hoped that he would be covering this discovery for the near future and he was excited at the possibilities it could present for his career.

As 10 a.m. rolled around, the entire morning was spent with speculation and excitement around the station. All the cable news stations had picked up the story and had live feeds from Geneva. By now the entire world was tuning in to see what these scientists had discovered. James by then had a pretty decent understanding of what could be going on. The Large Hadron Collider had been researching the Big Bang, so the discovery had something to do with some natural energy source. About six people were gathered around the television hanging on the wall over a small fake tree as 11 a.m. rolled around.

"Good afternoon ladies and gentlemen, soon we will be bringing you live to the press conference from Geneva regarding a major discovery."

The announcer spent the next minute giving a background on the Collider. "Now we go live to Geneva."

"Today is a great day for all of humanity," said Alfred Linchkin, lead scientist at the Large Hadron Collider. "Thanks to the contributions of our dynamic professor and scientist Frederick Slater, we have uncovered one of the major secrets of the universe. We have been able to successfully recreate the Big Bang, and produce a sample of dark matter. This dark matter that we created is now able to produce power thousands of times more powerful than anything else on Earth. The typical spaceflight would take 214 days to get to Mars using typical rocket fuel. With dark matter we will be able to get there in 30 days. We will no longer have a need for fossil fuels. We have found a cheap, highly efficient, and naturally occurring energy resource."

Alfred paused to gather his thoughts. "Our scientists have calculated that there are two sources of this new fuel source somewhere on this planet. Unfortunately, we have no way of knowing where to look, so we have asked for help deciding where to look first. The UN will vote on the order of which we will be searching for the two sources of black matter."

"The UN? That is strange... Why would they need the UN?" James thought to himself.

"Rejoice everyone. We have found the discovery that the world has been waiting for. No more waste, no more pollution, now we will have a clean and abundant energy source that we hope to be able to recreate on a larger scale with more research. We will update you once we have had time to discuss the vote with the Secretary-General."

The scientists turned away from the podium amid a flurry of camera flashes and walked back into the building they came from.

James and his colleagues were all speechless immediately following the press conference. "So now we will no longer be slaves to the Middle East, but slaves to whatever two new countries have the black matter," joked Andy Lawson. He was a business reporter. The crowd gave a small chuckle but even though he said it as a joke he was still right. Who would have this new energy source? What will this do to our cars and transportation? What will this mean for everything?

James was eager to get the story on the UN voting selection but he knew he wouldn't. James really didn't know what kind of story he could pull out of this. He wanted to do something great but being the low man on the totem pole doesn't get you very far at this station. The best he could hope for was some kind of local coverage of the international search for dark matter.

James walked back to his desk to sulk. He just knew that nothing would come of this. Charlie came around the corner, surprised to see his friend so down with all the big news buzzing around. "Hey whoa man what exactly could be getting you down right now? The entire world is excited for the future and I come in here to find you wound up in a ball."

"Charlie," James said as he looked up from his desk, "I just know that despite all this good news, I won't be able to get anything from Cruise. I work my ass off trying to do well for myself and this paper and I feel like I am just not being respected."

"Well you need to find a way to channel all of that negative energy into something positive." Charlie walked over to James and put a hand on this shoulder. "Look brotha, you have to get this through your head. As long as you continue walking down the straight and narrow path, it is not going to get you very far. Just sitting in line behind Susan and Daniel is not going to get you that big break. You need to come up with something different and unique that those two senior reporters won't want."

Charlie's words brought an optimistic smile to James's face. "Yeah maybe you're right," his smile dimmed. "But what is out there that would be any good? Either one of them will undoubtedly cover the UN voting. All the top countries will be covered by either one of them in one way or another..."

Charlie jumped in mid-sentence, "Exactly! So why not try for something less desirable? Why not try to cover one of the worst countries you can find? Maybe instead of reaching for the crumbs of the 'best' countries out there to cover, you should cover the worst and get an angle that no one else is giving. I mean, I guarantee neither Susan nor Daniel would want to do it."

"Ehh, I don't know about that one ol' man. You really expect me to cover some shitty place like North Korea or an African war-torn nation?"

Charlie walked around his desk and sat down in the guest seat and looked at him face to face. "If it gets you out of this office and in the field you're damn straight you better go to some shitty place. Everyone will already hear enough about the UN search from a western perspective. It would be brilliant to try and cover the worst nation on the list and show us if there is any hope, any optimism, and any semblance of faith that just maybe they would end up being the country where they find the dark matter. I mean think of it, this stuff will change that country forever right? Why not see if the worst of the worst have any hope left in them?"

"It sounds interesting, Charlie, it really does, but how do I pass this with Cruise?"

"You're worried about old Kenny boy?" Charlie chuckled deep in his chest. "Let's just say he owes me one."

"The boss owes you one huh? I could only imagine…"

Charlie had a look on his face that his actions were pure. "We played 18 the other day and I beat him so he owes me a favor. I can call it in with you, young'n."

"Well I appreciate the kindness Charlie, I really do. You have been kind to me ever since I showed up here. Where would I be without you?" James had a hearty feeling back in his stomach. Maybe Charlie's plan might just work out, he was thinking.

"James, not only are you the only other brotha in the station, but you are a Trojan and we always look out for each other. I just want to see you get on your feet and move."

"Thanks again. I appreciate it."

"I will talk to Kenny later today. He will give you the story; no doubt in my mind. Just make sure you don't let me down, OK?"

"All I need is a chance and I will prove myself to be a great journalist."

"Keep up that attitude and you just might make it out there, son."

___

Jose awoke in silence two days later in his hospital room. He had lost a lot of blood which induced a minor coma. He saw the IVs in his arms but was reluctant to pull them out. "Where am I?" Jose asked to himself.

He looked around the room and saw a call alarm and pressed it, hoping it would bring someone who knew what the hell was going on. Last Jose remembered, he shot that man who was shooting at everyone. Who was that man? *What* was that man? Was he hallucinating when he saw his eyes turn yellow? Were Bill and everyone OK? There was so much going through his mind, he needed to see someone. He was still in a daze but his mind was swirling with questions on what was happening.

After a minute or two there was the creak of the door opening and in walked a hefty older woman who was seemingly his nurse. She waddled into the room and stood over Jose. "How are you, Congressman? Glad to see that you are awake. You had the entire country worried. Be careful not to move suddenly. You lost a lot of blood at the convention center before they brought you here."

Jose slowly sat up and greeted his nurse with a welcoming smile. "What happened, where am I?"

"You are in the county hospital. You were shot in the shoulder and you have a concussion. I am sure you remember the shooting. Several people were shot and rushed to the hospital. Some did not make it. We were hoping you wouldn't be one of them. I will see if any of your family or staff is here who could fill you in on the details of exactly what happened."

She left the room in a hurry to see if there was someone ready to help him. Seconds later in walked Carmela, Jose's mother, and Sharon, his communications director. "Oh son, I am so happy to see you are awake," said Carmela with tears in her eyes.

"I am happy to see you too mother. What happened? Who was that man? Is he alive? Is Bill alive? What happened with…"

Sharon cut him off. "Calm down Jose and take a deep breath. What happened was very traumatic; maybe it's best if we tell you the news later."

"What do you mean later? I want to know if my friend is alive!"

Carmela grabbed his hands to calm him down. "Son, Bill is dead. I am sorry. So are the shooter and four other people. Several others were shot as well. Everyone feared the worst with you when you fell into a coma. Everyone is calling you a hero. Your headfirst dive is what the entire country saw. The cameras weren't stationed to see the crowd so everyone just saw your dive from the stage."

Jose sat up straight and put his head into his hands and sobbed. "My friend Bill is dead. I am no hero. I should have warned everyone when I first saw him. I knew he was up to no good."

Carmela rubbed her hand on his back to soothe him like only a mother could. "Please son, it is going to be OK. We must not let evil conquer the good. If we gave in, then the terrorists and Satan win."

"So he was a terrorist? Who is this person, Sharon?"

"Nobody knows who this man is. He has no family, no property, and no record at all. Everyone thinks he must have been hired by the Mexican cartels because of your tough stance on immigration and border protection."

"God damned cartels!? You really think that they had the balls to go after a U.S. Congressman?"

"Reports are that he was a European gunman who one of the cartels hired to take you out if you won. There is no video record of him coming into this country at any airport or border crossing, so they are saying that he must have crossed the border illegally."

"So these cartels really think this is going to stop me? This is only going to give me strength to stop illegal immigration forever."

"Well Congressman, since Bill is not here anymore I have to be the one to tell you this. You are undoubtedly a famous young Congressman now. I cannot tell you what to do with your newfound fame, but I can tell you what not to do. Do not let this opportunity slip by you. I understand people are dead and we are very sad about that, but this is a big event in your career. You need to put your face out there and make a bigger name for yourself and your message against illegal immigration. Go on the television shows, do radio interviews, and show the country that you are strong and that you can be a leader in a tough situation."

"You're right, Sharon, I need to honor my friend Bill but I also need to press forward and do everything I can to gain from this."

Carmela had a concerned look on her face. "Are you sure it is best for him to go back out there so soon after this horrible attack? Maybe you should take a couple of weeks off to mourn Bill and heal yourself. Being a congressman is no small task. You do not need to be recovering from your wounds while trying to make the rounds."

"I understand your concerns, mother, but I think this is the best thing for me. Once I get out of this hospital bed I will be going on an all-out media blitz. I am sure the nation will want to be hearing from the new hero."

Sharon and Carmela spent another fifteen minutes talking with Jose before they gathered their things to get ready to leave. "I will come by and see you tomorrow, son." Carmela leaned in to give Jose a kiss on the forehead. "Get some rest, son. I love you."

Carmela gave him one last hug and she headed for the door. Sharon stood there with her purse in hand. "You are getting a lot of requests for interviews. Just take the next week to relax and get your strength back. Things are going to start moving very fast for you, Congressman." She leaned in to give him a hug goodbye. "It's nice to see that you are OK. Get some rest, Jose." She turned around and left Jose in his room to himself. He took the opportunity to get some much needed rest.

Jose took the next few days to himself and got the sleep that he needed. He heard about the discovery of dark matter from his mother later that week. "A new resource, huh?" questioned Jose as he sat forward, still with a tender shoulder from the gunshot wound. "Do you understand what this could mean for the world? We will be able to completely back away from all our ties to the Middle East."

Jose was raised in the world of 9/11 and he still had a dislike for Islam and terrorists. "We just have to hope and pray that the two nations with the dark matter are nations that will work compatibly with the rest of the world." The results of the UN voting would be posted in a little over two weeks.

By the middle of the next week Jose was reenergized and ready for work. He had his swearing in to be Congressman in January, so he had time to finish up his state senate duties and make the rounds. His first priority was getting himself on television as much as possible. The nation was still grieving over the shooting and they wanted to hear from the hero of the convention shooting. The first request that Jose decided to entertain was a live interview on the most popular day time television show in America, the Lisa Malky Show. Lisa Malky was a billionaire hostess who started her own television station with all her own creative content. She was eager to get the young Congressman in her studio for the first interview. Jose knew this would be a prime opportunity to showcase himself to the nation and explain his views to the world.

So he had Sharon set up the interview and Jose prepared for his big debut to the nation. He spent the next few days going over his routine and sharpening his skills. He was going to wear his favorite black suit with a blue and gray tie. When the morning of the interview arrived he woke up early to meet with Sharon to go over some prepared questions.

"Remember, this interview is not just about you. It is about the victims who died that day as well. Always remember that," Sharon said as she was thumbing through a series of papers on the desk in the hotel room. Jose was deciding on whether to wear his shoulder sling or not. "You think it will make me look weak?"

Jose had all the confidence in the world but he had to admit he was getting nervous to be on such a big stage. Sharon could sense it in him and did her best to calm him. She knew this was a big deal and she cared deeply for the Congressman, so failure would hurt her as well. She was an aide to the Congressman, but she felt as though the years they had spent together in school made them friends before colleagues. "How could anyone think you are weak after what you did? Stop being negative. This is not the time."

"You're right, I need to calm down." Jose went over to the sink and mirror in the area outside the bathroom. He knew he was ready for this. All he had to do was ride the wave. His actions had given him that much.

Jose got ready for the limo that would take him to the studio. His hotel was in downtown Chicago and the studio was just 5 minutes away. He gingerly eased his way into the limo, careful not to put pressure on his shoulder. He and Sharon got in and they went off for the studio. They were greeted at the back of the hotel by Lisa Malky's assistant, Yvette. She had long blonde hair that was shining in the light of the day. Taller than the average woman, she had to bend down to look inside the limo to confirm that it was Jose.

"Good afternoon, Congressman," Yvette said as she was helping Jose out of the limo. "Shoulder is still tender huh, darling? I am so sad to see that. Lisa is definitely looking forward to meeting you. She is too busy to meet you before the show but we have prepared a set of questions for you to review before the interview. Not all of the interview will be scripted but this is just an outline of where she wants to go."

Jose took the paper and quickly scanned over the list. "Where are you from? How was your childhood? When did you first get involved with politics?" The questions went on and on and Jose quickly scanned them all through. He went into the waiting room to wait until he was called in by the director.

After about fifteen minutes the director came in and ushered Jose into a side room to the main studio. Here he went over again what type of questions the host would ask. Everything was ready to go and Jose was signaled by the director to walk onto the stage. He calmly strode his long legs across the glossy wooden floor. The audience stood to applaud the young hero as he entered the studio after an introduction by Lisa.

"Welcome Jose, everyone," Lisa said as she stood up clapping to greet Jose. He smiled and waved with his good arm to the crowd. Lisa walked over to guide the Congressman to his plush red velvet seat. Jose sat down tenderly with his shoulder still sore in the sling. "Congressman we are all so glad to see that you are OK."

"Thank you for your concern. I received so much mail in the hospital. I still haven't had a chance to get through it all."

"Do you consider yourself a hero?"

"A hero?" Jose paused slightly as he searched for the true answer. "No, I don't consider myself a hero. I only did what any other person in my position would do. I couldn't just sit there and hide as he was targeting the audience. He had his head turned from me so I took the opportunity to make a move."

"Well even if you try to explain it like it was normal, I know that I, and the rest of the country, think you are a hero for what you did."

Jose knew he could bask in his glory on national television if he wanted, but this wasn't about himself, it was about his friend Bill and the others who died. "The real hero is Bill Knotts, my chief of staff, who ran to save me when he easily could have run away."

The crowd agreed when they erupted into a round of applause for his fallen friend. Jose started to gather moisture in his eyes and he began to remember his old friend. "He was a great man. He had a wonderful family and he was a wonderful friend. It pains me inside to know that he won't be there to raise his children, but I know I have to do what I can to be there for them. I just don't know how I am going to move on from him."

Lisa, with her long, brown hair perfectly set against her light mocha skin, responded carefully to the softening congressman. "I know he would want you to move on. You have too much potential to let yourself lose your zeal for success and life due to the loss of your friend. I know it must be hard but we cannot let evil people accomplish what they set out to do."

Jose knew she was right. "These cartels..." Jose trailed off as he calmed his inner anger. "These cartels are growing in strength, so much so that they are spilling their influence across the border. Americans must rise together with our Mexican brothers to end the influence of drugs and illegal immigrants flowing over the border into our cities."

Lisa jumped in. "It is easy to say that drugs are all bad, but do you really think all illegal immigrants are bad? You must admit that they have good and bad attributes."

"We cannot support these people who come here illegally, do not pay taxes, receive government assistance, and bring down the quality of our public education system."

"I think everyone here who does not know you would like to know where this hostility toward illegal immigrants and drug smuggling came from," Lisa said, looking from him to the audience.

"Well, I myself am the offspring of an illegal immigrant and drug mule for the cartels. I have been ashamed of it from the moment I was old enough to understand what those things meant to me and my community."

"If your father were still alive today what would you say to him?"

"I would tell him thank you first and foremost, because I would not be here without him. After that, I would ask him why he had to sell his soul to the devil by working for the cartels. I understand that he made it here to this country with the help of the cartels, but he should not have traded a good, honest life in Mexico with a crime-ridden immoral life of an illegal immigrant with ties to the cartel in the United States. I don't care how poor and down on his luck he was, nothing is worth risking your eternal soul."

"So you feel as though it should have been his faith that prevented him from coming to America? Are you a strong Christian, Congressman Valdez?"

Jose knew she was not a Christian, but he answered truthfully. "No, I am a very weak Christian. I have no problems admitting that. Faith does still play a role in my life. I may not be in church every Sunday, but I do pray every now and again for the health and success of my family and friends."

Jose paused to refocus his mind on the original question. "Yes, I do feel as though his faith should have prevented him from selling himself to the cartels. Nothing good comes from drugs or the drug money they acquire. Look at all the death and destruction the cartels cause on a daily basis in Mexico. We may not know for a fact if the shooter was from the cartels or not, but look at our country and the crime and violence they cause here. Kidnappings, murders, rapes, all allegedly carried out by cartel operatives in the United States. I am here to say that their days of power are numbered! I am here to be a leading voice against the sin and depredation flowing out from these cartels. They tried to kill me once, and I will make them pay for missing their chance at taking me out before I get in office to make a major change."

The crowd exploded into applause for the fiery young Congressman. They could smell the fumes of hate and revenge on him as they cheered on.

"OK, let us move on from the incident at the convention center. We are all excited to see what kind of Congressman you will be once you take your seat in the House. Everyone I have talked to about you calls you the next big thing in the Republican Party. What do you say about that?"

The audience was silent, and Jose could sense each member's interest in how he would answer. He drew in a deep breath, adjusted his sling ever so slightly, and replied.

"I am very flattered by all of the good press I have gotten since I put my name in the hat to be a Congressperson. I would like nothing more than to live up to the expectations of my friends, family, and peers."

"What do you plan to work on first when you get to Congress?" Lisa glanced down at the notecard in her hand and back up at him with a smile.

"I plan on pushing for comprehensive immigration reform and finding a solution to the millions of illegal immigrants who are already here. I also plan on increasing the capability of our counter terrorism departments to help stop terrorists, both domestic and foreign."

"How do you plan on stopping a lone gunman, whether they are a deranged lone killer, a cartel assassin, or a Muslim radical?"

Jose had thought a lot about this. "We need to do a better job of monitoring suspicious individuals. If someone is buying large amounts of weapons, putting hate speech on the internet, or associating themselves with known criminal or terrorist entities, then they should be monitored and singled out in the community. No longer will we succumb to the wills of the few who want to do harm to the many."

The crowd erupted in applause as the young Congressman displayed why he was looked at as the next star as he raised his voice with force and determination. "No matter how long it takes or how hard I have to work, I will bring security and safety back to our streets. I will make it where you can leave your front door open again without fear." Jose continued on forcefully, knowing he had his audience riveted. "There was a time in this country before 9-11 that we all loved and trusted each other. No matter what it takes, I promise I will bring that back to this country."

The audience couldn't help but burst into another round of applause. Lisa waited until the crowd quieted to finish up the interview. "So your platform is to bring safety and security back to America? Quite a noble quest young Congressman. I will be supporting you all the way through until you reach your goal. I would love for America to return to a place where you could raise your children in safety and security. Thank you for coming today Jose and good luck in a few weeks when you start your new job."

"Thank you, Lisa. I hope to come back sometime."

"Most definitely, Jose!"

With that the audience clapped one last time as the lights dimmed and the interview was over.

Lisa leaned in to Jose after the cameras and microphones were off. "Very good interview, Jose. I know it must have been hard for you to get through it but you did a wonderful job."

"Yeah my shoulder is killing me right now."

"If you are serious about bringing safety and security back to America no matter what, then I think I have some people that you may want to meet. I am part of an organization that is trying to bring change to this country and I think you may be just the man to help us realize our dreams. I will have Yvette give you the information before you leave the studio. We will be having a meeting next week. I would love for you to come and join me as my personal invitee."

Jose couldn't believe what he was hearing. He had done a good enough job that Lisa Malky, the most powerful and successful woman in the country, hell the world, was inviting him to a private gathering.

"Being a Congressman is going to get me right to the top," Jose thought to himself as he was easing his way off the chair to stand. "Thank you, Lisa. If your organization is something important to you then it must be good. I will definitely go. I need all the help I can get. I want to make an impact, Lisa. I want to be great."

"If you are with me then your greatness is guaranteed."

With that they hugged and said their final goodbyes.

Jose met briefly with Yvette and exchanged information so she could give him further details on the meeting next week. Feeling like he made a major stride in his career that day, he got back in the limo, confident and cocky.

"Lisa Malky wants me in her organization. Can you believe it?" he said to Sharon.

But she was not quite as ready to leap into the positive pit. She knew Lisa was powerful, hell one of the most influential people in the world. The thing that bothered her was that Lisa Malky was known to be one of the most power hungry and sinister forces in this country. She couldn't be fully trusted and she wanted to make sure that Jose knew that.

"Jose, I want you to be careful with Lisa."

"Careful? What could possibly go wrong? She is going to help my prestige and my platform. I can't see the danger in that."

"She doesn't just want you because she thinks you're a great guy. She has to be getting something out of it."

Jose turned his head suddenly to challenge her assertion. "Why can't she just see the potential in me as an influential young congressman?"

"First she is a Democrat, so what is her interest in you anyway? Second, she takes orders and suggestions from no one. She is a one-woman show. I know you may not care as much as I do but she is not a religious person. Can you really trust someone with no spiritual accountability?"

"Just because she is a Democrat doesn't mean she would not want me in her organization if there is a way I can help. When you start getting around the top dogs the D or R next to your name just does not matter as much. I know she sees the capabilities in me to get the job done." Jose took a pause to adjust his sling as his arm was getting a little sore. "I don't plan on being anyone's puppet. I am the congressman, not her. If she wants something from me she will have to come to me as a peer. I am no man or woman's stepping stone."

Sharon had her head down, worried about the words that her boss and close friend were speaking. She knew this entire situation sounded fishy. She wanted to trust him, but her strong feelings for Jose only made her want to protect him from others and himself.

"And religion? Who cares about religion right now? There are plenty of good people who are not religious people. Lisa and I both want the best for this country. That is all that should matter. If she is not a Christian, who cares? The way I see it, I am only a Christian because it gets votes. I don't go to church, I hardly ever pray, and I don't care for the most part. Right now all I care about is getting this country safe and protecting my friends and family. I will do whatever it takes to get that done. My power and influence are growing every day, every show I go on, every interview I complete. I must use my influence now to get what I need done in the Congress. Lisa, Boone, and any other multi-millionaire who wants to join my team, will be openly welcomed."

Sharon could tell he was still on a high from the successful interview and the invite from Lisa Malky. She knew she was fighting an uphill battle so she decided to fold her cards in the conversation. "Just be careful of what steps it will take for you to gain the power you seek, Jose."

"Don't worry about me. I can handle myself. I've handled myself my entire life with no hitches. Just let me take control of my own destiny." With that Jose rolled over on his good shoulder and closed his eyes to relax on the short trip back to the hotel. The rest of the limo ride was in silence as they both went into a daydream about their futures.

Jose left Chicago for New York because he had another interview scheduled with Charles West, one of the top cable news hosts in the world on ABS News (American Broadcasting Station). He really shined in this interview, reintroducing his platform on immigration reform and domestic security. Jose felt that an immigrant should have come to this country legally to be considered a true citizen with no conditions. It was clearly very controversial but Jose was a true Republican. Beliefs like those endeared him more to the Right and created more hatred for the young Congressman from the Left. He finished this interview successfully and had a day off before being scheduled for another interview in Los Angeles the following day. He had several phone interviews and radio appearances as well. He was very busy in his week leading up to his meeting with Lisa Malky.

Jose had done a great job in using the tragedy to boost his career. His poll numbers were soaring, his approval rating was extremely high, and he was getting nothing but good press. He was the hero for now. He could do no wrong in many Americans' eyes. He was the bilingual savior of the Republican Party.

By the end of the week Jose was worn out. He didn't schedule any more meetings for the weekend so he could get some much-needed rest and spend some time with his constituents. Jose was excited about the meeting with Lisa. As that Monday came, he was bubbly and nervous about meeting potential new supporters. He had flown back to Chicago, where the meeting would take place at Lisa Malky's mansion.

"I wonder what they want from me," Jose thought to himself. "I have to just relax and get a feel for everything that is going on before I try to make any major decisions. I want to see if they have anything that can help me achieve my goals. With all the good press I have right now, I don't want to jeopardize it by making a foolish mistake."

He adjusted his dark navy blue suit in the mirror and massaged his shoulder to quell a small burst of pain. He was tired of wearing his sling, and he decided against the wishes of his doctors and took it off. He left the hotel for the limo that Lisa sent for him. It was long, sleek, and shimmered from the hotel lights glimmering and swinging above in the Chicago night time wind. Jose eased himself in and off they went. Her mansion was 30 minutes out of the city so Jose took this time to himself to read the internet on his phone.

He read on his phone that the UN vote was coming up. He was excited to see where America would fall on the list. He knew that if a country friendly to the United States happened to get control of the dark matter, it would ensure our future for hundreds of years. Jose read on that they were thinking of ways to harvest the dark matter from space. "The lead scientist, Professor Frederick Slater, has not yet released his patent for the engine prototype to the public. He wants to remain in control of all use of dark matter for the time being. A personal flying automobile and a shuttle to space to harvest black matter are being discussed behind closed doors, our sources say."

"Very interesting," Jose thought to himself. "I wonder if America can get a head start on rebuilding our worthless space flight program. This is going to be the future."

Jose finished up reading the article and put the phone back in his pocket as he neared Lisa's mansion. The driveway was wide and curving left and right through the trees as he neared a large, white gate with gold-tipped metal rod spears. The limo driver pulled up to the intercom and spoke to someone on the other side. A few seconds later the large gate broke open at its center as the gates swung backward. The limo carefully pulled in on the smooth, black, paved street lined with tall lamp posts. As they came around the corner, the road opened up to a large street that led to the parking area in the front of the house. There were several nice cars and limos parked here, undoubtedly belonging to other members of this organization.

Jose was welcomed once again by Lisa's slender, blonde assistant Yvette. "Welcome, Congressmen Valdez, Lisa and our guests will be very glad to meet you."

Jose had no idea who else would be there but he was getting excited just by looking at all of the other cars and limos in the parking area. "Right this way, sir." Jose couldn't help but notice the slender, young blonde. She was voluptuous and curvy in all the right places. Her pouting pink lips were set perfectly against her tanned, creamy skin.

She led him up the stairway into the front door. When it opened it took a minute for Jose to adjust to the dimly glowing light. He could make out several figures as he walked through the door. First he saw former General Lee Doughney. He led the U.S. forces in the first war against Iraq. He was a balding and aging man with a few light brown hairs desperately clinging to his pineapple shaped head. Next he saw two mysterious looking tall men, both white, looking at him and whispering to each other. As he walked further into the dim hallway he could see it led to another door which he was to walk through. As he entered, the light burned bright in his eyes as he adjusted to the well-lit opening entryway into the mansion. There was a large white staircase with gold encrusted pillars, winding up and to the right with a jutting balcony off the second floor up above. In this room he saw the pudgy billionaire owner of several hotels in Vegas and Atlantic City who went by the name of Calvin Dempster. Jose looked next to him, and there was former speaker of the House Allan Jamson. The two were engaged in a heartfelt conversation, as neither noticed the young Congressman entering the room. Jose followed Yvette as she walked through the room.

"Right this way, Congressman." She led him into the next room which was a large open room with several chairs and a projector and screen set up. There was an announcement over a loudspeaker hidden somewhere in the walls. "The presentation will begin in 10 minutes, please make your way to the main room."

Yvette turned her beautiful face back around toward him and smiled. "Please take a seat or take advantage of the food servings at the tables along the wall over there." She pointed toward the far wall. Jose wasn't hungry so he just took his seat and waited for the presentation to begin. Several people were now flowing into the presentation area from several doors located around the room. Jose couldn't make them out because the lights were dimmed in this room, but he knew they had to be powerful and successful people. He just sat there annoyed that he didn't bring his sling, and awaited Lisa or someone he could talk to.

As the time neared, in came Lisa, wearing a long blue dress with her hair wrapped up in a bun around a black pin. She asked everyone to take a seat. "Welcome my friends, I am glad you are all here. This is the fifth meeting of the year for our organization, The American Protectorate, for those who are here for the first time. We are here to discuss a major breakthrough for the future of American innovation and domestic security."

She walked across the stage to the podium where she picked up a handheld clicker to change the power point slides. "I would like to proudly announce, after years of secret testing, the introduction of the X-chip."

With that the screen changed and that is when Jose saw the chip for the first time. He didn't really know what to think. "A chip? How is a chip going to protect this country?" he thought to himself as he sat patiently waiting for the next slide.

"This chip will revolutionize the way we shop, the way we travel, our entertainment, our health, and our security."

"This chip will be inserted subcutaneously into the hand or forehead of a recipient. The chip will be able to produce three dimensional images or a video stream straight from its source. It will act as a computer and a laptop all on your hand and you can click and move things around on the screen with your free hand. It will act as an active debit card, simply needing to be scanned to purchase something instead of carrying around a purse or wallet full of cards or cash. It can make phone calls and record conversations, record a person's movements throughout the day, and tell you when a person is sleeping, eating, walking, or running. This chip will also detect cancer before it starts, and by setting the frequency to a specific setting, it can help put a person to sleep or give them energy for the entire day, eliminating the need for sleeping pills or coffee. This chip will hold your electronic identification, so you will be able to cross the border into any country without a passport or ID because they are already embedded into the device. I brought all of you here to show you that with this new device, developed by the Zynot Company, we will finally be able to live in a device-free world where crime can be easily recorded and prevented. Several other countries have begun using the X-chip with their citizens and they have gotten back rave reviews. I feel with some of the stars we have in this room today, we can drum up enough support to get the American public to buy into to this new product." The crowd graciously lauded Lisa as the lights slowly came back on.

Jose was stunned. He had never heard anything about an X-chip before but he was very intrigued by everything that Lisa had to say. He had to learn more about this chip and more about this organization. Jose looked to his right when the lights cut back on and there was famous musician and actress Juanita Mills. She made eye contact with the Congressman when he turned his head and she instantly smiled. "Hello, Congressman! I had heard you would be with us today but I didn't think it was going to happen."

"What is this organization? What do you do?"

"We are here to protect the culture, security, financial success, and future of the country through scientific research. I have been coming for a little over a year now."

"Well is the chip thing new to you as well?"

"I have heard rumors of the high tech chip before but this is the first time I have seen the end product. I am excited about it, aren't you?" Her eyes lit up at the thought of the technology they had just seen.

"Yes I must say that I am, but I would like to learn more about it."

She glanced toward their host with a smile. "Well I am sure Lisa will give you plenty of time to get acquainted with the chip and our organization. I am just excited to see the Hero of the Convention Center here in front of me. How is your shoulder? Is it still healing OK?"

"Yes it is but I should have brought my sling tonight. I was being too macho for my own good."

"Ha ha well hopefully you learned your lesson. You do not have to show off or be someone you are not around us. Most of us are famous or successful and there is no sense of competition among us. We are all here to protect the future of the country."

"Well thank you for sharing some insight with me, Miss Mills. I am still fairly new to the national spotlight and I will need some help along the way."

"Well you are off to quite a start, Congressman. And you can call me Jay."

"Then you can call me Jose."

"Maybe we should exchange numbers and I can help ease your transition into our new group, if you decide to join, which I hope you do." She took his phone from his hand and put her number into it, then handed it back to him.

"Well this is all so new to me. I just want to get a grasp on everything before I jump into anything new."

"I understand. The world has so much planned for you, Jose. Please do not be afraid to seize the opportunity."

"Thank you for your help and kind words. I will give you a call sometime and we can talk more about this American Protectorate and what you all have for a long-term plan for this country."

"I look forward to hearing from you."

With that Juanita gathered her things and stood up to leave. "I am going to speak with a few other members, I suggest you go and speak to Lisa. She seems to be free at the moment. She is one of our founding members so you can get a lot of information from her."

"Thank you again Jay. I will be listening to you and watching you on the big screen as much as I can from now on."

"If you are in town for one of my shows I can get you a backstage pass. I am always in Dallas because my Grandmother lives there. Maybe we can meet up sometime for a get- together." With that the beautiful celebrity with medium length black hair turned and walked toward another group of members.

Jose took this chance to go up to Lisa to ask her a couple of questions. Everything was so new to the Congressman. He hadn't even been sworn in yet and he was already with celebrities in secret meetings. He couldn't believe his luck! He had just met the Grammy award winning artist Juanita "Jay" Mills. Now he was going to try and get more information from Lisa about this organization and what he could do to help.

"Jose! I am so glad you made it," Lisa careened toward the wounded Congressman, giving him a heartfelt but careful hug.

"What an exciting presentation, Lisa. I have so many questions to ask."

"Well I will be mailing everyone here an extensive packet with all the information you could ask for about the next X-chip and what it could mean for this country and the world long- term."

"How did you get involved with the X-chip and the American Protectorate in the first place?"

"Well, Jose, the American Protectorate was started by me, William Beard the CEO of Jester Electronics, and former speaker Allan Jamson. After 9-11 we felt as though the business and entertainment community needed to do more to protect the fabric of our society from outside hostilities. So we banded together to combine our power in order to shape legislation and public policy domestically and abroad in order to help protect the safety of our economy and our culture. The X-chip has been in research stage for the past decade, starting in 2002 and continuing to this day. It was in response to 9-11 that the American Protectorate began researching and testing a new product that could reduce crime, increase innovation and our economy, and protect against health concerns from the everyday cold to stage 3 cancers."

"This chip has the power to do all of that?"

"Yes it does. All we need now is a front man to help push the chip on the American public. That is where you come in."

"Me? What could a freshman member of the House possibly do to help?"

"You are in a position of power. The country is in love with you, Jose, whether you want to believe it or not. You are a hero. Your power is strong right now, and with the right moves it will only be stronger. We are here to help you realize your potential. What other way to kick off your new life as a powerful Congressman, than to endorse a product that will revolutionize the entire world?"

"It sounds exciting Lisa, it really does, but I need to think about it and talk to family before I make any major decisions."

"Well we will all be here to help you, Jose. We are all your biggest fans. Although we are a secret organization, we are very open about our support for each other. We are here to gather our power to make this country return to its former greatness. Return this country to a place where you can leave your front door open again just like you said during our interview. We need you to be our man, Jose. There is no rush but please remember that terror can strike at any time. It is in your platform that you want to protect against future attacks, right? Well with the chip, we can monitor suspicious individuals and prevent them before they can execute their attack."

"That sounds great, Lisa. I just have to do some more thinking before I commit to anything."

"OK, well we will be patiently awaiting your response."

With that they hugged goodbye and said their parting remarks before Jose turned to walk out. Several people had left ahead of Jose as there was a line of cars leading out of the mansion complex. This new X-chip sounded like the perfect opportunity to get him involved in something big before his opponents had a chance to jump on it. Jose planned on talking to his mother about all of these new events. Jose was excited and he knew that his future was looking bright. As long as he could find a way to harness the public outcry for security and safety, he could find himself in a comfy and positive position for his future.

Chapter 4

The world had been reverberating for the almost three weeks since the press conference announced the discovery of dark matter as a viable resource. Professor Slater had a busy schedule ever since the announcement, going on shows, being interviewed, and generally having no time to himself. The UN vote was due in two days and he was flying to New York to meet with UN Secretary-General Lenz Krause tomorrow. He was a strong-willed and very successful politician. He helped negotiate a settlement with Iran over their nuclear program, successfully bargained for the release of seven European sailors captured off the coast of Africa by Somali pirates, ushered the overturn of Russia's anti-gay policies, and negotiated an open-trade policy between the United States and Cuba. He was the hero of his German people and the world.

While Freddy was waiting for his flight to New York City, he had a few minutes to catch up with his girlfriend, Jennifer. "Hey Jenny, my flight leaves soon but I have some time to talk before I get on the plane."

Jennifer sighed, frustrated that she has had very little time to talk to her boyfriend since his discovery. "I am glad you are busy but you need to pace yourself. You still have so much more work to do; I don't want you to lose an edge because you got burnt out."

Freddy knew she was right. "I need to take some time off before we begin the search for dark matter. I think I will try to fly out to Colorado and visit everyone before the big search."

"How long are you on leave from the University?" Jennifer wondered aloud.

"Well they know I am going to be busy with the new discovery so they are giving me as much time as I need."

"That is good. I am sure they are happy that one of their professors is the most famous scientist in the world, with the most important discovery in science in a generation."

"Yeah I figure they are very pleased with my work so far, but there is so much left to do. I may not be able to teach for a long time. I still need to be hands-on with the development of my engine and many other things relating to dark matter and energy. Depending on what the secretary-general says, I may be using my patents to develop a new space craft that could mine the universe for dark matter. I haven't been able to calculate whether dark matter exists on other planets in our solar system, but now that we know my goggles work we can transfix their material to a telescope and search the planets."

Freddy paused to check his watch for the time, to see if his plane has started boarding yet. The aroma of the breakfast sandwiches served at the airport restaurant was killing Freddy, causing him to gaze longingly in the direction of the source of this smell, dreaming he had time to get one. Jennifer snapped him back into reality, "Hey! You were saying something about a special ship to mine the planets. Tell me more. I don't have much time before your flight, and I never get to talk to you."

"Sorry, sweetie. Now back to what I was saying. We will have to develop a space craft that can travel long distances quickly with my new engine. The world is changing in front of our eyes, Jenny. Once we find the dark matter here on Earth, we can calculate how great the need is for a space mining program."

"I just hope the dark matter isn't in the Middle East or China. We need it to be in a place that will work nicely with the rest of the world."

"Yes, Jenny, we are all worried about that. But we just have to hope the desire for human progress and prosperity will supersede any previous diplomatic relationships."

Freddy adjusted himself in the cold hard airport seat. Just as he did, he was recognized by passersby in the airport. "Congratulations, Professor Slater." "Good luck with the search!" They were a middle-aged couple who recognized him, and spoke English in a heavy accent. It was weird for Freddy to be getting so much attention, but as long as it was good attention it didn't bother him much.

"I have to be going soon, honey. I just wanted to let you know how much I love you. I hope to be seeing you soon if I get some time after this meeting."

"I love you too, Freddy. I just want you to be careful with who you trust. You are a famous and soon to be rich and powerful man. Just know that not everyone appreciates science as a tool for the betterment of mankind. Some people just want to keep all the success to themselves."

"You have nothing to worry about my dear; nobody is out to get me."

"I just want you to be careful."

"I promise I will be careful."

"Thank you. I love you and good luck with your meeting with the secretary-general." "I love you too, Jenny."

"I will be praying for you."

Freddy stopped and thought to himself, "A lot of good that is going to do." Now that Freddy had accomplished his goals, he owed his success to no one but himself. He had done it on his own and some magical God from the sky was not going to help or hurt his future success. But instead of getting into a religious argument before getting on the plane, he simply said, "Thank you, honey. I will talk to you soon."

He hung up the phone and got up just as the airport announced boarding for the plane to New York.

After a long flight and a taxi to his hotel room, Freddy relaxed and got some sleep. When he woke up he spent some time just walking around, caressing himself in the aromas and sights of the big city. Late at night after he spent time cruising the local late night food spots for dinner, he made his way back to his hotel room. Many people recognized him on the streets and asked him questions and wished him good luck. He hadn't made up his mind if he liked his newfound success yet. He was used to being recognized on campus with his students and faculty, but now he was a global figure. He had to adjust himself to this newfound fame.

He got his clothes ready for the next morning and went to sleep. When he woke up he felt ready to go. The taxi ride through the city in the morning was refreshing. When he got to the U.N. he arrived at the front desk and said he had a meeting with Secretary-General Krause. The secretary looked at her computer screen and confirmed the interview. She told him to go to the 38th floor and check in there. So Freddy went up the 38th floor and checked in at the counter. He sat for a few minutes and waited. About ten minutes later out walked the stout figure of a forceful man. He was taller than most people at about 6'0", but as stiff as he kept his neck, it added an extra inch or two. "Welcome to the U.N., Professor Slater. Right this way, please."

Freddy stood up and shook the man's strong hands as he greeted him with a smile. The two walked casually back to his main office. The room had miniature palm trees lined against the wall and a spectacular view of New

York City from his window. "Please take a seat, Professor, we have much to discuss."

There was a large, black leather couch with two side pillows tucked into the corners. Next to it was a large glass table with four wooden legs that held it in place. There were two blue sitting chairs situated around the table that gave the perfect place for face-to-face conversations. Freddy took a seat in one of the blue chairs and got comfortable. Krause took a seat and began in his trademark deep raspy voice, "Professor, we are on the verge of a golden age in humanity." He reached to the table and took a sip of his hot coffee. He looked up from his cup and began again. "What we need now is the world to come together and work as one toward the dream of a new and better Earth. With this new resource, the entire world will be better off."

Freddy was very intrigued by what the secretary-general had to say. He was world famous for his conversational skills, so Freddy was careful to listen and choose his words carefully. Freddy responded, "Well, Secretary-General, I…"

Lenz Krause interrupted, "Call me Lenz, please."

"Well Lenz, I certainly share in your vision of a better world, but I fear that once this resource is discovered, it will result in a similar situation as with oil. The rich will get richer and the poor and hungry will continue to mire in the misery of their birthright."

"Yes, there was a time that I used to think that way. I was pessimistic about the world. I never thought that things could get any better. Then one day, I just looked at myself in the mirror and realized that it was because of people like me, who were indifferent to the way the world worked, that bad people reign supreme over this planet. I sold my sportswear business and became a politician, determined to do everything within my power to help the world become a better place."

Freddy wished he had the secretary-general's passion and optimism for a better world. "I have my doubts that we can create a heaven on Earth."

Krause smiled a welcoming smile and responded, "It is already underway as we speak. All we need now are a few more steps to take place and our future will be secure. This is where you come into the picture, Professor."

"You can call me Freddy."

"Well Freddy, the UN needs your help in becoming the international force that it must become to secure the freedom and safety of the entire world."

Freddy was puzzled but he was interested in what the secretary-general had to offer. "What can I do to help?"

"Well you have not released your patents for public use yet, and I understand your hesitation in doing so. You do not want this to become a fight for the richest and most powerful to control the market on dark energy related products. That is where we come in. This decision could very much come in handy for our organization here."

"I am not interested in giving my patents to just anyone. It's not about the money because I know I could get very rich from my prototypes. I just want to make sure the world is a better place from my discovery."

Freddy looked at the secretary-general intently. The secretary-general seemed to understand Freddy's intentions and nodded.

"Well listen to my proposal. What do you think about giving your patents to the UN, to be designed, manufactured, and shipped around the world at a price the average consumer could afford?"

"Does the UN have the power to do something like this? Would I have controlling power over all research and products?" Freddy didn't take his eyes off the secretary-general's face.

"Well the UN has the power to do this most certainly. Yes, most definitely you will have complete control over all aspects of dark matter and dark energy related products. I would like to hire you full-time to be our Advisor of Science and take care of everything hands-on. Are you interested?"

Freddy couldn't believe how wonderful this proposal sounded. He really could make a difference in the world like he wanted to do all along. If he could control everything through the UN, he would have the power to change the world for the better. "I am not ready to commit to anything today but I am very interested. I see a lot of promise with this proposal, and I could see us working together to make a better world."

"We want the same things, you and I. Someday soon you will trust me like a brother. I will earn your respect through my actions though, not by my words. I am ready to dedicate my life for the betterment of all mankind. With your help, Freddy, I think that dream of mine just might come true."

"I only hope to make an impact, Lenz," Freddy said. The excitement and passion came through in his voice. "I just want to leave my mark on this world."

"Stand by me and I know you will, Freddy."

Freddy stood up. "Thank you very much for meeting with me today and offering me such a prestigious position. I will have to talk it over with my friends and family first."

"Take your time please, Freddy. We will both be hands-on with the global search for dark matter, so I do not want to rush a decision when I know we have plenty of time to spend together. We will keep in touch by phone until the search and we will see how things progress as time moves forward."

"Well that sounds like a wonderful plan, Lenz. It was a pleasure meeting you."

The powerful Lenz stood from his chair and reached his hand out to engulf the professor's. "Take care and God bless."

Freddy was astonished again. Freddy was very fascinated with the older man and could not wait until his next opportunity to talk with him. Freddy left the office and left the United Nations Building. He spent the rest of the day catching up on some much needed rest and relaxation. He decided he would fly to Colorado the next morning to see his friends, family, and girlfriend. He would get the news of the UN vote with them. Freddy knew he would be busy going around the world for the foreseeable future so he wanted to spend as much time as he could with them before he had to go back to New York.

"Damn it, Charlie. It's fucking December now. It's been weeks and Cruise still hasn't approached me about the dark matter search. You said he owed you a favor." James was tired of waiting.

"Relax, young buck, he will talk to you. The vote is in a few hours, just wait until then and he will probably approach you with the idea that I gave him."

James sat back down in his chair and tried his best to relax. He wanted in on the action so badly. "OK, I will wait for the UN vote and we will see what happens after that."

James swung around in his chair and faced his computer to do some more research on the vote and the logistics of the search. The whole world was tuning in to watch the votes come in live. Everyone wanted to see who was picked number one and who was last.

The next few hours went by quickly for James as he anticipated the results of the UN voting. His interest in the television piqued as he heard an update. "New Zealand has the early lead on votes," the anchor said.

"New Zealand? I would hope it's not in freaking New Zealand of all places," exclaimed James in his own head. As the results kept coming in, New Zealand remained the strong first place winner. In last was Somalia, followed by Syria and North Korea. James did not think any of those places would be fun to cover. He was thinking that maybe he could cover one of the worse countries but one that was a little safer. He scanned through the list, "Columbia, no. Pakistan, no."

He continued to look through the list. He came across Ethiopia. "Ethiopia huh? Well that doesn't sound all too bad at all." James did some extensive research on Ethiopia for a good while, to see if it were some place he would be interested in. "Good climate, plenty of Christians so I do not need to be afraid of a terrorist kidnapping me, interesting modern culture yet still rustic and good looking food. This is looking like the place for me."

So Ethiopia it was. He would petition Cruise for the job to cover Ethiopia. The votes came in and Ethiopia ranked 129 out of 158 so it was poor but not in the extreme. "I just know that Cruise will let me get this. I know it."

So the hours went by and Kenneth Cruise had still not come by his cubicle. As the day was heading to a close James had all but given up hope of getting to cover a country. Just as the day was ending, he saw Cruise leave his office and walk right toward him. "Is this it? Is he coming?" James wondered to himself. The hairs stood up on his neck and a ripple of sweat beaded across his forehead. Cruise came walking right up to his cubicle, "Hello, James, do you have a minute before you close up and leave?"

"Yes, Mr. Cruise, I do," James tried to say as calmly as he could, hoping he didn't give away that he had been waiting for him all day.

"Well I was talking with Charlie the other day and he said you were interested in writing an onsite story in a foreign country dealing with the search for black matter."

"Yes sir I most definitely do. I have been doing research and I think Ethiopia is the perfect fit for my writing. They are a struggling country but they are trying to overcome. A discovery of dark matter there would completely change the landscape of the society. I am sure they are excited in some way and it would be a pleasure to go out and cover the search. I have the utmost confidence that the stories I will produce will be good enough for as long as the search lasts. I can only hope that the search lasts as long as Ethiopia. It's worth a chance."

"OK well I am going to give you the go-ahead on this one. I think you are a good writer and I am going to give you a chance to make a name for yourself. If it is successful, you could be looking at more foreign coverage in the future."

"I look forward to the opportunity, sir."

"I trust you will give me your best. Good luck James and try to not have too much fun while you're in Africa. Remember this is a business trip not a pleasure trip."

"Yes sir I will remember, thank you." With that Kenneth Cruise walked out of the building, presumably to go home early.

James was ecstatic. He clasped his fists in front of him in a victory pose and took a deep breath, letting out the tension he had felt all day. His mind raced with possibility. This was his big break. He had to go and thank Charlie and tell him the good news. He almost ran as he skipped his way to Charlie's nice top shelf office.

"Hey my man, Charlie, guess what?" James practically yelled as he quickly forced open Charlie's door to his office without knocking.

"What happened?" But one look at James's face and Charlie broke out into a grin. "You got the job didn't you?"

"Aw man how'd you guess?"

"Because you got a smile a mile wide on your face, and I told you I was going to come through for you."

"Well thank you again buddy, I appreciate it. I have to tell my friends and family that I will be going away for a while!"

"You have friends? No freaking way!"

"Yeah ha ha really funny, Charlie. Well we should go out and celebrate. I am guessing I am due to be leaving as soon as possible so let's enjoy the night while we still can. I hope I come back from Africa a changed man. I have never been before."

"I've been before," Charlie said, shutting down his computer.

"What do you think about it?"

"It's beautiful," Charlie said, standing. "It will definitely change you."

"Well I am excited most definitely. Dinner is on me tonight."

"I'll take that any day." With that James got his things together and they left to go celebrate.

Chapter 5

Jose flew home to Dallas after visiting Chicago for a few days. He planned on spending the next few weeks before his term began meeting with donors and constituents. He had plenty of people to thank for his miraculous victory. He came home, threw his suit jacket on the bed and turned on the television to relax. When he got settled in his lounge garb, he grabbed his cell phone and called his mother. "Hey, Mother I am just getting in from Chicago right now," he said to her as she answered the phone with a loving hello.

"How was your visit with Lisa Malky?"

"It was great! I learned so much and met so many great people. Can you believe I actually sat next to Juanita Mills?"

"You mean the Grammy winner? Wow son, I bet she is even more beautiful in real life."

"Yes she is spectacular. I don't know how much I am allowed to say right now but let me say that something big is coming here soon, and I could be at the forefront of it."

"Really? How exciting! But remember that a lot of people are going to be looking to make money and gain power through your success. Be careful who you trust."

"You don't have to worry about me, Mother. I know what I am doing." He was getting a little tired of people telling him to watch his back.

"Watch your tone with me son. I am still your mother and I am only looking out for your best interests."

Jose's tone softened. "OK, you are right. I'm sorry. I am just on the verge of a major boost if I play my cards right. I am on my way to the top."

"I love you and hopefully you will stop by sometime soon. I am glad that you are home."

"I love you too, Mother, and I will see you soon." He ended the call and went to put his phone back in his pocket when he felt the vibration of a text message. He turned his screen back on and to his surprise it was a text message from Juanita. It said: "Photo shoot in Dallas tomorrow. Are you going to be free for dinner afterward?"

Jose was shocked. He really didn't think he had made that much of an impression with the beautiful young singer. He quickly responded back that he would clear up his schedule for her and he was excited to see her. Jose really hadn't dated in a while but he thought twice that he shouldn't get too ahead of himself. He had just met her and she probably wasn't even interested in him like that. He would take this as an opportunity to learn more about the American Protectorate and any other organizations she may be a part of. Jose knew that if he was going to change the world, he would need to start growing his power base by joining more organizations. He had a charity breakfast tomorrow and after that he was free until dinner with Juanita. Jose knew they would be loyal donors as long as he produced and won elections. He settled in for the night and got ready for the big day tomorrow.

Jose woke up to the sound of his alarm and the feel of a crisp December morning in Dallas. He was excited about his meeting with Juanita. He couldn't stop thinking about her attractive style, beautiful green eyes, and soft pouting lips. He had to refocus himself on his charity breakfast which came first in the day. He would be meeting several important people there who helped during his election. He showered and put on a dark gray suit with a navy blue tie. He had time to eat before he heard a knock on the door. It was the driver who would take him to the breakfast. He finished up inside and left for the car. He got to the event about twenty minutes before breakfast was served. He walked around and mingled with his constituents and his donors before he sat down at his table. At his table was his long-time confidante, Ron L. Boone and several other key donors. After a good breakfast he was due to deliver a speech to the crowd. He got up and went to the podium amidst a cascade of applause. He delivered his speech flawlessly. He focused his speech on passing immigration reform and the drug war. Jose was passionate about his speech but in the back of his mind he could not stop thinking about Juanita Mills. It was strange to him. It was almost like she implanted herself into his brain somehow; making him pine over her since the second she got up and left him at the American Protectorate meeting. The speech was over and Jose went to be greeted by his loyal supporters. He shook hands and gave hugs and thanked everyone for coming. It was a successful event for Jose.

After the event Jose went back to his place to relax and read up on the Zynot Company from the internet. They were based in Chicago. Their website said they were an advanced technological services company. The website had a lot of their products for sale but nothing on there said anything about the X-chip. He was cautiously optimistic about the X-chip and what it could mean for his future if he jumped out in front of it. It could revolutionize the world. Jose was only growing more confident in his plans. He sat and daydreamed about his future in politics and in the world.

It was seven-fifteen when the phone rang and it was Juanita on the other end. "Hey there, Jose, are you ready for our meeting tonight?"

She said it in a very playful way. "I am looking forward to it. When am I going to pick you up?" "

Well I am just now getting finished so give me an hour to go to the hotel and shower and change."

"OK, just text me when you want me to leave."

"OK, I will. See you soon."

About three hours went by when Jose got a text to leave his house. He left his downtown condo for the hotel which was a few blocks away. When he got there she was waiting outside for him near the valet attendants. She looked remarkable. She had on tight black jeans with an off- white turtleneck sweater. She was a fashion setter in America. Girls wanted to copy her style, and boys wanted a girl who looked like her. She was spectacular in how she carried herself. She knew she was beautiful and she made her presence known always. There was a small crowd gathered around her, asking her for autographs and pictures.

When Jose pulled up he got out and walked toward the crowd. Instantly the crowd recognized their new Congressman. A man with a cane and brown suit came up to Jose and shook his hand. "It's a pleasure to see you in person, Congressman. You are a hero to me and my family. I wish you the best of luck in your upcoming term."

"Thank you for your support," Jose said as he turned his attention to his date. He walked up to her and said to the crowd, "I am sorry but I have to steal her from you. We have reservations to make."

With that he took her slim and graceful hand into his and led her to his car. "Please step in, Jay."

Her curvy and toned bronzed body squeezed into her outfit. Jose was in a daze over just how beautiful she was in the full light. He guided her into the car and closed the door behind her after she was settled. He looked up as he made his way to the driver side door and saw a scene that he swore he had seen before. There were two valets running to open the doors of a white van, two children playing on a yellow bench near the door to the hotel, and an old woman smiling at him as he turned his body toward the door. He had sworn he had seen this scene before but he had never been to this hotel and to his knowledge he had never seen these people before. But no, he was sure he had seen this before. It was strong déjà vu. It was like he was living a dream in real life. Jose shook it off. "No way I could have seen that before. I must be hallucinating," he thought to himself as he got into the car. "I made reservations at the Casa de Avue, a new Mexican restaurant that just opened. I asked for a special table away from the guests so we could have our privacy. They have made special arrangements for our arrival."

She turned with a soft and curious look on her face. "Seems like someone is trying to impress me. That is the perfect way to not impress me."

Jose stumbled on his words, "But, no, I…"

She cut him off to spare him the excuse. "I am just giving you a hard time. You need to learn to relax."

She put her hand on his shoulder and said, "If we are going to be partners in the AP and good friends, then you are going to have to be able to take some serious shit from me. Don't be an old man. Act your age, Mr. Serious."

Jose put a smile on his face. "You don't have to worry about me, little girl. I can handle whatever you think you can dish out."

Jay pushed him with her hand that was rested on his good shoulder. "Oh I am a little girl huh? I can show you who the little one is."

"That sounds like a threat," Jose said as he brushed her arm away from his body.

"Politicians don't take kindly to threats. I know people." Jose pointed his finger in her face and said, "Maybe it's you who will be doing the learning here, Miss. And another thing, how do you get off…"

With an evil smile Jay quickly opened her mouth and bit Jose's finger that he had pointed at her. "Ouch," Jose exclaimed as he pulled his hand away from her.

"What was that for?"

"It's rude to point your finger in someone's face." She stuck out her tongue and wiggled her hands as she laughed heartily at his expense. Jose couldn't help but laugh at her. She was acting stupid and childish but mature and witty at the same time. He was instantly enamored with her. He had never seen anyone like her. She was so beautiful and confident, but silly and playful at the same time. She turned her attention away from him to look at the radio. "What do you have in here? What kind of music do you like?"

She thumbed through the radio stations that were preset. There were some rap stations and some smooth R&B, which was exactly what Jay, was looking for. "Oh nice, you have 105.5 programmed. I always listen to this station when I visit Dallas." She turned the music up and moved her body to the soft rhythmic beat. She reached down suddenly and began scrambling her hands through her purse to find something.

She pulled out a cigar. Jose's eyes widened in surprise.

Well at least he thought it was a cigar until she said, "Hey you want to take this blunt to the head before we go eat? It will make the experience so much better."

Jose hadn't smoked since college. "No I do not use that stuff anymore. It is bad for you anyway. And even if I wanted to I couldn't because of my job. Not everyone can be a famous entertainer and do what they want."

Jay noticed that some of the edges of the blunt were coming undone and she licked them and pressed them back down. "If you don't want to smoke with the cool kids, then don't be a pussy and tell me it's because mommy might find out. Just say you don't want to smoke, and I will still accept you."

Jose glanced at her out of the side of his eye as he drove. "OK then, I just don't want to smoke. I don't think it has any benefit. To be honest I am disappointed that you smoke."

"Oh lighten up, will ya?" She lit the rolled cigar, rolled the windows down, and puffed a little on the end to get the flame going strong. In a cloud of smoke her green eyes were shining in each passing street light. Jose could hardly keep his gaze from her and concentrate on the road, but he reminded himself that it would be weird to stare at her on the first date or meeting, or whatever you want to call it.

He opened his window so he could get some fresh air. He hated the smell of smoke, especially now that he wasn't a smoker. It had been years since he had smelled the strong fragrance. Jay just turned the music up louder and danced as she puffed on her "magic stick." She was amazing, singing beautifully as she joyfully danced. She knew the words to every song that came on during the drive to the restaurant.

Jose just sat back with a smile on his face. She was really something he had never seen before. She fascinated and mesmerized him with every movement and every glance. Jose couldn't explain it, but whatever she was doing, he was drawn to her.

They pulled up to the restaurant and drove up slowly to the valet. He had on a long sleeve white shirt with a shiny black tie. He reached down and opened the passenger side door. As she stepped out into the light shining from the building, the valet instantly recognized who she was. "Welcome, Miss Mills! I was instructed to have you go through the side stairs entrance. Just walk this way with me after the Congressman gets out."

He held out his hand and Jay grabbed it, looking back to see if Jose had gotten out of the car yet. A second valet had opened Jose's door and he got out and began to follow the enthralled young valet as he led Juanita back to the side entrance. There was a small staircase that stood against the side of the building. A single light stood above the dark wooden staircase. "Right up these stairs, you two just knock on the door. They should be expecting you."

Jay walked out ahead of him and Jose noticed the valet checking out her body. "Wow I can't believe I actually saw Juanita Mills," he mumbled to himself as he shook his head. Not paying attention to where he was going, the valet ran right into Jose.

"Oh I am sorry, Congressman. Have a great night!"

"Thank you for your help. Here is your tip" Jose said as he tipped him and then made his way up the staircase to catch up with his friend.

Jay, eager to get inside from the December cold, knocked furiously on the door, "God, hurry up!"

A waiter quickly opened the door and welcomed Jay. "Greetings, Miss Mills. Welcome to the Casa de Avue! Please step right this way."

He held the door open for Jay and Jose as they made their way into the dim candlelit hallway. "Just head down the hallway until you see a door on the left. Your private dining room is located there. I will notify the waiter that you have arrived. Have a great night."

"Thank you," both Jose and Juanita said in unison.

They chuckled and shared an awkward moment of eye contact, which caused Jay to smile but turn away. Jose moved in front of her to pull back the chair facing away from the door and Jay stopped him. "No I will take the other seat if you don't mind."

Jose really thought nothing of it. The seat had a better view of the room and it faced the door, things which at this time Jose would think nothing of. "OK sure, here have a seat, Jay."

"I am not used to men pulling out my seat for me. I wouldn't even let them if they tried. However, for the Hero, I will make an accommodation."

She swayed her slender hips down into the chair gracefully. "I hope you understand that this is only a friendly business meeting," she said as she sank her body down into the chair.

"Of course it is, Jay. I hope to be able to learn a lot from you. I did not take this as a flirtatious invitation." Jose pushed her chair under the table.

She turned her head with a wicked smile. "You couldn't handle a girl like me anyway. I am way too much woman for a guy like you."

Jose was taken aback. He was not used to women being so forward and talking trash like that. "I... well... I think you will find out from me that real men don't have to brag. If I did happen to grab a woman like you, I guarantee I would handle my own. I have had my fair share of experiences on the street."

Jay laughed heartily at his comment. "If you were from my streets we definitely wouldn't have come to some fancy ass restaurant just to hang out and shoot the shit. Do they even have beers here?"

"I happen to think going out to eat here was a great idea. Just wait until the food comes out and then say something after you taste it. I know it will be worth our time."

"I will give it a try for you, hero," she said as she winked and smiled at him sarcastically. "You sure are making me bend away from my norms tonight."

"Hey you are the one who initiated the entire thing, including coming up to me at Lisa Malky's house. So don't give me a hard time. This is who I am."

"Spend enough time with me, son, and you will forget who you are..."

She looked him right in the eyes as she said it. Just as she finished her sentence, the door opened and in came a chubby, mid-thirties looking Hispanic man.

"Hello, Juanita Mills and Congressman Valdez. I am Hercules, your waiter for the evening."

They both smiled and said "hello" to the man as they opened their menus and began looking. Jay spoke, "I think we are going to need a little more time. Just bring out some chips and the avocado spicy dip. What beers do you have on tap?"

Of course Jay was speaking for both of them, something that really irritated Jose. He kept his cool though, just relishing the new experience of this different kind of woman.

"We have Hanz, Chinst, Oregona, Golden River, and Delush."

"Hmm," Jay thought to herself for a moment. "What are you drinking, hot stuff?"

Jose thumbed through the menu to the drinks page. "I'll take a Roy Rogers, please."

Jay looked at him as if he just told her he hit her mother. "No, he will have the Oregona, and I will have the Hanz, please. This is a celebration of taking his first step on the pyramid."

Jose looked at her quizzically but with frustration as well. He opened his mouth to protest but Jay butted in. "No do not say anything but thank you. Please lighten up a little bit. You are not running for Congress anymore.

You made it. Sit back and enjoy the perks of the good life. It is time for you to go back to your college days! There are only, what, 200 of you people? You should take that as a sign that you can basically do whatever you want and get away with it."

Jose laughed inside but still held his face sternly. "First off, there are 465 members in the House, and 100 members in the Senate. I just haven't had a beer in a long time. I have been busy with my campaign. I guess I have never really had the time to party and drink a lot in the last few years."

"Well you need to relax and have a good time. We have all night to drink and talk. If you want, we can take a taxi to my hotel and you can take it home."

Jose thought about it. He never really drank anymore but this was a better time than ever to drink. He had this beautiful woman urging him to drink, making it nearly impossible to say no. He hadn't been really drunk since college, so he thought it would be best to have a few but keep it easy.

"OK I will have a few drinks tonight, but not enough to take a taxi."

Jay smirked and flashed her emerald eyes. "OK, that is fine. But you sound like a punk. Hopefully after you spend a little more time with me you can loosen up."

Jose just ignored her. "Whatever you say, doll."

Jose grabbed his menu and held it up in front of his face blocking his view of her. "I think I already know what I want, how about you?"

When he looked up she had her face down looking at the menu, contemplating what she would be eating.

"So tell me again how you got involved with the American Protectorate?"

Jay looked up from her menu. "Come on, Hero, do we have to talk about that right now? Let's talk about something fun. What's the craziest thing you have ever done?"

Jose was again frustrated that they could not get down to business. "Come on," she repeated, "tell me, what's the craziest thing you have ever done?"

Jose thought about it for a second and came up with easily his best answer, "I had sex on the fifth floor of the library at school and the middle of the day."

Jay let out a rich laugh, and responded, "That is great. I would never expect that from a square like you."

"I am not a square," Jose retorted forcefully. "I was captain of my college basketball team. I was a jock. I just turned it down a few notches after I started getting serious about my political career."

"You still are lacking in many ways, young Congressman. You need training on how to be fun again."

"I don't need any training, especially from a girl like you."

"What is wrong with a girl like me? Just because I am from East Phoenix there is something wrong with me?"

"No I don't mean it like that. I meant a woman so young."

"I am not even that young. I have plenty of experience in my 23 years."

"You keep on thinking that," Jose responded.

Jay shrugged. "OK fine. Let's talk about the AP since you are so interested in learning how I became involved. I joined the American Protectorate a year and a half ago, about a month after my first Grammy Award. I went on Lisa's show, and after it was over she invited me to a meeting. I went to the meeting, and I was hooked. They were talking about preserving and spreading American culture and that is very important to me. My grandfather fought in WWII in Italy, so I have a tradition of patriotism in my family. That is where he met my grandmother, in Rome, after it was liberated. She was a volunteer nurse for the Allies and my grandfather was wounded by German soldiers on the initial surge into the city. She nursed him back to health. Before he left to fly back home to America he proposed to her and she accepted. They moved back to America where they had to deal with the racial bigotry from both sides of the family. My grandfather was black and my mother was full-blooded Italian, so they moved to Phoenix away from Mississippi where my grandfather was raised. That is where they had my mother. I am sorry I am rambling."

Jose smiled. "I wasn't going to say anything but I appreciate the family lesson."

"Do you want me to continue? I can give you a quick background on my life and you can do the same."

"Sure continue."

"Well when they got to Phoenix they moved downtown because it was cheap and crime wasn't too bad. They raised my mother there. My grandfather passed in 2003; he was 77. My grandmother is named Domenica, she is 85 but she has the spirit of a 40-year-old. My grandparents raised me. Both my father and mother were killed in a car accident shortly after I was born. I wasn't in the car. I was at my grandparents' place."

"I am sorry to hear that. I am sure your grandmother is a wonderful person."

"She is amazing! You must meet her someday. She actually lives here in Dallas."

"Oh well in that case, I will definitely meet her."

Jay's eyes lit up as she talked about the woman who raised her. "She is a great woman. She calls herself a Prophetess. She thinks she hears messages and has visions from God. She is really a sweet woman, but sometimes she can be a little crazy."

"Well she doesn't sound like anything too bad."

"She can be a handful sometimes. You know if I am telling you that, she must be a whirlwind."

The waiter came back and took their orders and left. "I like Hercules; he is a good man. I am going to leave him a big tip," Jose said as he munched on more of his avocado dip.

"Now you go," Jay exclaimed with an inquisitive smirk in her eyes.

"Well, I was raised here in Dallas by my mom. She was brought here by my grandparents from Guatemala. My grandparents died before I was born, unfortunately. My father ran off on my mom when she was pregnant with me. He died in a car accident in Oklahoma on his way out of town. So I guess we both grew up without knowing our fathers. Sad, but that is probably what gives us strength to make it so far on our own hard work."

"Maybe you are right that it gave me strength, but it also has its downside. I am horrible with finding a good man. I am sure you know of my love affairs from the tabloids."

Jose knew the story, everyone did, but he played it cool. "I heard something about your ex-boyfriend Landon Rondell cheating on you."

"Yeah well he not only cheated on me, but it was with my former band mate. On top of that he made a sex tape that got out on the internet. It devastated me!"

"I am sorry to hear that. Yeah maybe dating a horny, young sex symbol might have been a bad idea."

"I am a horny, young sex symbol. Does that mean you wouldn't date me?"

Jose stumbled for a quick response. "I, uh, didn't mean it like that."

"Save it. I have heard it all already. It isn't fair that I get a bad rap just because I am young, sexy, and fun. That is part of the reason I joined the American Protectorate. I want people to take me more seriously."

"Well just because you are young doesn't mean I don't take you seriously. I very much take you seriously. I just think because you are a beautiful pop star, people expect the worst rather than the best when it comes to intelligence and wisdom. Some of the lyrics to your songs may rub people the wrong way as well."

"Well the lyrics to my songs are important to me. I have sex, I drink, I smoke weed, and I get crazy. I sing about myself, nothing more, and nothing less. If people don't like it, they can change the station or change the channel. And if YOU don't like it you can just take me home now."

Jose was once again taken by surprise by the aggressive stance of his precious young compatriot. "No, I don't mind you at all. You are very different from any woman I have met before and that is a good thing. I like uniqueness in a person. I consider myself a unique individual so I am drawn to others who are like me."

Jay continued after an awkward and dramatic pause. "One of my first reasons for joining the AP was to gain more respect from the community and my peers. The close second is because it is focusing on protecting American beliefs. I believe strongly in the right to free speech, and an organization that puts its efforts into protecting that is something I want to be a part of. Also their commitment to preserving American culture drew me to them. I love music. It is a gift from God."

Jose sighed sarcastically, "I could tell."

"Shut up! I am not ashamed of my love for music." Jay started rubbing the sides of her body and around her stomach. "It pours through my soul and my body. It gives me life."

Jose was in a trance over the seductive motions of the green-eyed beauty. "The third reason I joined the AP was because of their pursuit of higher forms of media. You already heard about the X-chip and what that could mean for the radio and television business. It would be a new medium that I could get ahead of instead of coming in behind. I want to be cutting-edge, ahead of the trends and making them instead of being a worthless follower. I see that you and I share that ambition."

"Yes, I think we do. I want to be a leader for this country and for Latinos world-wide. I have a few ideas on how to do that but I just need a little help on getting them implemented."

Jose was interrupted by the door opening and three waiters, including the jolly and wide Hercules, bringing in their food on separate trays. "Hot plates so be very careful." Hercules swung the plates down over the table in graceful form, holding each plate with a white towel to avoid burning himself.

"Enjoy, Lady and Gentleman. I will come back in a few minutes to check your drinks and see if everything is OK." With a smooth move, the three men were gone and there they were with a table full of food. They ate and barely spoke for the next fifteen minutes.

Jay looked up from her finished plate and said, "So you are ready to tell me more about your plans? Maybe I could help."

Jose had just finished his food as well. "Right now I don't have anything concrete, just a general outline of what I want to do."

"Go on, please."

"Well I want to save Mexico from being an impoverished and crime-ridden country. When we fix Mexico, we fix illegal immigration. I support amnesty but only if there was a punishment for coming here illegally. There must be a system we can use to keep illegals out, and prevent the ones already here from committing crime."

"You could always use the X-chip to monitor them and use it as a form of punishment for coming here illegally. Make it a condition of obtaining citizenship. That would be humane and it would give you a huge boost in popularity."

"That is an excellent idea, Jay. However, we can't get to that part until we find a way to increase the wealth of Mexico."

"Give me some time and I will think of something. I am good at problem solving."

"Most of my other political beliefs are just generic in order to stay in good terms with the party, a party that is growing more and more radical every year. I have to say I am a practicing Christian, even though I rarely attend church and have almost no relationship with God."

"Yeah I rarely attended church too, and then I found this church here in Dallas that I sometimes go to with my Grandmother. Mostly I just do Bible study by myself or with my Grandmother, though."

"So you consider yourself a Christian? I guess I do too but I just haven't put a lot of effort into it lately. Maybe that will change soon though. I have had an itch to get back into my Biblical studies; I only just need a partner in crime who can help keep me on task."

"I could definitely be that for you if you wanted me to help. I love God and everything He has given me. I wouldn't be where I am without Him. I would love to get that spirit back inside of you. You definitely need to meet my Grandmother then. She is a very uniquely spiritual person."

Jose grinned. "OK you keep talking about your grandmother. It seems like I just have to meet her now."

"Wonderful. Unfortunately, I have some news for you, one thing good, and one thing bad. Which do you want to hear first?"

Intrigued, Jose said, "Good."

"Well the good news is that I am actually having fun on our first business meeting."

"OK, so what is the bad news then?"

"The bad news is that I am getting bored. There is this great club downtown that I always go to when I am in town. We are going tonight."

"Really? A club? I haven't been to a club in years. Are you serious?"

"Yes! Why don't you liven up a little and relax? I am not going let anyone hurt the Hero."

"You don't care that people are going to see us together? I am sure Congressmen aren't too hip in your crowd."

"You are a hero, whether you are a boring Congressman or not."

"OK maybe I should try to not be so boring. Maybe you can help me with that too."

She gave a nod and an impish smile. "Damn straight I will."

So Jose paid the bill and the two left out the side entrance to the valet station. Jose got his car keys from the valet and they pulled off for the club. Just as Jose started driving Jay spoke up. "Hey can you take the long way there so I have enough time to blow these trees?"

"You are smoking again?" Jose questioned as Jay pulled another fat weed-filled cigar.

"Honey I stay high as much as possible. I wish you would smoke but I guess we need to take things slowly, don't we?"

"I just don't think it is smart for a Congressman to be smoking marijuana. It would be one thing if I lived in a state where it is legal, but they would have me by the balls in Texas if I were caught smoking."

"Relax, no one would know you were smoking."

"No, I am just not comfortable with all that."

With that Jay shrugged her shoulders and took the lighter flame, which came out the nozzle of a miniature metal gun, and held it to the tip of the blunt. "You just don't understand yet the power of this plant. It was given to us as a gift. It is from the original Garden of Eden. Did you know that? God had always intended us to smoke weed as a way to reach closer to Him."

"Where on earth did you hear that nonsense from? I never heard that in any church growing up."

"That is because it is the dirty little secret that the Catholic Church covered up when they first put together the books of the Bible. Ever since, Christians have had a negative view of marijuana. They unfortunately classify it as a narcotic and dangerous drug."

Jose took a right turn onto the next street and glanced at her. "It is a narcotic and a dangerous drug. You know how many people are dying in the drug trade in Mexico right now? How about on the streets of Chicago? Black and brown people are deemed criminals far too often over this silly plant."

"You have so much to learn and so little time." Jay took a drag on the cigar.

"What is that supposed to mean? I have done my research on marijuana. It destroys lives, leads to other more dangerous drugs, and it makes you lazy, unproductive, and lethargic."

Jay slowly shook her head in disbelief as she took another deep inhale of the sticky herb. "No," she coughed a little and caught her breath, "those are all lies told to you by the government to keep you from the truth. They want you to believe that marijuana is a bad thing because they do not have control over it. It is a gateway to spiritual awakening. It is a pathway to enlightenment. It gives one a supernatural power over their mind that only a few know how to utilize."

"You are saying some pretty deep stuff there lady. How am I supposed to believe all these things you are saying when my whole life I have been told something different?"

"I will have to show you. Do not worry though, the night is young and fortunately we have just enough time to get you ready. I just hope you have your seatbelt on because I am about to take you on a wild ride."

With that Jay took another few hits on the blunt. It was nearing its end and Jay had her eyes closed in a trance as she took the last few puffs on the brown wand. Jose had taken the back way so they had a good 15 minutes before he got to the valet. "Just pull right up. They will take the car. They should be expecting us."

"How could they be expecting us? You didn't call or anything."

"I already made plans earlier in the afternoon to come here."

"How did you know I was going to say yes?"

"Because I had faith in you, Jose. Also, because I knew you couldn't say no to this pretty face," she said as she puckered her lips for an air kiss.

They pulled up to the front of the club, with Jay singing the lyrics to one of the songs on the radio. The black tinted sedan rolled smoothly to the curb with the crowd looking to see who would come out of the car. When the valet opened the door and the crowd saw that Juanita was inside, they went crazy. Everyone tried to lean in to get a good look at her, screaming, "Oh my God! It's Juanita Mills!" and "Look it's Jay Mills. I can't believe it."

Everyone was pulling out their camera phones to get a snap of the famous actress and music star. People barely noticed when the Hero of the Convention Center got out of the car and headed around toward the valet station. One person blurted out, "Hey there is the Congressman," and Jose looked up and waved toward him. While Jose may be famous in some crowds for his efforts that election night, this was the crowd that Juanita was an icon in. An usher from the club came up and met Juanita, telling her and Jose to follow her to the entrance. She said she would lead them to their VIP table. The club had a long line of waiting patrons, and they all clapped and jeered the Congressman for being out with the dynamic young superstar. "Good luck, Congressman," someone cheered out as they made their way to the entrance.

Once inside they were led up to the third level, where the main dance floor and stage were for the club. They made their way to the table and Jose gave a tip to the usher who led them there. Jose had had a few beers at dinner and they were running through his system quickly. "I need to go to the bathroom," he yelled to Jay over the loud hip-hop music being played in the background.

"OK, I will wait here with the bottle just in case someone tries to get cute and take it. You go and I will probably go when you get back."

With that Jose waved a small goodbye to Jay, and made his way toward the signs for "Gentleman" and "Ladies," shining neon green on the far side wall. He stood in line like everyone else, expecting nothing special from his important status. After a few minutes and a couple songs, Jose was up and he took his opening in the middle stall. He was careful not to let his black collared shirt touch the sides of the stall. Lord knows what could have gotten on them. After he finished using the bathroom he washed his hands.

A few of the other men in the bathroom recognized him and said hello to the Congressman. He said hello back graciously and made his way out the door.

It was then that Jose began to feel it. The room started to turn in on his peripherals, and his eyes were strangely focused in on whatever he was looking at. He looked toward the bar, and he saw three bartenders. One tall white guy with an American flag and eagle tattooed on his arm, one black guy with dreadlocks, and an Asian girl with dyed blonde hair. It didn't make any sense to him, but he somehow knew each of them would be standing there at this exact moment without ever having been there before in his life. He scanned the crowd to the right, and once again he saw a scene he had seen before in his brain somewhere.

It was a hefty black woman arguing with what appeared to be her boyfriend. She was holding a drink in her hand. Jose now remembered that she was going to throw it at him, and just as the vision came to his head it happened. Jose was having strong déjà vu again. It was so strong it was making him dizzy, and his head started to ache. As he turned the corner toward the back of the room where the VIP was, he had another strong sensation, like he was supposed to be there, seeing someone who he was supposed to fall in love with. It was a strange sensation but he knew exactly what it was telling him. He put his hands to his eyes to rub them, trying to make the sensations go away. Just when he opened his eyes, they focused on one beautiful woman in an off-white, tight sweater. It was Jay, and she looked absolutely spectacular. "But how could this be happening?" Jose thought to himself as he reached for a side rail to gather himself.

He had seen this scene before somewhere in his past. He felt he was live in a dream. He felt like was going to wake up from some vivid slumber, but it was all real. As he made his way closer to Jay the feelings slowly began to subside and he was back to normal. "That made no sense," he said audibly and loud enough for Jay to hear as he was walking up the steps toward their table.

"What made no sense honey?" Jay asked him.

"Oh nothing I would consider serious. I just had some really bad déjà vu is all. I can't explain what just happened but it was weird."

Jay looked up slowly from her drink, with a curious expression on her face. "Déjà vu, huh? That sure is strange to be getting déjà vu so randomly. Was it strong or just a little flash?"

"No it was strong. It was like my brain was in a movie I had already seen."

"Very interesting. Maybe you should tell my Grandmother what happened when you see her. She is very much into those kinds of things. She might be able to help you."

"OK I will, but for now I am going to drink to get that feeling to go away."

Jay reached for a glass and poured him a good amount of vodka from the tall, slender, and curved bottle on the table. She poured from the cranberry juice container to mix the elixir for Jose. "Here you go, just relax and have a good time. Let's just dance and enjoy the night."

Jose took the glass from Jay and began drinking. Jay then left for the bathroom leaving Jose alone for a good 15 minutes to drink by himself. By the time she came back, Jose was feeling a little tipsy. She made a few cracks at Jose for stumbling on his speech already and then poured herself another drink. The two laughed and drank for a while longer before Jay asked Jose if he wanted to dance.

"Well I haven't really gone out and danced like this since college, so don't laugh at me if I mess up."

"Will you stop being such a pussy and come on with me, Mr. Hero."

Jose took this insult and compliment in stride. He was growing accustomed to it from her, unfortunately.

They meandered the river of space the crowd gave them until they made their way to the middle of the dance floor. People noticed who they were but they were too focused on dancing themselves to bother them. They danced, close at times, to plenty of songs that night. They would spend breaks going back to the table to get more liquor. They were both pretty drunk and having a great time when all of a sudden the lights came on and the DJ said, "It's 2 a.m. so closing time. Please start making your way toward the door."

Jay stopped dancing on Jose and she turned around and made a pouty face, "Damn I liked that song." The alcohol made her wave in the current of the air conditioner. Jose was drunk too, and this made him very tired. He had a meeting with a man named Chester Begg the next afternoon, so he needed his sleep.

Jose was thinking of making him his chief of staff. He needed to get his staff in order because the swearing in would be in a few weeks. "Dear, I have had a lot of fun tonight but I have to raise the white flag," Jose said in defeat.

"You can't be serious. The night is still young. I am sure I can find another party for us to go to or we can just hang out at my hotel."

Jose and Jay walked out together to the murmurs of the crowd around them. "I have an important meeting tomorrow. I really would but I can't. I had a great time tonight, though."

"Oh yeah I forgot, it's Mr. Congressman with all his important meetings bullshit. Well if you weren't such an old man we could be having so much more fun. I understand, though. If you have a meeting tomorrow, you need to get your sleep. I just hope for the few times I get to see you at AP meetings or around the town, you can loosen up a bit."

"I have already come out of my shell a lot for you tonight. You are so damn demanding."

"Hey don't curse at me asshole or you'll be going to your meeting tomorrow with one testicle."

Jose smiled and raised his hand for a cab. "Feisty…" Jose retorted.

A cab came swerving into the lane and stopped in front of the Congressman. Jose opened the door for Jay and then went around and got in himself. Several people had gathered around them to take pictures and ask for autographs. When the two got in the car the crowd erupted into applause for the pair. The Hero with the Princess will be all the tabloids talk about in the next few days.

"Please take her to the Olianda Hotel and then take me to the Shadyside Condos on Shadyside Avenue."

"OK, Congressman," the cabbie responded. "Buckle up please, and let's go."

For the first few minutes of the ride there was silence, and then Jose spoke up. "So when is the next AP meeting?"

Jay looked up from her cell phone to respond, "I am not too sure. We usually meet about once every other month. Sometimes we meet in Chicago, or New York, or Miami. It is usually on the East Coast or Midwest because that is where the majority of the members are from."

"I am fascinated by this X-chip. I can see so many possibilities with it. From what I see, it could completely change the media landscape of not only America, but the world."

"It has a translation option as well so you can speak into it and it will translate what you are saying into any other language. It is quite the amazing project. I just hope our fellow Christians don't try to stop us."

"Why would Christians be trying to stop the X-chip?"

Jay looked up at him with a, "you can't be serious" look. "Well most Christians believe that in the end times there will be a mark of the beast given to them in the hand or forehead."

Jose nodded his head in agreement as the memory of the mark of the beast came back to him. "Ah yes I have heard of that. I thought most of those types of Christians believed the world would end in 2012? Since the world clearly isn't ending any time soon, you would figure that they would lay off the conspiracy theories."

"You never know with Christians, though."

"You say Christians as if you are not one."

"I am not a 'Christian' in the typical sense, but I do believe in Christ. He was definitely a real person. I just do not agree with all the social constraints of the Christian community. They got it all wrong. Christ did not want us to live like slaves, bound up and afraid to live. He wanted us to be free and experience life to the fullest."

"But there are rules to following Christ. You shouldn't be out having sex, smoking weed, and being crazy. I don't think He would approve."

"As long as in your heart you know you believe that Christ will wash away your sins, you can sin as much as you want. A white lie is just as big of a sin as me being in an orgy or killing someone. All sins are washed away, remember that."

"I just have never interpreted the Gospel that way before. You say your Grandmother is a Prophetess, does she approve of all of this behavior?"

"Well she doesn't know about all of it. She just knows I am trying to be a better person. I always take what she says to heart because I know she has been called to action by a higher power. Maybe I am just not ready to call myself a Christian. It would be a lie. I don't go to church enough and I never pray. I do believe in Christ and I wish I could worship Him more. It's crazy but I have never really come out and said this to anyone before. Maybe there is a reason we met each other. It was dark at Malky's house and I just randomly sat next to you I swear. When I realized it was the Hero of the Convention Center, the new Congressman, I just had to talk to you. I am glad I did." Jose turned his shoulders to face her, "I am glad you invited me out. I also think I met you for a reason. I kept getting this weird déjà vu, it has to mean something. I know God is telling me this is the right path. I am definitely eager to start our Bible study."

Jay clapped and smiled with her pouty lips, then raised her arms in the air and yelled "Hallelujah!" at the top of her lungs. It startled the driver and made him swerve a little in the lane.

The driver spoke up., "Miss Mills, your hotel is coming up in a few seconds."

Jay grabbed Jose's hands and placed them in hers. She softly said, "Thank you for a good night, Congressman. I hope all goes well at your inauguration. I will text you my email and my FaceNet account. If you ever get any free time just hit me up! I come to Dallas all the time to visit my Grandmother so hopefully we can run into each other."

The car pulled into the entrance and the valet came and opened the car door. The two said their final goodbyes and she got out of the car. Her tanned skin glowed in the hotel lights as she made her way to the entrance. Jose was in a trance. What an incredible night. He had not gone out like this since college, and he definitely hasn't gotten drunk in a while. He spent the rest of the car ride home thinking about when he was going to talk to her next. Bible study excited him, especially because he was going to need the spiritual guidance in his position as Congressman.

He got to his condo and paid for the cab. He stumbled his way into the building. He was greeted by Earl the doorman. "Hello Congressman, let me get that elevator for you."

He ran out from behind his desk to push the up button. "Crazy night huh, Congressman? Make sure you eat something before you go to sleep to soak up that alcohol."

"Thanks, Earl," Jose responded slowly as the elevator doors opened. Jose went up to his floor, strode into his apartment, and grabbed an apple as he made his way to bed.

He woke up the next morning groggy and slightly hung over. His meeting with Chester Begg was in the afternoon, so he had some time to kill in the morning. Instead of going to the gym he decided to go to his mother's house. He had promised her he would come by. He had plenty of things to tell her about the day before. So he drove to the apartment complex where he was raised.

People on the street recognized him and said hello as he walked toward the entrance to the building. He got to the door and knocked. His mother came and answered the door wearing a pink robe and blue dragon styled slippers. "Jose! My son, it is so nice to see you. Come in baby I have breakfast ready."

Jose came in and took off his coat and sat down at the table. "Just take a seat," she yelled from the kitchen. "I am bringing you your plate."

Jose made himself comfortable as he waited for breakfast to come out. In a few minutes, his mother arrived with a plate full of food. She brought chorizo sausage burritos with eggs and bacon, pancakes, and a glass of orange juice.

"Eat up, son." She went back to the kitchen to make her own plate as Jose started to eat his burritos.

"I had a great day yesterday. I can't wait to tell you about it. The breakfast was great and the night with Juanita Mills was even better."

Carmela had a wide smile as she placed her plate and drink on the table. "Go ahead. I am listening."

"Well the breakfast went fantastic. I really had a chance to reach out to some of my most prized donors. I really think I am hitting a good stride in my speeches, too." He took a swig of his OJ and continued. "When I get up on the stage I have a confidence that comes from deep inside me that I am doing something great. I can feel it in my soul. I just can't describe the feeling. It's almost as if I am destined to make an impact on this world."

"Destiny is in our hands though, son. We have the choice to shape our own destiny."

Jose looked up quizzically. "I thought you believed that God has a master plan for you? I thought you believed that your life is already mapped out for you?"

"No son, those aren't exactly my beliefs," Carmela responded. "I believe that God already knows the decision you are going to make, but it is up to you to decide for yourself. God has given us free will to decide our own fates."

"Well I decided mine a long time ago. I wanted to change the world; end the suffering of my people here in America and our neighboring countries."

"Well I just want you to focus on the small things, son. You keep getting caught up on the big grand picture instead of focusing on the details.

Little by little you can change the world but it takes time and patience. Nothing is given to you in one night. If you really want to save the Latino people in this country, it starts by you being an example to them. I hope that I raised a son who is strong in his beliefs, but cautious in their application."

Jose had a mouth full of food as he nodded his head in agreement. When he finished he replied, "You raised me to have a good heart, Mother. I am just looking ahead to the future because my future looks very bright. The possibilities are endless."

"Well your future will only remain bright if you concentrate on the present," Carmela smartly retorted to her son. "So, tell me about Miss Mills. Was she as spectacular as she seems on television?"

"I just don't know how to describe her mom, but she is absolutely one of a kind. We talked about life, love, God, and of course, the American Protectorate. She called it a business meeting but it felt like a lot more than that to me. She actually wants to start doing a Bible study with me; can you believe that?"

Carmela got up from the table and began to gather up the plates and dishes. "That sounds great, Jose. She is absolutely beautiful and she seems like a real firecracker on the news."

"Yeah she is a firecracker, but still elegant and confident in herself. There isn't another woman like her that I have ever met. Another crazy thing is that I kept having this crazy déjà vu that night, almost like I was supposed to meet with her that night or something."

Just then there was a loud crash. Carmela tripped over herself and she dropped the plates and glasses on the hardwood floor. She stammered to catch her breath and get the words out as Jose rushed to her side to help her up. "You said what? Déjà vu? Are you sure it was déjà vu?"

Jose grabbed her under her arms and helped her up as she gathered her balance. "Are you OK, Mom? What happened? Did you trip or did you faint? You want me to call the ambulance to come get you?"

Carmela refuted him soundly, "No I am perfectly fine. Do not worry about me. Now get back to your story. Tell me about this déjà vu."

Carmela slowly picked up the items she had dropped. Jose leaned down to help, but she waved him off.

"Well it was a crazy feeling. It was strong. It was almost as if I had seen the scene before in a dream or something. The music, the people, the atmosphere, it was like I was already there before. It made my head hurt, to be honest with you."

"Well that is remarkable, Jose. That is a very weird experience. Maybe you should talk to someone about it. How about going to this new church I found just out of the city? The pastor's name is Rich Urban. I could give Pastor Rich a call and you could go and talk to him."

"A pastor… Mom, you can't be serious. Give me a break. I never even go to church. Why would I go to a random pastor to talk to him about déjà vu of all things? It doesn't seem that important."

"It may be important; you never know. You need someone to look out for you spiritually. I can only do so much as your mother."

"I don't need anyone looking out for my spiritual health. I think it is just fine. Plus, I am about to start Bible study and everything. The last thing I need is a pastor getting all into my business and my personal life"

Carmela shot a sideways glance at her son. "Well he already knows a little about you. I have been emailing with him. He knows I am the Congressman's mother."

"Mom! You know I hate it when you go and tell my business to other people."

"I am sorry. I just needed some spiritual help regarding you and me. I felt like we were growing apart. I don't want you to lose trust in me."

"What reason would I have to be suspicious?" Jose said, thinking that it was very strange that she was talking to a pastor about him.

"No it's nothing, I promise," she said as she turned and looked down and away. "Now tell me more about Miss Mills."

Jose, for the first time in his life, didn't quite trust his mother. He knew something was up but he couldn't call her on it. "Well, she was great, like I said before. She isn't all glamorous and stuck up. She is a real down-to-earth woman. I can appreciate that. I didn't quite agree with her taste in smoking, but maybe I could look past it as we become good friends."

"Friends, huh? I really hope that's where it stands. You remember what happened to this girl and her last relationship. You don't need anything crazy like that happening with you. Your career is at stake. A reputable Congressman shouldn't be gallivanting with a young and frivolous girl like that." Carmela placed the items on the table and sat down at the table.

"Oh," Jose said as he sat back down at the table. "You heard about that huh?"

"Of course I heard about it. The story was all over the news and late night comedy shows."

"Well none of that was her fault. The guy cheated on her, remember that, and her friend was a whore."

"That still shines poorly on who she would choose as a man to date. All I am saying is be careful. She could easily be trouble. You don't think she's a little too young for you?"

"Why do you keep talking about this dating stuff? We are just friends and that is where I plan on keeping it. I am not looking to date right now anyway. I have way too much on my plate. She is just a cool young woman who is spiritually in a place that I am comfortable with. Her social life means nothing to me. She is going to be young, and in the spotlight. There is nothing I could or would want to do about that."

Carmela nodded. "I like that you are more interested in improving your spiritual life. I just wish you would go see my new pastor. He is absolutely amazing. The Holy Spirit is just pouring through him. He speaks to you. You must give him a try at least once for me. Go with your new little girlfriend," she said with a wicked smile on her face.

Jose got mad and rolled his napkin into a ball and threw it at her. "Stop that, I am telling you. I am not interested in dating right now. I am just enjoying being a young 30-year-old Congressman. I don't know what it was but she was just hypnotizing. I couldn't stop thinking about her. It was like she was in my head or something."

"What do you mean in your head?" his mother said with a worried look on her face.

"I am talking about the image of her. Those eyes, that smile, and her hair. I distinctly remember all of it. It's like her smell is still in my nostrils."

Carmela wrinkled her nose and waved her hand. "Eww don't be talking about her smell. I don't want to know about any of that stuff."

Jose sighed. "Mom, don't be vulgar. I said I am not going to fool around with her or date her. I don't understand why you are having such a hard time believing me."

"I believe you son; I am just giving you a hard time." Carmela set her head in the palm of her hands at the table. "You know you look just like your father."

"You know, you never talk about Dad. I really do wish I could have met him. He would be so proud of me now. I am doing a lot of what I am doing because of him. Did you love him?"

Carmela sat up at attention. "I did love him. It was just that our love could not last. I wish there was something I could have done to prevent him from leaving that day but I couldn't stop him. He just couldn't bear with the fact that I was having his child. The weight of it was too much for him. Who knows if he would have come back for you. The only thing you can look at is that he decided to run from me. I don't know why God took him from you but He did. He was just in the wrong place at the wrong time. I just always go back to that day and wish there was something I could do to stop him from leaving me."

"It is sad. My father is in heaven watching over me, but I don't get angry. It gives me courage. It gives me faith that one day I will meet with him again and I can tell him that I love him and ask him if he is proud of the work I did."

"I know he is proud of you, Jose." Carmela got up and kissed him on the cheek and gave him a hug. "You are making us all proud, Son."

Jose looked at the time on the wall. "I need to be leaving now, Mom, I am sorry. I am meeting with a man named Chester Begg. He has a lot of experience working on the Hill and he has references from several of the other members. I think he may be the man I am looking for to fill my spot for chief of staff."

"Oh good. That is exciting. I know the inauguration is coming up soon so you need to get all that stuff figured out. Good luck with your meeting and I love you, Son. Always remember that I love you and I would do anything to protect you."

They gave each other one last hug and Jose left the apartment. He was excited about putting his staff together, but there were a few things on his mind that were bothering him. First, what would his mother be talking to a pastor about? Why did she sound so fishy at times during breakfast this morning? Why couldn't he get Juanita Mills off his mind? It was like she was a catchy tune that he got stuck in his head. All of these things bothered Jose but nothing would come of it anytime soon. He had a swearing in ceremony to get ready for.

Chapter 6

It had been a very busy day for Freddy since it was his last full day in Colorado. The air was chilled in a light December storm. Freddy had held a farewell seminar at the University of Colorado at Boulder. There he had a chance to talk about many of his dark matter related inventions. He showcased his suspended flight automobile, high speed train, airplanes, and space craft prototypes. Freddy was the star of Boulder. Everyone had congratulations and questions for him. Many of his students came to the seminar to wish him good luck on the search. They also were saddened at the fact that the professor would not be available to teach for an extended period of time.

Freddy really loved his students. He appreciated their passion for science and learning because it gave him more strength to pursue his own goals and dreams. Freddy made sure to connect with everyone important today after his seminar because he wanted to foster good relationships before he left. He still didn't know where the discovery of dark matter and his inventions would take him in life, so he wanted to make sure he could come back to CU at any time he needed.

After a long and fruitful day at the university, Freddy left to go see his friend Lawrence DeRossi perform at a local club in downtown Denver. The sun had already set and downtown was abuzz with locals and tourists out for a good time on a Saturday night. Freddy was lucky and found a good parking spot across the street from the club. Freddy had on a suit and an overcoat in the chilly December Colorado air. As he opened the front door of the club a rush of warm air flowed into his face. A familiar sound filled his ears as he stepped through into the dark, shadowy room. It was Lawrence sitting on the stage in the glow of a bright stage light in the dim darkness. He was playing his bass guitar and singing his famous song called "Tomorrow We Run." It was a love song about a young couple hiding from the law and making their escape to Canada. The crowd was singing along to the lyrics and swaying their heads to the rhythmic beat. Freddy made his way to the dimly lit bar to order a drink. He sat and listened to the gentle voice of his friend.

"The sun is setting. It's almost time to run," Lawrence, who went by his stage name of DeRossi in public, softly sang the first line of the second verse, and then the crowd chimed in and finished the sentence, "Go get the cash girl, don't forget my gun."

Lawrence chimed in, "I will walk with you when the sun stands still," the crowd responded, "Move the tides with our love."

Lawrence got up from his seat, letting the black leather strap hold up his white-faced guitar with black trim, and he grabbed the microphone with both hands. He used the power of his entire body to yell out the next sentence. "We will live with the stars until," "The Lord calls us home from above!" His guitar player, a 28-year-old friend named Casper, whom Lawrence and Freddy had met while at CU, peeled his electric guitar into a hypnotic guitar solo that had the crowd clapping along with the beat. When it was over the crowd went quiet and listened to the buttery soothing voice of DeRossi that they had come to know and love.

He finished the song and the crowd erupted into a standing ovation. DeRossi was a big name in Colorado and around the college scene and the crowd definitely represented that. The main lighting came on signaling the end of the show as Lawrence made his last few thank you remarks to the crowd. Just as he was about to turn and walk off the stage he took a quick peek at the crowd and then the bar and he saw Freddy sitting there. Lawrence gave a great big smile and grabbed the microphone again.

"I have a treat for you all right now. There is a very special guest at the bar tonight." The crowd all looked toward the bar wondering who it was. "We have Professor Slater, the discoverer of dark matter. He is going to change the world I can tell you that!"

The crowd all looked toward Freddy and he blushed from the attention forced onto him from his friend. The crowd splashed a round of applause on Freddy. DeRossi waved him to come up to the stage and say something. Freddy got up and slithered his way through the chairs and people to get to the stage. Freddy grabbed the microphone. "Thank you so much for your support during this exciting time. We begin searching for dark matter next week, so stay tuned everyone."

DeRossi took the microphone back and thanked the crowd for coming and reminded them that he had two shows there the following weekend before he would be taking a hiatus from live performing to work on his new album. DeRossi put the microphone back on the stand and walked over and gave his friend a hug. He guided him, with his right arm draped over his shoulders, toward his dressing room located in the back of the club. When they arrived Lawrence closed the door behind him and told his friend to take a seat while he got changed out of his sweaty shirt.

"Great crowd tonight, Lawrence," Freddy said, smiling. "You are really starting to hit a great stride in your career. We are both finding success, which makes me very happy. Who would have thought that a couple of goofballs from Colorado could make it in this crazy world? When is your new album coming out?"

Lawrence came out from around the closet door to answer him. "Sometime next fall if all goes as planned, but we shouldn't be talking about my little bit of success. You are changing mankind forever with your discovery and inventions. I am so proud of you, man. You are making the entire state become washed with pride."

"I know I should be excited because things in my life are great but I still feel an empty feeling in my stomach. We are uncovering the final secrets of God, and that should make me excited, but for some reason it doesn't."

"Do you feel like you are killing God?"

"I feel like I am definitely helping. I have created something that only God had the power to do. I am disproving the notion that men are subservient to a magical being in the sky. Men can accomplish anything we set out to. The only things we have left to conquer are the skies of the great beyond. I feel that is coming in the very near future once I find someone to help build my prototypes."

"Yeah I heard about how you are keeping your patents to yourself. I think that is a great idea. Wait for the highest bidder! Really take it to 'em. You have all the leverage."

"Lawrence, it is not about the money. You should know that."

"Yeah you're right I was thinking about what I would do."

They both laughed and Lawrence came and grabbed him close. "You need to do what makes you happy."

"What would make me happy is if Jennifer came on the trip with me. I really love her, Lawrence."

"That is serious to take her on such an important expedition. What do you think she would say if you asked her? You have been dating her for six years now, right? Maybe it is time to make a move beyond girlfriend."

"I don't know how you read my mind, but yes, I was thinking of asking the big question after we found the dark matter. I am extremely nervous about it. The problem is getting her to go. I know she can't just take off from work during the school year. Christmas break is coming up but there is no guarantee I could get her back on time to start the second half of the year."

"Just ask her and roll with the flow. The important part is that you decided to ask her to marry you, not so much the timing. Wait, have you asked her tight-ass Pastor Father if you can have his daughter's hand in marriage?"

Freddy cleared his throat and shook his head slightly in disapproval of bringing up the subject. "No I haven't. I really have my doubts that he would be OK with it. Every time I see the man he gives me a lecture about science and God and how I need to get my life right with Jesus. Why don't these Christians understand that by bothering people who are skeptical like me, all it does is drive us away?"

"I hear you brother. I can't stand when those people come to my door asking me about God every Saturday morning. I believe in the power of the universe. I can feel it in my music. I don't need some Christ to tell me what to do when I can tap into the powers of the world through my music."

"You lose God through your music while I lose him through scientific research and reason. I am just glad we are in the same place. I wish I could say the same about Jennifer. She is always talking to me about God. Her father really did a great job in brainwashing her. Getting me to believe in Christ seems like her number one priority all the time. I am hoping that if she accepts my proposal, she will accept me for who I am and stop proselytizing every other sentence. If she weren't so hot, I would have dropped her because of it a long time ago."

They both laughed as Lawrence got up from his seat to stretch his back.

"You just keep pushing the boundaries of science and God lovers will have no choice but to accept the reality that man in the modern age has grown past the need for a God."

"Well, I see her tonight after I am done with you. If she says yes she will go, then I will ask her father about the marriage."

Freddy took a deep breath and let it out slowly, and then he leaned back in his chair and clapped his hands to get Lawrence's attention back from the mirror. "You are the first one I am telling about this so keep it quiet. The new UN Secretary-General offered me a very interesting proposal."

"Oh great, he is trying to get your patents, isn't he?"

"Well, yes, but he is offering me something that no business executive could offer me. He wants to make me Advisor of Science for the U.N. and develop and manufacture my products to be made around the world and sold at a reasonable price. I do not want to create a price war with my products. I want the prices of my products to be low so the average man can afford them. I care more about the welfare of the world than making a profit."

"But there will be a profit, you know that. How much of the profit would you be getting?"

"I didn't talk to him about that. I think he could tell I was the type of man who did not care deeply for such things. I can see that he doesn't care for material wealth as well, just like me. I will have more time to feel out the Secretary-General on our search, but I am definitely warming to the idea of working with him. I know all of my research would be improved ten-fold with the power of the U.N. behind it."

Freddy paused in thought, remembering the positive and confident aura that surrounded the strong-willed German Secretary-General. "I do not know how to explain it, but there is greatness behind that man. He has a presence that surrounds him that emanates power yet grace. He is quite the remarkable man. I have only had a chance to meet with him once, but in that brief meeting he wowed me beyond my highest expectations."

"I guess I am just going to have to trust you on this one. I hope he is half the man you are saying he is. There has to be a large benefit for him if he gets your patents."

"Of course he will gain something if I work with him. I am not worried about that though, for some reason. I can feel that he wants the same things that I want in this world. He wants to create a heaven on earth, and I think with my inventions and his position, we might just have the power to start the process."

"Yeah, screw waiting for a magical white-clouded paradise in the sky when we can create that right here. I just want you to be careful. You know I will always look out for you, Freddy, through thick and thin. I hope you will remember that after you get all your success and money."

"I will not change, Lawrence. I promise. I will always be the nerdy and warm-hearted man from Greeley."

Freddy stood up and buttoned his jacket. "It is time for me to go, Lawrence. I only had time to stop by for a second."

"OK, no problem. Sorry if I kept you too long talking your ear off. I am just excited for what's going on in your life."

"No, it's OK. I am right on time. I am supposed to be at Jennifer's around eleven." Freddy walked over to his friend and extended his arms outward. "Come here buddy. I won't be seeing you for a while probably with all that I have going on."

Lawrence came in for the hug and embraced his longtime friend. "Just make sure we keep in touch with phone calls or FaceNet whenever you get a chance."

With that the two dear friends departed, their futures seemingly bright, but uncertain in a time of change.

Freddy made his way out of the dimly lit bar to his car. He got on the highway and headed back to Boulder where his girlfriend lived in a house by herself. When he arrived he parked in the driveway. He took a moment to look in the mirror to get himself together. He popped in a piece of gum and got out of the car and walked to the front door. He had the keys ready in his right hand, with a copy of the key to her house on his key chain. He opened the door softly, being careful not to wake her in case she was already asleep. When he came in she was up watching television.

"Freddy! Baby!" She got up quickly from her comfortable spot on the couch and ran up to him, giving him a warm embrace. She pulled back from her affectionate hug and gave him a loving kiss. "I have been waiting all day for you. This is our last night together before you go, and I want to spend every minute with you."

"I am surprised you still have energy for me. I have been over here non-stop since I got in from New York."

"And I appreciate that very much Freddy baby. I am in love with the smartest man on the planet and I do not have shame in admitting it."

Freddy smiled and went in for another kiss, but Jennifer blocked him with her hand. "Do not even waste your time getting worked up big boy. You know I won't do anything to alleviate that evil thing in your pants."

Freddy tried in vain to kiss her again but she bobbed her head to the side and pushed him away in retreat. She ran quickly in the other room, pursued vigorously by her frustrated lover. "Come on, I have been dating you for six years now. Time is up on me waiting for the goods." He lunged at her but she quickly skirted past him up the stairs where she ran into her master bedroom and locked the door.

Out of breath and stumbling up the stairs after her was Freddy. Defeated and down in spirit, he realized he would be relegated to another night of dreaming about her pleasuring him. He banged on the door in vain. "Please, I beg you let me in! Just let me stick the tip in. I promise that is all I want to do."

Jennifer in disgust answered back, "Eww vile. No way would I ever let any man, especially a God-less heathen like you, near my non pollinated flower."

"Fine I give up. Just open the door. I will be nice, I promise."

Jennifer put her left index finger to her chin to contemplate the sincerity of his words. "Well I guess it isn't exactly spending time with you if I am hiding behind this door."

She slowly opened up the door to let him in, but once he got a chance he pushed it completely open, causing Jennifer to fall back. Freddy took this chance to advance quickly on his wounded prey and he scooped her up in his arms. With her body already moving in the direction of the bed, Freddy simply grabbed her and lifted her up off the ground to place her on the bed. He jumped on top of her and pinned her down. "One of these days I am going to just take what I have been waiting for."

Jennifer was squirming in his grip beneath him. "No! Never! Let me go you barbarian."

Freddy held her still. "Apologize for calling me a heathen, and I will let you go."

Jennifer, still struggling, took a moment to think about it. "But you are a heathen... and an asshole on top of that!" She kicked her legs in an effort to propel herself out of his grip.

"No, that was hurtful and ignorant. I am a very spiritual person at times. Just because I do not believe in your God does not make a bad person."

Jennifer calmed down and smiled as she stopped struggling. "OK, I am sorry baby. I was just playing. You have never been sensitive before about my ribbing. Is everything OK? Is something on your mind?"

Freddy knew she couldn't have known about his plans on proposing, so he did his best to keep his cool under pressure. "No, everything is OK. I have just been thinking a lot about God and if what I am doing is really going to help mankind."

Freddy eased his grip and she put her hands around his. "God has a special plan for you, Freddy. He wouldn't have given you so much responsibility if He didn't have a purpose for you. I am not worried about the dark matter being evil at all. I am only worried about what it will do to men who are full of hate and greed."

"Men never fought a major war over coal, so there is hope that we can peacefully harvest and utilize a new power source."

"True, but men have fought war and done great evil over oil, and other natural resources."

Freddy quickly decided that he was not going to argue with her, because she had a degree in history and he was certain she could rail off several examples to prove herself. "Let's just hope for the best, Jenny. I will do what I can to ensure that this resource is not misused for evil."

"That is why I love you, Freddy. Even though you may not have an active faith in the Lord, He is moving through you always. I can see it in your eyes. You have so much power in you that the Lord is waiting to tap into if you can just see the truth."

"I told you I am not ready to start going to church and doing all that stuff. Maybe one day soon I will try, only for you, but I make no promises."

The blue in Jennifer's eyes vibrated with happiness. "You mean it? I have been trying to get you to go to church since I met you. You really are ready to finally go with me? I promise it is nothing scary."

"Yeah I think I might be ready to do it, just to make you happy and show you that I am willing to change to make our relationship healthier. But if I go to church you need to do something for me."

"Yeah what is it, baby?"

Freddy paused to gather himself. "I want you to come with me on the search for dark matter."

Jennifer smiled, but her thoughts quickly crept to her responsibilities. "You know I am almost on break, but no way will you be done in time for me to make it back for the second half of the school year. You know I cannot afford to have a sub for God only knows how long before you find the dark matter."

"I knew you would say I no. I shouldn't even have asked."

Jennifer quickly tried to mend the situation. "No, I am not saying no because I don't want to go. I am saying no because I can't go. Those children need a teacher who can devote their time to them. Flying around the world would be a major disservice to them."

"Yes you are right. I was just hoping for the best. This is a major moment in my life and I wanted to share it with you."

"I will be there with you in spirit, always supporting you. I love you, Frederick Slater." Jennifer extended her head upward and kissed him softly on the lips.

Jennifer leaned her head back down against the pillow, and Freddy rolled himself off her, vanquished another night by her purity.

Jennifer peered at Freddy. "So tell me more about the search. We saw the list on the news when they announced it. I thought it was hilarious that every single diplomat voted for their own country first no matter what kind of turmoil may be going on there. I hope you are prepared for a lot of travel baby because there is no regard for distance when it comes to the list. I saw New Zealand was first but Sweden was second. That is a rough plane ride."

"OK, let me answer your first question. The search is starting simultaneously around several sites in Sweden, with the main search starting from the capital, Stockholm. That is how we are going to be setting up each country. The main force will have me and other key diplomats and scientists from the capital, and the rest of the staff flying at other strategic spots around the country. We are hoping for two days in each country searching for 10 hours a day. Obviously the two days will not work for countries like Russia, and won't be necessary for countries like Taiwan, so it is just a goal for the average country."

"Ooh very exciting!"

"Yeah there should be no surprise that every country voted for itself. The impact of finding this new resource within their country's border would change their lives forever."

Freddy kicked off his shoes and started to unbutton his shirt, sitting up to do so.

"Tell me about the Secretary-General," Jennifer said. "You briefly talked about him when you first came home but haven't really brought him up much since."

"Well I am sorry I haven't been keeping you in the loop like I should be. He left a very strong impression on me. He is older and wiser than me, which is good, and dedicated to the improvement of mankind. He is willing to put his reputation on the line to do it. He wants me to give the rights to my patents over to the U.N. for production and sale under their supervision."

"Wow, I didn't know they had the power to do that. What is the catch? He just wants your patents and that's it?"

"Yeah apparently he does have the power to do it, he assured me of it. No, he doesn't just want my patents for himself. He wants me to become the Advisor of Science for the entire U.N. I would be in charge of all scientific research and implementation for the U.N."

"Well that is surprising. It sounds like a very lofty position. I hope that wouldn't require you to move from Boulder," she said with a looking of longing for him as if he had already decided to leave her.

"I don't know where I would be working. The subject never came up. I would assume New York because that is where the U.N. Headquarters are."

"Well I am very concerned about you moving away. That would really put a dent in my heart."

"Well why wouldn't you come with me?"

"That is something I would do for a husband, not a boyfriend." Jennifer rolled her eyes and turned her head to look at the ceiling, awaiting a response.

"Well that is a very serious thing, marriage," Freddy said. "I can't say I haven't been thinking about it. I just have a lot on my plate right now. I couldn't handle it."

Freddy was trying his best to downplay his true thoughts. He knew he was on the verge of asking her the big question, but the last thing he wanted to do was be coerced into making a decision.

"Well nobody is trying to make you do something you do not want to do," Jennifer wisely replied. "I am just telling you that I am not going to move across the country from my family and friends for any man who isn't at least my husband. I think that is a very fair and reasonable approach to the situation."

"Well, I have the entire search to think about where I want to take my life. After such an epic expedition I expect to come out a different man."

"Hopefully you don't change too much. I like you just the way you are."

"That is why I need you around me to keep me in check…" Freddy paused but continued on not waiting for a response. "So what do I think about the Secretary-General? I think he is a good man with good intentions. Nothing in his past or present gives me a reason to doubt his future."

"You speak highly of this man. Be careful, no man of power is without his own personal aspirations. You only know a fraction about this man's personal life outside of what you see in the paper and on cable. I just want you to be really careful of who you trust from now on. Things are different. You are no longer going to be just a professor from Colorado. Now you are going to be shaping the destiny of our species. You have a lot on your plate, and Lord willing you are able to handle it. Beware of this shiny new thing you see as a new potential friend; his true intentions for you are unknown at this point."

"Well the search will give me plenty of time to pick his brain and try to understand him better. I will take your warning to heart. Lawrence told me to be careful about him as well. I am glad to have the two closest people in my life looking out for me, but you are both just going to have to trust me on this. He is as genuine as apple pie, or whatever they eat in Germany."

"I love you, Freddy. I just want the best for you at all times. I will support you no matter what you decide to do with your life."

"I love you too, Jenny. Now let's get some sleep because I have to wake up early in the morning for my flight to New York. We are then flying out to Sweden from there."

"OK, baby let me get the light. I love you and good night."

With that she reached for the remote control to the fan and clicked off the light. They both quickly acceded to the lure of sleep as the warmth of their bodies under the blanket protected them from the sting of coolness in the chill Colorado air.

It was a relaxing drive out of the busy and bustling city of Los Angeles to the quiet suburb of Chessfield, where James grew up. Here, there was almost no threat of gang violence and crime that plagued other sections of the Los Angeles Metropolitan area. It was about 30 minutes from L.A., but the drive was well worth it to get away from the pressure and pollution of the big city. James pulled up to his parents' house early morning before they left for church that Sunday. He was so excited to tell them the news about his new assignment that his hands were sweating. He had only kept the news from them the last few days because he wanted to make sure his assignment was concrete before he announced it. He strode along the pavement leading to the front door, taking time to smell the sweet fragrance from the flowers growing along the wall leading to the door. He knocked on the front door and then tried the door handle.

"I don't understand why they lock the door when they know I am coming," James complained to himself as he jiggled the handle trying to get someone's attention from the other side. The first to the door was his mother. She was a woman of medium height with a slender shape and a graceful aura that surrounded her at all times. When she opened the door she welcomed him with a great smile. Her pearly whites sparkled in the sun as she said, "My boy, we have all been dying to see you and hear the big news you have for us. Please come in. Take off your coat and go to the kitchen to see your father. We are just finishing up breakfast."

James walked forward and gave his mother a hug and kiss on the check as he took off his jacket and placed it on the coat rack. His father was scraping his scraps off his plate as he heard the heavy footsteps of his son walking toward him in the kitchen. "James is that you?" questioned his father as he erected himself from his bent position over the trash can.

"Yes, Dad, it's me. I am glad I wasn't too late and missed you both before church," James replied. "Yeah well we decided it would be worth missing a little bit of church to see you and hear the big news," his father said. James' father was a strong and sturdy man, but after years of basketball in school and for recreation, his knees were getting the better of him.

James walked over to him and helped him into his chair as his mother came around into the kitchen to hear his announcement. "Do you want me to get Kira? She is studying right now for finals but I am sure she can spare a minute to hear the big news," James' mother Miani said as she made her way toward the staircase to go grab her daughter.

James stepped in to stop her. "No, I will go tell her myself after we are done talking first. I am sure you both will have plenty of questions after I am done telling you the news. Go ahead and take a seat next to Dad and I will tell you."

Miani took a seat next to James' father at the dinner table and said, "Go ahead my dear, tell us what you have been keeping from us for the past few days."

James walked around the table to face them both, thinking quickly of the best way to tell them he was leaving. "Well," James started then paused. "I finally got my first big assignment from work."

They both smiled and said, "Really, amazing news" and "Congratulations."

They quickly asked for more details questioning: "What is it?" "Where will you be doing your research?"

James gathered his breath and said, "I am going to be covering the U.N. dark matter search from a unique perspective. I chose a country toward the bottom of the list to cover their outlook on the search and their prospects for being the lucky location of dark matter."

"Oh that sounds wonderful that your boss allowed you to cover a story hands-on like you always wanted," chimed in his mother.

"Well what country are we talking about?" His father questioned him sternly and with concern.

"Ethiopia," James said with cautious optimism.

"Oh my Lord not Africa!" exclaimed his mother as she grabbed her husband closer to her to support her from falling out of her chair.

"James, do you really think it is wise to be going to Africa in its current state of affairs? If I am not mistaken, Ethiopia borders Sudan and Somalia, both horrible places," his father said, worry in his voice.

"It is not perfect but I think I can manage my way to find a good story there. They are mostly Christian, and even though their government doesn't promote a free and loving democracy, they are still not as bad as you might think. I have started to do my research on Ethiopia and statistics say their GDP is the highest in the region, and it is growing. I think if they were lucky enough to find the dark matter there, it would completely transform their democracy from authoritative into representative. I do not know how to describe how I feel about it. I just feel excited and like this is exactly where I am supposed to be right now."

"Well the Lord works in mysterious ways," Miani spoke up. "If this is where you are supposed to be then He will guide you to your right path. I have to have faith."

"I have been praying for an opportunity to prove my worth to not only my job, but to Him above. I am hoping that this is truly a response from the Lord that I have this opportunity."

"Son," his father Franklin drew in a breath and spoke deeply. "I trust that you are ready to embark on such an endeavor; I am just nervous about you going all the way to Africa all by yourself. You have no idea what kind of trouble you could run into. You must let us think about what to do about that. Go, go, tell your sister the big news and let us get ready for church."

"Well I am glad that you are not taking the news as poorly as I thought you would."

"Of course we are excited for you and your blossoming life son," Miani said. "We are with you every step of the way. We love you, and we are just trying to look out for you. Now go tell your sister. We are already late. Church is about to start in ten minutes."

James walked over and hugged them both, then left the kitchen as they were standing from their chairs.

On his way up the stairs he saw the familiar artwork that graced the peach colored wall. There was music blasting as he neared the top few steps. He could hear it was Niles Nightly, the buzzing rap star out of Detroit. He got to the door and knocked, but there was no answer so he tried the handle to see if it was locked. He creaked the door open to see his sister lying on the bed on her stomach facing away. James instantly recognized the turquoise pajama bottoms bent at the knee, with her feet swaying adorned with black socks with a matching black top, showing off the colors to her new sorority Nu Iota Ro.

"Hey bugger," James exclaimed over the music, but to no avail. She was entranced in the new song on the radio. James walked over to the bed and hit her foot. "Bugger I got news; it won't take but a second."

With that Kira looked up from her text book and flipped around to see who hit her. "Oh hey James, let me turn this down," she said as she reached for the remote to the mp3 player stereo.

"What was that you said?" asked Kira as she wedged a piece of paper into her book to keep her place at where she was studying.

"I got news. Remember I texted you I would come tell you in person."

"Oh yeah I remember. Well you got me from my studying so go ahead and tell me."

"Well, I am going to Africa. Ethiopia to be exact, I am going to be doing an ongoing story on their reaction to the search for dark matter."

"Wow I can't believe it. I am so excited for you! Oh my God that is so cool. I can't wait to visit you! You are going to have so much fun. I am definitely going to have to come visit you."

"Well you are definitely taking it better than Mom and Dad. They almost had heart attacks. They are worried for my safety because Africa is dangerous. Like I can't take care of myself."

"Well now that I think about it, yeah it is a little daunting thinking that you would be in Africa all by yourself. I am sure you will make new friends though so I am not worried. I just want the best for you, big brother. I know you have been waiting for a more challenging assignment at work and I am glad to see you are finally getting it after all this time."

"Yeah all my hard work finally paid off it seems. I would love for you to come and visit. The drinking age is 18, so maybe you could bring a friend and go out in Addis Ababa after I get my apartment there. It's the capitol of Ethiopia in case your dumb ass didn't know."

"Shut up," yelled Kira as she threw an eraser at James' head. "Well I am just excited for you James, you really deserve this. Maybe we could have a going away party before you go so all of your friends can see you one last time before you leave for Africa. When are you going?"

"I plan on going sometime in early January after I get my passport approved by Ethiopia for work and any immunization shots I might need."

"Maybe we can do something for New Years in L.A.? That would be a lot of fun to get all the family and friends together for one big sendoff. I will keep you posted. You should go talk to Mom and Dad before they leave for church. It was nice to see you, big jerk. I wish you would call me more often. You better FaceNet me all the time when you are in Africa."

"I am sorry for not calling you as much as I should. I will definitely keep in touch with you when I go overseas. I am sure I will have plenty of things to tell you about. See ya later sis, and keep in touch about this party. I think it is good idea. I need to tell my friends as soon as possible so they don't make other New Year's plans."

"OK let me get back to studying. Talk to you soon."

With that Kira flipped back around and put her feet back up, opening her book back to the correct page and putting her music back on. James retreated back downstairs to see his parents one last time that day before they went to church. By the time he got downstairs they had changed into their church attire and were waiting for him in the main living room just outside the front door.

"Son we are very excited about your new job in Africa and we wish you the best of luck…" said his mother Miani. "But," James finished her sentence.

"But I feel like you really need to take someone with you to help protect you from people that may want to harm you. Me and your father talked about it, went through our options, and we think we came up with a good compromise."

"Go ahead," James impatiently asked.

"Well we think you should take your cousin Justin."

"Justin? Are you kidding me!? He…"

"Now, Son, just hear us out please," his mother began as James shook his head.

His father cut in to say, "Go ahead, Miani."

"Well, James, you know that Justin just had his two boys taken away because of an alleged domestic battery," Miani continued. "He is going through a lot right now. I think giving him a chance to get a fresh new start for a couple months, or however long it takes you to finish your work in Africa, will be good for him. Not only that, but ever since you got to college you stopped spending time with your cousin. I think this would be healthy for your relationship with him."

"Yeah I stopped hanging out with him because all he does is talk trash and drink. I got tired of it."

"You know your cousin has lived a different life than you," James' mother said. "I wish you would just take a second to understand him."

"Well I do not want to have a conversation about Justin and his problems, it could take hours. For you though, I will think about it."

"Go by his place later please and just talk to him about it," Miani insisted. "I think it would be a great idea. Just give it a chance in your heart."

"OK, I will go over and talk to him about it. Maybe he needs a break from all the nonsense with his baby momma."

"Thank you", said a triumphant Miani, "now let us run to church. Go over his house this afternoon and we will talk tonight."

"OK have a great time."

They hugged and all left the house together, locking the front door and leaving in their respective cars. James really didn't have that much to do outside of visiting Justin's house. He was hungry so he headed back to his apartment in the city and ordered a breakfast burrito from this local Mexican spot, and then met up with his cousin in the afternoon.

He had called Justin before he got back to Los Angeles to let him know he was coming over. When he pulled up to his apartment complex in Ascerty, a relatively low income and high crime city in the inner L.A. metro area, he was greeted by the sight of three young kids, two Black and one Mexican, running with arms full of beers away from a shouting overweight Asian man who was obviously the shop owner of the liquor store just down the street. James just laughed at the kids being bad and locked his car and headed in toward the apartments. When he got to the door he smelled a familiar scent of special flowers floating out the windows of his cousin's apartment.

"I thought he quit smoking," James thought to himself as he rang the doorbell. Justin answered the door in a wife beater and black basketball shorts. His belly slightly protruded from his waist, evidence of too many beers and too little exercise by the former Ascerty High School football legend. He had a blunt in his mouth and a weak smile on his face. "Hey lil cuzzo, come in. It's cold outside today for some reason."

He walked James into the apartment kicking children's toys and clothing out of the way to make a path toward the couch. "Sorry, I haven't really felt like doing much cleaning since they took my two boys away. Just sit on the couch. Here take this, you want a hit right?" asked Justin as he took a quick puff on the blunt before offering it to his cousin.

"Yeah thanks, I do not mind smoking today. I probably won't have much of a chance to do this where I am going."

"Africa, right?"

"How did you hear about it already? Those damn Jenkins sisters talk too much."

"Yeah my Moms called and told me what was up."

"Did they tell you that I was supposed to come over here and ask you to come with me as my travel companion?"

"Naw Nigga they definitely did not tell me that shit. Go with you to Africa huh?"

"Yeah I would help pay for your trip until you get settled and find something to do out there. I know your Lindal car factory is closing soon."

"Yeah the company is going out of business. I am sure you have heard. My life is falling apart all around me my nigga. I need something to go right for me for once. Maybe if I get out to Africa and get established out there, I can get my kids back. That bitch Niona doesn't work and she has a different nigga running through her every night. If I didn't push that bitch I would still have my kids. She is in no condition to be taking care of my boys. I was so stupid I lost my cool."

"We all make mistakes, Justin. We are all just here to support you. Don't get too down on yourself."

"Whatever, Nigga, stop being gay. I just think going back to the Mother Land, back to Cush and Kemet, would bring a spirit back in my heart. I lost a lot of faith in myself as a man lately, and a journey home to Africa, might be exactly what I need to get my life back on track. I will definitely go with you cuzzo. I have no more life to live here in Ascerty and

Los Angeles. All these bitches are played out, all these niggas are jealous and conniving on me every step I take. It would be good to really take a step back from this fast lifestyle on these L.A. streets to get a different perspective on life. I have never really left L.A. except for occasional trips to Vegas or TJ."

"Well I am glad I came over here and asked you then," James said as he took another hit of the blunt and passed it to his cousin. "To be honest I was a little afraid of going all the way out to Africa by myself."

"That's because you are a square ass, pussy ass nigga from fucking Chessfield trying to go out to the land of true niggas. You will need a big nigga like me, who nobody will fuck with, to protect you," exclaimed Justin as he flexed his muscles at his cousin.

"You just worry about writing that gay shit that you write, and I will worry about gettin' that money and all the fine ass Cushite women my big dick can manage at once."

"Glad to see your recent struggles haven't changed you too much...," sighed James as he reached for the video game controller. "Let's play some Gridiron '16. I would love to smoke up all these blunts you have rolled and tap your monkey ass in some football all afternoon."

"Let's do this shit!"

James and Justin played games all that afternoon, trying to reestablish a fading bond between them as they both tried to mentally prepare themselves to take on the challenge of their lifetimes in traveling to Africa. James had about a month to get ready to leave. He had to finish up his reporting on the Middle East before he left, so he would be busy the next few weeks leading up to his party on New Year's Eve. James had told his family and friends he was leaving, now all that was left was for him to do was to research and prepare himself for what he hoped would propel him into the global journalism spotlight. He just had to stay focused and keep his eyes on the prize in front of him.

Freddy saw that it was snowing lightly in a passive breeze that December morning in New York City. His girlfriend Jennifer saw him off at the airport that morning with tears, knowing he would be busy for the foreseeable future. She was so proud and happy for him, but she was nervous about where her future with him might lead. Freddy already missed her and everyone else in Colorado. As the plane pulled up to the terminal Freddy got his things together to prepare to get off the plane. He had his flight paid for by the U.N., so he had deluxe first class tickets. With such an early flight, he had the entire row of four chairs to himself. He got much-needed relaxation and time to study his work without being bothered by curious passengers. Everything from now on until the finding of the two dark matter sites would be taken care of by the U.N. Freddy was excited that he would get a chance to travel the world, staying in the most luxurious hotels and eating the best food the world had to offer.

He just hoped he had the energy to search practically every day with very little breaks until the dark matter was found. As he gathered his bag and briefcase, he made his was off the plane and walked through the airport toward baggage claim. He was recognized by several people who wished him luck on the search. People wanted to stop and talk with him about his discovery and his prototypes but Freddy was in a hurry to stay on schedule and unfortunately couldn't entertain them.

When he arrived at baggage claim there was a short Hispanic man holding a sign that said Slater. Freddy approached him and asked if he was his driver and the man said yes he was looking for the famous scientist Frederick Slater. The driver got his bags and they left for the parking structure where the driver had left the limousine. After loading, the pair took off for Midtown, New York City where the U.N. was located. It was about a 30-minute drive there in the Sunday traffic. Freddy arrived at the U.N. with a flurry of cameras and reporters lining the entrance waiting for top scientists and politicians involved with the search to arrive.

When he got out of the limousine all the reporters recognized him and they gathered around the door to ask him questions. Two representatives from the U.N. came to the door and helped out the young scientist amidst the screams and roars of the crowd. They hovered over him and helped push the crowd open enough for them to get through. One of them spoke to the crowd, "No questions will be answered until the search begins tomorrow!"

When they got to the front doors of the U.N. building, the security guards took over in escorting Professor Slater to the elevator. Once there, Freddy had a chance to catch his breath. He wasn't expecting so much calamity on his first day on the job. He made his way up to the Secretary-General's floor and went to the receptionist. They alerted the Secretary-General that the professor was there for him. After a few minutes of waiting, Lenz Krause walked out of the back area with a gaggle of men flocking around him.

"Greetings, young Professor. I am so glad to see you made it here safely. Please staff, leave us to be alone. There will be plenty of time for all of us to talk together later today and on the plane ride to New Zealand tonight."

With that, his staff said their goodbyes to Krause and their hellos to Freddy as they made their way to the board room to continue their discussion on what to do if certain countries have the dark matter within their borders.

"Come right this way, Professor. We have much to discuss." The full-bodied former European football great led the professor back to his office. They sat in the same red seats that they sat in before when they last met. "Professor, Professor, the world is all in your hands now. They are hanging at your every word and every action. Please, if you would be so kind, fill me in on the details of the current status of the LHC in Geneva and your prototypes and machines that are dark matter related. I hear so much nonsense in the press about the things you have invented and will unleash on the world. I would like to hear it from you directly now that you have had a little time to see what works and what doesn't. I hope your travels back home to Colorado went well."

"Yes they did go well. I was very happy to have had some time to see my family and friends," Freddy smiled at his new friend. "Well where do I begin? We had time to repair the Large Hadron Collider and make alterations to try and prevent similar malfunctions from shooting beams in rapid succession. In our second attempt at finding dark matter, we were also successful. We examined the differences in our two samples and realized that the density of the two samples were different. In the second test we used more particles in the beam, so the collisions were more violent. That is just a theory of mine as to why we have two different densities but we are testing right now to find out. When we find the dark matter in our two locations, I am sure they will both be of a different density now that we know they come in different variations. The power and longevity of the denser dark matter is much greater than the lighter density sample. We will have to test everything when it is found. Even though density determines how great the power will be, even a low density sample has great power and will be very valuable."

"Very interesting," Lenz said as he nodded his head. "Please continue, there must be more."

"Yes there is more," continued Freddy. "We have begun testing the material I use for the gravitational distortion goggles on different telescopes to determine if we have the power to see if other planets have dark matter. Tests have been unsuccessful so far but hopefully we can find a solution to manipulating the material to work with the telescopic vision."

Freddy reached down to grab the mug on the table full of fresh water. He took a sip and then continued, "The engineers at the LHC have been trying to design the line of automobiles that will be produced. I have been working with them hands-on and I think we have come up with some really interesting ideas on our cars and trucks. I believe with more testing of my theories, we will come up with a formula to finally create the first flying car. Our engines are that powerful and compact. The final prototype I think I should tell you about is our spacecraft. We have been testing our small engine to see how much fuel would be necessary for a trip to, let's say, Mars. I realized that the amount necessary for a trip that far, at a tremendous speed, carrying a large load of equipment for mining and exploration could be easily attained.

"Unfortunately, everything we have planned for the expansion of the limits of mankind can only be fulfilled if we have friendly host nations of the dark matter. Let us keep our fingers crossed."

Lenz had his legs crossed, and his hand on his chin thinking of the possibilities. "I can see such a wonderful future with your machines," Lenz scooted forward in his seat and leaned in for effect. "I trust you have had time to talk the Advisor position over with your friends and family. What conclusion did you come up with?"

Freddy sat back in his chair. "Well, to be honest, I do not think I will be comfortable making any kind of decision until we find the first dark matter site. It is just too soon to commit to anything right now. I need to feel things out. I am very interested though. Now that you brought it up, could you tell me more about it?"

Lenz sat back in his chair and uncrossed his legs. "Well what I have envisioned is dividing the world into ten zones of operation, controlled by one core research and manufacturing zone. Each zone will have a main center for production and distribution. In this way we can control all production and distribution of all dark matter products. The General Assembly will still be located in New York, but UN headquarters will be moved to the new capital of dark matter related research and production. It will also be head of the ten zones. The main UN will have a peace keeping army, and each individual zone will also have peace keeping forces to ensure safe and reliable delivery. I have been doing my thinking about where the main capital of the new UN would be, but it will strongly depend on where the two dark matter sites are located.

"These are just the ideas that are running through my head. What do you think? Does it sound like something you would be interested in?"

Freddy was interested, and he let Lenz know that. "Yes, I think it sounds like something I could definitely see myself doing. If I had complete control in order to ensure its usage for the betterment of mankind, it would really help me sleep at night. I am just worried that once my products are put out there that people will reverse engineer them and use all my ideas for copycat products."

"With the power of international law on your side, your inventions will be protected. We will come down hard on any copyright infringement."

"Well it is safe to say I am getting excited about the prospects of working with you. I have a lot of respect for the things you have done, Lenz. I know your ambitions are pure. I just need to see where the dark matter is located first, and then I will make my decision."

"Fair enough, my friend. We shall wait until the dark matter is found first, and then we shall make a decision on what to do with your inventions and expertise. The UN bus will be leaving tonight around 7 p.m. to get to the airport. The flight is at 9 p.m. We will have plenty of time to talk during our travels, my friend. Please, go find your colleagues! I am sure they have much to talk to you about."

"It was a pleasure catching up with you, Lenz. I will talk to you soon."

The two stood up and met and shook hands. When they made eye contact Freddy just got an overwhelmingly safe feeling from the man. Everything he did just exhibited confidence and reliability. The two said their goodbyes and parted ways. Freddy went off to the conference room downstairs to try and find some of his fellow scientists who would be accompanying them on the search.

As Freddy approached the multi-door half circle that was the front of the conference room, he could hear a familiar voice. "Oh do be careful with those boxes boys, there are very valuable items inside of them."

It was Colleen Embers, fellow LHC scientist who was there with him during the discovery. "Oh please, oh watch out!" exclaimed Colleen as the men were dodging pieces of cloth and paper on the ground as they were carrying out the equipment used for a presentation on dark matter that was staged at the UN the night before.

Freddy walked up quietly behind his fair-skinned and long-legged prey. Colleen was still barking out orders to the poor men just trying to clean up and do their job, when Freddy leaped upon her causing her to scream and swing her arms wildly at her assaulter. "Get off! Get off! Get off!" exclaimed Colleen, still unaware of whom the attacker was.

Freddy let go of her waist and stood up laughing at her expense as she shuffled her clothing around and fixed her hair. When she looked up and saw that it was Freddy who mauled her, her anger quickly turned from raging to gone. "Oh Freddy, how could you scare me like that! Ugh, you almost scared me half to death. I thought one of these brutes moving the boxes got his eye on me after I came in here. Do not ever do that again," she said as she swung at him but missed as Freddy dodged her.

"Well besides all this childish nonsense, I am very glad to see you. We have all been working hard in the labs testing and developing. It is nice to see you after a much-deserved vacation."

She opened her arms and asked Freddy for a hug. "You just want to get close to my junk you cougar, stop trying to seduce me."

"First of all, if I wanted to get close to your junk, I would have long ago found my way to it. To be honest, you are not the kind of man who could satisfy me anyway," she said as she measured the size of her fictional man's member.

"You will never know until you find out. Maybe one day when I am not in a relationship I can give you a call," Freddy said as he winked at her.

"I am sure your girlfriend would be excited to hear you are already making plans for after you break up."

"You wouldn't!"

"Damn sure I would!"

"OK, OK, we'll stop. Come here, old lady," he said to the woman only ten years his elder. She gave in and received his kindness by accepting his hug. She missed him. They had worked together every day since he was hired on staff at the LHC and they grew very close. They were an office couple, but nothing ever came out of it.

"You have no idea how much activity there has been at the LHC! Everyone is excited about your discovery. There were reporters lined up at the entrance to the LHC every day since the press conference. You are the talk of the world, Professor Slater. I am just glad I am a part of this."

"Yes, it has been a whirlwind of activity since our discovery but we still have so much further to go. The only limitations are how hard we can dream."

"Well everyone on staff has been trying to come up with new inventions that can be used with your dark matter. From ovens, to motorcycles, and from lamps to beard trimmers, we have been all over the place trying to invent new and creative ways to utilize dark matter. We have been working nonstop. I am glad we get a chance to take a work vacation and travel the world searching for dark matter. I sure do feel for the lower staff who will be working around the clock on your inventions and theories while we are gone. Are you hungry? Let us go to the cafeteria and get some food before our flight leaves in a couple hours."

"Yes I am hungry. It was a long flight, thank you for the offer. Let's go."

The two walked and talked through the hallways to the elevator, and then down to the floor with the cafeteria. As they approached the doorways they could see plenty of people there getting an early dinner or eating before the flight if they were part of the search party. "Hey, Professor Slater, over here." It was the UN Ambassador for the United States, Jeffery Willis, an elder black man. He was waving at him to come over there.

"After you get your food come sit with us," he said. So Freddy and Colleen got their food and settled at the Ambassador's table. There with the ambassador to the U.S. was the ambassador to Tunisia, Mago Eshmun, and the ambassador to Cuba who was also the president of the General

Assembly, Gonzalo Moreno. All the men would be accompanying the scientists on the search for the dark matter. The three men introduced themselves to Freddy and Colleen. As they sat and talked, they mostly focused their conversation on Freddy's inventions and wishful sayings in regard to where the dark matter would be found.

They were very polite but selected their words carefully. It was part of what made them skilled enough to be in their high level political positions. They ate and talked, generating positive feedback between each other as they got ready for the trip around the world that they were preparing for. After a good meal and conversation, they all decided it would be best to go to their respective staging rooms to prepare for the flight and double-check their bags. As they were leaving they all got a text that the bus was in the parking lot. When they were ready they were to call and have their bags picked up. Colleen and Freddy talked as they walked through the corridors of the United Nations. They walked into the staging room and saw Alfred Linchkin, head scientist of the LHC facility, and Henry Hangruler, Freddy's old rival and fellow LHC scientist.

They all welcomed each other with hugs and handshakes, excited for the trip that was about to change the world. They talked briefly about progress on tests and improvements in replicating the beam shots without damage. As they talked the time came for them to go and they called to have all of their bags packed in the bus. As they arrived to the bus it was sparsely full. There were only about 20 people going on the flight, including the five scientists from the LHC. The rest were UN representatives going along with the search for their own personal reasons. As Freddy ascended the stairs last behind his four comrades, all the passengers on the bus cascaded their applause upon Freddy. Everyone yelled out congratulations to the young professor. Many people told him thank you. The entire congregation of scientists and politicians gave their utmost appreciation to the work that Freddy had done. As Freddy said you are welcome, he accepted his praise gracefully and took his seat. When they got to the airport everyone was excited for the search to begin. They boarded the private jet and took their seats. The flight to Wellington, New Zealand was about 18 hours, so everyone had plenty of chance to catch up on sleep and be refreshed and ready to start the search as soon as they landed.

When they landed in Wellington it was late afternoon in the summer there, so the sun would be setting late. They had enough time to get to the helicopters and search the southern half of New Zealand before the sun went down. They all had gotten plenty of sleep in the luxurious and spacious private plane. When they landed they had been up for an hour talking about the search together, getting their riding partners settled. The 20 people in the main UN search party would be divided into five helicopters. Each person would be equipped with a set of gravitational distortion goggles and a telescope to look out below for traces of the dark matter. Riding partners would rotate each new country searched based on random selection from out of a hat.

They took the drive from the airport to the military base where the helicopters were stationed. Everyone was nervous but eager to get started. As Freddy climbed out of the bus he relished the beautiful weather of a New Zealand summer. "When it is all said and done I want to retire here," he said as he looked to the sky, shading his eyes from the sun while doing so.

Colleen answered, "Not a bad choice, Professor. With all the money you will have coming in, each of these countries should be trying to persuade you to join their country!"

"Not everyone wants to import Americans, especially these days," said Henry with a matter-of-fact sense of truth to his statement. "

Oh stop, the world may not love America but they certainly love Professor Slater," Colleen responded to Henry's taunting.

"Well who knows if I will even want to retire, a lot of that stuff depends on my wife," replied Freddy, trying his best to ignore Henry's agitation.

"Speaking of wives," chimed in Colleen, "When are you going to pop the question to that little doll school teacher of yours? You have been dating for long enough, stop torturing the poor girl."

"This really is not the time to talk about this, seeing as we are all about to leave in different helicopters, but yeah I have been putting some serious thoughts into proposing to her. I actually invited her to come to the search with me. I was going to propose to her when we found the first dark matter site. Unfortunately, she could not tear herself away from her kids to come with me for so long."

"Oh how absolutely wonderful to hear. She will be a very lucky woman. I think you are making the best decision. Even though my marriage did not end well, it was still a magical gift from God that we were able to create a healthy bright-eyed young boy who is soon turning into a man. If you truly love her, I say go with it! You only live once, right?" said Colleen as she walked up close to Freddy and draped her arm around his shoulder in support of his difficult life decision.

"I do not know if that is the best decision mein friend. The day I married my wife she stopped working out and stopped giving me blow jobs. My life is hell when I am home. I am hoping this search takes as long as possible," exclaimed Henry as they neared the location of the helicopters.

Alfred caught up to them from behind and heard what Henry said and responded, "Please professor, do not listen to the grumblings of our German counterpart. Marriage is a beautiful thing between two people that love one another. Take some time to really think about what you want to do on our search. I believe the universe will place you exactly where you need to be. If you are meant to marry, then it shall be so. The universe has already decided."

"Well I do not know about all that, Alfred," replied Freddy. "I just know that I do in fact love her and I am ready to take things to the next level in our relationship. The search will give me plenty of time to think over how I am going to do it and when. I really love her, guys. I think now that I will be financially secured soon, it will be a perfect time to start a family."

They all came up to the helicopters and said their goodbyes as they split. "We will talk about this later tonight when we get back to the hotel," said Alfred over the noise of the helicopters chopping the air above.

Freddy was in the helicopter with Francis, his fellow LHC scientist from France but with an English mother. He was also accompanied by Jeffery Willis, U.S. Ambassador, and Harold Mandible, Australian Ambassador. The search on their first day was wildly uneventful. The helicopter dove and dipped its way through the countryside on their planned route through the country, but they did not see any gravitational distortion from their goggles. The day was filled mostly with Francis talking about his ideas on dark matter related products.

When they arrived back at the home base in Wellington, the entire search party was worn out. They had flown and searched all day. They were ready to get some much-needed rest. The search party took their bus to a nice hotel near the military base in Wellington. Each participant retired to their room to refresh themselves for another day of searching and another day of travel the day after.

In the morning the next day, Freddy got up early to go get breakfast, hoping nobody else would be there so he could get some time to eat in peace. Unfortunately, Alfred had beat him there and waved Freddy to come and sit with him. "Professor Slater, great morning. I hope you got good sleep last night. Please, I hope you have a minute. We have not had a chance to talk since you left to see the Secretary-General."

"Yes I do not mind. I have more than enough time to go back to my room and get a little extra sleep before we have to get ready. How are things with you and your wife and kids?"

"Ah my family is doing wonderful. My daughter just told me she is having a son! It will be my first grandchild so I am very excited. Besides that, things are going well. My son is going to college in England this spring for a program at his school so he is excited about that. I could talk about my family all day but that is not important. What is important is you. A little birdie told me that the Secretary-General Krause offered you a top position in the UN as the Advisor of Science."

"Well you definitely did not hear that from my side. What are your feelings on the entire thing? I know we are making progress at the LHC on my ideas and dark matter research, but if we had the power of the world behind our research we could do wonderful things," Freddy told him as the excitement of the subject woke him from post slumber fog.

"Yes, dear Professor, the power of the UN would greatly increase our capacity for testing and research. I do not want to be the one who tips the scale with your decision one way or the other. I think it would be best to keep my opinion to myself."

"No, I insist Alfred, please tell me what you think. Your opinion is very important to me."

"Well I just feel that your opportunity to succeed is limited at the LHC. You could help push science to new frontiers with the power and protection of the UN behind you. Your inventions on the open market could net you billions of dollars, but it will only leave the rich richer, and the poor still poor. With the UN on your side, you can put the world to work building and selling your supplies, and mining the earth for dark matter. You need the capital from somewhere to get all of these things started. The Large Hadron Collider budget and the European Organization for Nuclear Research funds are not enough to test and develop your ideas and prototypes on a large scale. With the UN's international support, you could control your workforce down to the last man. You could build plants in poor countries and make your Dark Matter Magnet Vacuums available for purchase by the lowliest soul. Working with a man with as much clout as Krause will only help the operation. If I were you, I would take the position."

"Well that is a very good answer with very good points. I am worried about what would happen if I just opened up my products to the market. It would be much like how the oil production is done now. Only the rich can prosper because they control the operation. You are right along with my thinking when you say that working with the UN will prevent corruption and greed from taking over the operation. I want the money to go back to the people."

"You see that," Alfred said as he pointed to the sky, "You do not need to pray to some sky god to be a good person and want to change the world for the better. Speaking of Christianity, what are you going to do about your girlfriend Jennifer and her religion?"

"Ugh, I really do not know what to do about Jennifer and her faith. To be honest, I told her I would actually go to church with her."

"No you didn't!"

"Yes, I did. I am not saying that I believe or will believe anything, I just know that there is something more out there than just this."

"Yes, it is the universe beyond that works through all living things on all planets. We all operate with the same heartbeat, a cosmic energy that flows through all stars. You are right that there is something beyond, but there is something within as well. We have the energy in ourselves to shape the world, become god-like men. Forget about all that church crap."

"I just hope once I get everything up and running I will have some time to myself to reflect on my life and what I want it to mean. There is just so much going on in my life right now. It is a whirlwind. Thinking about God and the universe is so much more than what I want to do. Everyone has their own unique way of looking at the world. I just try to soak it all in and learn from everyone."

"Well very nice, young Professor. The world is lucky to have a man like you in charge of the dark matter. You have a great soul. Please, Professor eat. I will retire back to my room and read the papers online. Have a great morning and let us hope we find some dark matter tomorrow!"

"Nice talking to you, Alfred. It was good catching up. Yes, let's hope we find that dark matter sooner rather than later."

With that the elder Swiss man slowly eased his way back to his room leaving Freddy some much-needed time alone. He thought about a lot of things that morning, but the most pressing thing was Jennifer and how much he missed her while working. He really did love her. Her being a virgin made things worse for Freddy but he appreciated her religious conviction. He wished he could have some of it in his life somehow but he could never see himself as a Christian. He just wasn't cut out for it. He was open to going to church just once to see what happens, but beyond that he just could not see himself being interested. Jennifer would just have to understand if she was truly supposed to be his wife. Freddy felt he could work around it but the work would have to come from both ends.

Freddy finished his breakfast and went back to his room to relax and get some sleep before the bus was due to take them to the military base and the helicopters. He awoke to his alarm on his cell phone, with a little extra energy for the day. Freddy was extra happy that he would not have to fly over water in the helicopter as he had done the previous day when they searched the southern half. He got to the bus a little early and took his seat in the back without being bothered by anyone. As people came shuffling in, Secretary-General Krause went to the seat next to Freddy.

"Good morning, Frederick. I hope you got some good sleep last night."

"Yes, I did. The beds here are very relaxing. I am glad you sat next to me. I have been doing some thinking. If I were to agree to work for the UN and give them my patents, then I want complete control over where the manufacturing sites would be located. I want control over all worker contracts and negotiations. I have been talking with people who are helping me feel much better about making this decision in your favor. Even though I told you I would wait until we find the first dark matter before I made my final decision, I would just like you to know that your prospects are looking good."

Krause had a wide smile on his face. "Great to hear, my friend. There is no rush. Let us find the dark matter and then our arrangement can be solidified. I hope you believe me when I say I want to create a heaven here on Earth. With you on our side, we very well could come close to doing so."

"I believe you, Lenz. It is just so nerve-wrecking thinking of where this stuff could be located. It will literally shape the world for the next thousand years," Freddy said as he turned from Lenz and looked out the bus window to the crowd of reporters gathered. He turned back and looked at Lenz again. "I am just scared of what could happen if this stuff fell into the wrong hands. Who knows what kind of weapon of mass destruction could be made from dark matter. None of my research has even taken me there. We need strict control over all dark matter. Do as best as we can from keeping it out of malicious nations' hands."

"Well we will work out all of the details once we find the stuff. We just have to hope and pray that God put it in suitable places."

"Hope yes, we must hope."

When everyone was checked off as being present on the bus, they took off for the military base and the helicopters. They got their partners selected and they went to their perspective helicopter. It was another long day of flying for Freddy and the crew. They searched and looked out from beyond the metal birds to see if they could find their pay dirt but to no avail; there was no dark matter anywhere in New Zealand. The helicopters all flew back late in the afternoon, bringing back the downtrodden crews aboard.

"Well check the first one off the list," exclaimed Henry as Freddy walked up to the bus Henry was leaning against, waiting for the last of the helicopters. "Only one hundred and fifty-seven more countries to go. Ugh this could take forever! Someone tell me again why we didn't just search continent to continent instead of country to country?"

Out of the small group gathered by the bus, Colleen spoke out. "It just would not have been fair to search continent by continent. This is better for global relations to have a fair vote select which countries would be searched first. You are always Mr. Grumbles, aren't you Henry?" she questioned him.

"Well like I said before, I am enjoying the vacation from the wife and kids. It is just so daunting the amount of travelling and searching we are about to do to find this special stuff. I do see though that it would probably be cheaper and faster to search in person than transfixing the gravitational

153

distortion material onto satellites and searching the world that way. So I will stop complaining."

"Music to my ears," Colleen said in a snarky tone.

Freddy chimed in, "So what country do we have next?"

Secretary-General Krause pulled out his smart phone to check the list. "Sweden, Egypt, and England are the next three up on the list."

"Exciting, I always wanted to go to Egypt," Francis said. "I also get to visit my mum in England while we are there."

Freddy was excited for more of the search but he missed Jennifer. They had talked on the phone a few times since he left Colorado but it just wasn't the same. He missed the feel of her lips upon his as he woke up in the morning next to her. The more he thought about her the more he thought about marrying her when he got home. Each new day he was psyching himself up to make the big move. His first action would be to visit her father when he got home and tell him he wanted to marry his daughter. It was the only way. Freddy had too much respect for the old coot. Just because he did not believe in his religion did not mean he did not like the guy. He was just very aggressive and domineering at times which intimidated Freddy, who was a laidback and mild-mannered person. Jennifer's father also could be a tight ass at times, which frustrated Freddy, but with things in his life going so well he really was trying to look at things more positively.

"OK, here come the last two choppers," Lenz said, as he gazed into the distant blue sky.

The crowd stopped their conversation as the wind picked up and the helicopters landed. Out shuffled the remainder of the group. Everyone greeted the others and headed into the buses to retreat to their hotels. Now that the search in New Zealand was over, they had the rest of the day to relax and explore the richness of Wellington.

The flight to Stockholm, Sweden would be about 23 hours, so Freddy went off to explore on his own that Tuesday night without having to entertain any of the others. The flight was Wednesday morning at 9, and they were due to arrive in Stockholm at 8 p.m. their time. Freddy got a good night of sleep after a wonderful night out and a great dinner at this spot he found walking around Wellington. He was thinking about how long this search would take. He knew his colleagues at the LHC were trying to find a way to expedite the gravitational distortion goggles creation process. It took Freddy months to create those 20 goggles by himself.

With time the LHC, and hopefully at some point the UN scientists, would be able to mass produce the goggles in order to distribute them around the world and end the search. Freddy awoke early again to get some breakfast before any others were up. This time Alfred was not out there eating. He went back to his room to relax and read the paper. Front page on the local paper was that the search was unsuccessful in New Zealand. The country was dismayed because they lost out on untold fortune.

Departure time neared and Freddy got his things together. He left for the bus. Some people were on the bus already and Freddy took a seat next to Colleen for the trip to the airport. Freddy talked to her about his butterflies regarding proposing. Colleen just told him to relax and let it come naturally. Sometimes planning out a proposal doesn't always mean it will be better. Spontaneity can be very romantic. Freddy took her words to heart and they spent the remainder of the trip horse playing and joking with each other.

The plane ride was smooth for the first several hours, but as they neared the northern hemisphere the turbulence grew worse and worse. Stockholm was recovering from a snow storm in the last week, so the air pressure was low and choppy coming in. Good news was that the air was clear except for some scattered clouds. Bad weather would undoubtedly delay

155

the search at some point, but Freddy was happy it was not this day. They arrived in Stockholm Wednesday night and relaxed. They saw the nightlife of Stockholm on a weekday. The next morning, they took a bus to the military base where there were fifteen helicopters ready for use in the search. Sweden is considerably larger than New Zealand, hence the need for more helicopters. They would search the more populated southern half of Sweden first that day. After hours of searching, nothing came up.

The crew once again retired to their hotel rooms or went around the town. The next day did not bring any more luck on finding the dark matter, so they prepared for their next trip to Egypt. After a long flight and another two days of searching, Egypt's borders produced none of the dark matter. The next on the list was England, and after two days of searching there they came up empty. They searched five more countries after that up to New Year's Eve weekend.

Then they took some time off for the holidays and to relax and reenergize. The LHC was still unsuccessful on finding a way to mass produce the gravitational distortion goggles. They had only produced five more since the original test for dark matter. Freddy was getting homesick for his friends and family. Talking to them on the phone was comforting, but he missed the Colorado air. With nine countries down out of one hundred and fifty-eight, the task looked daunting. Freddy was thinking he would give in and share his patents with the UN to increase research capacity and find a way to mass produce his goggles. He would give it another few months and if there was still no luck, he would tell Secretary-General Krause about his desire to end the search quicker and the decision to share his patents with the UN. For now, Freddy would be a quiet soldier, spending his mornings to himself whenever possible. Media coverage of the search was making Freddy a star worldwide, but he was not concerned for such things. All he wanted right now was Jennifer and to make her happy however possible. If changing the world was part of that then he would accept it.

They had several countries on the list to search with a break planned at the start of March, 2017. Until the break in March the search must go on in 2017, and the whole world was watching Freddy and the search team to eagerly see where the dark matter was located.

Chapter 7

It was New Year's Eve, 2016, and the city of Los Angeles was poppin'. Everyone was out to have a good time. James and his family and friends were among those looking to have a great send-off into the New Year. James was moving away to Ethiopia to cover the dark matter search with his cousin Justin Rawlins. James' younger sister Kira had worked all month on her big brother's send-off party. All his friends and local family showed up to wish the young journalist off for a successful trip.

The official party was heading toward its end at about ten o'clock at night, and James was contemplating going out with his cousin for more drinks at a popular bar down the street. "Come on cuzzo," Justin said. "This is gonna be our last chance to go out and get some American pussy before we go to that dark meat only diet. Justin needs to be bustin' open some slut tonight, that's the damn truth."

"I don't know, Justin. I had a long day with the party and I kinda just want to go home, smoke a blunt, and pass out. I have a lot of work left to do before we leave on Monday."

"Oh come on, you do not want to find some fine ass bitch to kiss on when the clock strikes twelve? I know you haven't had any pussy for a while stop actin' like a bitch. What if I could get a blunt delivered to us? Would that help change your mind?"

James turned his head to Justin as the question garnered his interest. "Yeah that would help change my mind, who you gonna get it from?"

"TJ."

"What? I thought you stopped hanging out with that guy. Is he still bangin' and slangin'? I thought you told me he was going to quit?"

"You know it ain't easy to just walk away from a gang, James. That nigga really does want to get a new start. He just hasn't had the chance to find an opportunity. That is a good reason I am doing what I am doing. I am tired of being in this hustler lifestyle. I want to try to do right for once, get my kids back, and change my life around. Just give him a chance. I grew up with the nigga."

"Yeah it is unfortunate that you did. I just don't trust him. He is always out for himself. Just like every other nigga from Los Angeles. It is always about how good he looks and how he is perceived by others."

"The nigga lacks confidence. He has always been mediocre at everything he has done except for the street life. He flourishes with pushin' and hustlin' on a daily basis. The streets were his text books."

"Well call that nigga up," James hastily replied. "Looks like everyone has just about left. By the time he gets here everyone will be gone."

James kissed his mother goodbye and shook his father's hand as they climbed into the car. "Thank you for the party lil' sis. I am gonna miss you. I hope you can come out and visit like you planned. Let's just keep our ear to the ground and see how things go for me out there before we plan anything."

Kira ran up to him and gave him a big hug. "You better come by and see us before you leave. I already miss you, James," she said as her eyes started to well up with water.

"It will be OK. This is for the better. Hopefully this will set me up so I can come back to L.A. and get you your own place."

"That would be so sick. I would love that. Have a safe night and don't do anything too crazy with your crazy ass cousin."

"OK, I will try to make it home at a reasonable time."

"Love you, bro!"

"Bye Bugger, love you."

With that she jumped in the back seat of the car and they pulled out of the parking lot of the Boomerang bar and arcade. James went back inside to go see Justin. Just as he walked in he saw Justin leaning over the shoulder of a brown-haired woman at the bar on a stool. He was whispering something in her ear as she swung around violently in her chair and gave him a solid slap across his face with her right hand. Justin backed his head up quickly, smiled and walked away, seeing James standing toward the entrance he made his way toward him.

"Ha ha that didn't go as planned."

"Oh my god what happened?"

"I saw her eyin' me so I just went over and told her how big my dick was and asked her if she wanted to see stars tonight. I must have been a little too forward with her."

"Yeah, ya think you big monkey?"

"Fuck you don't call me a monkey and don't call me big. I am a solid Nubian god. A mighty black man, all powerful, and ruler of the world."

"I don't know where you get this stuff from."

"I have been doing my research on Black Power and there is great stuff on the internet. Black men are gods and we are more powerful than any other man on this planet because we are the original. We used to rule this planet in ancient times."

James gave his cousin a sideways glance. "Stop fucking bullshitting me, where are you getting this nonsense from?"

"Just a bunch of random websites for now, but I am going to look into it more when I get to Africa and try to find my real calling on this earth."

"Well good luck with all that. I hope in the process you will be looking for a job and staying out of trouble."

"You know me cuzzo, you got nothing to worry about," Justin said with a wide shit eating grin on his face.

"Yeah fucking right. Speaking of trouble, where is TJ's ass? It has been long enough."

"Knowing him, he smoked a blunt before he got up to leave and that is what took him so long," Justin said, looking down at his phone checking to see if TJ had texted him. "I hate waiting on niggas to smoke."

Just as James was talking TJ sent Justin a text saying he was outside. "Let's go, this skinny yellow nigga is here," Justin said, as he put his phone into his pocket. The two walked outside and Justin pointed to a black sedan with tinted black windows parked near the back of the parking lot. James and Justin walked up to the car and knocked on the windows to get TJ to unlock the doors.

As the two opened their doors a large plume of smoke came barreling out of the car. TJ had already lit the blunt waiting for them to come out to the car. James got in the back seat and Justin in the front.

"My niggas!" TJ exclaimed as he gave them both a handshake and passed Justin the blunt.

"Damn this smells like some strong ass bud, my Nigga," Justin said as he took the blunt in his hands and took a hit. "When did you get this shit? This ain't the same bud we were smoking yesterday."

"I just picked it up from my homie Darrell up the way."

"That half Black and Mexican nigga you went to high school with?" Justin questioned.

"Yeah, that's the one."

James got settled in the back seat and then spoke up. "Damn I have been waiting for a blunt since the party started."

Justin passed it backward to James.

161

"So I heard about ya'll two lucky niggas going out to the mother land." TJ pulled out another blunt and sparked it. "Good luck with that, I really mean it. So where are ya'll niggas going tonight? I can give you a ride cause ya'll two look drunk as fuck."

"Yeah we have been drinkin' a little bit," said Justin, taking the second blunt from TJ as James passed his back up front.

"I would love to go to Laragra for our last night on the town before we leave. So many fine ass bitches be there and I know the Latinas will be out tonight. That is what I am looking for before I go on a salsa drought in Africa."

"Nigga you're tripping', fuck Mexican bitches," said TJ, with a scowl on his face.

"Ha ha nigga that is only because you got played by that bitch you took home last weekend," Justin said. "Don't hate on my Latin spice because you couldn't handle your alcohol."

"That bitch came over with a bottle of Vodka and got me fucked up just to rob me. She took all my coke and 300 dollars. If I ever catch that bitch out somewhere I swear I'ma kill her."

"Damn some girl did you dirty like that?" James questioned.

"Yeah just like I said, she jacked me for my shit. She was fine as hell though with a big ol' fat Mexican booty. You know how them chicas be rollin. She just caught me slippin'."

The trio continued passing the two blunts around until they were finished. "So since this is ya'll twos last real night out, why not go out with a bang?"

TJ reached into his glove compartment and pulled out a bag of small white pills. "You ready to roll tonight? I got some premium molly here for ya'll niggas, no cost just have fun on me tonight."

"Oh hell ya my nigga you always come through with the best shit when I need you," said Justin with a wide smile on his face. James was a little more reluctant than his eager cousin.

"Molly? Isn't that ecstasy? I have never done that stuff before. I only smoke weed you all know that."

"Come on you Chessfield nigga, loosen up a bit. You need to expand your horizons. You are about to go to the motherland on an all-expenses paid trip. You need to start experiencing life to the fullest before you get out there and waste an opportunity of a lifetime," Justin said as he took three of the pills from TJ.

"I will be watching you tonight so you do not have anything to worry about. I am your big cousin; just trust me. I wouldn't do anything to hurt you."

James was conflicted in his head about what to do but the coercion by his cousin egged him on to try the drug for the first time. "How is it going to make me feel? I am a little nervous."

"It is going to make you feel like you are king of the world. Everything gets ten thousand times better, I promise. Just give it about forty-five minutes to an hour and the party will get real crackin'. You got some water, TJ?"

"Yeah I got a couple bottles you guys can take 'em."

Justin opened up and took the pills of molly as TJ handed two to James. "OK, here goes nothing," James said as he grabbed the bottle of water and took the two capsules.

"Let's just have a fun New Year's Eve. Who knows how long before I get to come back home and do this again."

The pair was ready to party for the night sufficiently intoxicated on their drugs of choice. The alcohol from the farewell party was still running

163

through their veins. "Do you have any condoms, my nigga? I don't think I brought any and I am determined to get some trim tonight," Justin said as he opened and searched through the center console.

"Yeah I got some in my glove compartment. You don't need any more kids nigga, that is for sure."

Drunk, high, and rollin', the pair got a ride to Leragra, one of the most popular spots in all of L.A. "So ya'll two are good for the night right?" TJ asked as he pulled up to the back street behind the club near the parking lot.

"Yeah, we can take a taxi back here to the car at Boomerang or just take it home. Thanks for the ride TJ and stay safe out there," said James as he got out of the back seat.

Justin got out of the car and headed over to where James was standing. TJ pulled off the curb and blasted his way down the street, turning the corner with the blaring of his tires telling the world how little he cared for driving the speed limit. The pair went in the bar and night club knowing that their lives were soon to change and they wanted to just let it all go tonight. They weaved their way through the crowd to the bar. "We got a little over an hour till the clock hits twelve so let's get some more drinks in," Justin said. He went over to order the drinks and left James standing there, looking out onto the crowd to see what was going on.

As he scanned the horizon he caught eye contact with a lovely young brown-haired Hispanic chick. She smiled and turned away back to her friend to continue their conversation. James, starting to feel the effects of the liquor, weed, and molly all at once, was instantly in a trance over this girl. He tried his best to play it cool and not look at her. When Justin came back up to him James told him he saw a pretty chick and her friend looked good too, when Justin looked over to where James was talking about, both of the women were looking in their direction smiling.

"Oh man they want it cuzzo let's go talk to them," Justin said.

The two, with cocktails in hand, walked over to the two pretty Hispanic girls who were both in their early twenties. "Hola mi amor, como te llamas?" Justin said, asking them their names in Spanish to try and seem down with the Brown.

"My name is Cecelia, and this is my best friend Lola. You do not have to try and speak in Spanish to impress us but thanks for the effort."

The shorter one with the blue eye shadow named Lola was who caught James' attention.

"Hello Cecelia, this is my cousin James. This nigga here is about to be famous so you are lucky you had a chance to meet him before he makes it big."

"Oh really, what is it that you do?" questioned Lola as she smiled at the tall and handsome James.

"I am a journalist for the L.A. Dawn and I am about to do some special reporting from Africa. Hopefully what I do can shine some light on the positives of Africa, you know, change our perspective of the Mother Land."

Justin blurted in, "And he hopes that they find the dark matter there. If they do, then he would be super famous for his reporting ahead of time."

Cecelia, with an impressed smile on her face, turned to her best friend Lola. "Ooh he is sexy and about to be a star! My friend here has been looking for a good man to hang out with. She just got out of a bad relationship."

Lola hit her friend in protest of sharing her personal life. "I am not looking for a relationship right now, just looking to have some fun tonight."

"Well," Justin said as he walked over and put his arm around Cecelia. "We can be you twos hosts for the night. We got weed, we got molly, we are gonna go buy some more alcohol after the place closes so why don't you two just bring in the New Year with us?"

"That doesn't sound like too bad of an idea. What do you think, Lola?" Cecelia prodded her friend to answer.

"Yeah that doesn't sound too bad. You seem like cool and nice guys."

"Perfect," Justin said as he clapped his hands. "Let's go get another drink and then hit the dance floor to bring in the New Year."

The foursome walked pair by pair to the bar to order their drinks. They stood near the bar and finished their drinks and talked, getting to know each other better and warming to the idea of spending the night hanging out. As they were about to hit the dance floor the effects of the drugs were really starting to hit James. His skin was tingly and the music was bumping sweet noise into his head. He was feelin' himself, his new girl Lola, and every song that came on. James grabbed Lola's hand as she put down her drink on the counter and they headed off to the dance floor, with Cecelia and Justin right behind them. Lola was a foot shorter than James with amazing curves, a thin waist, and sexy full lips. As she pressed her ass against James midsection the vibration of the music and feel of her rubbing in tune against him to the music gave James wonderful sensation.

He had to try and concentrate to keep his manly composure and not embarrass himself with his new play date. They swayed and gyrated together to each new song, sometimes dancing face to face, and sometimes dancing with his front to her back. They were having a great time. As the songs went off and the clock neared 12, the pairs grabbed each other and counted out loud with the rest of the crowd down from ten. They got down to one and both Justin and James went in for the kiss and were met with success. The short kiss ended and James and Lola looked deep into each other's eyes and smiled. As they both looked over to the other pair, they saw that they were in full-on make-out mode, darting their tongues deeply into each other's mouth.

In the darkness they were not making a scene but James and Lola could see them as they were standing right next to them. The music came back on but James couldn't stop hugging Lola. She smiled and laughed at him, knowing the effects of the molly. She walked him over to a plush orange couch against the wall as she was getting tired of dancing all night. "So we have been dancing a lot but it is getting kinda boring. I would be having a lot more fun being on some of the stuff you are on," she said with a menacing grin. "

Well my cousin is the one who has that stuff on him. We can get going and take a taxi to a hotel room or something and keep the party going if you want," James said as his pupils were wide and his speech slightly slurred from the alcohol.

"Let me go get Cecelia and Justin and we can get going, which would be way more fun that staying here all night till close." Lola left him there to go get the other two. James had a chance to catch his breath and try to compose himself. The room was fuzzy, his eyes were spinning, and he kept grinding his teeth. His put in a stick of gum to stop his teeth from grinding but nothing could alleviate the effects of the alcohol. He knew he had to calm down his drinking when he got to the hotel so he wouldn't get sick the next morning because he had work to do.

The trio came to James and Lola grabbed him as the other pair walked toward the exit. "Come on big sexy man let's go," she flirtatiously whispered to James as he stood up. They walked out and called a taxi.

On the way to the hotel in the taxi, Justin gave the girls some molly, which they gladly took with a bottle of water Cecelia had in her purse. They had the taxi stop at a liquor store down the street from the hotel to pick up some blunts and alcohol. When they got to the hotel they were excited and ready for a party. They got to the two-bedroom hotel suite and put music on and started dancing. Everyone was feeling themselves with alcohol, weed, and molly flowing and blowing freely. As the night wore down to a close in the wee hours, the ladies said they were ready for bed.

Justin took his cue and took Cecelia to his room, and James, rather reluctantly, took Lola to his. Yeah they had kissed earlier but James was not really interested in pursuing her tonight. He really felt like his life was blessed with an opportunity from the Lord, and he felt that sinning in celebration wasn't the best way of handling it. He had made poor choices all that night and he just wasn't sure if he should cap it off with the ultimate mistake. James sat in the bed fully clothed on top of the covers. Lola sat down next to him.

"What is wrong? Did I do something wrong? I thought we were having a great time."

"I don't know Lola, I just got this big break in my career and I owe a debt of gratitude to God. I don't want to piss him off any more by making my night more filled with vice."

"Oh I understand. Yeah the last thing I wanted to do was get involved with a man tonight so soon after my heart was broken. I just got lost in your eyes and your body. You have just been speaking to me the right way all night. You're a sexy gentleman most women are not lucky enough to find." Lola paused after her sentence as they both heard the moans and screams and banging coming from the other room. "Wow that sounds hot," Lola said as she uncrossed her arms and turned toward James. "I am not telling you to act against God, but this is only one night. We will probably never see each other again. Just give me one night to release myself onto you and we do not ever have to see each other again."

James was hesitant. Here was this fine ass chica lying here begging him to service her for the night. "Give me a minute to think of it."

"Well let me give you something to help you make your decision." With that she leaned in with her butter soft lips and kissed him softly, only opening her mouth to share her tongue with his after a few seconds. They kissed and James closed his eyes, intoxicated by numerous substances and by Lola's taste. His hands moved up to caress her body. Both their hands explored each other as both proceeded to take their clothes off. In the glare of the moon her silhouette was breathtaking to James. He gave in to his innermost instincts and conquered Lola for the night as many times as he could before they passed out in a heap of sweat and love, succumbing to the sweet embrace of slumber as their muscles and their minds were worn out from the long night of party and passion.

James woke up beside his conquest the next morning still groggy from the night before. Neither of them had any clothes on and it took a quick second for James to remember what happened the night before. He put his hand on his head and shook it, "Ugh what was I thinking? I have so much work to do before I leave and I am hung over and buzzin' from the drugs."

His movements woke up Lola, who slowly stirred from her sleep and sat up, covering herself with her blanket in the cold winter morning. "Good morning, sexy man."

"Good morning. It is good that you got up because I need to go back to my car. I have so much stuff to get done today and tomorrow before I leave on Tuesday morning. I had a great time with you. We have to end it too soon."

"Well I understand. I knew going into this that you were going away. I will give you my number anyway just in case you come home and want to hang out again."

James went and woke up the other pair and everyone got ready and called a taxi van to come get them to take them to the bar and back to Boomers. When James finally got back to his car at Boomers he and Justin parted ways. They were going to go to the airport together driven by Justin's mother on Tuesday morning. Their flight was at 6 a.m. on Tuesday and they would arrive in Addis Ababa, the capital of Ethiopia, through London at 1 p.m. East Africa Time. In Ethiopia the clock starts at 6 a.m. instead of 12 a.m. in the West, so they would actually be arriving in Ethiopia at 7 a.m. James got his last-minute errands and obligations done at work and around town for the next two days and got all his suitcases ready for travel. There would be a driver to take them to his apartment when he arrived in Addis Ababa. He had scheduled meetings with several politicians and community leaders that night after he arrived and had a chance to settle in and explore the city.

When James awoke the morning of his flight he was extremely excited but nervous. He got the text from his Aunty Lynette that she and Justin were outside waiting for him early that morning. The entire ride Justin's mom was telling them to check in with everyone back home constantly, and to be careful. She did her research on Ethiopia and saw that there were a lot of bad things going on there: an authoritarian one-party ruled democratic government, female mutilation, abduction marriages, and tremendous poverty. "Everyone has a chance, Aunty Lyn. The point of my reporting is to shed light on the hopes of the downtrodden. The dark matter could be anywhere so everyone should have hope that it is in their backyard."

"Yes I understand but I don't understand why Africa, and why Ethiopia? It is so dangerous there."

"When I saw the name as I was searching countries it just stood out to me. Call it a hunch or a gut feeling, but I could sense something in my soul that this was where I was supposed to be."

"Well I am hoping it is the Lord who called you there to bring them some hope for a better future. Those people need it."

"We all need it."

Lynette looked to her son in the passenger seat to get his feelings on the matter but he had his mp3 player blasting through the headphones in his ears. "Hey!" she yelled as she took her right hand off the steering wheel to smack him across the chest. "You should be paying attention to what we are talking about. Did you do any research on Ethiopia?"

"No, I didn't need to," Justin said as he sat up. "I know I am supposed to be going to Mother Land. I have been having this sensation in my head way before I heard about this Africa stuff that I was supposed to help lead my black people to greatness. Maybe I can do that here. There must be a reason my life is falling apart here in Cali. My spirit is trying to push me to a different place."

James was happy his cousin was having a positive outlook on their journey together.

"You and me will do great things out there, Cousin. We just need to stick together and rely on each other through thick and thin."

They were pulling up to the airport and Lynette spoke up. "Yes you two must lean on each other for help in such a new place. Here we are. Let me get out and give you two hugs goodbye."

They all got their luggage and took it to the curb, hugged Lynette goodbye and checked their bags in curbside. When they got inside they got breakfast at a fast food joint in the airport, talking as they walked to their gate. "So my nigga how was that Mexican bitch the other day?" Justin asked. "We never got a chance to talk about it."

"She was great but I wish I hadn't had sex with her at all."

"Aw come on do not tell me you are gonna start acting like a pussy right before we go to Africa."

"It's not about being a pussy at all. I just have been feeling really spiritual lately. I am feeling such strong urges to get closer to God. I am hoping I have a chance to do that when I get to Africa."

"God? Man you need to get off that white man's God bullshit. Black man is God. I may not have been doing research on Ethiopia but I have been learning about new movements in the black community. First I read about the Black Israelites but I wasn't feeling them. Then the Black Phoenix Society was cool but they are only in New York and Chicago. Then I found a website about the Order of Horus and I saw that they have a chapter in Addis Ababa. Let me tell you all about them, maybe you might like what you hear and we can check them out."

"Yeah it sounds interesting, what is it about?"

"Well they teach that the Black man and woman have the power of the heavens within themselves. We alone, the descendants of the American slave trade, have the power of Christ within us. The order teaches how to attain the spiritual enlightenment of 360 degrees of spiritual knowledge and power. We, the black man, are gods and were worshipped around the world in ancient times — all around the world. If we harness that power, we could rebirth the next great prophet. The return of Horus is imminent the website says, and only by the stolen saints returning to the mother land will Horus return to lead us into the Golden Age of black civilization where we rule the world once again."

"That is amazing stuff, Justin. I have never seen you so eager and informed about anything in my life. You are really serious about this stuff."

"Yes, I feel like these people are speaking to me. I am not saying you have to come right away to a meeting, but when you have some free time between your interviews and writing maybe come check them out with me. I will go and check them out first to make sure it isn't bullshit, but their website looks legit."

"Yes it sounds interesting but I will make no promises. I will have plenty to do in Addis Ababa in a short amount of time. You never know, the dark matter could be found tomorrow. I need to make some stories happen quickly before we have to come home. They sound very interesting though. I do not know how well that kind of thinking will go with my push toward God but for you cousin, I might give it a try if I am in the mood."

"Well I am excited about that and our trip in general. What I am not excited about is this plane trip. It is nice though that your job sprung for first class tickets the entire way. I have never ridden first class before."

"Well it will make the trip just that much better, I can promise you that. I think our plane is pulling up now."

James looked out the window in the cold mist of an early year morning and saw his plane pulling up to the terminal. "Here we go, Cuzzo," said Justin and he grabbed his cousin and pulled him in closer. "This is gonna change things forever!"

They loaded on the plane and they took off for London. The ride was relatively smooth except for the landing into London. It was full of turbulence and high winds. After they landed at London they walked to their next plane. James and Justin talked about a lot of things on the first leg of the trip, but James felt like this was a good chance to prepare Justin for what was in store in Ethiopia.

"OK Justin listen up. Ethiopia has an authoritarian one-party government so you need to be careful of what you say in public, observe how things are run, and don't criticize the conditions of poor people. You really do not know what will get you in trouble so just lay low when we first get there. After some time has passed we can feel our way around how to act and what to say. Remember, I am meeting with government officials so having a cousin making bad noise in the streets is not good news for me."

"OK, I understand. Tell me a little more about their government because I am interested."

"Well Ethiopia used to be ruled by an emperor, then the Communist party took over. They were toppled and a military junta was installed. They were overthrown by this current party, the Federation of Democratic Ethiopians or FDE, and they have been ruling in a one-sided fragile democracy ever since. They have a notorious history of crackdowns on opposition, politically and in the media. Lately things have been improving though on that front. They have elections in 2018 for a new prime minister and opposition parties have been left alone for the most part. I think Ethiopia is really trying to change their image and emerge into the modern world as one of Africa's shining lights. Let's hope that we are arriving at just the right time to capture all this for our audience back home."

"Nigga, we got this," Justin said as he shook the hand of his cousin. "You get the perspective from the top and I get the perspective from the bottom, you know, from the streets. I can help you any way possible. Ethiopia doesn't sound so scary at all. Let's just hope we never have to go to Somalia or anywhere crazy."

"Sounds good, Justin. Remember my work out here is priority number one. That is what is funding this whole operation."

"I'll be careful, I promise." The Air East Africa plane rolled up to the terminal right on time. The pair boarded the plane and enjoyed another first class flight on the Los Angeles Dawn's dollar.

They arrived in Addis Ababa at 7:25 a.m., which would be 1:25 p.m. on a western clock. The beautiful green rolling hills and lush green trees everywhere were a sight to see. Ethiopia from the air was a beautiful place. Both James and Justin couldn't wait to get off the plane and check out the airport and the environment. When they got off the plane they marveled at how modern the airport was and how sweet the air smelled. "We are finally home, cuzzo," Justin told James as he pulled him close. "Look at these beautiful people and this beautiful building. Addis Ababa truly is the New York of Africa."

They walked to the baggage claim and saw a man with a sign that said James Anthony on it. "There is our driver right there," James said as he led his cousin toward the short and fair- skinned man with curly locks of black hair.

"Hello there I am James Anthony from the United States. Are you my driver?"

"Hello," the man exclaimed with a wide smile and heavy accent. "Hello Mr. Anthony my name is Abal! I will be your guide and translator while you are here in Ethiopia. I was hired by your newspaper company back from the United States so I aim to please in all ways possible."

"Well thank you for meeting us, Abal. I look forward to seeing the sights and sounds of this wonderful country in my spare time, but for the time being I need to be focused on business. I need you for my meetings tomorrow with the prime minister and some other government officials.

Make sure you get me an hour or two early so we can get some food before I meet with them."

"Yes, sir, Mr. Anthony."

"Please, Abal, call me James. I am sorry for not introducing you first, but this is my cousin, Justin. He came with me on the trip. He will not always be with us when I am handling business but you will see him plenty."

Justin stepped forward and shook Abal's hand in a classic Los Angeles style. "What's up my nigga? You gotta show us all the hot spots in this city where all the pretty girls are."

Abal countered his handshake with a customary African embrace. "My friend Justin, you will find that Addis Ababa has plenty to offer when it comes to beautiful women. I am not the best advisor on how to get them home with you but they are ripe for the picking."

Justin smiled and laughed at his new friend's style. "My nigga, me and you are gonna get along just fine. Just teach me all you can about the customs here so I don't get myself in trouble with the ladies."

"Yes we will have plenty of time to learn all about Ethiopia, but for now let us go get your suitcases and head to the town car. We will then travel to the hotel downtown and check in. We will talk the whole way about everything you need to know about being here."

They walked to the baggage claim and got their luggage and headed off to the car. James was in amazement that Africa had advanced this much to have such a fine looking airport and high rises. It was nothing like the news in America said about Africa. They talked all the way to the car and to the hotel about everything that goes on in Addis Ababa and all the customs of Ethiopia. Abal also gave them a short history lesson on the country and their current government party. Abal supported the opposition party silently but felt comfortable telling the new visitors his feelings without fear of reprisal. He said that things had recently begun getting better with more of an international presence in Ethiopia watching how the government behaved. It allowed for more leniencies on different political parties having meetings and holding rallies.

They arrived at the hotel and checked the bags in and got themselves situated to go out on the town and explore with their guide. They took showers and changed clothes, getting themselves ready to announce their presence in Africa. Justin took an exceptionally long time to get out of the bathroom, giving Abal and James some time to get to know each other. Abal was an only child of middle class parents who owned a grocery store in town. He went to Addis Ababa University where he majored in History and English. After he graduated he started working as a tour guide for a travel company using the skills he learned in both his majors at school. He wasn't married and didn't have a girlfriend, which was shocking because Abal was a decent looking young man at a good height. He said that luck just hadn't been on his side with the ladies but he hoped that it would change soon. Justin got ready and they left together for a local restaurant.

The restaurant served traditional Ethiopian dishes. Abal picked their dinner for them and his choice was fantastic, leaving both James and Justin breathless and full to the brim. After that they went to the state-of-the-art shopping mall to check out the latest fashions, and buy some local clothing. The cousins and Abal spent several hours there buying some new shirts and shoes. They loaded the cargo in the truck and headed off for a night club as it had turned night by the time they left the mall.

Abal had a change of clothes folded pristinely in the trunk in case his guests wanted to go out to a disco. He took them to the hottest spot in Addis Ababa, the Stone Temple bar and club. The line stretched out down the street as they pulled up looking for a spot to park in. After parking they walked up to the line. "Watch this," Abal said as he led the cousins down past the line and up to the front. The security guard looked up and saw Abal walking toward him and immediately unlatched the rope's hook and waved him in.

James and Justin were stunned, as they walked further into the dimly lit club James leaned in and asked, "How did you get us in like that?"

Abal answered, "They know I am good for bringing big spending foreigners to their club so they always let me in for free without waiting in line."

"That's great. Let me get us some drinks." James walked up to the bar to get some beers and Justin began scanning the crowd for his newest prey. His tight shirt was showing off his bulging muscles and it was getting the attention of several women in the crowd, who could also tell he wasn't from there. A curious pair of light brown women approached him.

"Where are you from? You look like an American football player."

"I am American," Justin answered with his master swag turned on, "and I used to be a football player. Who won the bet?"

The girls laughed. One of the women pointed to her friend. "I bet her for who would be driving home. I won so that means I get to drink if you will buy one for me."

"Oh baby I will buy you way more than one if you want. My cousin just went up to the bar. Let me go get him." Justin walked smoothly over to the bar to talk to his cousin who was waiting to grab the bartender's attention. Justin leaned in to James' head so he and Abal could hear him. "Hey my niggas I got some fine ass women interested in me because I am American. I am sure I can get one of them home with me tonight. You two can fight for the other one. Get some cocktails for my chick. The other one isn't drinking. She is driving."

James grinned at the good news for Justin and placed his hand on Abal's shoulder. "Abal, my friend she is all yours. I feel like women need to be the last thing on my mind right now."

Abal nervously smiled at the gesture. "Thank you, James, I will try my best."

James ordered the drinks and passed them to Justin and Abal as they made their way over to the women to go drink and dance with them. James just walked over to the corner in the club to watch them and everyone else who was having a good time. He didn't know what was wrong. He was in the prime of his life having a once-in-a-lifetime experience in Africa and he didn't want to go out and get some with his cousin. James had been reading a lot of his Bible on the airplane ride over here and he really felt that the Lord was speaking to him somehow. His life was moving in a direction that was taking him toward success, but he didn't want to forget that it was God who blessed him with this opportunity. He hadn't been going to a ton of church before he left for Ethiopia, but now that he was standing there in the club immersed in the stench of alcohol and sweat, and with the sight of scantily clad women and desperate men, James felt as though he needed to break away from this kind of sinful behavior and start focusing more on living a pure kind of life. Sex was great and he loved women but it just felt so empty to him lately.

He wanted to wait until he could really make that connection with a woman before jumping in the sack again so soon. Lola left a bad taste in his mouth since New Year's. He wanted to prove to himself and to God that he didn't need to be the same man that he used to be. An hour went by with James sitting there entertaining himself with his thoughts. The two pairs of new lovebirds came up to James and said they were all ready to go home.

It turned out that the other girl ended up drinking and James was the only sober one left. So James ended up driving them back to the hotel where he retired to his room while the foursome stayed awake and partied with some beer and liquor they got from the store. James was exhausted from the day of travel and sightseeing, so even though the four of them were making considerable noise, he managed to go to sleep at a reasonable time.

He looked forward to his day of meeting top officials the next day, knowing he had to be in the zone to get the best story out of these people. James was also nervous about Justin. He wanted the best for his cousin. He thought that coming to Africa would give Justin a clean start to try and improve his life, but it turned out that Justin was starting off acting just like he did back in California on the Ascerty streets. Always chasing women and trying to show off. James wanted Justin to grow up and see that life isn't all about getting pussy and drinking. James hoped that maybe if Justin saw him take a turn toward the Lord and a better way of living, that he will think about making better decisions. With the music and the giggles of women in the background, James finally went to sleep, ready for his big day tomorrow.

Chapter 8

     Jose woke up in his new D.C. condo with an awful hangover. He and his friend CC, whom he knew from high school, and his friend Lorenzo Daugherty who played with him at Texas, had hung out all weekend celebrating. Jose had taken Jay's words to heart and decided to let loose and have some fun with his friends in celebration of his swearing in to Congress. It was early in the morning but Jose still had time before he was due at Congress to vote on a Speaker of the House. In addition to the parties with his friends, Jose attended several high-end political functions, where he had a chance to meet with many of his upcoming colleagues. Through his talking with the members he learned that most of them were voting for Harold Yaster Jr. He had been the House Majority Leader for the past two terms of Congress. He helped lead the Republican Crusade against the previous president, Democrat Steven Olando. Those on the left felt like the Crusade was waged because of his skin color while others, like Jose, felt like the Crusade was waged because of his extreme liberal actions. The Crusade faded in the last year of Olando's second four-year term, but some were grumbling about bringing it back to elevate Mark Knight's presidency. Jose considered himself a child of the Crusade, and he came to Congress to enforce his will on the other side.

     Jose rolled out of bed and rolled his head around his neck to stretch after sleeping on it wrong. He walked out of his room stumbling, eyes burning from the sun and crumbling with crust. He saw his friend CC passed out on the couch, one leg draped over the top of the cushion with a small blanket strewn across his chest. Jose walked up to him and tried waking him up. "CC, hey man wake up. I have to get ready to go up to the Hill in a few minutes."

He shook CC a little bit to see if he would wake, but when it didn't work he resorted to using more violent measures. Jose punched him in the chest which caused CC to sit up and quickly open his thin slit eyes to see what had just attacked him. "Oh for fucks sake Jose, what the fuck? I am trying to sleep."

"I have to go to Capitol Hill for the private swear-in soon. I was wondering if you guys are gonna come with me or stay here and wait."

"I don't mind staying and getting more sleep. We just have to be there for the public swearing in ceremony. Ask Lorenzo if he wants to stay in. Be careful though remember he brought that Asian girl home last night."

Jose walked quietly up the stairs in his condo to the location of the guest bedroom. He could hear muffled sounds as he came closer to the door but nothing definitive that they were busy so he decided to open the door. It was a mistake as Jose was greeted to the sight of the beautiful slim figured woman bouncing and moaning on top of his friend. She heard the squeak of the door and stopped riding his friend to look.

"Oh I am so sorry!" Jose exclaimed as he went to close to door. The woman, initially shocked by the intruder, smiled at Jose as he was closing the door and simply went back to screwing his friend. Jose walked back over to CC who had fallen back asleep in the minute that Jose had gone upstairs.

"OK fuck it. I will leave them here," Jose thought as he sashayed his way through the empty beer cans and liquor bottles on the ground to get back to his room. He had a special coal black suit tailored for today that was hanging covered in the closet. Jose took a shower and got himself ready in the bathroom before he got himself dressed and left for Congress.

He was driving himself for this early morning vote and private swearing in ceremony but would take a limo with his family and friends for the afternoon public swearing in ceremony. Jose had butterflies in his stomach as he pulled up to the private parking lot next to the Cannon House Office Building. He checked in with the security guard and parked, quickly walking to his office to get a cup of coffee and meet with his Chief of Staff, Chester Begg, who should be there that day waiting on him.

He walked on the pearly white marble floor to his room. There he saw Chester watching cable political television covering the early morning House vote for Speaker. He heard Jose open the door and stood up to greet his boss with a great smile and hearty handshake. "Good morning, Congressman! I am glad to see you made it through the weekend in one piece."

"Yeah it was crazy but it was good to get all of that out of my system as I get ready to pour myself into this job for the next few years."

"Well the news coming out of the media is that Harold Yaster Jr. is a shoo-in to win the Speakership. I think it might be best to just roll with the flow on your first vote. Voting for the winning man will help give you some leverage in the coming months. Plus, your vote is an important one as you are the hot new politician on a national scale. Use your power wisely, Sir."

"Yes it does make the most sense to vote for Harold. I think he earned his position through years of hard work and dedication to the party. I look up to him. He is a political hero of mine. He was a strong figure during the Crusade, and I know he will be a strong person to help dominate the Democrats over the next four years."

"Well grab a cup of coffee and let's go to the floor to vote and get you sworn in soon to be Congressman!"

Jose grabbed a fresh cup of the finest coffee and headed toward the floor with his chief of staff. They ran into several other old and new members and all heaped praise on Jose for his courage and leadership. They looked forward to working soon with Jose on key legislation, including the immigration problem. As they made it to the floor of the House, the blue floor was a striking contrast to the glossy dark brown wood. The steps led down to the front and Jose walked off to the side of the room to take his seat.

When the vote was officially called for, Jose was eager and giggled to himself in his head and he happily walked to the front to cast his vote. He made his vote for Yaster Jr. and walked back to his seat to talk with his fellow Republicans who were seated next to him.

Congressman Jackson Batay came over to Jose and ushered him away to the corridors by themselves to talk. Batay was the Majority Whip during the last session of Congress and he was unsure if he would take the position again for this session. "Young man, great Hero, the world's eyes are upon you. Let me be the first to really welcome you to the club. We are all expecting so much out of you Jose. We all want you to be great and accomplish great things while you are here. Everything within my power I can help you with, I will do. Just remember, that gaining favors will come in handy when you need a vote for something important one day."

"Thank you, Congressman Batay. I appreciate and welcome all advice, especially from such a respected and seasoned man such as yourself. What steps can I do to improve my impact and my political skills?"

Batay seemed glad that Jose would even ask him the question. "Well first of all you need to improve your movements and gestures. I have seen you speak on television and you could be ten times more powerful with your speeches with the right hand movements and proper tone. I have a couple of books I want you to really study in your spare time. Have you ever heard of NLP?"

Jose thought deep in his memory banks but nothing rang a bell. "No, I am sorry I have not. What is that? How do you learn about things like hand gestures and tone of voice? I took speech and debate classes in college but you are saying I am still doing something wrong?"

"Yes, the books I am sending you will help you understand what you are doing wrong. We need to mold you into a more perfect form," Batay paused and looked out toward the crowd to see if anyone was coming, then turned back to Jose. "NLP is a powerful communication tool used by only the smartest and most advanced thinking people. It will improve your ability to sell a message, sway the masses, and control the audience. Your God-given abilities are tremendous by themselves, but with the help of my NLP book, you will be a super elite player in the political field. I want you to stay ahead of the curve and not come up behind.

"You have too much potential to be a lemming in this crowd of pawns. I am here to look out for you, hero. I was assigned to be your guide. By all means, step out and make a name for yourself on your own, but listen to me and let me be your guiding voice in the fog of doubt. With the resume you are bringing to the table, you will go far with the right crowd behind you. Keep on being yourself, keep on charming the crowd and pushing the envelope, because the farther you push yourself the farther the party will go. We are all here to support you, Jose, remember that."

"Thank you very much for such kind and insightful words. I will take them to heart."

"Yes, yes, now let's get sworn in so we can go back to our families and show up later for the cameras." The former Speaker of the House announced that the vote was in and all the members gathered around to see who was elected the new Speaker. He reached inside the white envelope, pulled out a folded slip of paper, and read it aloud into the speaker, "Harold Yates Jr. is our new Speaker of the House."

Everyone clapped and congratulated the tanned-skinned handsome figure, who even in old age could still cause a crowd to gather with his good looks. Congratulations rang out from around the chamber as the Democrats began filing onto the floor to begin the swearing in process. After all the Congressmen were present, the new Speaker called everyone to order and asked them to raise their right hand. They repeated the Oath of Office for Congress and officially became sworn in on January 4th, 2017.

Jose shook hands with several nearby members and after a brief moment of talking with them, he went off to find his Chief of Staff Chester Begg. He met with him briefly and then they went their separate ways before they had to meet up again later for the family and friend photo and video public swearing in ceremony. Jose called his mother and told her he would pick her up at the hotel in twenty minutes after he went home and picked up his friends.

He called CC and he answered, finally awake after being in such a deep, alcohol-induced slumber. CC said he and Lorenzo cleaned up the place and they were ready to go to lunch. Jose drove his car back to his condo and picked up Lorenzo and CC and went to go pick up Jose's mother Carmela. When he got to her she was wearing a fuzzy and warm black coat over a stunning black dress with stylish black boots. She wanted to look nice for her son's big day.

"It's a shame you never got married, looking as hot as you do," Jose said as he greeted his mother and gave her a big hug and kiss.

"Hello son, or should I say Congressman," she turned to face the tall pair of men walking up behind Jose on the sidewalk. "Good afternoon, CC and Lorenzo. Thank you again for coming to support Jose. You know we don't have any family here in the United States so it is nice for you to come be our family for today."

CC spoke up first. "Aw no problem Miss C, anything for ol' Jose. We are all just so proud of him and his achievements! We wouldn't miss this for the world."

"Yeah Miss C," chimed in Lorenzo, "Jose is like a brother to us. His success is like our success. We will support him 'til the end."

They both came and gave Carmela a hug and then headed off for the limo that had pulled up just in time. They decided on going to a local Mexican restaurant blocks from Congress. They went and had a great time, catching up on the latest news of CC and Lorenzo and talking spiritedly about Jose's upcoming career. They finished the lunch and headed off for the capitol. The limo dropped them off near the main house chamber, where the cameras would be set up to record them swearing in for the public. Their appearance time was in fifteen minutes so they were just on time. They got there and waited in line behind several other Congressmen and women with their families.

It came time for Jose and his crew to go up to the new speaker and get sworn in. Jose chose his mother's family Bible, passed down for four generations, to be sworn in on. The group gathered around Jose and the speaker and everyone smiled for the cameras except Jose, who took this moment very seriously. He was not coming to Congress for fun, he was coming to handle business and that is what he wanted to portray. Speaker Yaster Jr. said the oath to Congress and the Constitution and had Jose repeat. After they were done reciting they shook hands and all turned toward the cameras.

Jose forced a smile but inside he knew he was ready for war. They finished up and left, ready to take a guided Secret Service tour of all the monuments and museums they could fit in before they closed. As the group headed for the limo which would take them to the World War II Memorial,

Jose got a call. He told everyone to get in so he could answer it outside. He looked at the screen and it was singer Juanita Mills. The two had stayed in contact by text and the occasional phone call since they had dinner, but Jose was still surprised she was calling.

"Hello, Jay, how are you doing?"

"Hey, Hero. I just saw you on the news, hot stuff. I wanted to say you looked great. Kinda serious for my taste, so I hope Congress doesn't turn you into a serious asshole. Congratulation on your big day is what I called to say first and foremost. I wish you the best of luck, my friend."

"Thank you for your support. I never thought you would be watching politics in the middle of the day but I will take a compliment from you anytime. I have to get going but we should talk sometime soon. I will tell you how my new job is going."

"That would be nice. Remember we have to start having our Bible study when you have a chance to come back to Dallas. Just tell me your schedule and we can plan it. Maybe we can start doing some lessons together soon on FaceNet or something."

"Yeah that sounds good. I will probably be back in Dallas this weekend if you want to hook up. Remember, it is your job to keep me in line with the Lord. I am giving you that responsibility."

"Whoa that is a big deal but I take on your challenge. You can trust me. I will try to keep your life as close to God as I can take it. Yes, I will be in Dallas this weekend so just call me and we can meet up."

"OK, I really have to go. Nice hearing your voice, Jay. Take care."

"Goodbye, Hero. Talk to you soon."

With that Jose and his family and friends went off to explore the richness of Washington, D.C. He was a freshman Congressman, ready to take the next step in pushing his agenda and maybe pushing his friendship with the stunningly beautiful Jay Mills to a more personal level.

Chapter 9

James was in a deep sleep when he was woken up by a loud knock on the door. He rolled over and said, "Come in," loud enough for the knocker to hear him.

"James, you are late. I thought you would already be up and dressed by now."

Groggy still, James grabbed his cell phone and saw that he forgot to set his alarm. As his eyes adjusted to the sunlight he saw that Abal had put on a full black suit with shining black shoes. Confused, James asked him, "Hey what the hell? Where did you get that suit from? I don't remember seeing that in the car?"

Abal responded, "I drove home early this morning when I woke up to shower and change. I ended up passing out from a mixture of the alcohol and being very tired. I don't know what happened with your cousin and those two women."

Just as he said that they both heard the door opposite of theirs in the hallway open up and the two women, with hair matted and wild, walked out the bedroom toward the front door. Justin, in a pair of sweatpants and no shirt, walked gingerly behind them out of the room. He noticed the door to James' room was open so he poked his head inside, gave them both a wide smile, and gestured a thumbs up with his hand that his night had gone wonderfully. He walked the two ladies out, out of view from James and Abal.

"Wow he is such a dog. I don't know how he does it."

Abal looked at him confused. "A dog? What does this mean to be a dog?"

"He is a dog, you know… he humps everything around the block with no discretion. He has no control over his penis."

"Ah yes I understand now. I thought getting the ladies was important to American men? I was surprised when you excused yourself and went to bed."

"I am just not in the right mindset to start sleeping around out here. I was sent to Africa to tell a story, not to get distracted by women. Not only that, I am trying to live my life better in the Lord's eyes. My life has been filled with blessings and I do not want to forget that."

"That is very interesting, James. I admire your faith and your pursuit of a better way of life. I am too weak right now to change my life in that direction. Or maybe it is just that I never had proper guidance or motivation. I don't know what my problem is. I want to go out and party and have fun while I am young, but I don't want to sin and make the Lord upset with me. It is a struggle trying to balance out living my life to the fullest and being obedient to the Lord."

"Well it is nice to see that you are a Christian. I didn't want to scare you off with my ramblings about the Lord."

Abal responded, "You will find that there are many Christians out. Excuse me, James, I am sorry to change the subject but you must take a shower and get ready. I will iron your shirt for you. Please go wash up."

"OK I will, but yes, I am interested in meeting other Christians while I am here in Ethiopia."

With that James got up to go get his boxers and his undershirt to head to the shower. Just as he got to the door Justin came back from walking the girls to the taxi.

"Justin be bustin' open, on, and in these hoes!" He roared and beat his chest like a maniac, "I am a black man, and I am god! No man can touch me and no woman can resist me."

James rolled his eyes and just headed to the shower. "Congratulations, Cousin, those girls were sexy. I really don't need to know the details. I am just glad you had a good time our first night out in Addis Ababa. I really do not have time to talk. I am running late for my meeting. What are you going to do while I am gone?"

"I am going to check out the Order of Horus. They have an open meeting in about two hours. I am extremely excited."

"Well, have a good time. Remember, if you find anything or anyone worth interviewing let me know as soon possible."

"OK, will do, Cuzzo. Good luck with your interviews."

James went to the shower and Justin went back to his room to go to sleep before his meeting.

As James was in the shower he was thinking over his assignment. James was going to video record every interview and put them on his blog page on the L.A. Dawn's website. He would also put the interviews in print and hopefully get them in the paper if they were good enough. At the very least, everything he did would be best found on his online blog page. As the water ran over his wide and strong chest, it helped calm him down as his nerves were starting to get the best of him. This was his first interview of a world leader. He had to do his best not to disrespect him on the first visit. He would have to try and garner his respect while still asking the tough questions that everyone back home wanted to know. There was a knock on the door as James was lost in thought. Abal, hardly waiting for a response, peaked his head through to yell at his boss, "James we must go soon, hurry up please."

Abal ended his plea quickly after James answered in the affirmative and left the bathroom door for his spot on the couch. He turned on the television and watched the news, waiting for James to get ready. In ten minutes James was out the shower with his teeth and hair brushed. He went into his room and got dressed in a couple minutes. Abal had prepared some breakfast earlier in the morning so James grabbed a plate as they both headed for the car. James ate his delicious Ethiopian breakfast in the car on the way to the prime minister's office.

When they pulled up to the gate and got clearance, they found the nearest park. James put on his suit jacket and both he and Abal made their way to the entrance. The building was a spectacular hue of grey with beautiful overhangs. They went inside the building and signed in to the guest chart. They were about seven minutes early, and they headed up to the floor where the media room was set up for the interview. As they neared the room the director saw James coming and went up to him. "Good morning, Mr. Anthony, my name is Demeke. Glad you found your way here all right through the traffic. Please right this way…"

He led them to a couple of seats moved up against the wall. "OK so we have the interview set for thirty minutes. You can ask as many questions as you want in that time frame. The prime minister has given you full permission to ask any questions you desire. He is an open book."

"Thank you, Demeke, for all of your help. I trust that you will email and mail me a copy of the interview as soon as possible so I can get it up on my website."

"Yes sir I will."

Demeke went to the camera and checked inside and outside to make sure everything was working properly as they were waiting for Prime Minister Mehari Amanuel. A few minutes passed by and then, coming out of the hallway, were Prime Minister Amanuel and two of his staff. He had a wide smile and a slightly chubby bulge coming out from his stomach. His soft and jolly face gave the impression of a man who did not follow the cruel behavior of his ruthless father. "Mister James Anthony, welcome to Ethiopia! I take it you have had a chance to indulge in the splendor of Addis Ababa by now. How do you like our fair city? Are we catching up to the United States?"

James received his open-armed gesture and went in for a quick hug, feeling it might be customary to greet officials in such a manner as an invited guest. "I love the city and everything I have experienced in your country so far. I am hoping that with time I will grow to love Addis Ababa and this country even more. Yes, some things in the United States are worth mimicking, but most things are not. I like that Addis Ababa is technologically advanced yet still with a rustic African charm. The wealth of your natural beauty should never be replaced with modernity. That would take away from the entire experience."

"Yes, yes, I agree! We must keep Africa, Africa."

After a quick introduction of his assistants and Abal, they walked over to the staging area where the camera was set up and took their seats. As they sat down, Prime Minister Amanuel leaned in and whispered to James, "I take you will be nice on me for our first interview. I am in an election and negative press from overseas could be what puts the opposition in over me. We cannot allow the Muslims to gain another foothold in Africa."

"I will be as nice as I can allow myself to be, sir. Please do not worry."

"Thank you, James," with that he turned to Demeke and said, "We are ready director, so please let us begin."

"Welcome to this Los Angeles Dawn's special report on the new Ethiopia and dark matter. I am L.A. Dawn reporter James Anthony, and I would like to welcome my guest, first term Prime Minister Mehari Amanuel."

The camera turned to Mehari and he waved to the future audience. "We are here to discuss Ethiopia, its future, and where dark matter could fit into its plans for a better tomorrow. So Prime Minister, Ethiopia has taken a major turn toward modernity in the last several years since you took office after your father passed away. Where do you see this country going in the next few years in regards to innovation?"

"Well, as you know our world class Chinese funded light rail system in our fine capital has been completed ahead of schedule and below budget. We are expanding the downtown area, adding more shopping centers, high rise apartments, and condo complexes. We are also giving 190 million birrs, which is about 10 million U.S. dollars, to the University of Addis Ababa's expansion. They will offer more classes, hire more professors, build more dormitories, and allow in more students. We are trying to build our school into a top flight world class university, and we need a serious investment from the public to make that happen. We also just approved the building of a high speed railroad system, but we are still searching for the funding before we begin construction."

"That all sounds good, Prime Minister, but let us talk about the real problem in Ethiopia, which is the same problem for a lot of Africa nations, and that is poverty. What do you plan on doing to address the needy, poor, and malnourished?"

"We have enacted a complete retooling of the agricultural system of Ethiopia. This starts by addressing poor irrigation techniques, which waste tons of water every day, and deliver poor circulation for large farms. We will also be hosting free educational classes on agricultural techniques used by farmers around the world. We hope that through investment and education, we can strengthen the backs of the lower class agricultural workers. We also need to focus on educating the young and impoverished at a young age. We need to teach them to read, write, and use computers. This can be done with determination and will, and with my guidance we will have them both."

James continued with his questioning, "What makes Ethiopia worthy of having dark matter found within its borders? What would Ethiopia do with an important resource? What kind of global force would you want Ethiopia to be if it found this source of new wealth and power?"

This was the question the prime minister had been waiting for. "We are very excited about the prospects of finding the dark matter within our borders. We feel, as the diplomatic capital of Africa, we are very well suited for the dark matter. We have great relations with our neighboring poor countries, and we would do wonders in being able to improve their wellbeing if we had the dark matter. We also get along well with Western and Eastern powers. We are the perfect blend of advanced and rustic, West and East, rich and poor. If we had dark matter within our borders we could lead the world to a better place by showing that money and power would not change our core convictions. Muslims will still get along with Christians, the dominant will still get along with other minorities, and we will spread the wealth to all classes of people.

"Africa has been waiting for an opportunity such as this. It has been too long that Africa has been sapped of her natural resources for the benefit of other races of people. First and foremost, a discovery of dark matter within our borders will go to help the black man and his problems. This is all in God's hands now. If He so chooses for us to be bestowed with the honor of having dark matter, we will gladly take on the challenge."

James finished up asking his questions and he wrapped up a very well done interview. This was James' first taste of the big time, interviewing a big shot in a foreign country, and he nailed it. "Thank you very much, Prime Minister. I hope to be coming to you for another interview in the future as things progress in the dark matter search and your re-election efforts."

"Thank you, James, this was wonderful. I hope to be seeing you again sometime. If you have any questions or need any help, feel free to call me at any time."

The Prime Minister exited the room back to his office with his two staffers eagerly following behind him, feeding him updates on current events around the country.

James and Abal left for the Federal Parliamentary Assembly buildings, home of some of the best and brightest minds Ethiopian government had to offer. They had three interviews set up with members from the House of Peoples' Representatives, which was the lower chamber, and two interviews with members of the House of Federation, the upper chamber of Parliament.

James and Abal were busy all day with the interviews. James came away very satisfied with his performance and the honesty and candor of his interviewees. After a long day they left to retire for the night in the comfort of their homes. Abal drove James up to the hotel and dropped him off. He said he would be there early the next morning for James' next round of interviews with business leaders.

When James got to the hotel room and put the key in, he could hear music playing loudly in the room. He tried to push the door open but something on the ground was impeding the movement of the door. As he forced the door open bit by bit, he poked his head through the door to see what was blocking the way. There were towels on the floor, and just as he looked up to see where his cousin was, he caught a gust of wind that blew the familiar cloud of sweet smelling marijuana smoke into his nostrils.

"What the fuck, Justin! Come move these damn towels!"

It was impossible for him to be heard over the loud music so James just kept pushing, inch by inch, as the towels gave way. He hurried into the room once he had enough space to avoid any more smoke being blown into the hallway. He came into the main area of the hotel room and saw Justin sitting on the couch with a magazine in one hand and a blunt in the other. Justin was not paying attention to his surroundings, as he was completely entrenched in the magazine.

James went over to the stereo on the counter of the opposite wall where Justin was sitting and turned down the music, startling Justin from his focus on the magazine. "What the fuck Justin? Where did you get that bud from?"

"Hey, Cuzzo, what is up my naga? I have so much stuff to tell you about my day today. Here come take a seat," he said as he put the magazine in his lap and patted on the open spot of the couch next to him. James kept the music turned low and walked over and took his seat.

"What is up? So where you been all day? My interviews went well. Oh, and what the fuck is a naga?"

"My brotha, a naga is a black man, given a power from the heavens to be men of god-like power. I learned all about the Naga and how black men ruled the world from Dr. Cameron Berihun today. He is the leader of the Order of Horus."

"Horus?"

"Yes Horus, the Egyptian god. His prayer energy will be reborn in a black man who will rise to lead black people into a golden age of wealth and power. Dr. Berihun said his return to the Holy Land is imminent."

"Wait, Holy Land? Like Israel?"

"No, Naga, it is here in Ethiopia. The Garden of Eden was here, in Debre Berhan, about two hours' drive from here. That is where the Holy Land of the original man, the black man, is located. There in the Garden of

Eden God will unveil a great wealth to the black man. It was all seen by Dr. Berihun in a dream years ago and it will soon come to pass."

"This all sounds like a bit much to take in right now after such a long day," grumbled James and he stood up and began taking his jacket, shirt, and tie off. "How do you know anything this guy is saying is legit?"

"You can feel the power emanating from his body as he speaks. He is talking of a great and brand new world where the black man is in control again. You have to give him a try, or at least interview him. He says that the dark matter is located at Debre Berhan, I am sure that would be an exciting story for your paper. He also says that in order for Horus to return to save our people, he must be in charge of Ethiopia to bring about an end to the rampant sin and evil deeds being done in this country, and around the world, by black people."

"So he says the dark matter is in Debre Berhan? That is very interesting. My readers would probably eat this guy up. How does he know the dark matter is there?"

"He says a great light will appear in the sky just like it did for Zara Yaqob when he decided to build the city. It is there that the dark matter, and the Garden of Eden, will be found."

"Fascinating stuff Justin, it really is. Excuse me if I have my doubts about believing this guy. He does sound very interesting, to say the least."

"Well I am not here to convince you of anything. I am definitely convinced though, and I put in an application for a job as security. I also put in an application to become a cleric in the Order of Horus. I think I found what I am supposed to do with my life, Cuzzo. God meant for me to come out here to Africa. I could feel it all along. Something special is about to happen to me, and all black people, in the very near future. I can just feel it in my soul."

"Well maybe you should temper your expectations a little, Justin. There have been plenty of big mouths and charlatans talking about new paradise for followers. Many of them end up being hoaxes and scams for people's money. Just be careful, Justin, is all I ask. We are supposed to be out here looking out for each other. I do not want you to get into to anything outside of our control."

"Nigga… I mean, Naga, you do not have to look out for me. I am sure of this. I have all the confidence in the world for Dr. Berihun. Nothing he says is about money or power. It is all about salvation and spiritual purification for our people. It is all about positivity. You will see, I promise. He can sway even the most jaded and hard-headed man."

"Well when is the next meeting?"

"He has a beginners meeting in two weeks here in Addis Ababa. He left back for Debre Berhan to his compound in the mountains. That is where the clerics stay. It is like a monastery."

"Good, that will give me time to interview all the people I need before I indulge in this endeavor with your man Dr. Berihun."

"You will not be disappointed."

James and Justin talked a bit more about the Order of Horus and then decided to go downstairs to the hotel restaurant for dinner. The beginning of their lives in Africa had gone well, but James was still determined to produce more quality work for his job. The election in Ethiopia was four months away and even though the deadline for running for the position of prime minister was two months away there were still plenty of quality participants to interview.

James was excited for his prospects of success, with or without the dark matter being discovered there. He hoped that his move toward living a more Christ-inspired life would reflect in the success of his work. God had been blessing him all up until that point, so James expected more of the same, especially if he changed his life for the better. He needed to find a church when he had more time. He hoped Abal could help him find an English-speaking non-denominational church in Addis, but his schedule was busy as well.

James would put it on the back burner for the immediate future, but planned on getting to it sooner rather than later. James also hoped that his cousin's foray into this new cult would not impact his career. He was optimistic about the future but he just had to keep an eye on Justin. Going to the newcomer's event in two weeks would give him a chance to check out this Dr. Berihun and make sure he was legit before his cousin got in too deep.

Chapter 10

Jose, with his visiting mother and friends, all took the afternoon flight from D.C. to Dallas on a chilly Friday in early January. Jose had flown back to Dallas to meet with constituents and backers, most importantly of which was oil Tycoon Ron L. Boone. He had his meeting with Boone tomorrow, freeing him up to meet up with Juanita "Jay" Mills that Friday if she was available. Jose pulled up to his condo and parked in his space. As he climbed out of his car he pulled out his cell phone and called Jay. After several rings she answered, "Hello there Hero, what do I owe for the pleasure of this call?"

"I told you I was going to be in Dallas this weekend. I wanted to know if you would like to meet up at your place or mine to Bible study together."

"Oh that sounds tremendous Jose. I was just finishing up with my grandmother. I can come right over after I shower and get ready."

"Sounds good, Jay. I will text you my address. I have two parking spaces so park in number 213 on the second floor parking garage. You should see my car parked in the space next to it. My unit number is 296 on the second floor. If you have any questions or get lost just call me."

"OK, will do."

They got off the phone and Jose made his way up to his room. He changed out of his suit into a more comfortable outfit. He did not want to overdress for such a casual date with Jay. At the same time, he did not want to look like a scrub in front of one of the most beautiful and sought after women on the planet. He went to his closet and rummaged through his clothes looking for the right look. As he was frantically searching through the walk-in space, he stopped what he was doing and yelled at himself, "What the hell are you doing, Jose? Calm down and get it together."

He did not know why he was in such a flurry of thoughts and anxiety. He tried not to think of Juanita in sexual terms because Jose was not that kind of person, but he could not get the warm feelings and butterflies out of his stomach.

Frustrated, Jose just grabbed a pair of jeans and a white t-shirt. He did not want to get in the habit of overdoing it with Jay. He tried to convince himself that his only interest in her was to further his career and hopefully further his spiritual development, which had been severely lacking in the last few years.

Jose paced around his apartment trying to calm his nerves. He decided the best way to take the edge off would be to grab a beer while he was waiting for Jay. An hour went by and Jose was a couple beers in when he got a text from her saying that she was on the way. The buzz of the alcohol eased Jose's tension and soothed his nerves. He knew he couldn't keep acting like this every time he was about to see Jay. It was just that she left such a strong impression on him the last time they hung out, that he was nervous about where this altercation could lead as far as his feelings for her. Things were moving so fast for Jose's heart. He could not control what he was beginning to feel for her. She had a spell on him.

There was a loud knock on the door that interrupted Jose's thoughts. He got himself together mentally as best he could, then went to the door to get it. Just as he was approaching there was another loud knock at the door and he could hear Jay on the other side saying, "Hurry up, it's cold in your building!"

Jose opened the door and greeted Jay with a smile. "Sorry for not coming faster. It can get a bit chilly in the hallways here. They do not do a good job of heating it. Come right in."

Jose asked, "Would you like a tour of the place before we start? Where is the Bible study book? All I see is that you brought your Bible."

"Yeah I looked at some Bible studies at the Christian store and online, and they were just boring. I think we would have more fun if we just read the Bible to each other and teach ourselves about its meanings."

"OK that sounds interesting. I haven't just read the Bible straight through in a long time."

"We are going to start with the New Testament, and if that goes well we can do the Old. My Grandmother Domenica says we should skip the first few chapters of the New Testament and start with John."

"I would love to meet her the next time I am in Dallas. It really is not hard for me to fly home from D.C. on the weekends to do whatever I want. D.C. is a great city but I am a Texan, and I love it out here. Oh and I was meaning to ask you a question. I was sent some books by one of my Congressional friends about NLP. I was wondering if you would like to study them with me?"

"What is NLP?"

"Well from what I learned from the internet, NLP is the verbal and physical science of communication. It is supposed to teach me everything I need to know about communicating with my peers and with my constituents. I am very excited to learn about it. Congressman Batay insisted that I learn as soon as possible."

"Sounds very interesting," Jay said as she clapped her hands together loudly and smiled brightly at Jose. "This is going to be a lot of fun. I am glad you decided to be my little learning friend. Hopefully we have a lot that we can learn from the books and from each other. OK let us get started. Turn your Bible to John. You know his name was the Beloved One? He was really quite special."

"Very interesting, look we are learning from each other already. Would you like me to read first?"

"Yes please do."

Jose got his Bible out and began to read the passages of John aloud to his new friend. He read for about fifteen minutes and then passed the duty of reading to Jay. Before she started to read she went in her purse and pulled out three blunts. "I like to smoke before I study the Bible. It really gives you understanding on another plane. I suggest you try too but alas, you are a square."

"I am not a square. I am a Congressman. Haven't you heard of Congressmen being asked to resign over drug usage?"

"Yeah and I have heard of some who have kept their jobs. It is OK, sweetie, I promise. As long as you let me smoke I won't have a problem with it."

She pulled out a pink lighter and lit the marijuana cigar. Jose saw her eyes roll into the back of her head as she took the first big hit to her lungs. "OK, I can read while I smoke."

She started reading the verses of John as she smoked her three blunts. Over twenty minutes later Jay spoke up, "You know, as we are reading about John the Baptist in this chapter, do you find it interesting that they thought he was a prophet reborn, like Elijah or another great prophet who returns in the end times?"

"I never put any thought into it. I just kinda glazed past that part as I was reading. What do you mean a prophet reborn? Are prophets coming back to Earth or something?"

"Yes, as I have been taught by my grandmother and my elders, there are great prophets that will be returning to the earth to decide the fate of human kind in a struggle between the darkness and the light."

"Come on, I know the Bible says some crazy stuff but I have a hard time believing that these Biblical figures are going to be reborn. Wait, you aren't one of those people that believe the end of the world is coming, are you? I thought all those people disappeared after the Mayan prophecy was a bust."

"I believe what my heart tells me to believe. My grandmother has seen visions of the future and I believe she is not lying. She says the end of the world is coming soon. I have done my own research and I really think something big is about to happen. We already discovered a new resource, which is a huge earth-changing event. Who knows what other crazy things we have in store for us in the upcoming years? I also do not believe the Mayan prophecy was wrong. They calculated the end of the age not the end of the world. We are in the beginning of the Age of Horus. We have entered into a new Age of Enlightenment."

"Well call me a skeptic. People have been calling for the end of the world for thousands of years with no success. Nothing has changed. The world has moved on. Man does not have the power to stop turning the world, and I honestly believe God isn't done with us yet. We have so many more horizons to break through as a species. Why would God turn in the cards right now?"

"I don't have a good answer to that. I just have feelings that I follow. I hope the Lord is not planning on ending us soon. I hope He lifts us up. I believe that is what He is going to do. Not destroy this world, but recreate it through the will of His faithful servants. I for one will be a ready and willing soldier for the Army of believers.

"Speaking of dark matter, I came up with a plan for you to use to solve the immigration crisis. They have to be finding sites to manufacture this stuff right? The way I see it, dark matter related products will require global production, not just localized in some faraway place. You should look into speaking with the discoverer of dark matter, Professor Frederick Slater, about setting up a manufacturing center in Mexico. The tens of thousands of jobs would certainly help alleviate the United States border crossings, and the added income will boost the military's ability to protect its citizens' new wealth."

"Wow that is an amazing idea, Jay. Not only that, but the UN would see to it that the global production is safe, so they might even send some soldiers to Mexico to help fight the drug cartels. Everything is a win-win situation for me. I am going to get on that right away. There must be a way for me to contact him through our UN Ambassador. He is busy with the search now but if I request his time early he might grant me an audience."

"It wouldn't hurt to try, sweetie. I told you I am a bundle of ideas. How do you think I write all the lyrics to my songs without being extremely creative?"

"Yeah I never thought about it like that. Well you have earned a little more of my respect. I really appreciate it."

Jay smiled and batted her eyes, and blushed a little at the compliment from Jose. "Let us get back to the Bible, shall we?" Jose's question pierced the clouded and uncomfortable silence in the room.

"Yes, we should. Take a look back at John 1:8 when they talk about John the Baptist. It says, 'He was not that Light, but he was sent to bear witness of that Light.' What do you think that Light is?"

"Well the Light is just a reference to Jesus."

"Well you are right and you are wrong. What Jesus did was bring the Light to man through His birth. It is a Light that we can all absorb through attaining the same spiritual knowledge and power of Jesus. Look at John 1:9, it reads, 'That was the true Light which gives light to every man coming into this world.' What it is saying is that the Light that Jesus brought has been given to every man of this world. It is our responsibility to bring it out and reach the level of Christ."

"OK I am following you, but what do you have to do to bring out that light within us?"

"You must learn the true ways of the world. You must learn to harness the spiritual power that is within you. Only then can you be at one with the Light inside of you. That is why they call this the Age of Enlightenment. Men will finally be able to find the Light that has been hidden within us. I am still in the beginning stages of my training, but if you are interested in learning more, you must come see my grandmother."

"OK, next weekend I will fly back to Dallas and I can meet your grandmother. I am too busy these next few days. I am definitely interested in learning about this 'Light' you speak of, and how attaining it can help me grow in spirit and in life."

"Once you start learning the secrets of the elders, your life begins to change. Anyway, let us continue reading. I will start, I believe we left off at John 17. I will just finish off the story of Jesus."

So Jay read through the remainder of John and finished at the beginning of Acts. "Oh the story of Jesus and the Gospels is so enthralling and inspiring. I swear I haven't read them in ages. I am glad we did this," she said.

"I am glad as well. Reading the parables and really absorbing Jesus' message really does something to my soul. Well now that we finished our first reading together, let us change subject and hit up this NLP book and learn about what this stuff is."

"Yes I am very interested in this NLP thing. Sounds like something I could use for my music."

"Let me go and get the books. Wait right here. Do you want anything to drink while I am up? Maybe we could order some Chinese and watch some movies if you don't have plans for the night." Jose tried to sound casual about the movie suggestion.

"I would really like that, thank you for the invite. I really only party and drink in moderation. It is hard to see, but I am trying to shed my rock star and sex symbol lifestyle for something more modest and humble."

"I could only imagine the pressures of stardom in the entertainment business. I am sure it will be difficult being a Congressman, but I will garner nowhere near as much attention as an entertainment superstar."

To change the subject, Jose asked her, "What do you want to drink? I have water, lemonade, and some bottles of Chinst and Delush as well. I already hit up some of the Chinst winter lager before you came."

"Give me a Delush please. I am excited to learn about this NLP thing. Hurry. Go get the books."

Jose turned and left for his room where he put the package that was delivered overnight from D.C. to Dallas. He tore open the package and saw the book named, "Path to Success: The Essentials of NLP." It was written by a Dr. Dirk Waters from Mesa, Arizona. He grabbed the book and went to the fridge to get a Chinst and a Delush.

"Thank you, sweet cheeks," she said as she took her cold bottle of beer from his hand. "So what do we have here?" she said as she was looking at the books.

Jose handed them both to Jay. "Here, take a look at them while I put some music on. There is a cable channel that plays really great music. Let me put it on."

As he was going for the remote, Jay was thumbing through both books. "They look very interesting. I hope we learn a lot."

Jose quickly found the channel and put it on low so it could be a background noise to their reading. He found his seat again and asked Jay, "Whom do you want to start reading?"

"I will start since I already have the book." Jay opened to the first page and began reading. "Here I go, 'If you are here reading this book, then you are here because you are willing to open your mind. The secrets you will learn in this book will open you to a brand new world. It changes the very way you exist. However, we do urge our readers to not use their newfound knowledge for devious and negative actions. We are here to guide you to a more positive and successful life. Use our knowledge wisely.' Whoa that sounds serious. I hope they are gonna teach us some crazy ass shit in this book. I am excited! Aren't you, Mr. Hero?"

Jose smiled, "Yes I am excited! I never even knew this stuff was out there. If it is so powerful why don't more people use it?"

"I don't know, baby doll... Maybe everyone does use it, and we have just been ignorant to it this entire time."

"The smarter we become, the better."

"The smarter we are the more powerful we are. It will only help us. OK, let me continue." Jay read a few more paragraphs; she was absorbing everything she was reading aloud. "So from what I understand, Neuro represents the brain and how we process what comes in and what goes out, Linguistic is the language we use to communicate with others, and Programming is our behavior. Let me continue reading."

Jay read until she got to something interesting. "Here look at this, we can only take in up to nine parcels of information at any one time, but the brain is overloaded with over two billion pieces of information per second. The book is offering us a way to focus our minds on what we want and need to accept into our receptors. Let's keep reading."

Jay was very excited. They had just started reading about NLP and she was already so interested on what they were teaching. "It says here that the best way to communicate with people is to have a goal in mind for every conversation and work your way backward in your head until you get to where you are so you can map where you want the communications to go. Here is something about how we process information, listen, 'There are five representational systems that make up how your brain processes information: Visual, the things that a person can see with their eyes; Kinesthetic, the things you touch and feel physically; Auditory, the things that you hear; Gustatory, what you taste with your tongue; Olfactory, what you smell with your nose. We represent these representational systems with the first letter of the word, but we will primarily focus on the first three as they are the most important, V, K, A, respectively.' OK remember that Jose."

"I got it. You want me to read yet?"

"No I am enjoying this. Maybe when I want to smoke some more marijuana we can switch because my high is starting to wear off."

"OK, continue reading."

"OK. 'Most people shade their communication toward one of the three main rep systems. So if you know if a person communicates with primarily auditory phrases and words, you can use that to gain subconscious agreement with them.' Here they list several V, K, and A words and phrases that I am sure we can use for later. That is fascinating. I never knew that the words that I use have a pattern. 'By using the knowledge of the V, K, A systems, it allows one to create rapport with the person they are communicating with. Rapport is the active relationship, positive or negative, that a person has with another. You can either build or destroy rapport quickly communicating within or outside of a person's preferred rep system. An effective way of reading a person's rep system is by watching their eyes. When you ask a person a question, by reading their eye movements, you can see if a person is accessing pictures, feelings, or sounds.

"'While looking at a person, up and to the left means Visual-constructed, meaning that they are accessing the creative part of their brain. Up and to the right is Visual-remembered, meaning they are accessing a stored memory. Left movement without movement up or down is Auditory-constructed, while to the right is Auditory remembered. Down and the left is Kinesthetic, and to the bottom right is Auditory dialogue. By remembering these eye movements, you can not only tell a person's rep system, but if a person is creating a lie when answering a question.' Wow Jose that is fascinating. We should totally use this on people and test it out one day."

"Yeah, if what they are saying is legit then that is some powerful knowledge. People have been able to read our eye movements this entire time!"

"I know crazy, huh? Let me keep reading, 'Rapport is an essential part of NLP. Creating it and destroying it are essential ways of controlling any social situation. You build rapport by being in congruence with a person's VKA type, and you destroy rapport by purposely operating outside of it. Ways to identify a person's VKA type is through the words they use and their eye movements. Another important step in creating rapport is through a process called coding. Coding is the strategy of delivering coded speech, to deliver a hidden message with your words without the listener being aware. You do this by having layers of meaning within your speech. So if you are visiting a friend's house and the temperature is too cold, you can ask him a simple question about where he would like to travel to that summer. His subliminal messaging will pick up the thought of summer, and being warm, and he will immediately think about how cold it is in the house compared to how warm he would be on his vacation. Then, without seeming rude, he responds to your command to have him change the temperature on the thermostat to a higher level. This strategy of language coding takes some practice, but it is very effective. Another important aspect of NLP is mimicking. This is the process in which you move your body into a similar position as the person(s) you are speaking with. Going into congruence with another person creates a greater sense of bonding and comfort with one another.

"'Going out of congruence weakens the communicative bond, giving an easier way to leave the social interaction. The ultimate 'out of congruence' maneuver is turning your back to the subject you wish to end communications with. Now with the ability to read a person's VKA type, and the ability to codify your words, and the ability to mimic, you will be able to manipulate any conversation or social situation in your favor. The remainder of this book gives helpful tips on becoming stronger NLP users, but you have all the base knowledge you need to succeed in the world of NLP. Now is the time where you must go into the world and practice these skills in order to become effective at using NLP. Good luck knowledge seeker!'

"Well that was exciting, Jose! It is like an entirely new world just opened up to us. We must make one promise to each though."

Jose looked at her curiously, "Sure, what is it?"

"We must never use NLP against each other maliciously. For any reason! Deal?"

"I believe that is fair. I promise."

With that they shook hands and then Jose said, "So you still want to watch that movie? I have a ton of movies On-Demand with my cable box."

Jay perked up and remembered about the movie plans. "Yes, of course I will watch a movie. Could you grab us some more beers while I go through the movies? Do not mind me. I am just going to smoke while we get ready for the movie."

Jay reached for her purse and pulled out two more blunts. She came well prepared for a long night with the amount of pre-rolled blunts she brought. She lit one of them up while placing the other on the table and grabbing the remote. The cable was still playing soft R&B music, which made Jay sway in the beat. She refocused her attention on the mission at hand and began surfing through the movies while Jose grabbed two beers in each hand for his guest and himself.

"I found a good movie, Jose," she yelled from the main room. "Have you seen 'Contra Costa'?"

"No, but I have heard good things from a good friend of mine who saw it with a girl he took on a date."

Jose put the beers down on the table and left for the cabinet in the hallway leading to his room to gather some blankets for the cold January Texas night. He gathered up the blankets and headed back out to the main room. Jay had gotten herself comfortable on the couch, laying her head on the far side of the couch on a soft off-white pillow.

Jose laid a blanket on top of her and she said thank you, batting her soft brown eyelashes at him with a wickedly seductive smile. Jose landed himself on the opposite side of the luxuriously soft and wide couch and laid down, crisscrossing his feet and ankles with Jay in the middle of the couch.

They both got comfortable within reach of their beers, and Jay started the movie.

It was growing late, and between the warm blanket and the warmth of the alcohol in his blood, Jose was getting extremely tired. There was still a sizeable portion of the movie left, so Jose figured he would just close his eyes for a minute and wake back up by the end to see Jay out. He closed his eyes and before he knew it, he had given in to the lure of sleep.

The sun's rays peaked through the blinds and reflected off a metallic vase on the dinner table, piercing into the eyes of Jose as he tried to sleep. This intrusion forced his mind to wake up, and Jose rolled over on the couch to avoid the optic interference. As his mind began to gather its awareness, he suddenly remembered he was there watching a movie the night before with Jay Mills. Jose pushed the covers from his chest and sat up to look at the other side of the couch. Jay was not there.

"Damn, my dumb ass falls asleep in the middle of the movie. It is no wonder she left. I am such a fool. I hope she wasn't mad."

Jose was beating himself up as he drug himself from the couch. When he stood up and looked at the coffee table, there was a hand written note with the lipstick form of a kiss on the outside. He opened it and read what was written. "Dear Jose, thank you for a wonderful night of learning. I had a great time. I will be in Dallas next weekend visiting my grandmother if you want to meet up again. Maybe you can come over to my grandmother's for dinner? She might be able to help you with your déjà vu situation. Text me and let me know your schedule. Remember to find out about that manufacturing center in Mexico. We have another American Protectorate meeting in three weeks, so make sure you clear your schedule for Saturday the 28th. Look forward to seeing you next weekend; I really enjoy spending time with you. Hit me up. P.S. I left you a present on your forehead."

Jose was flustered with positive feelings after reading the note. He hurried to the bathroom to look at the mirror. He went in and turned on the light and when he looked, he saw a giant red imprint of a kiss from Jay's supple light brown lips. "I can't believe she kissed me," Jose exclaimed in his head. "I wish I was awake to feel her skin on mine."

He could not help but begin to give in to the feelings he had for Jay, which grew every time he talked to her or saw her in person. Just as he was in a daze of thoughts surrounding the young starlet, the alarm on his phone blared out its annoying tone, springing Jose from the trap of his own thoughts. "Oh yeah, my meeting with Boone," he remembered. "This will be a perfect opportunity to try out some of my new NLP skills."

Jose turned the shower on in the bathroom and went to his bedroom to gather his undershirt and boxers. After his shower he put on a bagel and started some coffee as he sat down to watch the morning news. "Still no updates from the dark matter search which has begun again in Italy today," said the young Hispanic female reporter, standing in a yellow waterproof jacket.

The screen switched back over to the host. "Is there any update on the release of patents to the global business community?"

The picture turned to the reporter. "Professor Slater has announced that he will make that decision after the discovery of the first location of dark matter. Rumors are flying around the press that he will end up sharing his patents with the UN for exclusive worldwide production. More on that news as it comes in to us here on the ground."

The host said thank you and they switched over to local weather. Jose's bagel and coffee were ready so he put on the cream cheese and added sugar and cream. After he was done he left for his car. "So they are going to be producing it through the UN? I have to get an inside connection with the

UN to sway him to build in Mexico. He would have to understand the immense positives of building a manufacturing center in Mexico. All I need is a chance to talk to the professor, and I will be able to convince him!"

Jose arrived at the downtown hotel restaurant right on time for his meeting with Ron L. Boone, wealthy oil tycoon and also his prized financial supporter. Boone was there, drinking a Bloody Mary and reading the newspaper at the table. Jose told the hostess his guest was already there and she showed him to his seat. "Howdy there Jose my friend, how is your mother doing?"

"She is well. I am stopping by to see her after I am done here with you. I will tell her you send your regards."

"How are things going with your new lover, the lovely Juanita Mills? I saw you two had some pictures together in the paper."

"I just was with her last night. She is a lovely woman. We are not lovers though. I don't think either one of us are interested in the other like that."

"Well son, you are young and single, so why not give her a try? She obviously has had her share of shitty men in the past. Give her something new and exciting."

"I can say she is very appealing to the eyes, but I don't know if our social lives match up. I won't close off myself from the idea just yet, for you Ron."

"Excellent, now let's see to it that we get to grubbing soon before I eat the container of pepper for sustenance."

Jose noticed that Ron used two visual words early in the conversation. "Maybe Ron is a visual person," Jose thought to himself. "I will use more visual words and see if it makes an impact on the conversation."

They both scanned through the menu and when the waiter arrived, ordered their breakfast. Jose was the first to speak after he left. "So let me illuminate what my plans are right now. I am thinking real big right now, Ron."

"Well lay it on me, brother."

"I think I found a view to a solution to illegal immigration and a solution for citizenship for people here illegally. So first for the illegal immigration: I plan on pitching a plan to the head of the dark matter search, Professor Frederick Slater, to build a manufacturing center in Mexico. This will dramatically alleviate the need for illegals to leave Mexico because there will be an influx of thousands of low-skilled manufacturing jobs. Second part, we strike a deal in Congress in which both sides would be happy to give citizenship to the illegals that are here. We make them agree to sign on to a new project where they would be monitored by a microchip inserted subcutaneously in the forehead or hand. This microchip is the cutting edge of technology, and the illegal Mexicans will get a chance to be on the forefront of history.

"These microchips allow you to watch television and movies anywhere, translate to any language, navigate any map. It is every technological advance in the last 15 years implanted into a small microchip. It is amazing, it…"

"Sorry to interrupt but I know all about the X-chip."

"You do? How?"

"I am one of many minor investors into the product."

"Are you in the American Protectorate as well?"

"No I am not because I declined membership. I am only interested in affairs that improve my pocketbook. I am not into social movements, even if they would help a product I am invested in."

"Well, I am glad to see that you have a background in what I want to do then. What do you think about my plans on using the X-chip and the dark matter production?"

"I think these plans reveal a focused and determined leader of the new world. The future of America is bright and your vision for a safer and more stable immigration system is in clear sight. I can see the headlines now! You would be a hero to Hispanics worldwide. With that kind of power, you could really move and shake in the political nexus in this country. I could see a speakership, the Senate, hell even the White House if plans are seen through to the end."

"To be honest I am just interested in doing a good job where I am right now. I am not even thinking about my next step career wise. I am happy just where I am."

"Well if you don't want to think about your future, I can do it for you plenty fine."

Jose noticed that Boone crossed his legs, so Jose, slyly crossed his as well. Jose noticed that Boone put his napkin down on the right side of his plate when he was done eating, and Jose did so as well. To Jose, it seemed that the NLP was working wonders on the conversation. Several times Boone remarked on how wonderful he felt about Jose and his future, and that he just had great warm feelings about him. Throughout the entire conversation Jose came in and out of congruence and focused on visual wording.

After about an hour and a half of eating and talking, they wrapped up their meeting and went their separate ways. Boone approved of all of Jose's ambitions and gave his full support. It was important for Jose to keep Boone in the loop and behind what he was doing considering the millions he had spent on Jose's campaigns.

Jose left the hotel for his mother's house. When he arrived he knocked on the door. She answered with a dark purple robe on and black slippers. "Hello Jose, come in please. It is very cold outside."

Jose kissed his mother and stepped into the house. "So how are you doing my son? How was the meeting with Ron L. Boone?"

"It went well. He really supports all my plans I told you about yesterday in the airport when we talked. He is a really great guy and he has always been there for me since we met while I was in college."

"That is great to hear, Jose. How was the Bible study with Juanita Mills?"

"It was great. I really learned a lot. She is really an amazing person, Mother. Ron told me to keep my mind open to the idea of dating her. I just really don't know. We really do have a great time together, but I just have so much work on my plate and I don't know if I could handle her lifestyle."

"Well just be careful, son. You know I want grandbabies so I am not going to be negative about her. I just want you to be careful. She is so beautiful but sometimes the pretty ones are the craziest."

"You ain't lying there, Mother, I can tell you that. I just don't think she is like all the rest of them. She is different. There is something really special about her and I can't put my finger on it."

"Well since you are in such a spiritual mood with this woman, why not take her to my church next weekend? I know you are going to be busy at a fundraiser tomorrow but next weekend you are going to be free. Please, do it for me."

"OK fine. I told you I would do it before so I will do it. Maybe I will get in a good word and message for my new pursuits on Capitol Hill."

"Thank you my son. You will not regret it. I won't even tell Pastor Rich you are coming so you do not have to feel obligated to meet him."

"Thank you for that. I really do not want to hang around mingling with everyone. I just want to get in my spiritual refresher and get out."

"OK, you do not have to talk to anyone if you do not want to. Just come and experience his message. Since I am going to be out of town next weekend I will not be there, but do not hesitate to call me and tell me what you think. I am going to try and watch from my hotel room on my computer."

"Mother! Do not wake up early on a vacation to Vegas to watch church. Go out and have fun with your girlfriends."

"OK, OK I will not watch. You know I try not to gamble though because I hate losing money and it is a sin. Even though I am in Sin City does not mean I have to partake in all the debauchery."

"Do whatever makes you happy, Mother, I was just kidding. You just need to take time to yourself and relax. Get away from this cold and nasty weather and go soak in the hot tub."

"I think I will do that. Now let's watch this movie I rented. I hear it is amazing."

So the mother and son sat down and watched a movie together. Jose spent some quality time with his mother before going over and spending time with a few more donors over dinner that night. He flew out to D.C. Sunday morning.

Jose was on the Foreign Affairs and Veterans' Affairs committees. During Jose's first week in Congress he got acclimated with the process of law making. The Republicans still controlled the House so bills were constantly being pushed out that required Jose's attention. Jose put together a great staff of mostly Texans for his D.C. and Dallas offices. His big plans on using the X-chip and fixing the immigration problem needed to be taken care of sooner rather than later. He personally called UN Ambassador Jeffery

Willis' office to request a live FaceNet meeting regarding a pressing issue. The office contacted Mr. Willis on the search and he accepted the request to have a meeting. He said he would have some down time on Thursday night D.C. time.

Jose had been eager for the FaceNet interview the entire week. Ambassador Willis had an opening before they set off for their next search mission. He was located in Brazil so he was three hours behind Jose in Washington, D.C. Jose had his staff set up the monitor on the big screen television in his office. The computer sat in front of his face as he primed himself for the camera. Jose signed into FaceNet and awaited the invitation for a chat from the ambassador's laptop. A minute went by, and just as Jose said to Chester, "I bet he over slept...", the laptop flashed an incoming call window on his screen. Excitedly, he pressed the OK button and sat up straight in his chair.

"Ambassador, I thank you for giving me a little of your time."

"No, the pleasure is all mine, Hero. To what do I owe this conversation?"

"Well, Sir, I am in need of some of your assistance. I beg you listen to me a brief moment and tell me what you think of my idea."

"I'm all ears."

Jose paused to take in a deep breath. "Well I think I found a solution to our illegal immigration problem. However, the only way I will get my plan to work is through your help."

"What do you need me to do?"

"I need you to talk to Professor Slater and get him to give me a face-to-face meeting. I want him to build a manufacturing center for North American dark matter products in Mexico. It would almost immediately dry up the need for Mexican workers to leave over the border."

"Well I'll be damned, Congressman, that is a brilliant idea. I would love to share it with the professor when I have a chance. Professor Slater is a good man, Congressman Valdez. It is safe to put your faith in him. I cannot say that about all the people you associate yourself with. For you, Hero, I will try my hardest to make this possible for you."

"Thank you very much, Ambassador. You are doing a great service to this country."

"Save the pleasantries for the ignorant and the women, we are on the verge of a great battle between those with the light and those without. Remember this: It is not yourself who guides your steps toward success. Give honor to the One who makes the path straight for your footsteps, and be weary of those trying to take you off your path."

"Very thought-provoking, Ambassador. I will keep your words in my heart."

"Yes, yes indeed. Hopefully by the time the world really needs you, your preparation will be complete. I eagerly look forward to that, Jose. In the meantime, I can only tell you to prepare yourself to fight the demons that will be coming to your doorstep."

"Yes, of course I will. I know you have to run, Ambassador. But thank you so very much for your time, your help, and your advice."

"Pray for the world, Jose. We need this dark matter to be in an ideal location. Until I talk to you next, Congressman Valdez, be well."

Jose had a great finish to a busy week on the Hill. After a hard week, he flew out to Dallas Friday morning. He attended some meetings and some events for all of Friday and then after he arrived at his condo he called Jay.

The phone rang several times and just as Jose was taking the phone from his ear to hang it up he heard a voice on the other end. "Hey there,

Jose, me and my grandmother were just talking about you. What great timing."

"Oh how funny. Well I am free tomorrow to come over and meet your grandmother. Maybe we should do a Bible study over here first and then I can ride over there with you?"

"Oh that sounds like a lovely way to spend my Saturday."

"Oh, and my mother is insisting I go to her church tomorrow. She told me to invite you to come. How does that sound? I am not trying to kidnap you the entire weekend, I promise."

"That doesn't sound all too bad, the first part or the second part."

Jose laughed in his head. "Well," Jose said, "I am about to watch TV and relax after a long week. Tell your grandmother I said hi and that I look forward to meeting her."

Jay responded, "Yes I will do just that. Enjoy your night, Hero, goodbye."

Jose went into his bedroom and took off his dark navy blue suit and his custom made shoes. He was enthralled with the prospects of spending more time with Jay. She frustrated him because he could not tell if her playful and flirtatious banter was serious or just a ruse. Jose got himself together and turned on the cable just in time to catch the college football playoff game between Arizona State and Ohio State. He decided he would sleep on the couch that night so he went and grabbed a heavy down blanket and his favorite pillow.

Jose tried staying up through the game but the wear and tear of his busy life bled him of his will to stay awake. He went to sleep with a smile on his face, dreaming sweet thoughts of Jay Mills.

With plenty of time in the day before Jay came over at 4 p.m., Jose ran some errands and stopped by the library to study. He enjoyed going into a dark corner and studying books on a variety of subjects. He would usually read about other religions and cultures, current events, history, and science. He wanted to spend every minute of the day doing something productive. After hours at the library he went home and got ready for Jay to come over.

As Jay's arrival time approached, Jose got nervous again like before and indulged in a little liquid courage. He took a couple shots of premium vodka and cracked open a beer. About a half an hour past four, there was a knock at the door. Jose opened it to see the beautiful maven of pop culture standing at his door shivering in the cold air conditioning.

"Damn I hate the cold air in these hallways!" she said, pushing past him to get into the warm living room. "Your asshole condo managers need to fix that."

"Yeah they do," Jose said, closing the door. "It really is the only downside to living here."

"OK, let's get started. Dinner is at seven so we have plenty of time to read and relax before we have to go over there."

Jay got settled on the couch as Jose went to the refrigerator to grab her beer. As he came back around to the main room he could hear the clicking of a lighter. Jay had taken a couple blunts out of her purse and was starting up the first one. Of course she offered the Congressman but again he said no. So they both cracked their books open to Acts where they had left off. Jay began, "Before we get started you should know that most people have come to the conclusion that Acts was written by Luke."

"I did not know that, very interesting."

So Jay began to read aloud the passages of Acts. They got to Acts 1:20 which refers to the field in which Judas spilled his blood. "Let his dwelling place be desolate, And let no one live in it," Jay paused, then put a frown upon her face. "You know in Matthew they tell a different story for

225

the Field of Blood. It says that Judas went to the Jews to give the money back. They did not want to keep the money in the treasury because they considered it blood money, so they bought the field that Judas died in to bury non-Jews."

"Why are there two different stories for the same field?"

"I know right! This is why I get frustrated with the Bible sometimes. If it is supposed to be a book written by God, how could there be two stories for the same thing. It makes no sense. Then they want us to have perfect faith in a book that has flaws itself. Christians can be such hypocrites sometimes."

"Well I think most Christians put too literal of an interpretation on things. Instead of thinking of the two stories as literally what happened," Jose said, "maybe they are both supposed to symbolize something unique. So the burial of non-Jews in the field could symbolize the final disgrace done upon the Savior by the Jewish people."

"I guess I never thought of it like that. Sorry if I come across as so jaded. Christians are some of my fiercest protestors. I just think it is unfair. I believe in Christ, shouldn't that be enough? So what if my music is a little provocative? I am young and wealthy, so I am just trying to have some fun."

"I think the problem is that you are seducing young men through your music and movies. It isn't your fault you are beautiful. It is the record company and movie industry's fault that they promote you as a sex symbol."

"Yes it is frustrating but it is part of the territory. Anyways, let's continue."

They got to Acts 2:4. "And they were all filled with the Holy Spirit and began to speak with other tongues, as the Spirit gave them utterance." Jay stopped reading from the Bible and asked, "Have you ever spoken in tongues before, Hero?"

226

"No, I haven't. I don't even really know what it means to speak in tongues."

"Speaking in tongues is when the Holy Spirit fills your soul and you speak out in a language you have never spoken before, or in an incoherent language that only the Lord can understand. It truly is a beautiful thing when done correctly. Only people who are one with the Holy Spirit can truly speak in tongues. No way could I speak in tongues now like I used to when I was a more spiritual person in my younger days."

"Well you have to remember that we are wealthy people. The chances of us getting into heaven are like a camel through a needle point."

"Oh nice, you are learning. Yes you are right Jose and I worry about that all the time. I just hope that when I get older I have a chance to really sit down and get my life in order spiritually."

"Well what we are doing is a good first step toward making some improvements."

"OK, let me continue," she said as she flipped the book back open. She read for several pages, briefly stopping to add in a few comments about things she had learned growing up with her grandmother. They finished Acts just in time.

"Are you ready to go? You want me to grab you anything before we leave?"

"No I am OK. I am ready to eat! I am starving. I will text my grandmother we are on the way. Hopefully dinner is ready."

So they got their things together and left for Jay's grandmother's house. It was about 30 minutes out of the city to get there. When they got off the freeway it was a well-developed area. They drove for about five minutes off the freeway and got to her development. "Lone Star Acres" was the name of it. A mixture of simple and elaborate homes sprawled along well-paved roads. Jay pointed out the house as they pulled up in her car. It was a quaint yet elegant home with a well-kept front yard. Several garden gnomes smiled coarsely at Jose in the dusk sunlight.

"Oh I am so excited for you to meet Grandma!" Jay clapped her hands and hurriedly opened the car door to rush to her grandmother's front porch. "Hurry up Jose I am hungry," she yelled as she opened the latch to the gate that encircled the front grass area of the house. Jose quickly pulled the keys out and got out of the car, responding favorably to the pleas of his friend. As Jose came up to the front door, Jay had already rung the door bell and knocked.

"God, it's freezing," she complained as she moved close to Jose and draped his arms around her to keep her warm in the cooling air's breeze. The door slowly opened much to the joy of Juanita. She dashed off Jose's arms and ran to the crack in the door. "It is me, Juanita! Open up Grandma D it is freezing out here!"

The door opened all the way and there stood the most adorable and tiny old woman Jose had seen in a while. She was very short, no more than five feet, and her hair was black with spots of grey breaking through. Her wrinkles were not as developed as you would expect for someone who lived through World War II. "Oh dear, please come in, sorry for taking so long you know I move slowly."

The three walked into the main entryway of the house and Jay introduced Jose.

"Grandma Domenica, this is Congressman Jose Valdez, Jose, this is Grandma D."

The two exchanged hellos and a pleasant handshake. "Yes, Congressman Valdez, the Hero. I have heard so much about you in the news and from my granddaughter here. I hope you live up to at least half the hype."

"I hope to exceed your expectations, my dear."

"Very good start, handsome. Now please let us walk this way into the dining room. Would you like some wine? Juanita, get the Congressman some wine. You two relax while I bring the food in."

Jay and Jose walked into the dining room. Jose took a seat beside the base of the table and Jay went to the wine cabinet to pull out a bottle and glasses. She came to the table and poured Jose and herself a glass. She leaned in close to Jose and whispered in his ear, "Thank you for coming, I really appreciate it."

She put her hand on Jose's good shoulder and gave him an appreciative smile. She put the wine bottle down and took her seat across the table, leaving the head chair for her grandmother. Jay and Jose talked briefly and soon Domenica brought in the dishes. Assortments of chicken and pasta dishes were lined up by Domenica along the end of the table. After the last dish was delivered she sat in her chair and put out her hands to both Jose and Jay. "Let us pray for this dinner."

They joined hands around the table and Domenica gave a short prayer. As she was praying she grabbed Jose's hand tighter and tighter. As she ended the prayer she looked at Jose, "Young man you have a lot of prayer power. You must be a very special one indeed. Jay you watch out for this one, he has great things in him. Now let us eat."

They ate and talked about Jose's new job as a Congressman. Jay had a new movie she just signed up for that they talked about as well. That is when Jay remembered to bring up the déjà vu. "So Grandma D, Jose said he had been having some strong déjà vu a while back. What do you think it might be?"

"Oh déjà vu you say? It could mean something, or it could be nothing. Come here son, move your chair around here so you can look into my eyes."

Jose moved the chair and got into position. Domenica held out her hands and grabbed Jose's. She looked deep into Jose's eyes and saw a pattern she recognized. "He has the markings of a seer. You are going to be a very great man. It means that if the Lord needs to deliver a message about the future to mankind he will use you as a seer by giving you dreams of the future. Most of these dreams will be in code and you need a person of great knowledge to decipher them."

"You could see all that just from my eyes?"

"Yes, Congressman, the eyes are the gateway to the soul. There are markings on everyone's eyes that give one an impression of what their souls are made of. These markings change as the person's soul develops and grows stronger or weaker."

"How do I know if I am going to become a seer?"

"You won't know. It is only if the Lord needs you for something. We must monitor the situation and prepare you. If you are going to be a seer you need to be in tune with the Holy Spirit and grow with the Holy Spirit. I have been in your shoes. I was a seer before I became a great prophetess. It was not revealed to me that I was a prophetess until years later after it was revealed to me that I was a seer. Speaking of being a seer and dreams, maybe you two could explain why I had this dream last night. It was revealed to me in a dream that the two stories of Judas' death described in Matthew and in Acts are both true. One is an account of the present Judas' death, and the other is the story of the future death of Judas reborn."

Jose and Jay both looked at each other with an astonished look on their faces. Jay spoke up, "Wow Grandma, we were just having a discussion about that very thing earlier today. It was making me frustrated and testing my faith."

"The Lord is giving you both confirmations that you are on the right path spiritually. Continue to do the Bible study. You will see that the Lord will give you messages when you are in tune with the Holy Spirit. As long as your heart is receptive to the Lord He will continue to speak to you."

"That is amazing," chimed in Jose. "I can't believe the Lord just sent us a direct message like that. That has never happened to me before."

"Well, Congressman, you need to prepare yourself for a world you never knew was there. The battle between the light and the dark is around us every day. The devil never sleeps. He never stops thinking of ways to create doubt and angst in believers. Just continue to immerse yourself in the Bible every day. Pray and seek guidance and the Lord will deliver His will onto your heart."

Everyone had great feelings of warmth in their souls. The Lord was reaching out to touch them all at that moment. "Are you almost done with your food Jose? I can take your plate." Jay stood up and took everyone's plates to the kitchen. She came back and told her grandma that she would do the dishes after she dropped off Jose at his condo.

"So tell me about your family, Jose. Where are your parents from?"

Jose looked down, uneasy with having to answer the question. "Well, my mother is from Guatemala and my father is from Mexico. He died in a car accident when my mother was pregnant with me."

"Oh dear I am so sorry for asking. I didn't know. I am sure you know that Juanita's parents died in a car accident as well. It is very sad and unfortunate for both of you to grow up without both parents. I will pray for you, Congressman."

"Thank you very much for your kind words. It was a struggle growing up in the city without a father figure. My mother is a very strong woman. She had to supply the role of both mother and father. I am sure you are strong as well, raising Jay to be as strong-willed as she is."

Jose looked over at Jay and she smiled and blushed. Domenica answered, "Well me and Gerald did our best. Little Juanita was destined for greatness. All we had to do was steer her in the right direction and let her grow. It was amazing to watch. The amazing part about it is that I know the best is yet to come."

Domenica reached out and squeezed Jay's arm lovingly and with a warm smile.

"OK, we can stop talking about me now," Jay said.

"Yes, OK, we can. However, I think it might be best if we get going. We have to wake up early for service tomorrow at my mother's church and I don't want Jay out driving too late."

Domenica nodded in agreement. "Yes, it is getting late. I enjoyed your company very much, Congressman…"

"Please call me Jose. I insist."

"Well, Jose, the pleasure has been all mine. I would love to have you back soon. We have so many things to discuss. You have much to learn before you can reach your full potential. The light is yearning to come out of you. I can feel it. You just have to tap into the power of the Lord and He will do wonders in your life."

"Any help would be great. I trust you, Domenica. You are a good and wise woman. I am glad I came over here and met you. You lived up to every expectation and then some. I will definitely make my way back here when I have the time. It is convenient that you live in Dallas because it will help us be able to foster a strong relationship."

"I look forward to our next meeting. Good bye, Jose. I will see you when you get back here, Juanita."

Jose and Jay exited the house after hugs were exchanged and got into the car. Jay reached into her glove compartment and pulled out a pre-rolled blunt. "You know I always come prepared."

Jose just rolled his eyes and buckled himself in. "I had a great time with your grandmother. She is an amazing woman."

"We haven't even scratched the surface yet. We didn't even get a chance to talk about her being a prophetess and the things she sees and hears from the Lord. Those are the truly amazing things. That preview should entice you to make your way back here soon. And that confirmation! Wow, can you believe the Lord would speak to us directly like that? He is trying to get our attention, Jose, I can just feel it. I am excited for church tomorrow."

"Well this whole seer thing is crazy to me. Who am I to doubt her, though? I had to have had that déjà vu for a reason. I am excited for our next meeting. I think I can learn a lot about myself by listening to her," Jose paused and rolled down his window to get the smoke smell out of his face. "My world is moving so fast but I don't have time to slow down and relax."

"No you can't afford to slow down. Too much is happening in the world for you to relax. The world needs a hero for change and a hero for the Lord. You are that hero, Jose. I can feel it in you. Just like my grandmother felt your prayer energy, I can feel your spirit energy as well. It is strong. You come from a strong line of men. I wish you knew your father's family because it would answer so many questions."

"I wish I did too…"

Jay finished the blunt and they rode the rest of the way listening to the soft music playing in the stereo. They pulled up to the curb in front of his condo. "I had a great time, Hero. You made quite the impression on my

Grandma D. I know she is going to talk my ear off about you." "I had a great time too. Maybe some time in the future you can meet my mother. She would love to meet you. She thinks you are such a beautiful movie star."

"Aw how sweet. I would love to meet her. Well I will be back here at 8 a.m. sharp tomorrow. It takes about 45 minutes to get there and service starts at 9:15, right?"

"You are right. I will be out here waiting and ready. I hope it isn't too cold."

"Don't worry about it. I know you can handle it. Goodnight, Hero."

She leaned in and gave him a kiss on the cheek. Jose just smiled and played it cool saying, "Goodbye Jay," and turning and leaving the car. He had butterflies in his stomach. He just got a kiss by Jay Mills. He couldn't believe his luck. When he got to his condo he tore off his clothes and jumped in the bed. He was exhausted. He was eager to get a good night of sleep. As he dozed off, he hoped he could get a message out of church the next day.

Jose was deep into sleep when he entered the dream world. He was imagining that he was a shepherd. He was up in the hills of a lush, grassy land gathering up the sheep from the countryside to be put away in the barn for the night. He was worried about wolves coming to eat the sheep if they were left out. Comforted by knowing the sheep were in the barn, he forgot to close a large window which was low enough for an animal to jump through. Low and behold, when Jose came back out the next morning, all of the sheep had been slaughtered. Jose was devastated when he discovered the bloody scene the following morning. Just as Jose in his dream started sobbing, the alarm went off and he suddenly was awakened from his dream.

"What the hell was that all about?" questioned Jose in his head. The dream was so vivid and real, it felt like he was there. He didn't have time to sit and think about the dream because he had to get ready. He would tell Jay about the dream on the way to church.

Jose got ready and ate breakfast with a few minutes to spare so he made his way downstairs in the cold Dallas air to meet Jay on the curb in front of the condo. Just as the time arrived, Jay came rolling down the street. Jose got in the car and off they went to church. On the way Jose told Jay about the dream with the sheep.

"Oh my Jose, that is an incredible dream. Do you think you are starting to have visions?"

"I don't think it was a vision of anything just yet. I have dreams all the time without any meaning or significance."

"No, Jose! You cannot think that way anymore. We are on the precipice of the Lord's return, and He will definitely use His seers to tell a story to the people. You must believe in order for the Lord's will to manifest itself in you."

"Well I am having a hard time putting my full faith in everything you and your grandmother are saying. I have never heard any of this stuff before. It is all just so new to me."

"Don't worry, Jose. The Lord is perfect in his design. Everything will be revealed to you at the perfect time."

They chatted some more and Jay sparked up a morning blunt on the long trip outside the city. They finally arrived at the church. Jay had kept her windows down in the chilly morning breeze to air herself out before going into the church. She sprayed herself with a sweet smelling perfume and they got out of the car and headed to the church. It was a large building with a great white two leveled stairway leading to the front of the church. It was located on a slight hill, making it stand out in the surrounding area. As they approached the doors everyone was looking at them and talking to each other about them. The church patrons were shocked to see the dashing young Congressman with the world famous movie star and singer.

A few people came up to say hi to them both, but most were too intimidated to step up to them. "We should go to the top floor to avoid bringing any more attention to ourselves," said Jay as she made her way toward the staircase that led to the second floor.

"Yes, good idea. It is bad enough my mother already told the pastor about me. The last thing I want is for him to recognize me and call me to the front. I like to have peace when I go to church, especially since I have not been in such a long time."

"Yeah, Jose, I totally understand where you are coming from."

They made their way up the stairs and walked out of the side door to a large sprawling seating area with several rows of seats. The front rows were all taken so the two friends went to the third row up to find their seats. They got comfortable and waited about fifteen minutes until the procession would start. In the down time several people introduced themselves to the pair, and wanted to shake both of their hands. Movie stars and famous politicians did not come to their church regularly, even though it was a large church. The choir came out with the live band in tow behind them. A young Hispanic man came to the mic to announce that church was starting.

He gave some current announcements of the church and gave the mic to the bandleader. She was a soulful looking heavyset white woman. She wished everyone a good and blessed morning and the drummer slammed his sticks three times to time up the band to get ready to play. The music started and the band leader's voice was like heaven to Jose. Everything she was saying was really speaking to Jose. He didn't know what was getting into him. The music was flowing through his soul, causing him to stand up and raise his hands to the air in celebration of the feelings God was creating in his soul. Jay saw Jose's enthusiasm and joined him in celebration of the Lord. After the song was over Jose snapped out of it and sat down quickly. Jay joined him down in his chair and Jose whispered to her, "I don't know what came over me. I have never done that before."

Jay smiled, "It is called the Holy Spirit. He is trying to communicate with you. Just keep your eyes, ears, and heart open to the Lord."

A few more songs played and then out from the crowd came an elder white man with glasses and striking white hair. He was getting older in age but he could still move smoothly and quickly. He made his way to the pew, clapping along to the ending of the last song of this section of church.

"OK everyone, take your seats, take your seats. As most of you know, I am your pastor Rich Urban. I have been pastoring this church for 41 years now so hopefully you all can trust me when I tell you something. Well today I have a special message for, I am hoping, at least one of you here with us or watching online. I had a sermon all planned out and ready for this morning but the Holy Spirit woke me up out of bed and told me to write a new one. The Holy Spirit washed over my body and inspired me to write these words which I am going to share with you right after the offering. So please let's get a good song going and pass around the collection plates. Remember we are trying to plan a trip to Ecuador for this summer so any extra donations would be greatly appreciated. Now let me get out of your way and let the band take over for now."

The band leader went back to the mic and the band started up playing their next song. Ushers made their way through the columns of staircases to pass out the collection plates. Jose pulled out his checkbook and made a healthy contribution to his mother's church. Jay pulled out some hundreds to add to the pile. After the collection was over and the song was finished the pastor came back up to the pew to begin his sermon.

"Like I said before, I was awash with the Holy Spirit writing this sermon today. I hope this message reaches the person it is supposed to reach. First let me tell you about a story my father used to tell me growing up. My father was a pastor for a short time in my youth. I told my dad I never wanted to do it. He always seemed to know that I was going to grow up and be called to pastor my own church anyway. In preparation he would always tell me about the story of the confident shepherd."

Jay nudged Jose and had a look of amazement on her face. Pastor Rich continued, "The confident shepherd is an unwise Christian leader. Night time is approaching and he needs to take in his sheep to protect them from wolves. He casually brings in his sheep, confident the confines of his newly built barn would protect them from harm. In his aloofness, he leaves a window open as he leaves the barn for the night. When he wakes up the next morning he finds all his sheep killed. His mistake fed the entire pack the previous night. What my father meant by this story is that when you have leaders who claim to be Christian but are really led by the world, they will draw in their followers to a safe and comfortable place, only to have them become devoured by the world they live in.

"My father always warned me to never become that man who led others to their physical or spiritual deaths. Those people are destined for the darkest pits of hell. Leading believers astray is the worst sin a person can commit. Be wise if you are in a position of power. You must follow the Lord's word above all else at all times. Do not become too proud to do the Lord's work. Like in Leviticus 26:19, the Lord says, 'I will break down your stubborn pride.' He does not want stubborn men in the kingdom of heaven. Neither does He want self-promoters. We all care about how the world perceives us. How much money we have, how nice our cars are. We sell ourselves to others in order to achieve these worldly things. Politicians are the worst at this. They have to sell their own souls to get votes and money for their campaigns.

"Sure there are a few decent politicians out there, but most are too into promoting themselves to others for their own success to promote themselves for the Lord for only His satisfaction. Lord willing this sermon is reaching someone this morning!"

The crowd erupted into applause, complete with shouts of "Hallelujah" and "Thank the Lord."

"Now that we have gotten that out of the way, let us turn in our Bibles to…"

Jay nudged Jose again and leaned into to his ear, "Wow he was really speaking to you wasn't he?"

Jose just nodded his head and whispered back, "Yes, he was speaking directly to me."

The rest of the sermon was about self-aggrandizement and promotion, speaking directly to Jose's soul. He was really touched by the sermon. The Holy Spirit was flowing through him. He closed his eyes tight and raised his arms in the air in praise. After holding his eyes tight he opened them to see little colored flashing dots in his vision. He had never seen this before. He was thinking that the Lord was giving him a supernatural vision of lights. The sermon ended and the pastor called for all those who got a message of hope from his words to come down and get prayed over.

Jose felt compelled to go down and get prayed over for his salvation. He told Jay, "Stay right here. I am going down. I will be right back."

He went down amid the stares of all the church goers, amazed that the local Congressman came to their church to hear a sermon so well suited for him. He went down with many others to form a semi-circle in front of the pew. Jose got on his knees and raised his arms to the Lord. He began

239

praying for understanding and enlightenment to His will. The pastor came around and put his hands on Jose. "Lord, I pray for this young man that he will have Your love and guidance come into his life. Lord, protect this soul in his journey to Your embrace."

Jose felt a chill go down his spine and out into his body and his brain. He felt a tremendous pressure in his eyes like something was trying to force its way out of his brain. He fell back from his knees onto his butt, dizzy and lightheaded. Something had just come over him and he didn't know how to describe it. One of the church aides came over to him quickly to help him up.

"Sorry I was not there to catch you, Congressman! I was helping an elder get up."

Jose stood up straight and fixed his suit. "No, it is perfectly OK. Something just came over me. I did not expect to fall like that."

"It is called the Holy Spirit, sir."

"Well I hope that means the Lord is with me."

"The Lord is always with you; it is only up to you to see Him."

The aide left to help stand behind the next person in line and Jose left to go back up to Jay. When he got to her she was talking to several church goers who wanted to get a chance to talk to the superstar. "OK my guest is here, everyone. I need to get going."

The crowd surrounding Juanita let out a sigh of sadness as she made her way to the opening where Jose was standing. She came up to him and gave him a great big hug. "I am so happy for you! I saw the Holy Spirit come over you. The Lord is really speaking to you right now, Jose. You need to be doing a lot of prayer and meditation when you get home. Something big is coming your way, I can feel it."

"Yeah, I can feel it, too. Something is coming to me soon."

They walked out to the car and got in line to leave the parking lot. When they hit the highway Jay lit up another blunt and turned up the music. Jose was easily ignoring her antics because his mind was abuzz with excitement over the sermon and the rush he had when he was prayed over. He rubbed his eyes because he still felt some pressure behind them. He ignored it, hoping it would go away by the end of the day.

"I am just going to go home and get some much-needed sleep. I have a flight at 4:30 a.m. tomorrow to get back to D.C. These weekend visits are taking a lot out of me."

"Try not to come to Dallas that often until you get some time off. I can always fly to meet you in D.C. if you want to hang out. My schedule is much more flexible. We have an American Protectorate meeting in two weeks so I will just see you there."

"Oh yeah thanks for reminding me. I have to put that in my schedule. Well, thank you for the ride and coming to my mother's church. I had a really great time this weekend."

"So did I, Hero. I look forward to seeing you in two weeks. Now come here and give me a hug."

They hugged and said their final goodbyes. The two were magnetic for each other and they both could feel it. Every time they saw each other the force of the pull grew. Jose had to get his mind off this woman and back on his job where it belonged. She was making him stir crazy. He was looking forward to getting back to work and eager to learn more about the X-chip during the next A.P. meeting in Chicago in two weeks. If things worked out, he could become a national hero for not only America, but for Mexico as well. Even though Pastor Rich had just warned him, Jose was thinking big for himself.

Chapter 11

James had a great work week, leading him into a Saturday with nothing on the menu except the meeting of the Order of Horus with his cousin. He couldn't say he was particularly excited. He got great material from several politicians, business moguls, and community leaders in the last two weeks. His blog had been sparking some interest back home, almost doubling in views since he published his first Ethiopian article. Things were going well for his life, and he wanted to see the same for his cousin. Justin had been spending a lot of time with these Order of Horus people. James needed to make sure that they were not out to hurt or manipulate his cousin. Getting something out of this for his job was only a second priority. His cousin's safety came first.

He awoke to the familiar smell of potent Ethiopian cannabis. Apparently the compound in Debre Berhan, where the leader of the Order stayed, had a small marijuana forest. Justin said he had a special batch of plants growing deep in the forest which had amazing powers. The weed had the potential to give the people who smoked it visions from God. Well at least, that is what they were telling Justin. James had a hard time believing any of this stuff. So he crawled out of bed to meet his cousin on the couch where he was listening to music and brushing his hair with the blunt in his mouth.

"Hey, Cuzzo, good timing with the blunt," Justin said as he took a puff and passed it to him. James received it and took a deep inhale of the potent plant. "So are you excited for the meeting today?" asked Justin as he put the brush down and leaned back against the couch, stretching himself out.

"I can't say I am too excited, Justin, but I know this is important to you so I will go with an open mind."

"I am telling you, Cuz, this Dr. Berihun is legit. He is a great seer. He has visions from God. He is going to help get us all to the golden age."

"OK, I understand your passion. I am very happy for it as well. You have something positive and inspiring in your life now and I want you to reach your full potential. You just need to be careful of how much trust you put into these people."

"Like I said before, I know what I am doing. Just wait, you will see and feel what I felt that day I first went."

"Well I am open to anything. I am in Africa for a reason as well, I know it. Maybe this man will help me find a greater purpose." They finished the blunt with the medium grade weed and rolled up another. After that one was done they both got ready and went off to an early lunch. After they were done eating it was about time to make their way out so they stopped by the hotel to get cleaned up and headed off for the meeting.

When they arrived there were several people waiting around outside the building where they parked. The people in charge all had on crisp black suits and short haircuts. It was all very professional looking, not at all like he had expected. He expected men in long white robes and long dreads. They were handing out fliers to everyone who walked by the building. As Justin and James approached one of the men in a suit recognized him. "Brother Justin, come in. Is this your cousin you were talking about?"

The man's English was very good. It almost sounded as if he were from America. He had no African accent. "Yeah this is my Cousin James. He is a reporter for the L.A. Dawn like I said, and he wanted to come see if the Order was something he could write about."

"Hello James, my name is Mendeli. If you haven't noticed by now, I am not from Africa. I am actually from Trenton, New Jersey. I met the doctor at a seminar he had back in New York City promoting the Order of Horus. I went to one meeting and I was hooked. I travelled around the United States with Dr. Berihun and he invited me to come be a cleric in the Order and come back with him to Africa. It was the opportunity of a lifetime. I get to be on the front lines of the golden age of the black man. Please, please, come inside and find a seat. The proceedings will be starting in less than ten minutes."

James and Justin found a seat and opened up the program. Justin had seen it before, so he spent his time talking to the other clerics who were walking around. James was enthralled with the information in the program. "If this Dr. Berihun is even half the man he says he is, he will be a great interview," James thought to himself.

The place was getting really crowded from what James could tell. It seemed as though all the seats were filled and it was standing room only for the rest of the crowd trying to get in to hear Dr. Berihun speak. "This guy must be really something," James thought to himself as he saw the crowd swelling with anticipation. A cleric in a clean black suit came on stage and raised his arms to quiet the crowd.

"Please, everyone take your seats. Dr. Berihun is ready to come out as soon as the crowd is quiet."

Everyone got quiet quickly. "Now please, Dr. Berihun, we are ready." The back door opened and out walked several large bodyguards. Behind them was a good looking elderly black man with a well-tailored suit. He was very handsome and had spots of gray in his short cut hair. His face was clean shaven, and his jaw line was strong and noble. He walked with purpose and determination. He was not taller than the average man but his presence made him appear a man amongst boys. He made his way to the mic amid the applause of the crowd. Everyone gave him a standing ovation, welcoming him like royalty.

"Please take your seats. Let us begin," Dr. Berihun said to the crowd. All the people sat down and stopped clapping. "My beautiful Nagas, I am glad to see you on this wondrous day in Addis Ababa. My trip here was wonderful but my trip here is urgent. We are in the modern Age of Enlightenment, and our time is coming soon. We are vastly under prepared for the change that is to come to our world. We need so much change in our lives physically and spiritually, before we can truly ascend to our rightful place in human history. Now my Nagas, do not fret. We will be blessed by the Lord very soon. I saw it all in a dream. The Garden of Eden was here in Ethiopia, among you beautiful people of this land. We are the original man. Our forefathers once ruled this entire planet. The whole world, from China, to India, to South America, worshipped the Naga. The Naga were black men. Half man, half serpent. The serpent can never be killed; he simply sheds his skin and is born again. That is who we are as black men. We can never be destroyed. We are the embodiment of the clay that God used to craft his first human. Our design is perfect, our minds powerful, and our bodies strong. We once ruled this entire planet. All men bowed to the black man. They looked to us for guidance. We were God's children."

James was extremely impressed. He still held out a sense of skepticism, but the man was powerful indeed. James was thinking how great of an interview he would be. He settled into his seat and continued listening to the doctor. "The reason we lost our blessing from the Lord is because we turned from Him. We lost our way. We worshipped false idols and gave in to the temptations of the flesh. We cursed ourselves for generations. But the curse is being lifted through generations of prayer. The black man has a prayer power twice as powerful as the white man.

"Their spiritual capacity is only 180 degrees. But the black man can reach 360 degrees of spiritual power. Our power has allowed us to survive great tribulations. Our prayer power saved us from slavery, saved Ethiopia from foreign aggressors, and has done other wondrous things. The prayer power will fully manifest itself in the rebirth of one of the black man's greatest gods. He is the ancient black manifestation of the story of the Christ, given to us by a fallen angel in an attempt to mimic the future word of God. He is Horus, the patron god of Kemet and Nubia. Our people prayed to Horus to such a capacity, that his spirit will be reborn in human form, sent back to life to guide the black man through the golden age. We are waiting for that black man. He is our black Christ. His coming has been foretold on ancient monuments. He will rise out of the people who were taken from their homelands to be slaves in a foreign land. He will rise out of the American black population.

"But we need you all here to help raise the Holy Land back to being a beacon of black power and hope. We Americans and Ethiopians must work together to guide our people into the golden age. We will rule the world again. I have seen it. It starts when a bright light will be seen in the sky above Debre Berhan. The light will signify God's purpose for me to rule Ethiopia. The light will come on the last day of April this year, according to the Lord. When we see that light, rejoice my Nagas, the golden age has begun. The dark matter is here in the lands surrounding Debre Berhan.

"I saw it all in a dream I had years before when I was first inspired to move here. The Lord showed me on a map where the Garden of Eden was, and He told me there would be great wealth there that will give rise to the Age of the Black Man. When the scientist Professor Slater discovered the dark matter, I knew that it had to be what was in the soil. Around my compound the trees grow great, the bud is especially powerful, and all my vegetables grow twice their size. It must be the dark matter in the soil that is making the vegetation grow so strong. In one special place I know the dark matter is especially strong. I have discovered it all. Now it is my job to guide all of you to be better men and women in the eyes of the Lord, so He can put us back where we rightfully belong, on top. If you are interested in learning more about us, please talk to one of our clerics. I am also going to announce right now that I am running for prime minister of Ethiopia. I must be in charge in order for Horus to come back and return us to glory."

The crowd erupted into another standing ovation. Everyone was exuding happiness with the announcement. Justin looked at James and said, "It really is happening, Cuzzo. The world is really going to be ours."

The crowd began dispersing slowly and James told Justin he was going to go ask Dr. Berihun for an interview. James made his way up to the front to get the doctor's attention. He was surrounded by his bodyguards but talking to different people in the crowd who had questions. James raised his hand and got the doctor's attention., "Doctor, my name is James Anthony, reporter from the Los Angeles Dawn. I am doing an assignment on dark matter in Ethiopia. I was wondering if I could interview you?"

The doctor put a great big smile on his face. "Son, please come up here."

He told his bodyguards to let James pass and he went up to the doctor. "You are an American?"

"Yes sir, from Los Angeles. I work for the newspaper out there. I am doing a series of interviews and articles on the potential of dark matter in Ethiopia."

"Well it looks like you came to the right person. I would love to give you an interview. How about you come to my compound in two weeks' time? I will have one of my clerics give you my address and phone information. We need more intelligent American black men to join our movement. Hopefully you are interested."

"No, not particularly. My cousin thinks you are great though, so I will definitely give him all the support he needs. I find what you are saying to be fascinating but I guess I would have to have more proof before I believe you are truly having visions from the Lord."

"I am glad you are not so intimated by me that you could not speak your mind. I really respect you, James Anthony from the Los Angeles Dawn. Maybe you might have a future with me just yet. I look forward to seeing you again in two weeks. Take care, my Naga."

With that the doctor answered a few more questions from the crowd and took off out the back door with his body guards. James went back over to Justin and told him that he had an interview scheduled in two weeks. Justin was extremely excited that he would get to see the compound and hopefully meet the doctor and have some personal conversation. If the doctor was really right about the dark matter, then James' entire career would change for the better. He would have a leg up on most all reporters with the dark matter coverage in Ethiopia. All he had to do was make this doctor a great and compelling story and his paper will love it.

The flight into Chicago was bumpy but Jose survived. He had arranged to have a town car pick him up and take him straight to Lisa Malky's house. On the way there he called Jay and she was already at the mansion.

He arrived at the mansion and told the driver to wait for him and that he might be a few hours. The driver smiled and happily turned off the engine and relaxed. His company paid him by the hour. Jose made his way inside. He saw Jay mingling with some of the others and she broke away from her group to greet Jose. "Hey baby doll, we have some big news that Lisa is going to announce soon. I am glad you made it on time. Let's go take our seats. It is about to start."

They took their seats in the middle aisle. After a few minutes Lisa came out from a back room with a majestic blue dress on. She looked spectacular in her moderately old age. She came to the mic and got right to it. "I have great news for everyone. The X-chip was just approved by the FDA! We can start putting it on the market. All we have to do now is find an angle to get this thing moving."

Jay nudged Jose, urging him to speak up about his plan. He took her cue and stood up. "Hello, Lisa, I think I might have a plan to get things started."

"Yes, Congressman Valdez, I will get to you in one second. I must first give some bad news. Unfortunately, there is one setback with the availability of our product. For the first week the body thinks that the chip is a parasite and it sends eosinophil white blood cells to attack the chip. This greatly diminishes the eosinophil cell count temporarily. The FDA doctors say that anyone with asthma, or with a low eosinophil white blood cell count, cannot have the chip. OK now that I got that out of the way, Jose let us please hear your ideas."

Jose walked up to the front of the stage and went to the microphone. "Hello everyone I am Congressman Valdez. I am excited for the good news just like everyone else. I have been doing a lot of thinking about the X-chip and I think me and Juanita Mills came up with some good ideas. First, I would like to pass an immigration bill that grants citizenship to those who are willing to get the X-chip for monitoring purposes. We also need to make an agreement with Mexico that any illegal immigrant that we capture and deport must have an X-chip installed so if that person decides to return across the border they can be easily detected. Do not worry about me getting the Mexicans to play ball; I hope to have my other plan in place soon which will garner much goodwill with the Mexican government and people.

"I will also introduce a bill to bring the X-chip to our battlefields around the world. Think of the communicative and strategic possibilities for the average soldier in the field if they were to be equipped with instant video and audio communication. I think if we put our political might together we can create enough public support to get these new laws passed."

Jose clasped his hands together and said thank you to the crowd before he stepped away to the applause of his peers. They all thought they were great ideas to jump start the usage of the X-chip. They believed with so many high profile people using the X-chip the public sentiment would quickly be on their side. Jose and Jay mingled with the crowd for several hours, growing their social strength and making friends through the American Protectorate.

Lisa was very excited for Jose's plan. She instantly became his second biggest supporter behind Juanita. Everyone was just excited to get everything started. The plan would have to wait until Professor Slater was back in the States from his dark matter search. Until then Jose would continue studying the Bible with Jay online and in person, and he would continue to receive spiritual guidance from Grandmother Domenica.

A lot of things were changing in Jose's life. The closer he got to Jay and her grandmother, the further away he fell from his own mother and friends. They were sucking him in with sweet words and a sense of spiritual superiority. Jose was becoming addicted to them. The pressure in his eyes was still lingering. It felt as though he was on a plane flight high in the air. He planned on seeing a doctor when he got back to D.C. the next week. Hopefully they could do something to fix it.

Chapter 12

Debre Berhan is 120 kilometers to the northeast of Addis Ababa, which is about a two-hour drive with decent traffic. James, Justin, and their guide Abal made it to Debre Berhan about an hour before the interview with Dr. Cameron Berihun. They took the 1 highway to the small village of Aboto in the high forests just to the northeast of the city Debre Berhan and to the southwest of the Wof Washa National Forest Priority. Once they arrived in the small village they parked their car and hiked to the compound through the forest. Clerics from the compound came down to Aboto to guide them there. The forest was heavy but the trail was clear and lined with stones. The trail curved to the right and an opening came through the trees, giving view to a beautiful brown and white painted multilayered building. It was massive. The building was built high into the trees.

It really impressed all three of the guests. They made their way up the stairs and when they got to the top, the security guards radioed in to say that the doctor's guests had arrived. The clerics led them to an elevator which they took up to the top floor. When the doors opened there stood Dr. Berihun with his arms out and a great grin on his face. "Welcome to the Garden. I am glad to see you made the trip safely. I hope the walk here from Aboto was not too difficult. In my old age it gets harder and harder to make my way up here. It makes me never want to leave."

James responded. "No the hike was not too bad. I got a little sweaty but I should be nice and cool by the time the interview starts. This compound is amazing. How many people live here?"

"About 50 members of the Order of Horus live here. I would like to expand as membership grows. If I hear correctly, you are interested in joining our society, Justin. How have you enjoyed your time around the clerics in Addis Ababa?"

Justin, surprised that the doctor knew his name, stammered out a response, "Well… I… I really enjoy my time with them and with you, Doctor, sir. I am soaking everything up like a sponge."

"Well we always have more room for good strong clerics. There will come a day where we will have to protect our lands from foreign invaders, and the stronger our men are the better chances of success we will have. A large part of that also depends on if Hours is returned to us or not. We must create an ideal society before his return, so there is much work to be done. Let us go into my study. I have set up some chairs and a camera for our interview."

The trio, Dr. Berihun, and several clerics made their way to the study to begin the interview.

The lights were on and the camera set, so James began the interview. "This is James Anthony of the Los Angeles Dawn bringing you an exclusive from Ethiopia. I am here today with Doctor Cameron Berihun, scholar, professor, and head cleric in the Order of Horus. Thank you for joining me today, Doctor."

"Thank you for coming to my compound. The pleasure is all mine."

"Let us get started. Where were you born and raised?"

"I was born in Newark, New Jersey and I grew up outside of Atlantic City."

"Interesting, so what brings you here to Ethiopia?"

"Ten years ago the Lord gave me a vision of a beautiful Garden in the middle of the forest. There a tall man with long brown hair told me that here would be the foundation of the age of the black man. He took me on his shoulders and we flew out of the Garden, showing me exactly where it was. I built my compound on that very location. The angel in my dream was telling me that here in Ethiopia there was the Garden of Eden. The power of the Garden will regenerate its original inhabitants, the black race. I believe this sacred land will be the location of dark matter. That is what is going to bless us."

"Stunning revelation, Doctor Berihun, please explain to us what the Order of Horus is and how you came about starting it."

"Well in that same dream the angel told me that spirit of Horus would return to lead the black man in this new age. However, until the black race rejects rampant sin and degradation, Horus will not return. He told me that it was my purpose to rule over the black land to prepare the world for Horus to return. So I started the Order of Horus to recruit members of the black community who want help preparing for the coming of our savior."

"So how are you preparing for your run for prime minister of Ethiopia?"

"I am doing a lot of praying and reaching out to churches around Ethiopia. I will be doing a tour around the country starting in March and ending back in Debre Berhan to watch the revelation of the light of God."

"Do you think your fervent Christianity might unsettle the fragile peace between Muslims and Christians in this country?"

"No, I do not feel the slight differences between us would cause any trouble in the future. They want to eliminate sinful behavior as much as I do. This is about the progress of the black man worldwide, not about if Jesus was the Messiah or if Mohammed was the true Prophet. The religious tolerance we are famous for in this country will help to propel us to a future of cohabitation and peace."

"You spoke at your meeting two weeks ago about seeing a bright light in the sky? Tell me more about that."

"Well the great emperor Zara Yaqob saw a bright light in the sky signaling where to build Debre Berhan. I had a dream that that very same light will reappear to signal the beginning of the new age, and the location of the Garden of Eden, on the last day of April."

"Fascinating stuff, Dr. Berihun. We will all be eagerly awaiting the end of April. I heard you use the word Naga in replacement of the word nigga. Tell me more about where Naga comes from."

"The Naga are the black man, the serpent gods. We were worshipped around the world. The Naga were ancient rulers of India, China, Indochina, the Middle East, South America and North America. Statues like the Easter Island heads and the Olmec heads prove the Negroid had sailed to the New World long before the white man. Nubia and Kemet had the greatest sailors in the world. They knew the earth revolved around the sun. They also knew it was tilted on its axis and they knew it was round. They had all the tools available to make the voyages and they most certainly did. So I refer to our people as nagas instead of that vile word nigga or what it really is, nigger. I say, that horrible word does nothing but remind us of our forced servitude and our place in American and global society. It is a word that brings us down, while naga will uplift us. We have a proud heritage that we should not be ashamed to honor regularly."

"You are a world impacting figure, Doctor Berihun. I look forward to more interviews in the future."

"I look forward to it, James."

"Viewers, stay tuned to my blog for more exciting stories from Ethiopia, hopefully home of one of the dark matter sites."

The camera operator gave the cut signal and the interview was over. "Well that was exciting, Dr. Berihun. My audience should eat that up."

"I am hoping they do. We need to recruit many more North and South American blacks to our cause."

"Well I will do my part to try and help."

"Oh do I have you convinced in my visions, young James? I thought you were skeptical?"

"I am still holding out giving complete faith in you, but what you say sounds good. I want what you are saying to come true so badly. Black men have been feeding from the bottom of the bin for far too long now."

"Well that will no longer be the case, Lord willing."

There was a silent pause. "Do you have time to come relax with me and the clerics in the smoke room?"

"Yes we have time."

"OK, Justin, and Abal come as well."

Justin had a giddy smile on his face as they all walked to the smoke room on the other side of the complex. "This is dark matter marijuana I have been growing, from the strongest part of the forest. I have been testing the soil for ten years trying to figure out what was making the plants so strong. When Professor Slater announced his discovery, I knew it had to be dark matter doing it. Come right through here and we will experience the Lord's touch through His beautiful plant."

The inside of the room had a deep red couch lining the walls with ashtrays built into the fabric. A glass table sat in the middle of the room where there was an assortment of jars filled with different types of marijuana.

"Please Mendeli, roll us three well-sized blunts."

"So where did you go to school, Doctor?" Justin asked when everyone sat down and relaxed.

"I got my undergrad at NYU, masters and Ph.D. in Theology from Norte Dame, and a Ph.D. in African American Studies from Howard. Those are just criteria to judge a man in the physical world. What I am truly proud of is my 360 degrees of spiritual power and knowledge that I have attained through the years. Like I said before, only the black man can reach 360. The Arab and the Asian can reach 300, the Hispanic and White can reach 180. We are the most powerful beings on the earth."

Mendeli finished rolling and lit them all up and passed them around. "Now remember, this weed is a gift from the Lord. You can transcend your physical limitations and communicate with the Lord through this marijuana if you are meant to be spoken to. Only a few of us have had visions. Just do not be scared if you see something. Just remember what it is so you can tell us after you wake up."

Everyone began taking hits as the blunts were passed around the small room, even James. He had begun to have less interest in journalism, and more interest in the Order, so he didn't mind partaking. The effects of the marijuana were immediate on everyone. They all became immediately stuck. James' eyes rolled into the back of his head. He snapped back to reality as another blunt was passed into his possession. He drew in a deep breath of smoke and coughed it out violently, adding tremendously to the high he was already feeling. Once again his eyes rolled into the back of his head. This time, however, the extreme high he was feeling seduced him to sudden sleep.

It felt like he was asleep for hours when he suddenly could not breathe. He opened his eyes and he was in a tub full of fresh oil. He sat up in the bath of oil and drew in desperate gasp of air. He looked over to his right and he saw another man coming out of the oil in the same manner he did. Fresh oil was covering both of their bodies. In the dark James could not make out the other man's face. He could see he was Hispanic but the oil that was dripping from his face was covering his true identity. Just as James was getting up out of the bath of oil he fell back in and his eyes closed again.

When they opened he once again was short of breath. He took a dramatic gasp of air but this time when he woke up he was back in the smoke room with his cousin, Abal, and the clerics from the Order of Horus.

They all were in silence looking at him, hoping to make sure he was OK. "I think I had a vision. I passed out there for a second and I woke up in a tub of oil next to a Hispanic man. I could not make out his face. Do you have any idea what it could mean, Dr. Berihun?"

"Oil is used for many things in the Bible. It really could mean anything. There must be some purpose of having the Hispanic man in the oil with you, though. I do not have any answers now but I will research and get back to you if I find anything. You should be looking out for a Hispanic man who could mean something to you, good or bad."

Justin, on a cloud so high, said, "I can't believe the Lord tried to speak to you, James. I need the Lord to speak to me and help me out because He can see I am trying to change."

Dr. Berihun responded, "Yes, Justin, we all can see you are trying to change. Just keep studying and praying. The stronger your prayer power becomes, the sooner you can become a cleric. You have great things in your future, Justin, so just keep on the Lord's path. He will speak to you in due time."

The doctor put his hand on Justin's shoulder and gave him a comforting smile. "I am glad you all came to my smoke room and to the Garden. I would love to speak with you again, Justin. I will be in Addis Ababa after my Ethiopian tour at the beginning of April to visit my daughter who is head of the choir at an English-speaking church. I would love for you all to come to a service when I am in town and we can all go out to dinner afterward. I will have one of my clerics give you a concrete date when the time is closer."

"I look forward to that, Dr. Berihun. I had a great time on the visit," Justin said.

"The interview was great," James said.

Justin spoke up. "Thank you for inviting me to the Garden. I will continue doing security and working on my studies. I want to be a great cleric and help pave the way for the golden age."

After exchanging pleasantries, the doctor walked the trio out of the complex and back down to the village of Aboto. The three made a safe voyage back to Addis Ababa.

James had several more interviews and articles planned leading up to the next meeting with the doctor at the beginning of April. However, the doctor and his dream were on his mind constantly. What if the dark matter was actually in Ethiopia? What if he fell upon a personal relationship with the future leader of an abundant and globally respected Ethiopia? Things were looking good for James and he was excited that the Lord was doing wonders in his life. He found a small church in Addis Ababa but it still wasn't satisfying his need to be closer to the Lord. Maybe the Lord would bring someone into his life that would inspire a faith-driven greatness.

Chapter 13

Freddy once again tried to sneak out early for breakfast before anyone had gotten up. He was lucky to have beaten the search team this morning. As he sat eating his breakfast in the Tel Aviv hotel, he sat thinking of his girlfriend Jennifer. This was the last search location before the break. He would definitely have time to get back to Colorado to see her. He would only propose to her if he found the dark matter here in Israel. Chances were slim though. The country was small and they had had no success anywhere else leading up to this point. After he finished his breakfast he scraped the leftovers in the trash and put the tray in the holder. He wanted to go and get some more sleep before having to get up for the search but just as he was making his way out of the dining hall, in came Ambassador Jeffery Willis, the wise and purposeful politician appointed for the last three terms.

His morning wrinkles were strikingly waving into his skin. He immediately came up to Freddy. "Young man, how is your morning?"

"Pretty good, Ambassador Willis. I had a chance to get some food and now I am just going to relax before I have to come down to the bus."

"Good good, well I have been meaning to talk to you. Do you know who Congressman Jose Valdez is?"

"Yes of course, the Hero of the Convention Center. Everyone should know who he is. Why do you ask?"

"Well he called me to get in touch with you. He has some very interesting ideas working with the dark matter in North America. I think it would be wise for you to get in contact with him once you get back to the States. He is a very eager and intelligent politician, but most importantly, he has a good heart. I think he has what's best for this country in his heart, and he would like to work with you, if given the opportunity."

"I am very flattered. He is a big-time rising star so I would love to work with him. Hopefully I can help him out in whatever he is interested in. I make no promises though so make sure you tell him that."

"Yes, no promises. I will tell him the good news. His office will contact you when you are back in the United States to set up a meeting. Trust me, Professor, he will make a tremendous impact on your life before all is said and done. I would not do anything to harm you."

"I believe you, Ambassador. If he is half the man the media makes him out to be I would look forward to meeting with him."

"Well very nice. I will let you go back to your room. Thank you for your time. I will see you hopefully after a successful search."

"Yes indeed. Take care, Ambassador."

Freddy left the dining hall and headed up to his room. After about an hour of extra sleep the alarm went off and he got out of bed and got prepared for another day of search. It was the end of February but the weather was very nice outside. No rain, no wind, a clear and sunny day. Freddy got ready and headed down to the bus. It was about half full when he got on. He sat next to Colleen and the two playfully bantered while waiting for the rest of the search party to arrive. The Israeli army would provide five helicopters to search Israel and the West Bank.

Freddy's route would take him north along the coast and then eastward toward Nazareth. Everyone arrived and they pulled off to the military installment. They arrived with the choppers humming and buzzing, ready for lift-off. They all loaded up and took off. Freddy had on his goggles and his binoculars. He was in the helicopter with Henry and the Ambassador to Tunisia, Mago Eshmun. They made their way north for several hours, stopped and refueled, then headed east for Nazareth. They were coming around the bend and Freddy was looking lazily in the distance. He turned to his left as the curve of the earth was giving way to a rich and vast forest, and that is when he saw it. A beautiful soft dark substance glowed in the glasses vision. It was all over the trees and in the soil. It was everywhere. "Over there, look at the forest, it is glowing," he yelled to his companions. "Turn over there!" The helicopter pilot obeyed and swayed the chopper toward the heart of the HaSolelim Forest Reserve.

"It is so beautiful," cried Henry and he patted his friend Freddy on the back. "You did it, Professor. We did it! We all can rejoice in this great day."

Ambassador Eshmun was speechless. "Radio in to the other helicopters to return home and stop the search. We have found the dark matter."

Since Freddy's helicopter had flown the furthest from Tel Aviv, they were the last to return. As they climbed off the helicopter everyone was clapping and cheering for Freddy and his accomplishment. Colleen was the first to greet him when he was safely away from the chopper. "Congratulations, Freddy, you did it! You are going to save the world!"

Alfred came up to him next. "Now the real fun begins, Professor. Let us relax and celebrate. We can stop the search and focus on extracting the dark matter from here. Once we get the goggles tested for mass production, the entire world will be able to finish the search for us. Congratulations, Professor, all of your hard work has paid off."

He gave him a hand shake and a hug and allowed Freddy to be surrounded by the rest of the team to offer their congratulations and well wishes. For tonight they were going to party. Tomorrow the real work of getting the Israeli Prime Minister's approval for extraction would begin.

Adiel Tuchman was a dynamic figure in Israel. He overcame tremendous odds to get to where he got. He was an orphan who was adopted by a family of blanket makers. Elder Tuchman ran a very successful business, allowing the emotionally challenged boy to blossom into a confident and motivated man. He always used the fact that his biological parents abandoned him as motivation to go above and beyond. He wanted to show them what kind of son they could have had. Israel was in the midst of war with Hezbollah. The truce had been broken and terrorist attacks on Jews and night raids on Palestinians were frequent. Things were reaching a fever pitch in the streets of Israel. Some, like Adiel Tuchman, wanted all-out war to permanently rid the Promised Land of the non-believers. When he heard the news of the dark matter being found within his borders, he knew this was the opportunity to finally free Israel.

"Yes, let them in" Adiel said into the speaker on his desk. Coming into his office were Lenz Krause, secretary-general of the United Nations, and Freddy. They both walked confidently to their seats after shaking hands with the prime minister. Lenz spoke first. "So, Prime Minister, you must have heard the news by now. We discovered the dark matter in the HaSolelim Forest Reserve. We are very excited and want to clear the way for extraction."

"Well I think we need to discuss what Israel will be getting from this first and foremost, gentlemen. I am not about to carve up the beautiful God-given forests of Israel to quench the thirst of the Gentiles."

Curious and surprised by his comment, Freddy said, "What more could you possibly want from us? The wealth you will amass from the selling of dark matter should be enough of a prize to satisfy you."

"No, unfortunately it isn't. Israel is still divided amongst the Jews and the Palestinians. We cannot continue to live under these oppressive conditions. We will extract the dark matter ourselves and harvest it until later use unless we are allowed to relocate the Palestinians from our land and restore Jerusalem and the Holy Land to its rightful owners."

Lenz, astonished by the request, quickly mounted a response. "Move the Palestinians? Where to? They would never agree to something like that."

"Since the dark matter will make us so rich, we will gladly buy out every Palestinian property at fair market value. Not only that, but we will give a hefty stipend for the trouble of having to move. We understand how much of a hassle that could be."

"We need that dark matter, Prime Minister. The world is waiting to enter a new age and you are going to hold it up for your own selfish gains?" Freddy questioned the prime minister in frustration.

"God blessed our people with the dark matter because we are His people. In order for the world to benefit from your discovery, we must gain something in return."

Defeated, Lenz responded, "Well I have to get a vote from the UN before we can enact a forced removal of a group of people. If that is what must be done for the world to progress, then it must be done."

"But Lenz, no we can…"

"No, Professor, this is too important to the world to let it slip past us. We have no time to waste. We will vote on the issue tomorrow morning. Let us go so I can make the proper calls to set it up."

The pair shook hands with the shrewd prime minister and left the office. Lenz immediately set up a vote to take place back in New York City the next morning.

The public was festive with the news that Israel had the dark matter but upset that they were demanding a forced removal of the Palestinians. The vote took place amid a torrent of reporters flashing their cameras at each ambassador as they showed up. It was a very close vote, but by five

Ambassadors the U.N. declared that the Palestinians must leave Israel. The world was shocked, and so was Freddy, who already saw that his discovery was changing things for the worse. He was determined to get a hold on the situation by controlling his dark matter production.

After much thought he decided he would take the position as Advisor of Science and lend his patents to the United Nations for development and production. A final decision on manufacturing centers for each zone would be decided after the final dark matter location would be found. For now, Freddy was going to fly back to Colorado. First he had to meet with Congressman Jose Valdez, then he had to meet with his hopefully soon-to-be father-in-law to ask him for his daughter's hand in marriage, and then he would propose to Jennifer during his first visit to her church in front of all of her family. The entire flight home he was excited, his life was moving so fast, but he wanted it to be moving with Jennifer by his side.

Jose had seen several doctors in the last four weeks, trying to get an explanation for the pressure in his eyes. Just as he was running out of options to get the feeling to go away, it suddenly stopped. Jose thought everything was good going into his meeting in New York City at the UN with Professor Frederick Slater and Secretary-General Lenz Krause. He was early for the meeting, so after he checked in at the counter he sat back and read the newspaper. Jose was reading tons of news about the continuing dark matter search and Israel's decision to hold the world hostage for the removal of the Palestinians, which had tremendously angered the world, when a booming voice came at him from the door into the office.

"Congressman, Hero, I would like to know if you want something to drink?"

It was Lenz Krause and behind him a man of average height severely lacking in muscular wealth. Jose saw he was the scientist Frederick. "No, thank you Secretary-General. I just came from lunch."

"OK good, good. This is my colleague and discoverer of dark matter, Frederick Slater."

Jose got up from his seat and gave the shorter man a sturdy handshake. There was electricity in their handshake that shocked both of them. It was almost as if they were attracted to each other. "Nice to meet you, Professor. Your work is changing the world. I look forward to hopefully being a part of it."

"The pleasure is all mine, Congressman. I must have seen that stage dive a thousand times on the television. Let us go into the office and sit down. I would love to hear what ideas you have."

The trio walked into Lenz's office, with Lenz taking the big chair and Freddy and Jose sitting on opposite sides of the table. "So, let me explain what brings me here to New York to meet with you. I was wondering if you could listen to my proposal for building a North American production site in Mexico. I know the sites won't be final until you find the second dark matter site, but I implore you listen to my plea to build a mega manufacturing center in Mexico. Illegal immigration is bankrupting this country and ruining our schools. Drugs are flowing into this country at an all-time high. We need something to stem the flow of illegals coming over our borders. I think a mega center, able to produce all dark matter related products for North America, Central America, and the Caribbean, would be perfect for Mexico.

"First off all, geographically it is between all three areas in the North American zone. Second, they have an influx of highly skilled yet cheap labor. Taxes could be negotiated for a low price as well. Mexico needs this more than anything. But the United States wins as well. The manufacturing center would create thousands of high and low paying jobs, stemming the flow of illegals over our borders. The only way to end illegal immigration is to improve Mexico into a flourishing economy. To do that we need your help, Professor, because you make the final decision on all of this and the world is begging for your help.

"You can be the savior of millions of people living in poverty and starving themselves to sleep every night. Every place you decide to build and spread your goodwill will flourish under your righteous hand. As a personal favor, please build in Mexico. It would mean so much to my people here and in Mexico. Do not give me an answer now, please take your time and wait. Just know I am waiting for your answer whenever you are ready."

"Thank you for taking the time to share your thoughts with me, Congressman. I think what you are saying makes a lot of sense. I really do not need to build in the United States or Canada because they are very rich countries already. I need to build where I can make the greatest impact on people's lives. I think Mexico just might be the right place to make that dream come true. I will give it more thought, but I like what I had to hear. I will get back with you after we find the second location of dark matter."

"Thank you, Professor."

With that Jose left the office and returned to his hotel. On the way he started seeing floating rainbow colored flashing lights in his right eye again just like he did when he was in church. They went away and then he noticed a slight blur in the corner of his eyes. Hours went by and the blur got worse. He started to really get worried.

Jose scheduled a visit to the optometrist to check his eyesight. The doctor told him he did not have any answers because his eyes looked fine. The only idea the doctor had was to go to a neurologist because he thought it could be something happening inside of his brain. So he scheduled a visit to the neurologist March 13th, the following Monday, in D.C. Jose was really starting to get worried. He did not know what was going on with his eyes. He needed to be able to read and he was struggling with only one good eye. He decided to keep this entire thing a secret from his staff and the media. He wanted to know what he was up against before he decided to publicly fight it.

Chapter 14

Freddy kept going over what he was going to say to Pastor Gregory Inna, his girlfriend's father. Pastor Greg ran a very popular church just outside of Denver. He was well respected in the local and national church community. He published several books on the Holy Spirit, faith, the Gospels, and the End Times. He was well versed in scripture and a shining knight in God's Holy Army. Freddy's hands were sweating on the wheel as he got closer and closer to the church, where Pastor Greg was working on his Wednesday night sermon.

He pulled up in the parking lot and looked in the mirror. He had gotten a fresh haircut and shave before this meeting, since he had been rough looking after searching for the dark matter for so long. He texted the pastor that he was there. The pastor texted back, "I am in my office. The main doors are unlocked."

Freddy made his way to the office and opened the door. "Hello, Pastor. It is good to see you," he said as he walked toward him to give a healthy handshake. The pastor got out of his chair to greet the young scientist.

"Hello, Freddy. I am glad to see that the search went successfully for you. Does Jennifer know you are in town yet?"

"No she does not, and we need to keep it that way until your service on Sunday."

"Why is that, my son?"

"Well, Pastor Greg, I would like to have your daughter's hand in marriage. I want to surprise her by showing up to church and proposing to her in front of the whole congregation. I am here to seek your approval."

Pastor Greg put a wide grin on his face. "I will approve of your marriage only if you make one promise." "Yes, anything."

"You must honestly give Christianity a try. It is very important for me to have grandkids raised in the faith. I understand in the real world not everyone is Christian, but you must at least give it a try for me and my daughter's sake."

"Well that is an easy promise to keep. I was already planning on starting to get involved in church to ease the tension in our relationship. I know it is important to your family, and I am willing to really give an honest attempt at trying to understand your faith."

"Well good to hear, Freddy. Are you going back to the university to teach now that your search is over?"

"Actually... I meant to talk to you about that as well. I accepted the position as Advisor of Science for the new UN complex. I will be living wherever the complex is built. Unfortunately, Lenz Krause has not come up with the plans yet. We have to wait until the second dark matter is found before we can come up with a new capitol for dark matter."

"So you are taking my daughter away?"

"Yes, sir, that is my intention."

Pastor Greg closed his eyes and rocked back in his chair. He clasped his hands together and looked up with a stern and serious look on his face. "If you are taking my daughter you also must promise me to always protect her. And if you are ever in a position where her safety is not guaranteed, you must promise to send her back to Colorado. We can keep her safe here. We are preparing for the end times as we speak. We Christians have hidden chambers and tunnels all through these mountains. When the time comes, we will be able to hide. If by any chance that dreadful time does come and you are looking for us, look to the mountains. We will find you."

"This is a lot to take in right now but I trust it won't come to that. I don't see any reasons for Christians to have to worry. Nothing could change the faith of millions of Christians around the world. You all are in power, and you have nothing to fear."

"Your ignorance is ill-served for this daunting time. The signs are all around us, my son. You are going to play a major part in these times, Freddy, I hope you know that. You are in an extreme position of power and influence. You have sway over great men. You alone cannot change the path of destiny for human kind, but you could at least prolong it for another generation if the right steps are taken. Alas, I am unable to provide you with assistance for the unknown. You must look deep into your heart to see what the Lord is trying to tell you. Only the blood of Christ can save you and mankind, not technology and science. Remember that."

"I will try, Sir. I do not want to keep you waiting. Please invite all of the family to church this Sunday and tell them to keep everything a secret."

"OK I will, Freddy, take care."

They shook hands and hugged for the first time spontaneously, and Freddy left for his house. He had been telling Jennifer this whole time that he was stuck in New York at some more meetings. He had to keep a low profile by keeping the lights off in his house at night in case she drove by for some reason.

It was Sunday, March 12, a day that Freddy would always remember. He got his hair cut the day before, and went to the barber early that morning to get a fresh shave. He had spent his time in New York picking out the engagement ring, and he thought he made the right purchase. Considering how much money he had coming in, he did not want to skimp on diamonds. He put on his best suit and off he went to the Sunday service. Everything had been set up with Jennifer's family and the church. He would come in through the back door about 20 minutes into the service. He got there just in time and went around the back to where one of the church members was holding the door open.

She smiled and waved him into the building. They walked through the corridors of the church until they got to the side door behind the pew. The church member went in the main church and gave the thumbs up to the pastor who was sitting in the front row listening to the gospel music performed by his choir. He smiled and nodded, and when the song was close to being over he stood up and went up to the pew. "Thank you gentlemen and ladies for another beautiful song, everyone please take your seats."

The audience finished their applause and sat down, eager to hear the next part of the service. The pastor continued, "We have a special guest visiting our church here for the first time. He is a very close friend of the family and has travelled very far to be with us this morning. He has a very special message for the church that he would like to share with us. Please, everyone give a warm welcome to Professor Frederick Slater, discoverer of dark matter."

The whole crowd was surprised, but none as surprised as Jennifer, whose eyes and smile lit up the room. Freddy nervously walked out from the side door up to the pew and took the microphone. "Hello everyone, my name is Freddy. I am here to tell you today I have made two important decisions in my life, both of which should impact this church. The first message is that I am turning my life over to Christ. I have always been an unbeliever but I am going to honestly give my faith in the Lord a trial. With your support, I hope to become a healthy and faithful Christian one day."

The crowd erupted into cheers and applause of support. Plenty of people yelled out "God Bless!" and "Hallelujah!"

Freddy continued with the next part of his speech. "Unfortunately, that support will have to come in long distance form. As I have taken a position with the UN that will take me from Colorado. I also come to bring further hard news. I hope to be taking away one of your church members with me. Please Jennifer, come up here."

Jennifer, confused and frustrated that Freddy would be in town without telling her, and also upset over the news of him leaving Colorado, came walking up to the front of the church. "I have been putting a lot of time and thought into this decision. I know that this is the right thing for me. You are everything I have ever wanted in a woman, Jennifer. I am blessed to have such a warm, loving, caring, beautiful, and sensitive woman in my life. You are everything I dreamed of growing up as a youth. I cannot live another day without knowing that you will be mine forever. Jennifer," he said as he got down on one knee and reached into his back pocket, "Will you marry me?"

Jennifer had tears of joy immediately enter her eyes. "Yes, yes, yes, I love you Freddy!" She put on the ring as Freddy stood and they gave a great kiss for the entire world to see in the audience and on the internet. The crowd drowned them with clapping and shouts. It was a joyous day for the entire congregation.

In celebration, as many of the church that could make it went out to the local Italian restaurant. It was merry times for all, as the princess of the church and the king of Colorado would be married. Everything was looking up for Freddy. His career was taking off and the love of his life was now his. They would have to get married quickly because Freddy's duties at the UN would take him away from Colorado. Freddy was on the top of the world, nothing could stop him from saving the world now.

Jose's right eye was only getting worse. The vision was turning completely gray and blurry, unable to see anything. He was so nervous every day leading up to his appointment on Monday. As he waited in the neurologist's office he was too nervous to read a magazine or look through his phone. He simply wanted to find an answer to why his vision had gone blind in one eye. After a marginal wait the doctor called him back to one of the patient rooms. After another few minutes of waiting the doctor came in.

"Hello, Congressman, what brings you here today?"

"I am losing vision in my right eye. It is getting worse daily. I have been to optometrists and doctors and no one can give me any answers. I am extremely worried."

"Well you came to the right place, Congressman. In my professional opinion, I believe you have multiple sclerosis." "What is multiple sclerosis? I have never heard of it."

"Let me tell you about what MS is and what it does to the brain."

The doctor paused to mentally recollect all of the information he had on multiple sclerosis. "Every movement and function in your body is controlled by the nervous system. The nerves in your brain send out electrical signals to the different parts of your body to control everything you do. Each nerve cell is surrounded by a substance known as myelin. This substance allows the nerves to send out signals. Multiple sclerosis is what it is called when the body's own immune system attacks the myelin. When the immune system does this, it damages the nerve's ability to send communications to that particular part of the body. What I believe is happening to you is that your optic nerve is being damaged by multiple sclerosis, causing your vision in your right eye to fail."

"How can you be sure?" "Well there are two ways to detect MS but only one way to find out without a doubt. You can get a MRI, which will show the scars left on your brain from the MS, called lesions. The second way, and the only way to be one hundred percent sure, is to get a spinal tap."

Jose closed his eyes and winced at the thought of either scenario. "So I should get the MRI first to see if it even could be MS?"

"Yes, Congressman, we can see if there are lesions first before we do the spinal tap. If we can avoid the spinal tap that would be best, but do not worry. I have given many spinal taps and never had a problem. You can trust me, Sir."

"I do trust you, but let us hope it will not come to that. Let us hope that it is something else less sinister."

"I will schedule your MRI for tomorrow at the MRI Center on K Street. Pick the time that works best for you with the assistant up front. Do not be afraid, Congressman, because people with MS can live long and healthy lives as long as they manage themselves correctly. Unfortunately, because there is no cause for MS and no cure, I cannot guarantee your symptoms will not get worse with time. You may end up in a wheelchair or blind in one eye. It is a disease we are much uninformed about. Our doctors are trying their best to find better medicine and even a cure, but this disease confounds our brightest minds.

"Have faith, Congressman, if the Lord gave you this illness He can also take it away."

"Thank you, Doctor, for your words but I am still holding out hope this is something else before I start to think too hard about it. I hope to see you soon with better news."

Jose left after making the arrangements for tomorrow morning at the MRI Center. He called his mother with the news and then called Jay. Both wished him good luck with the MRI the next day.

Jose arrived at the MRI Center the next day in a town car driven by an experienced driver, Lenrie, an elder black man who knew every inch and crack of Washington, D.C. "We here, Bossman."

"Thank you, Lenrie, and I am sure I don't have to tell you that this is all a secret. You have always been trustworthy before so I have no reason to doubt you now."

"Come on, Bossman, you could tell me anythang and I wouldn't tell a soul. You are the Hero, my kids love it that I drive you around. They tell all the other kids at school and everyone wants to hear stories about you."

"I am very flattered, Lenrie."

"Good luck in there."

Jose walked up to the building and checked in. Very soon he was called into the changing room. He left on his boxers but changed into a blue gown. After waiting in the changing room for a few minutes he was called to the back where the MRI machine was located. As he entered the room he saw the monstrous contraption with the tunnel where he would be slid into. He wasn't nervous about claustrophobia; he was nervous about the sounds the machine would make. He heard the sounds were unbearable. His spirits were still up though because he still had hope that his loss of vision was not MS. He lay down on the sliding pad and tried to relax before the technician came in and hooked him up to an IV which would pump in the fluids that would illuminate his brain to the machine's scanners.

The prick of the needle hurt, signs of an amateur technician, but the pain soon subsided. After the medicine had been properly circulated it was time for Jose to enter the tunnel chamber. He was slid in by the technician and as the walls surrounded Jose's body he trembled at the thought he had to go through all of this. He was confused. If he was doing the Lord's work why would He be punishing him with this illness?

Following the MRI, Jose staggered to his feet as his brain calmed down, coming out of its punishment. He thanked the technician and made his way out to the car where Lenrie was sleeping. He woke the driver up and they took off for Jose's office where he had votes taking place later in the day. He still did not tell his staff about his affliction. He wanted to wait until the bad news was confirmed before he told them.

Jose had left Capitol Hill early afternoon that Monday in late March. He had just walked into his condo when his cell phone rang. He answered and it was his neurologist. He told him the bad news that there were lesions and scarring on his brain, meaning that he probably had multiple sclerosis. He also said that because they could not be completely sure, Jose must get a spinal tap.

They scheduled a spinal tap for Wednesday, the 22nd. Jose got off the phone and immediately started thinking of the worst. "If there is scarring on my brain then it must be something wrong with me," he thought to himself.

There was no dodging it now. He needed to have someone in town to take him to the spinal tap, so he called his friend CC, his Taiwanese-American best friend, to come to D.C. the next day. CC gladly agreed and gave solace for the bad news regarding the lesions.

Jose called all of his friends and family and told them the news. Nothing was confirmed yet but the signs were painted on the wall for all to see. Jose probably had multiple sclerosis. A nonhereditary disease with no cause or cure, was the worst of news for Jose. Everything was seemingly going his way ever since the assassination attempt, so to have such a big hill to climb physically, gave Jose nightmares that night. CC flew in on Tuesday and the two spent some quality time together.

On the day of the spinal tap Jose was nervous. "CC, I don't know about this, man. What if I sneeze and he tears a hole in my spine rendering me paralyzed?"

CC sighed and tried to calm his friend's nerves as they approached the hospital. "Your neurologist has performed spinal taps on maybe a hundred people by now. Each of his MS patients has to go through this. Do not be afraid, you are not the first and won't be the last."

With the motivation from his friend, Jose tempered himself and tried to get mentally prepared for what was coming. He was still blind in his right eye, and he knew he had to find out what was causing it. As they walked up to the front desk he felt as though he was as ready as he would ever be for this. They signed in and waited in the empty lobby. "So Jose, how are things going with Juanita Mills? I stopped by your mother's house the other day and we talked about how y'all are spending a lot of time together. Do you still think this is simply a business relationship?"

"I think it has progressed from that most definitely. I feel like we are in a weird place right now. I am starting to get feelings for her but I do not want to act on them and ruin a good friendship. I am torn on what to do about her. I just find her so beautiful and smart and witty, I have a hard time not thinking about her every day."

"I can't blame you, Jose, because she is one of the most beautiful women in the world. Just be careful and make sure you are acting with the right head when it comes to Miss Jay Mills."

"I will try, my friend."

Just then the nurse opened the door and ushered the two back into the medical room. Jose changed into his gown and got comfortable on the bed. After a few minutes in came the neurologist and the nurse. "Hello, Jose, please do not be nervous. I will take good care of you. Now, I want you to lay in the fetal position with your back turned toward me, please. Bring your knees up to your chest as close and tight as you can and hold it there perfectly still."

"OK, I will do that doctor." Jose got in position and the doctor readied the needle he would be using to puncture Jose's spine. He rubbed a cleaning liquid onto Jose's lower back where his spine protruded out. "OK here we go Jose, hold still please."

The doctor performed the procedure. Jose was extremely relieved when it was over.

"Now make sure you fixate yourself as flat as possible when you leave here. The spinal fluid that I took from you will leave your spine out of balance and you will become disoriented. If you stand or sit up too long your head will get dizzy and you will have to vomit. This will affect you for about a week so take time off from work and just try to relax."

The doctor wiped down the shot location again and put on a bandage. Jose sat up, "It wasn't too bad, CC. I could have done without the suction feeling but the worst is over. Hopefully I will never have to go through that again."

CC congratulated Jose on his courage and the two got their things and left the office. The nurse said they would schedule an appointment for treating the possible MS once the results came back in a few days. CC stayed with Jose until Friday to help him out around the house since he could not get up without vomiting. On Friday CC flew back to Dallas and Jay came in town to help take care of Jose while he was ill. Jose really appreciated all the help he was getting from his friends and family. This was an urgent and unfortunate situation for everyone.

Jay came into the apartment and immediately told Jose to go lie down on the couch before he got sick. His head was starting to get dizzy as he made his way back to safety, lying on his back. Jay brought in her bag of groceries. She was going to cook lasagna for Jose, her grandmother's recipe. The meal preparation and cooking took an hour and a half. In that time Jay and Jose talked about how their lives were going, updates on family, and their study of the Lord. They had made it about three quarters through the New Testament.

"I do not know what to make of this in regards to my faith," said Jose as he looked up from his pillow to meet Jay's eyes.

"What do you mean, my Hero?"

"I mean, I have been doing all of these things to try and please the Lord, and He afflicts me with this disease. Why, of all times of life, would this come onto me now when I am primed to change the world? How could the Lord be so cruel?"

Jay moved over on the couch closer to Jose. "My Hero, please, never blame the Lord for what the devil has done. The devil has dominion over this planet. He controls what is in the air and what is in the ground. The poisons men put into the earth are controlled by greed and power mongering. The devil is what gave you this disease, only the Lord can set you free. Be faithful, Jose, and you will be delivered from your illness.

"You are strong enough to handle it. I know I could not do it. Think about your friends, or your mother, what if she had it? You are not above the pain and torment of human existence, Mr. Young Dashing Hero. One eye, two eyes, no eyes, you must carry the torch of the Lord through the darkness to lead those who are blinded by the fire of the devil. No, Hero, this day, you will remain strong."

Jose looked deep into her emerald eyes. They held a passionate gaze, slowly gravitating toward one another for a loving embrace, when the phone rang on the table. It broke the silence and concentration of the two.

"Sorry, let me get that," said Jose as he quickly sat up and grabbed the phone off the table. He answered and lay back down onto his back.

"Yes, uh huh," he nodded his head to what the person was saying on the other end of the phone. "I understand. I will come into the office in two days to talk about treatment. Thank you, Doctor."

With that Jose hung up the phone and just closed his eyes. Even with Jay's encouraging words he was not ready to hear it from the doctor. "What happened, Jose? Was that your doctor?" asked Jay, wide-eyed and eager for news.

"Yes, that was the doctor. He said I have multiple sclerosis."

Jay hung her head hearing the news. "I am sorry to hear that, Jose. I am glad I am here to help you through this. If you need anything just ask me. I am yours until you get better. You are my dearest friend and we have grown close over the months. I do not want to see you suffer."

"I am not suffering. I am disoriented, tired, unable to concentrate on books or television, but I am not suffering. I can't say I feel great but I feel like I am prepared for the challenge. Your words inspire me. I was able to conquer every challenge that has come my way so far in life. I will not bow down to the evil oppressor of this world and let him have dominion over my body. I will do everything I can to fight."

"I will be right by your side, my Hero." Jay grabbed Jose's hands and pulled him in for a tight hug. She quickly released him and laid him back onto his back. For the rest of the weekend, the two dined on fine Italian cuisine and watched the latest movies. Jay tended to his every need. Jose called all of his family and friends to share the bad news. They each gave their condolences in their own way. Now it was time to fight back, and that started with his appointment to see the neurologist on Monday.

The neurologist showed him how to use the Simple-Ject device, which Jose would use to inject medication into seven locations on his body: Both sides of the hips, thighs, back of arms, and also the stomach.

Lenrie drove Jose back home. Jose talked to his staff and called his friends and family about the shots he had to take. Jay was showing him a lot of support throughout this entire process.

He really wanted to spend more time with her because she was constantly on his mind. The next possible meeting would be in Dallas when Jose would be going home to visit constituents and people close to him in a couple of weeks.

Besides his growing affection for Jay, he was primed and ready to take his immigration and military plans through Congress. All he had to wait for was the building of the dark matter headquarters in Mexico to start his plans, and that awaited the discovery of the second dark matter site.

Chapter 15

"Since you don't have a suit yet just put on some slacks and a dress shirt like you are going out," said James to Justin as he was finishing getting ready. There was a knock on the door so James answered and it was Abal. "Are you two ready to go? We do not want to be late."

"Yeah, I think we are about ready." Justin came out from his room with a white collared shirt on, black slacks and nice dress shoes. They all got their things and headed down to the car. The ride took some time because the church was on the other side of Addis Ababa. When they got there they saw the parking lot was quickly filling up. Justin, excited to see Dr. Berihun, said, "I hear Dr. Berihun's daughter is the best gospel singer this side of the Atlantic."

"I am excited to see and hear her. If these cars are any indication, we should be in for something good."

They parked their car and made their way to the entrance. Clerics from the Order of Horus were standing outside the entrance as security for the doctor who was already inside. The clerics recognized the trio as they walked up to the doors.

"Hey Justin, James, and Abal, the doctor said you three would be joining us. We have seats for you three in front next to the doctor. Come right this way."

They were led through the wide doors and down a side hallway that led to the front of the church. The cleric opened the door for them and pointed in the direction of Dr. Berihun as church was just minutes away from getting started. As they walked up to him he saw them and got up from his seat to greet the trio.

"Hello boys, I am glad you were able to make it today to my daughter's church. Please take your seats, the service is about to start. My daughter is the head of the choir in the yellow dress so you won't be able to miss her."

Everyone in the building took their seats as a man announced the start of the services. The band all came out and took their positions and then out walked Dr. Berihun's daughter. Her dress was form-fitting above the waist and flowing beneath it. Her beauty was unmatched in James' eyes, as he was mesmerized by her cinnamon skin and full, loving eyes. Her face had no flaws and neither did her body. She impacted James so much on first sight that he forgot to breathe as he sat there watching her stride up to the microphone.

"Welcome everyone to the Church on the Horizon. Please everyone stand up and sing along with us."

The drummer clicked off three hits of his drum sticks and the band began playing. The English speaking church was humming with pride and love for the Lord as they all sang their hearts out along with Dr. Berihun's daughter. James could not take his eyes off her. Her full lips and rigid jaw line were perfectly placed on her flawless face. He tried his best to fill his mind with thoughts of the Lord while he was in church, but Dr. Berihun's daughter was all he could concentrate on. Throughout the entire service, every time Dr. Berihun's daughter was up front James had butterflies in his stomach. He could not wait to meet her. The music was amazing and the pastor had a great message about responsibility as a Christian. When the service was over everyone got up to leave to their cars but the trio stayed with Dr. Berihun so they could meet his daughter.

As she approached the group James tried not to make strong eye contact as to reveal his attraction toward her. "My darling flower, please come and meet my good friends. Gentlemen, this is my daughter, Lilly."

They all said hello and Dr. Berihun introduced each of the three men. "I hope you liked my performance today. I am getting over a cold so hopefully I still sounded all right."

Justin responded quickly with a wide grin on his face. "No you sounded like an angel up there. It was a great performance."

James added in, "Yes I agree with my cousin. You were spectacular."

Lilly smiled warmly at them both. "Good! It is always important to try and make positive first impressions. Well I have to go in the back for our post service meeting, hopefully I run into you three soon on the campaign trail. It is refreshing to see some new American black men here in Addis Ababa. My father is great at recruiting them to his Order and I love meeting all of them so they can tell me how things are doing back home. I would love to sit down and chat with you both next time we get a chance. Take care. It was nice meeting you."

They all shook hands and she parted from the group. Dr. Berihun had the smile of a proud father on his face as she walked away. However, he had other business to attend to. He touched James on his shoulder to get his attention. "I have a proposal for you, James, and for you too, Justin. James, I would like to hire you to be my full-time communications director for my campaign and for my upcoming prime minister staff. Justin, you have worked very hard for Order of Horus since you first came to our beginners meeting. I think you have definitely proven yourself. I am inviting you to join our cleric program at my compound. You will continue to do security as a paid job, but in your free time you will become a full-time cleric. How do you both feel about this?"

Justin was quick to answer. "Oh thank you, Doctor I. have been eagerly awaiting this day. You will not be sorry, I promise you. I will be the best fighter, the smartest military tactician, and your most zealous Christian."

"I love the enthusiasm, Justin. We look forward to having you join our Order. Now you, James, what do you feel about my offer?"

James was sideswiped by the offer. He had not even thought about finding permanent work out here in Ethiopia outside of his work with the L.A. Dawn. The offer was very enticing to James because it allowed him to grow professionally. Also, if Dr. Berihun turned out to be right and the dark matter really was located outside of Debre Berhan, James would want to be right there in the thick of it with a very influential position. "Yes, Dr. Berihun, I will take that offer," James said. "It sounds like a wonderful opportunity to grow and expand my vocational horizons. I may not have the zeal that my cousin has for your Order, but I will be hardworking and loyal to your cause. The best thing that can happen for black people everywhere is for you to be right. I will call my boss immediately and tell him that I am resigning."

"Great news, James and Justin. I am very pleased to hear that you are both on board. I want you two to get your things together and move out to the Garden with me. Abal, I would like for you to come and be a translator for the Order. I will pay you triple what your current employer is paying you. We need good men who can speak the language of the people on our team. I want you all to move out to my compound and travel with me this month on my campaign around Ethiopia. We will only take a break from our duties for the celebration of the beginning of the golden age with the bright light in the sky at the end of April."

They all went out for lunch where they discussed further details on their future plans with the Order. Everyone was excited about the new world

Dr. Berihun was promising. The world would see soon if Dr. Berihun's musings on the new age were correct.

It was just over two weeks that Jose had been on his new medicine. The shots were mildly painful to not painful at all at times. It really just depended on his luck on picking a good shot location. He needed to take a trip home to relax and take some personal time to reflect on his new disease and his love life. Jay was in town and Jose had set up a dinner meeting with her and his mother Carmela. Jose was ecstatic to finally introduce his mother to one of his new best friends, and what Jose hoped would one day be more than that. Jose had given in to his desire to be with her but he was nervous about making a move. It was going to take time for him to ease into the right situation.

Jose got to his mother's house early to help her cook. When he arrived she was wearing her cooking apron and her hair was put up in rolling pins. "Hello, Jose, come in my son."

Jose gave her a kiss on the cheek and he walked in the house and kicked off his shoes. "It is hot today for April. D.C. in the spring time is the best time of year. I was actually a little sad to leave it when it is so beautiful."

"You needed to come home though, Jose. It has been too long and you have been through so much lately, I think you needed to come home and relax."

Jose got busy working on what his mother needed in the kitchen. "I am excited to meet your little girlfriend, Ms. Mills. All my friends have been asking me when I was finally going to meet her."

"She is not my girlfriend... yet."

"Oh really, is that how it is now? I thought you were so serious about keeping it a business only relationship?"

"I was but I just have grown to have feelings for her. She is obviously attractive, but our personalities just match up. She is exactly what I have been looking for. Someone not straight and narrow but who I can still take to dinner parties. She believes in God and she has really taken the time to teach me a lot of things I never knew. I tried my hardest to fight it, but I think I am starting to fall hard for her."

"Well don't fall too hard until I get to meet her. I can smell a bad one from a mile away."

"That is why I am bringing her here tonight."

They continued cooking and chatting about Jose's political life on the Hill. As the time for Jay's arrival approached in twenty minutes, Carmela went to her room to finish getting ready. She came out just in time to beat Jay, who knocked on the door and rang the doorbell to get out of the heat.

"Come right in Jay, let me introduce you to my mother. Mom, this is Juanita 'Jay' Mills. Jay, this is Carmela Valdez."

They both exchanged a friendly smile, handshake, and hellos. "Please come this way my dear, the food is ready," Carmela said as she walked over to the dishes to bring them to the table.

"I am so excited to finally meet you, Carmela. I wanted to see who was gifted enough to raise such an outstanding man. He is doing great things with his life, and no shortage of thanks goes to you for it."

"I did my best to raise him by myself since his father passed away."

"I know it was very tragic. I am curious, what kind of car was he driving when he got into his car accident? My parents were in a suburban that flipped over."

Jay looked intently at her eyes when Carmela answered. She clearly looked up and to her right when she answered. "He was in a truck. The truck did not flip. He hit a large tree just outside of town. It was very rainy that day."

Jay noticed that the whole time she looked up and to her right, which Jay remembered from her and Jose's studies of NLP, meant she was creating a visual image in her head, not remembering it, which up and to her left would signify.

"That is very sad that we both lost our parents and you lost your support for raising a child. I do think that we are stronger for it. Without that strength I would have never reached the level of success I have, and I don't think Jose would have either."

"It is hard to say. His father was a great man. He could have taught him so much."

Jay asked, "Do you remember the last thing he said to you?"

Carmela this time looked directly to her right when she answered, "All he kept saying was that he had to leave. I kept begging him to not go out in the rain and drive home but he did not want to stay with me that night. I think he was afraid of something or someone that night. I will never know what he was trying to run from when he got into the accident."

"That is too bad. Maybe I can try to research what happened to him. I know a lot of powerful people who can find answers to things."

"Well do what you must. I put the entire thing behind me a long time ago. I try not to bring up old feelings I had for him. It has just been so long and I have cried enough over him."

Jose spoke up, "Maybe it would be best to do some more research on what my father was doing before he died. All we know was that he was a drug mule and a technician. There could be so much more to him that we don't know."

"Well don't expect too much great news, Jose. He was a simple man."

"Simple men can do great things, Mother. OK, Jay, go ahead and find out what you can about him and get back with me."

They continued eating and talking. Jay and Carmela were getting to know each other but because of Jay's NLP signs she distrusted Carmela. Carmela could sense something was wrong about Jay but she could not put her finger on it.

Chapter 16

Freddy and Jennifer were coming in from a long night out. Jennifer fumbled for her keys, laughing as Freddy kept grabbing at her ass. "Hey, sexy gimme some of that," he mumbled as he groped her. "Stop it, you thug. Get your hands off me."

They were both drunk off alcohol and drunk in love. It wasn't like it was before they were married in haste. Their relationship was full of parties and constant sex. Everything had turned around for Freddy since the discovery of the dark matter. He was a hero at home in the United States and around the world. Everyone knew his name. "Come here now I command you as husband. It is time to service me."

He stammered into the house and undid his belt and pants. She saw that in his boxers was a raging phallus pointed in her direction. "Oh God no," she yelled as she ran away toward the bedroom trying not to hit the walls in her drunken laughter. The taxi driver was thrilled with his tip from the drunken pair when they got home. Freddy ran to the open bedroom door and saw his wife sitting on the bed with a wide grin on her face.

"OK come here hot stuff I will take care of that monster."

Freddy, excited by the news, started to take off his boxers and approach her, but just as he approached the bed and his boxers were half way down his legs, the phone rang. "Damn baby, hold on. It might be important. No one ever calls this late unless it is from overseas."

He pulled up his underwear and went to the phone. It was Lenz Krause. "Hey Lenz how are you? I hope it is important because you caught me at the worst time."

"Ha ha my friend I know it is late and you are probably attending to your matrimonial duties, but this is important."

"I just got word from Alfred Linchkin from the Large Hadron Collider that they discovered a way to mass produce the gravitational distortion goggles. We will have two hundred thousand produced and shipped by the end of the month. To keep demand from soaring we will set a limit to how many can go to each country and we will be charging a hundred thousand Euros per pair."

"That is quite a lot of money but I understand. If you feel this is the best way to go about doing this, then I will trust you. How is the District creation coming along? I told you that I want the North American District to have its manufacturing center in Mexico. Remember, that is very important to me. I am ready to find the second dark matter site and get back to work."

"No rush, Professor. Enjoy your time off with your new wife. Try to make some little Freddies in the free time. I already have some ideas of where the new UN capital will be. If the second dark matter site is in Europe, I want it in the Balkans. If it is in Asia, I will have it in Turkey. If it is in North or South America I will have two capitols, one there and one in Jerusalem. If it is Africa, I will probably have it in Southern Baghdad. Those are just my thoughts right now so you have a heads-up on what I am thinking. Is your wife ready for the move? I hope she is coming with you."

"Yes, she is coming with me. I don't know how excited she is about leaving her students but she loves me and she doesn't want me fighting this fight on my own on the other side of the world. She is a great wife."

"She is a good woman, Freddy, so do not ever let her go. I will let you get back to her. We will talk once the dark matter is found. Goodbye, my friend."

They hung up and Freddy got in the bed. "If they find the dark matter out here in the West we will have two capitols and we will be able to stay close. Let us hope for that."

"Not hope, pray my dear. I will pray for the Lord to keep me close to my family. I know the Lord will do what is best for us."

"Once we find the second source everything is going to change, and I will be on the forefront of that change. Please keep my head on my shoulders and keep me grounded through this entire experience."

"Yes I will. I love you."

"I love you too, Jenny." They kissed and made passionate love the rest of the night, taking in the pleasures of an early marriage.

By the time James, Justin, Abal, and some other clerics finished smoking, the sun had already set and the celebration was going to start in thirty minutes. They still had to make the trek down to Aboto and drive out to Debre Berhan. They rushed the entire way there down the mountain to the village. On their way out of the compound a delivery truck showed up with a small brown box. James was wondering what it was but quickly forgot about it in his marijuana induced haze. By the time they got all the way down to Debre Berhan, the city was absolutely packed with spectators who wanted to see if Dr. Berihun was right about the last day of April being the start of the golden age.

They found a park in the outskirts of downtown and made the walk to the stage. Justin couldn't believe they were late because he always wanted to be on his best for the doctor. They made it there just in time, as Dr. Berihun was walking up the staircase and onto the stage. Justin went and took his security position in front of the stage and Abal and James went into the large crowd of thousands.

"Welcome to Debre Berhan, the Holy City of Zara Yaqob and the location of the second source of dark matter. We have a pair of gravitational distortion goggles that will be here any day now that will prove me correct.

The Light of God will also prove that I am indeed a seer and a beacon of truth from the lips of our Lord Jesus Christ. I am his messenger, the messenger of the black man, sent to tell all of my Nagas young and old, that our time has come again. We will raise our status from the lowest to the highest once again just like in the ancient times. Ancient times where we ruled Africa, we ruled the Middle East, we controlled India, and we were worshipped in Asia. Those times will return, my loyal Nagas. Rejoice with me!"

The crowd erupted into applause for the head cleric. James was clapping when he looked to the right of the stage and saw Dr. Berihun's daughter Lilly standing there looking spectacular in all of her beauty. She was wearing a black blouse and dark blue jeans. She was looking over in James' direction and she waved at him. They had spent several moments together on the campaign trail over the last month of April. Now that they were done with the campaign they rarely saw each other since she stayed in Addis Ababa and James stayed in the Garden compound with Dr. Berihun and the clerics. After her wave and smile she turned back to her father who was about to speak once again now that he crowd's applause was dying down.

"Look to the sky, the hour of the Lord is at hand!"

Everyone looked to the sky but saw nothing. Several seconds went by and still nothing. People were starting to murmur in the crowd. Just as doubt was creeping in, in came a large object screaming through the skies. As it approached the atmosphere it ignited the object and lit up the entire sky around Debre Berhan. It burned beautiful colors, blues and reds and white. "Right now my Nagas, we have entered into the Age of Horus!"

He put his hands to the sky and started praying. One of the clerics came running onto the stage with a phone in his hand and interrupted Dr.

Berihun's prayer. He turned to the cleric and said, "This better be damned important, son."

"Yes sir, big news from The Garden compound." He handed Dr. Berihun the phone and the crowd stared on as he nodded his head to the person on the other end of the phone. A great smile crossed his face and he gave the phone back to the cleric. "You did good Naga, real well." He walked back up to the microphone. "My Nagas I have exciting news. We have found the dark matter everywhere around my compound in the forests, through Aboto, and they say it reaches all the way to Debre Berhan. Our time is here my Nagas. Great wealth and responsibility have come to us. Now the last step must take place. We must vote me in as prime minister of this country so we can begin the change. I have done all I can, the Lord has done all He can, and now it is up to all of you to heed our cries. The world will be ours, Nagas!"

Dr. Berihun had been up in the polls all week leading up to today, May 3rd, 2017 and Election Day. Dr. Berihun had his election party set up in Addis Ababa at his daughter's church. They set up big screens on the walls to show around-the-clock coverage of the Ethiopian elections. The vote was tight between all three major political parties. The three running for prime minister were Dr. Berihun, the current prime minister Mehari Amanuel, and leader of the Muslim Coalition Abba Fergessa. James and Abal were talking with one of the other clerics about the bright light in the sky a few days ago when Lilly came up to James and grabbed his shoulder. "Hey James, come with me for a second." James eagerly left the group, leaving Abal with a noticeable scowl.

"I am excited about tonight, James. I really think my dad can win by looking at these polls. The votes are really starting to come in and it looks like the prime minister has a lead but there is no way that can last. After the bright light of the Lord and the fact that we found dark matter here in Ethiopia, there is no way they can deny he was sent here by God to lead us until Horus comes to take over."

"It will be hard for your father to lose this one. I just hope that there is a peaceful transition of power. Each of these three leaders wants to be in charge with Ethiopia having the dark matter because untold amounts of wealth and power will be coming to these borders."

"Yes it will be very daunting times. That is why we need as many strong clerics like your cousin to be on our side fighting with us. How is his cleric training coming along?"

"He is getting the Biblical and philosophical stuff but the military training has been tough on him. He can do the entire regiment of physical things fine because he is an athletic freak, but he struggles with tactical thinking. It will come to him though with practice."

"Why don't you become a cleric? How can you deny that my father was sent to pave the way for Horus after the bright light and the dark matter discovery?"

"It has nothing to do with believing your father. I do believe that we are in a new age of the black man. I just do not want to try and conform myself to a group of people. I am comfortable with my own way of worship and living my life. I do not need a strict code of rules to control me. I am too much of a free thinker to conform."

"Very honest answer, and I respect it. Oh wait, there is an update in the votes. Let's listen."

"With 80% of districts reporting, we report that Prime Minister Amanuel is up by a considerable margin over the contenders. He is taking in sixty-five percent of the vote with Dr. Cameron Berihun coming in at nineteen and Abba Fergessa with twelve percent."

"What is this nonsense," yelled Lilly. "This can't be right at all. Something is incredibly fishy about this. How could we have come in so strong in the polls but be blown out by such a considerable margin? I cry foul on this one. Unfortunately, I do not know what else to do but to march in the streets and protest."

"If protest is what the people want to do, then that is what will happen. I can't believe this vote is for real." Another hour passed and the votes were all counted. Prime Minister Amanuel won by a large margin over his competition and people were not only upset in the church that night, but all over Ethiopia.

The next morning when people woke up and really realized what happened to their future of a world led by Horus reborn, they were mad. Millions took to the streets in protest. They did not go to work, they only protested. The Capital and every major city were filled with Christian and Muslim alike who were protesting for a revote because they felt it was fraudulent.

Lenz Krause, secretary-general to the UN, flew out to monitor the growing protest and bring more troops to protect the dark matter. He begged for the prime minister to allow a revote and not resort to violence, but the Amanuel family had a history of ruthless crackdowns on opposition protests.

First they were using rubber bullets, but then after he realized that water hoses and rubber bullets weren't solving the problem, he resorted to real bullets and physical violence. Hundreds of people died in the streets that week and the prime minister cracked down against his foes. But people still came out and marched, knowing that something must be done to bring the glory of the black race back to the world.

Then all of a sudden one day, the police and army just stopped attacking. There was an emergency radio and television broadcast of Prime Minister Amanuel. "Dear countrymen, first I would like to apologize for my behavior lately. I should not have allowed my generals to coerce me into firing on my own people to quell the protests. I was wrong for that. I had a dream last night, a wonderful dream. I was taken through the clouds to heaven where I saw black men, proud black men. They all told me that in order for us to reign again I had to step down. They said that the Lord commanded me in order to save my soul. The dream was so powerful that I woke up in tears, crying my eyes out. I am here to admit that I rigged the vote during the election. I concede my power over to a rightful winner of new elections which shall be held May 11th. Once again I apologize and I will leave the country for good. No more Amanuels will rule over this land with an iron fist. You deserve to a free and happy people, and a beacon of power for black people all around the world."

The new elections were held and Dr. Berihun won by a large margin in elections run, monitored, and counted by the United Nations. Abba Fergessa still did not trust the West loving and Christian siding United Nations with the vote. He would stop the Muslim protests for now, but beneath the surface was a steaming mad population of a large percentage of the country waiting to get back out in the streets and protest until Sharia law and Muslim faith dominated the land.

Chapter 17

"Hey, Professor Slater, I am sorry it took so long for me to call. It has been a little over two weeks since the dark matter was discovered in Africa. I had to attend to the Ethiopian uprising and revote because that was more important than anything else in the world."

"It is OK Lenz, I know you are doing your best to help the world become a better place. What news do you have on the capital and the ten zones?"

"I have decided on the capital, the zones, and the zone heads. The capital will be placed in Baghdad. The ten zones are as follows: Zone One is Western Europe led by Jeffery Talington, Zone Two is Eastern Europe led by Stanislas Cojeki, Zone Three is North America led by Barry Jolee, Zone Four is South America led by Iglesias Alundo, Zone Five is the Middle East led by Hamid Donislam, Zone Six is the Far East led by Shun Huang, Zone Seven is the South East led by Bua Phan, Zone Eight is Australia and New Zealand led by Michelle Banter, Zone Nine is North Africa led by Nazmi Cutar, Zone Ten is South Africa led by Yando Illidasy. The leaders of each zone will choose their own capital, except for North America which will be located in Mexico City, per your request. I have done my research on each of these fine men and women and I know they are up to the task of insuring safe production of our products and prompt delivery of all dark matter and dark matter related products.

"The original Zone Five leader is Hamid but he has fallen ill, my backup is Malik Jabbar from Southern Iraq."

"Tell me about this new Middle Eastern leader. That is such a volatile region to control, is he really up to the task?"

"He is an Iraqi, father was Shia and mother was Shiite. He comes from an old wealthy political family on both sides, so he was almost destined to be in the position he was in Iraqi Parliament. He is very popular in Iraq and neighboring countries as a sound voice of reason in a world of chaos and violence. If there is anyone with the ability to unite the Muslim people and the Middle East under a peaceful flag of progress, then it will be him."

"That is very exciting to hear. So now that we have the capital set, when do you want me to come out?"

"Well let's have you come on July 10th, the compound will be built to a point where we can start business by then."

"OK sounds good, Lenz. You did a great job in Ethiopia, by the way. You are as skilled a politician as they come. The world needs more people like you."

"No you are wrong, Professor. The world needs more people like you. Take care, my friend. I will see you and your lovely wife in two months."

Jay was rolling up another blunt as Jose was flipping through the movie stations on cable. "Damn, there isn't anything on right now. Maybe we can buy something."

Just then the alarm on his phone went off. "Shot time, oh great," he said with great annoyance. He went to the table in the kitchen where he stored a room temperature five-pack while he let the rest stay protected in the refrigerator. He got a pack of alcohol wipes and the syringe and went to the couch to shoot his body full of medicine.

"Where is it today, Hero?"

"In my thigh tonight. I don't look forward to it."

"Why not? There is a lot of meat on your thighs."

"Because there are also a lot of veins that I can't see on my thighs. I hope that answers your question."

"Just be careful, my dear."

He popped the syringe out of its plastic case and pulled off the needle protector. He wiped down his thigh with the alcohol wipe and prepared the needle. He pinched a lump of fat and in a second he plunged the needle into his skin and with a free finger he pushed down the medicine into his leg. Just as he thought it was a good shot location he felt the pain start to sear through his legs.

"Ah shit, ah shit, ah shit," he yelled as he pulled the needle out quickly. His leg started cramping up as muscles spasms and pain ran through his veins. "Fuck, I hit a vein! Oh my Lord it hurts so badly!"

Jay came over to try and soothe him. "What can I do? Do you want some pain medication from your cabinet?"

"No I will have to wait too long for that. Just give me some of that."

Jay had the lit blunt in her hand. "This?" she questioned as she held out the blunt to Jose.

"Yes, give me a hit. I need something now to stop this."

She gave Jose the blunt and he took a deep inhale of the sticky leaf. "Fuck me. I forgot how much I missed this."

The pain immediately began to subside with each new puff of the blunt. "Hey don't smoke it all up, pothead," Jay joked as she took the blunt away from Jose after he had several hits. "I don't even know why I tripped about smoking anyway. It is legal for me to get it medically if I want and no one will ever find out as long as I just do it in private. The pain from these shots is an annoyance. Plus, it will help relax me with this stressful job. I will only smoke with you, though."

"OK that sounds good with me. I brought plenty so we can get real high tonight to take your mind off the pain." She went into her bag and pulled out another pack of blunts and a bag of high-quality purple bud. She rolled three more blunts and the two enjoyed another night together on the couch watching movies until they both fell asleep.

It had been a month since the end of the protests and the swearing in of Dr. Berihun as prime minister. Things were moving fast in Ethiopia because of the discovery of dark matter. Port cities were booming with trade from the increase of wealth across of the country. Shipping of the dark matter to the countries around the world was increasing naval activity all around Ethiopia. The country was turning into a beacon of wealth for the entire world in a short amount of time. Skyscrapers were being built all around the country, investments were pouring in. Thousands upon thousands of workers came to work the extraction teams. They were paid high wages, with the setting of wages being made by dark matter discoverer Professor Frederick Slater. Thousands of people came for work and still thousands of jobs remained. Jobs were being created worldwide at each manufacturing center, creating an economic boom in each respective country. Stocks were soaring worldwide with the influx of wealth the dark matter was creating in all industries. Dr. Berihun was hard at work in Addis Ababa in his office, getting ready for a live announcement to the Ethiopian public on television.

"I think I am ready for what I have to say. We can start anytime you are ready, James," said Dr. Berihun, sitting in his desk chair going over his notes.

"OK, dim the lights and start the camera," said James, prepping the staff to get ready to shoot. "We go live in one minute." Everyone got in position. "Three, two, one, go."

"Hello my people, this is Prime Minister Cameron Berihun. I have had a chance to address the public several times but I have some critical announcements to make to you directly. First, we are going to do a total reconstruction of every school in the country over the next several years. High speed internet, desktop computers, and tablets will be provided to every school for each student. A high speed rail will also begin construction to connect the entire country. However, with great wealth and power comes great responsibility. As I promised when I campaigned, I am bringing the spirit of Christ into the lives of all our citizens. We must change how we behave in order for our savior to come to us. It starts with crime and sin.

"Homosexuals will have to pay a hefty ten percent surtax to continue to practice their immoral behavior in our country. Forced marriage by parents or by kidnap and rape is punishable up to life in prison. No more will our daughters and sisters be scared to walk the streets. Female mutilation is also a crime punishable by up to life in prison. These sentences will be heavy in order to break the sinful traditions that have been adapted here. Jesus must come to call us his brothers on the cross in order for Horus to return and save all of our people, Jewish, Christian, and Muslim. Several more social programs and harsher penalties will be enacted in order to create the perfect society. I will put up a bill to legalize marijuana. I believe that plants are not against the word of God. He put these things here to help us. If used correctly, in the spirit of the Lord, we can use this magical plant to aid in our spiritual growth and connection to the Lord. That is all I have to share with you at this time. For more updates on what I am doing go to my website and sign up for the newsletter. I love you all and may the peace of Christ be in your hearts."

The camera light turned off then everyone in the room clapped for the prime minister. "Prime Minister Berihun you did wonderful, such an inspiring message for our Nagas to hold on to as we make this transition," said Justin as he helped the doctor from his seat.

"Thank you, Justin. You have been such a helpful cleric ever since you passed the final test two weeks ago. I am glad I brought you on. How are things going with getting custody of your kids? Have you talked to them lately?"

"Thank you for asking sir. I hired a lawyer back in California to petition to the judge but my hopes are not high. I just don't see myself being able to tear them away from their friends and family and bring them to a foreign land. For now, I take satisfaction with video chatting with them once a week at least. They are so proud of me for everything I am doing here, probably for the first time in their young lives. I just hope to do right by them one day once I get established."

"I am sorrowful to hear you will not be able to get them out here. I will continue to pray for you and their health and happiness without you there to raise them." The prime minister turned to James. "Well, James, how do you think I did? Was everything said correctly?"

"You did a wonderful job, Doctor. Right on point with your delivery. The people love you. Everyone put their faith in you and you delivered."

"We have so much left to do before I have delivered on my task from God. We are getting there. It will just take time."

"Thankfully time is something that we have on our side right now."

"Time is never on our side, James. There is always someone out there plotting to take what God gave to us. We need to grow in strength so we can protect ourselves. I am putting a large amount of the budget on new military recruitment, technology, and weapons. If anyone wants to meet us in battle, we will be ready for them."

"Hopefully it will not come to that."

"Lord willing."

"Well at least this compound is relatively free of dirt and dust. God, it is unbearably hot in here."

Jennifer was doing her best to stay positive, but a summer in Baghdad was no fun place to be. There was no pool built in the UN compound yet, so the air conditioner and cold showers would have to suffice. "Well, I will make the best of the situation dear. We are here to guide the world to be a better place. I would not want to be anywhere else but by your side helping change the world."

Freddy put his suitcase on the bed and sat down. He grabbed the remote and turned it on. It was the UN feed so the stations were in English. "Let's just try our best to get used to things out here. There is a lot of work that must be done, and I am eager to get to it."

"When do you start working officially?"

"Tomorrow at three p.m. we have our first board meeting. I look forward to it."

"Very exciting for you, Freddy dear. I will try to find something useful to do with my free time. I hear there is an English speaking church here in Baghdad so I will ask to be escorted there to see if I can do any volunteering."

"That sounds good my love, but for today let's just relax and take in the sights as safely as possible. The armed guards will be very nice when it comes to kidnappings, but it won't stop a suicide bomber."

"Try to stay positive. We are here to help these people and I am sure they appreciate being chosen as the new capital of the new UN. Terrorist attacks are so rare here in the new Southern Iraq, we will have nothing to worry about."

Chapter 18

"Abal just texted me that he is here. Are you ready Justin?"

Justin was in the bathroom taking a long time to get ready. When he heard James say Abal was ready he finished up what he was doing and came out, ready to go.

"Let's do this! I am excited to see Kira. She is going to love it out here," Justin said.

"We need to show Bugger a good time. She is bringing a friend from her sorority, her name is Nancy Yonder. I have seen her FaceNet profile before and she is super bad. It sucks for you that you took a vow of celibacy until marriage because you would have been all over her."

"What the clerics don't know won't hurt 'em," Justin said.

They left the hotel room and went down to the front where Abal was waiting on the curb. They got in and off they went to the new Bole International Airport. It had been two months since Prime Minister Berihun had been sworn in, and one of his first priorities was to overhaul and upgrade every major airport in Ethiopia. The crown jewel of this project was Bole International in Addis Ababa. As they pulled up to the airport they could see cranes and construction everywhere, working to complete the new airport as quickly as possible. They parked and made their way to the terminal entrance to wait for Kira and Nancy.

Kira and her friend were both above average height in America, so they really stood out here in Africa. As they walked through the exit with their baggage the trio of men all approached them. Justin immediately had a devilish grin when he saw her friend Nancy. She had curves in all the right places with a beautiful face. She was clearly mixed with Hispanic, with long flowing mixed curly hair. James was the first to yell out, "Bugger! Hey lil sis how was the flight?"

She dropped her luggage and ran up to her big brother and gave him a hug, "Oh the flight was awful but it was all worth it. We saw the scenery landing and this place is beautiful. This airport is amazingly modern and look at all the construction everywhere! I can see that this place is changing fast. I came at the right time."

"Yes things are looking good for Addis Ababa. Hello Nancy, my name is James. This here is our cousin Justin, and this is our friend and translator Abal."

The men said hello and Nancy said hello back, taking special note of Justin and his impressive physical features. James introduced Kira to Abal. "Hello there, Kira," Abal said, smiling. "You are just remarkably beautiful, you must have some amazing looking parents."

Kira blushed at the comments. "Oh thank you for the compliment. Are you from here? You must have all the local girls all over you."

"Yes I am from here but no I do not have that special touch with the ladies just yet. I am learning from your brother and cousin though how to be a better man, and I hope that the next lady I date with reap the benefits of their teachings."

He winked at Kira and she smiled and blushed again. "OK, enough of the patty cake. Let's go explore the city and get some food," Justin said.

So the five of them left the airport and squeezed into Abal's car. Kira and Nancy experienced the new Addis Ababa and they immediately fell in love. Kira and Nancy loved all the attention they were getting from the African men on the streets, but both had their sights set on men within their own company. Kira and Nancy came at an exciting time for Ethiopia, but also a dangerous time. Muslim protests were back on that day. Not en masse, but small pockets of insurrection throughout the country demanding Muslims have a greater voice in the new Ethiopian government. Tensions were mounting, and wealth and prosperity were simmering the worst of the heat.

Freddy got to the board meeting door just in time before they closed it. "Welcome Professor, I am glad you decided to join us," Lenz said with a facetious smile and tone.

"I am ready for business. Let's get to it." The other advisors in the room took their seats and the meeting began.

"We are seeing tremendous global growth since the discovery of both dark matter sites. New dark matter products are flying off the shelves, and energy companies worldwide are turning to dark matter are a more efficient and safe source of power. Everything has been a success so far. The only people who are having negative side effects are the people in Zone Five."

Freddy interrupted Lenz. "That is the Middle East, right?"

"Yes it is. The price of oil is dropping as dark matter production grows. It is causing job loss and stock market declines. Malik Jabbar, the zone leader, is working hard to find alternative sources of wealth for his zone members. He needs a unified front to combat this growing economic problem. So he just called me yesterday to announce that he is going to set up a new Muslim Caliphate to rule over the Muslim populations of his zone and the world. He needs a new source of stability for the region and he feels that reestablishing the Caliphate will bring a new source of pride and confidence to the Muslim people in his region. What do you think about that, Professor?"

"I think it is a wonderful idea. Catholics have their Pope, who acts as a respected spiritual leader for those of his faith. I feel that Muslims having the same thing will only help ease global tensions between Christians, Muslims, and Jews."

"Speaking of Jews and Muslims, the removal date of Palestinians has been set to October of 2018. Israel is transforming for the better now that Palestinians are moving with large amounts of money to a new country. I think everything worked out for the better with that situation. We will wait until the final evacuation date has passed to make a final judgment, but things seem to be moving in the right direction."

"Everything sounds good, Lenz. This is an exciting time to be alive. That is for sure."

"Yes, the world is growing and prospering. Dark matter applied to agriculture is producing ten to fifty times normal yields. Everything is in abundance and the world is grateful to you, Freddy. Without you, none of this is possible."

"Let's not start patting ourselves on the back just yet; there is plenty more work to do."

The meeting continued for another thirty minutes covering issues such as technology development, wages for extraction workers, and how each zone's manufacturing center is handling the high amount of demand. Everything was looking good for Freddy and dark matter.

Kira and Nancy were enjoying the high life of African cuisine and travel. No expense was spared on the pair as they went on shopping trips and to day spas. James really wanted to cater to their every need. While things were going smoothly in the capital with the group of five, things were going poorly in other parts of the country. Justin had to report to Dr. Berihun for security so they brought the pair of visiting women with them to meet the prime minister.

"Yes, come in," said Prime Minister Berihun as he turned off the television to get ready for his guests. In came the group of five with Justin leading the way. They introduced Kira and Nancy to the prime minister and they shook hands. "This is a very exciting, yet daunting time to be visiting, young ladies. I want you to enjoy Ethiopia from the capital as best you can, but please be careful. Protests are growing in Harar and Muslim reinforcements are coming in from Somalia."

Just then a cleric came bursting into the room with urgent news from Harar. "Prime Minister, the Muslims are burning down buildings and churches in Harar. The Army Generals are requesting permission to go into Harar and quell the violence."

"Unbelievable, don't they realize that we are on the forefront of a new age for black men of all religions? I am not forcing them to accept Christianity. It is simply the model I am following to bring about the return of our savior Horus. Why don't they understand?"

Dr. Berihun slammed his hands on the desk in anger, but the cleric still needed an answer. "Sir, the generals are awaiting your response."

The prime minister took a moment to pause and then answered. "Bring in the military. Order must be restored, or I will look weak. Only a strong leader can bring about real change. My command is that they use rubber bullets at first, but if that does not stop them from attacking people and burning buildings, move on to real bullets."

The room gasped at this news. This was a history-changing move by Dr. Berihun. Everyone just hoped that he was making the right decision by meeting force with force. "OK, I am sorry ladies but it seems that I have some urgent business to attend to. Enjoy the Capital. Please, James, spare no expense on these two. I will compensate you for all you spend. Hopefully this rioting business will be over by next week."

Everyone left the room and Kira tried to stay positive. "I don't have anything to worry about with my big strong family and their big strong friend," she said to Abal with a smile. He smiled back and turned away from her affectionate gaze.

"Yes, we have nothing to worry about here in the Capital. There is plenty of security here. Now let's leave Justin to his clerical duties and we will take you two to lunch."

"Goodbye, Justin," said Nancy lovingly. Kira said goodbye too and they left Justin with the prime minister. Things were getting tense with the Muslim community in Ethiopia. Violence against them would not quell their voices but only strengthened them.

With the manufacturing center being built in Mexico at Jose's request, he had lavish praise heaped upon him from both Mexico and the United States. The thousands upon thousands of jobs created had stemmed the flow of illegal immigration, and poured tons of money into the Mexican economy. The UN agreed to move four hundred thousand elite trained troops into the area to destroy the cartels. With this success in his back pocket, Jose decided to push his two new bills through Congress. The first would be his New Dawn Immigration package. In this bill, every illegal immigrant could gain full citizenship by doing several things: They must install a X-chip on every family member, they must pay back taxes for every year that they were here, they must pass a basic English and U.S. history class, and they all must be vaccinated. The second bill would be his Active Field Bill, bringing the X-chip to all active duty military.

He was on the Hill all day pushing for his bills to be passed. Early reports were that his bills were gaining steam in both the House and the Senate. Jose's popularity sure did not hurt the popularity of the two bills. It was due for a vote in two weeks and Jose was doing all he could to fulfill his promise to the American Protectorate and bring the X-chip to the front of American culture. In celebration of the good news on his bills, he called Jay to tell her.

"Hey Jay, how are you doing today?"

"I am doing well. What is important is how you are doing?"

"Well my MS has been kicking my ass today. I feel sick and tired as all hell."

"I am sorry to hear that, but two things I need to say. You need to stop claiming the multiple sclerosis as your disease. Your words have power don't you know that? I thought you have been studying the Bible trying to gain the Light? You were well on your way before so do not stop now that you are sick. The Lord is testing your faith, and you must pass. He can and will heal you if you only have faith that you can be healed."

"Well how do I go about being healed? Do I have to pray or something?"

"Yes, prayer helps, but you need to have someone lay their hands on you. Grandmother Domenica is the perfect person. When are you free to come back to Dallas and meet with us?"

"In a little over a month I will have some time to come visit. My bills are the most important thing right now. That is actually why I called. It looks like both bills are going to pass. The AP is going to be so happy with me."

"Yes, we are well on our way to establishing a popular new form of media and technology. These are very exciting times. But you need to remember, this is also the time of the Lord in this new age. We must keep Him in our hearts to help guide us to victory."

"Yes, I understand. I will get back to studying tonight. I want to attain the Light. It is very important to me to try and get closer to God."

"You are doing well, Jose, much better than I thought. Just keep up the hard work and it will come to you."

They got off the phone and Jose got back to work in his office. His star was burning bright, but he still had more work to do before his plans would be complete.

Freddy came in the room and closed the door behind him. The advisors and Lenz were sitting and chatting about Ethiopia. Freddy was excited for the news he was bringing to the boardroom. "Gentlemen, we have discovered a way to transfix our gravitational distortion material onto a high powered lens. We are in the process of building an observatory and creating the telescopes now. We will have the power to look at all the planets in our solar system and search for dark matter. Could you imagine if we could find another global source for dark matter? We could convert the entire world to dark energy and dark energy products. We have also created the first dark energy battery. We only managed to create a small one for now, but with time we will develop larger batteries that can power machines, devices, and even cars, without running out of power for years. The devices and machines we have now require direct dark matter, but with the batteries, we can contain and easily ship the dark matter for them. It will change everything. Once we develop the new products and batteries we will send the blueprints to every manufacturing center and get them to work. Demand is high for the out-of-date products we already have, so it will increase exponentially with each new adaptation."

"That sounds very exciting, Professor. We have some bad news from Ethiopia. It seems the Christian leader, Prime Minister Berihun, has decided to quell the violence against civilians from the Muslim rioters by using violence. Several people were killed and the riots have been increasing. I am flying out after this meeting to get to his speech to the nation tomorrow night. Hopefully I can talk some sense into him."

"What does the new Khalifa think of these new protests? The vote for his rule was remarkably peaceful. It seems as though the Muslim people really took well to the idea of a new Khalifa."

"The Khalifa has denounced the violence on both sides and wants the Muslims to sue for peace to avoid more bloodshed. There are widespread reports throughout the Middle East that this stance is too lenient. They feel as though Muslims and Sharia should rule all the lands of the world, and negotiating with the infidels is a dishonor."

"Every religion has their radicals."

"Yes but no other religion in these times is as violent. I will go and do my best to quell the situation, so you and the advisors keep things running here while I am gone."

"Have a safe trip, Lenz."

The crowd was growing very large as James, Justin, and Abal made their way to the front of the stage for Justin to join the other clerics. After knifing through the masses of people, they got to the front where Justin joined his Order mates. James and Abal went off to the side of the stage. There standing off to the side of the main stage near them was Lilly in all her glory. She was wearing a beautiful African dress with her hair tied up behind her head. James went up to go talk to her while Abal hung back closer to the stage. Their conversation was healthy and energetic. James was incredibly interested in this woman, for her looks and for her intelligence. James got the feeling that she was interested in him too.

The international dignitaries and press core showed up and took their seats and positions around the stage. The crowd had grown into the hundreds of thousands to hear the prime minister speak, and he was ready to begin. Justin was on the far side of the stage watching over the crowd. "Dear Nagas, welcome to Addis Ababa. I am here to address the growing insurrection from our Muslim Nagas to the East. I am going to sue for peace because we do not need this kind of violence during our great time of glory. I will accept a Muslim representative into my council to help me cater to our very important minority. We do not want to ostracize such an important core to our society. It is our time to rule over this world with love and peace and respect, like our ancestors before us. Muslim rulers ruled the same way. We need to harness the spirit of our ancestors and grow into a greater society."

Dr. Berihun noticed a man wavering through the crowd as he spoke, but turned his attention back away to the crowd. Justin took particular note of him as he went through the crowd in haste. Justin was growing suspicious as he neared the front of the crowd, getting closer to the stage. Justin slowly started making his way down the side stairs and toward the front. He got there just in time. Just as the man got to the front of the stage he produced a black handgun and took aim at the prime minister. Just before the shot rang out, Justin ran and tackled him, taking the gun off target, causing the bullet to hit the prime minister in his left arm.

The crowd screamed and moved back as several clerics swarmed the assassin. "All praise to Allah," the man kept screaming as his struggles became useless against the strength of five well-trained clerics. They secured the gun, handcuffed him, and took him away to jail. Prime Minister Berihun returned to the podium. "For safety reason we must cut this speech short. Thank you for coming."

After all his messages for peace in the speech, the Muslims attacked him anyway. The prime minister was not only hurt by this transgression, he was enraged. After the speech he ordered a full military crackdown on the

Muslim forces against the wishes of his council and the UN delegation. The assassination attempt spoiled any goodwill there was left in his soul.

Chapter 19

Jose was doing his best to stay calm as his second bill of the day was being voted upon. His first bill, the Active Field Bill, passed with three hundred and thirty-two votes. His second bill was looking like it was going to pass with even more. He chatted with his fellow members of both parties on the floor as they came and went from their vote. Most members in Congress had tremendous respect for the young Congressman from Texas. He was a favorite in the chambers of Congress and the outcome of his two bills proved that. Everyone wished him congratulations, from his mother and Jay, to Lisa Malky, and even the president.

The country had finally solved the worst aspect of the immigration problem. The military was instantly excited with the news of their men being equipped with this state-of-the-art technology. They would be able to send detailed maps, have live visual feeds, and communicate in real time with every soldier in the world. It would change the way the military operated. The next part of his plan was to get the Mexican government to tag returned illegal immigrants with the X-chip in order to monitor them, so they could not attempt another crossing without being easily detected.

After that, Jose's plan would have been accomplished. The cartels were on the run, illegals were being stopped from crossing, and America was having an economic boom along with the rest of the world. It seems as though nothing could stop Jose now.

Jose arrived at Domenica's house just as the clock passed nine. He got to the front door and knocked to gain entry. Jay answered, "Come in, Hero, we have much to discuss."

He took off his shoes and made his way to the main living room of the house where Domenica was waiting. "Oh dear please come in, I hear you are very sick," Domenica said as she sat down in her large chair.

"Yes, I have become afflicted with multiple sclerosis. I have been having a hard time understanding why the Lord would allow me to get sick in my time of triumph in His name. Having this disease and taking this medicine is slowing me down and deteriorating my spirit. I would do anything to get rid of it. Jay says that in the Christian faith someone can lay hands on a person in the name of the Lord and they will be healed. Would you be interested in laying your hands on me? I would be honored if a woman of such Godly stature assisted me in my healing."

"The honor will be all mine, my dear. Please come over here and get onto your knees." Jose walked over to her and got on his knees. She stood up over top of him and reached her hands out to the sky. "Everyone close their eyes in prayer before I lay hands on Jose."

Everyone in the room closed their eyes in full faithful prayer. "Dear Lord, we are here today in Your holy name. Please bless this gathering with all of Your Spirit. We are here today to give peace and healing to one of Your faithful servants, Jose Valdez. He has been afflicted by the evil one of this Earth. Please Lord, in Your holy name, give faith and healing to Your servant Jose. In Your holy name," she said as she laid her right hand upon Jose's head. "Lord enter me and enter this man to give him healing and faith in his time of need. Deliver him from the bounds of pain and illness oh Lord, in Your holy name. Free this man of all affliction in Your holy name oh Lord. With Your love and grace, be free from illness."

The lights in the house flickered and a cold illness fell over Domenica as she felt the chill of the Lord's hand in her soul. She sat back in her chair and caught her breath. "I feel terrible, which is a good thing. When I feel sick after laying my hands on someone that means that it was a success. The only way it will stick though is if you deny the earthy medicine that poisons your body and soul."

"I will stop all medicine immediately."

"All signs of MS you have from now on are just tricks by the devil. You are clean and holy in Spirit."

"Thank you so much Grandma Domenica, my life has changed forever."

The pair got up and walked to the dinner table to begin dinner. Jay spoke up, "That was a very touching ceremony but I have some daunting news for you, Jose. So your mother says your father, Francisco Basurto, died in a car accident outside of Dallas, but there is no record of his death in any newspaper. I called some friends I know that know people in some cartels, and no one has ever heard of him. I am not going so far as to say your mother is lying, but something is not adding up. Maybe you should question her more at least."

"I can't believe she is lying to me. She has never lied to me. I don't even know if I want to ask her more questions. I am sure she has been through so much already over his death. She really loved him, and I don't want her to suffer."

"Yes, but you have been suffering your entire life without a father. What if he is still alive? What if his family is still around? There are so many questions left unanswered."

Domenica stopped Jay. "Juanita, please calm down. There is no need to get too excited over this new information. Trust your mother, Jose. She brought you into this world. Until you have reason to doubt her, I would not go asking questions unless the curiosity is just burning you up inside. Let the Lord take care of everything."

"Thank you, Domenica, and thank you, Jay. You have done so much to help me. I don't know how I can ever repay you."

"Just don't forget about us when you are president."

They all laughed and continued with a peaceful dinner. Jose was getting closer to the light with each passing day and Domenica could sense it. He was growing in power and she and Jay needed to guide him in the direction of the Lord. Jose did not doubt that he had been healed, but wanted to get confirmation that his illness was gone. So the next day he scheduled a MRI to confirm his blessing from the Lord.

"You two are sure you got all your stuff?" James questioned Kira and Nancy as he walked through their hotel room.

"Yeah we packed everything," Kira responded with a sad expression. She did not want to leave her brother with all of this turmoil in the country. She also did not want to leave Abal, whom she had grown very fond of during her vacation.

"I'll go get the guys so we can take down your luggage." James called Justin and Abal to come up and help take down the luggage. When they came up, Abal was getting the googly eyes from Kira and Nancy was looking lovingly upon Justin. They got the luggage and went down to Abal's car. The car ride to the airport was easy going, full of healthy conversation about the future of Ethiopia. "So what is going to happen now that Prime Minister Berihun almost got shot?"

"He is going to crack down hard on the Muslims, I am afraid. There is no telling what consequences his actions will have. I am sorrowful that this paradise for black men and women and Christians everywhere has turned into such a war zone," James said.

"There is no place for Islam in a Holy Christian nation. This was going to come eventually, good to get it over with right now in the early stages of the new Ethiopia," said Justin, full of bravado and confidence.

"Just be careful you three, there is no telling what kind of terrorism and violence the Muslim minority will bring to the people of this country until they get their way," Nancy said with worry on her face.

"We will be fine you two, stop worrying. We have the numbers, the money, and the power. What consequences could there possibly be for us cracking down on our own rioting population?" Justin questioned.

"Muslims have a new Khalifa,", Abal responded. "He would not look favorably to his people being murdered in the streets fighting in the name of Islam. The more brutal our attacks are against the Muslims, the more hostile the new Caliphate becomes. Lord knows how many altercations the old Caliphates participated in throughout human history because of the treatment of Muslims."

James said, "Let us hope it does not come to that and we can reach the peace terms Dr. Berihun described before the assassination attempt."

They pulled up to the airport and everyone got out saying their final goodbyes on the curbside drop off. Kira gave her brother, cousin, and her new friend Abal all hugs and kisses. Nancy gave everyone a hug but went in and kissed Justin on the lips with a loving kiss. They said their final goodbyes and they parted ways. "They are getting out of here at just the right time", James said. "Things could be getting a lot worse around here soon if things keep up. And what the hell was that kiss about?"

"Yeah they are leaving at a good time," Justin responded. "And that was a thank you kiss for me putting it down last night. You know me, Justin be bustin' open these hoes! Remember?"

"Glad to see the clerics haven't changed you that much. They would be furious if they knew about you breaking your vows so try to be careful of whom you fuck from now on, Justin."

The trio had the Sunday off, and they spent it relaxing now that the ladies were gone.

The trio showed up for work the next day on Monday eager and refreshed. When they entered Prime Minister Berihun's office, he was wracked with dread, they could see it on his face. "Come in boys, we have some terrible news."

The trio took their seats in the office as Dr. Berihun took a blunt out of the desk in front of him. He lit it and began talking. "We are headed to dire times, my friends. It appears the Khalifa and Zone leader Malik Jabbar are none too happy with our treatment of the Muslims in our nation. Instead of coming to our aid to end the protests, they have decided to call a Jihad against us. They are asking every able-bodied Muslim man to join a great army to vanquish once and for all the Christian forces in Africa. They want to unite all the brown people of the world under a common Muslim banner, from the Middle East down through Africa. It is part of his grand Muslim vision for the future.

"I, however, think this entire thing was a ploy to secure the dark matter resources for themselves now that the price of oil is dropping. I knew something was fishy once the protests started up."

The prime minister took a couple hits from the blunt and passed it. James spoke up, "What are we going to do now about protecting ourselves? The nation of Ethiopia, as strong a history of military success as they have, will not be able to repel a mighty Jihadi army of millions of fanatical Muslims."

"Yes, I have come to that conclusion as well. Soon we will take off for a recruitment trip all around Africa to ask strong black men to protect their Holy Land from the Islamic forces. Prepare your things, we will be leaving tomorrow."

"Oh Freddy baby I just heard about the Jihad declared by the new Khalifa this morning. Is there anything you can do to stop it?"

"Unfortunately I am not in a position to force change right now. We cannot enact an embargo against Zone Five because we are in Zone Five. We have to placate to the locals while still trying to respect Ethiopia's right to the dark matter through UN sponsored elections. I am worried about Malik Jabbar, the Zone Five leader. He is young and foolish, and too quick to resort to war for his own personal gain. I have no idea why Lenz would pick such a person. He may have seemed like a great neutral choice in a region divided by sectarian strife, but he should have looked at his quick rise to power at only twenty-eight and seen the warning signs. He never was going to be happy just ruling Five. He wanted more from the start. If I didn't know any better, I would think he staged those riots and protests in Ethiopia just to give the Khalifa a reason to declare war."

"You must not say these things to anyone but me Freddy, promise me that. If he gains as much power as he wants you might be working for him one day. Do not give anyone a reason to distrust you in these dark times. You must try to remain neutral politically and only show an outward focus on research and technology."

"If it were not for stupid religion, none of this would even be happening."

"Do not say that! You have come so far in your pursuit of Christ. Do not let the devil sway you in these horrible times. I need you to stay strong for me."

"It is hard to have faith in a loving and forgiving Lord when He sends His own people to kill and be killed in His name."

"The devil and his minions have gotten into these people, Muslim and Christian. These black Christians of Ethiopia may think they are doing the Lord's work, but they follow a false prophet. They must only turn to the Lord and his angels, not to the power of fallen angels and evil spirits hidden in the background of their movements."

"In these beautifully dark times, people will turn to anything that gives them purpose beyond living another meaningless life. Everyone wants to be great, and everyone wants to make a name for themselves. It is the pride of man that will be our downfall."

"Freddy, the love of my life, you must not forget the Lord. He sent His only Son to die on the cross for us to be saved. That is the only thing that matters, not science or war. Please do not forget that as we travel through life together. I pray every day that war can be avoided and man can live in peace, but the Lord knows that we are wicked at heart. He foretold our demise in the Bible for all to heed its warnings. Unfortunately, we ignore what is given to us right in our face. I want you to see what I see Freddy. I want you to open your heart to the Lord Freddy. He is at your doorstep begging to come in."

"I have to be honest my love, I do not have room for Jesus right now. I did my best in going to church and trying to learn about God but it just isn't satisfying me at all. Maybe I will come back to it another day."

"I am not going to give up on you, Frederick Slater, I love you."

Freddy looked her deep in her sparkling eyes. "I love you t…." Just then there was a loud knock on the door. "Professor! Professor! The council is having an emergency meeting right now as we speak, you must come now. There was a big discovery at the Observatory."

Freddy opened the door to speak to the messenger. "OK tell them I will get ready and be right there."

Freddy kissed his wife and got ready in the bathroom as his wife put his clothes out. He got dressed and went off to the Council Chambers. When he got there, the aids were running in and out of the doors and a sparkle of excitement was in the air.

"Freddy, we are glad to see you! Please sit down so I can break the good news to you." Freddy sat down and Lenz sat down as well. The other council members also took their seats and everyone ushered all of the aids out of the room. "Professor, we believe we have found an almost limitless supply of dark matter on Mars. One of our telescope operators saw the glow under the surface of the Red Planet. We confirmed it earlier today. All of our worries of over production are over Freddy! Now we have the needed political pressure to get the extra funding from major countries to sponsor a fleet of dark energy powered space shuttles produced here at the UN Capital."

Freddy had the widest grin in the room as this fascinating news really sank in. "I cannot believe all of this is happening so fast. Mars is the first planet we colonize, and there will be many more. There is no telling how much dark matter there is scattered throughout our solar system. This is a great day for the world amid so much bad news with the pending war. Let the press know if you haven't already. We want all neutral countries to heavily invest in a neutral UN space mining program. Every country will benefit from this so I do not think we will see any hesitation. Are there any new developments arising in Ethiopia?"

"Unfortunately no, I do not see a resolution coming to this at all. Neither side is interested in sitting down for a talk. Prime Minister Berihun believes he is destined by God to rule the Black Holy Land, and the Khalifa believes he was sent by God to spread and protect Islam around the world. It is hard to get people to the table when they both believe their God is going to win. I could only imagine what the world would be like with no God controlling the masses."

"I was just talking about that. I don't understand why each person's God has to command them to kill and hate the other for not believing the same way they do. I tried giving faith a chance and my heart is faltering. I really want to see God in my heart, Lenz. There is so much hate in the world right now, we need a loving God to come and save us from ourselves."

"I pray every day for the Lord's salvation, Professor. You must start to pray, not for yourself, but for the world."

"I go back and forth every day but I will try, for you and my wife and myself."

The meeting continued with phone calls to world leaders and planning for the space shuttle launch. They set a date for December 11th to be the day the shuttles launch. The entire world was excited for the Mars trip. Scientists and engineers from all nations would assist the astronauts with construction and extraction. The fleet would be thirty full sized dark energy powered space shuttles. They would be state-of-the-art technological marvels, with each capable of sustaining human life on board for ten years. This would be a truly global effort.

Chapter 20

James, Justin, and Abal waited outside the conference room with the other clerics as the meeting between Prime Minister Berihun, Zone Nine Leader Nazmi Cutar, Zone Ten Leader Yando Illidasy, along with several other top African politicians and pro-Christian generals was beginning to heat up. They could hear intense arguing between the men as they argued over the fate of Africa. An hour of top level negotiations ended and the parties came out of the room all smiling and giving positive vibes. Everyone left and the clerics came into the room to speak with the prime minister. "What news of the rest of Africa, Prime Minister?" one of the elder clerics asked the doctor.

"They all see how valuable the rise of the new Ethiopia has been to their countries and pocket books, and they want nothing more than to see us continue to thrive as a free black Christian nation. They will send us all the troops and supplies we need to defend North Africa from the Arab heathen invaders. By the power of Christ, they will be repelled and Horus will come to lead us to a great victory. I pray every day to have his presence revealed to me. It will come to me my Nagas, it will come to me."

The clerics, James, and Abal all went over the meeting with Prime Minister Berihun and they left feeling as though they accomplished what they set out for during this trip to South Africa. Their flight was leaving in four hours back to Addis Ababa so the Order and their two companions enjoyed a nice dinner and spoke of the grand future that the Lord was bringing to the black race.

Their flight was a long one, but they were all glad to make it back to home base. As they exited the plane there was a huge crowd of reporters waiting for them. James looked at Justin and said, "Something has happened while we were on the flight."

As Prime Minister Berihun came off the plane the reporters pummeled him with a barrage of questions. "What are your feelings on the discovery of the Naga Temple in India?"

"Do you feel like this justifies your message even more now that the Naga Temple has been discovered?"

The Prime Minister waved off all of these questions. "I have been asleep during my entire flight. I was not made aware of any discovery. What is the news from India?"

A middle-aged hardnosed reporter spoke up first. "Well sir, the Indian authorities have been notified of a great discovery. Developers were clearing out a dense patch of jungle for housing development when they came across a Naga temple. The temple had detailed maps of their holdings and churches all throughout the world. It depicts everything you said, Prime Minister. The Naga really were the rulers of India and worshipped by people all around the world. They discovered the New World and their origins were African. It is all detailed in the writings and carvings in the walls."

Dr. Berihun clapped his hands and shouted, "Lord be praised!" There were congratulations passed around between the clerics as another one of Dr. Berihun's messages has come to be the truth. He turned to the reporters and said to them, "My Nagas, go tell your newspapers that I said today is another glorious day in the eyes of the Lord of the black race. All the knowledge and power that was stolen from us will be returned. We are coming back to claim what is ours on this earth. Our history can no longer be wiped away by the lighter races. We are once again proven to be exactly who I said we are. Celebrate my Nagas, shout out to the stars that the black man is returning to his former glory."

As James, Justin, and Abal left the small press conference and headed toward the car, a beautiful woman reporter caught all of their attention. She came up to the trio and said, "I always see you all on TV with Dr. Berihun, are you very close to him?"

"Yes we are. We are all working for him in some capacity."

"How exciting! I would love to get closer to him for my work. Would you mind if we went out to dinner some time so we could talk about the Order of Horus and have some fun?"

Justin could see in her eyes that it was her intention to not only get information but to seduce him. "No thank you dear. I am really trying to focus on my studies and prepare for the impending war."

"Well, here is my card if you ever want to hang out." She gave him her card and walked away.

James looked astonished by Justin's actions. "Damn, she was fine cousin. What has gotten into you?"

"It is no more time for childish games, James. It is time to start growing up and being true to my word. Much like what happened with you with that Mexican girl in LA, sleeping with Nancy has been eating at my soul. If I am going to be a great cleric, it is time to start acting like one."

"I am glad to hear that cousin, I really am. Let us go celebrate the new you with a nice lunch and a fat blunt."

They left the airport and got lunch, gaining strength in themselves as their faith in Dr. Berihun and Ethiopia's future was rising in the face of impending war.

It was the last Saturday in October and Jose took a break from the action on the Hill to visit his family and friends in Dallas. He saw his friends and his mother on Friday, and had a planned dinner with Jay and Domenica at Domenica's house. When he arrived he could see a cloud of smoke coming from the backyard. Jose went to the side gate and saw Jay smoking a blunt on the back patio. "Just in time," Jose said as he came over to Jay while she passed him the blunt. Jose was thinking about how good Jay looked in the warm fall sunset.

"I have great news to share with you and Domenica when we get inside."

"Oh really, I can't wait to hear it!"

They finished the blunt and talked outside for fifteen minutes to air out a bit before they went inside. When they got inside Domenica was happy to see Jose. "Oh my dear you snuck in through the back, huh? I was waiting for the doorbell to ring."

He gave her a great hug and Jose and Jay took their seat at the table while Domenica got the food from the kitchen and brought it out to the table. After all the food had been set Domenica took her place at the head of the table and they prayed over the food. During the prayer, Jose thought that Domenica was taking a long time. When the prayer was over, Domenica turned to Jose and said, "Sorry if I took a long time. I know how annoying that can be when someone prays your ear off."

"Oh no it was fine," Jose said. He quickly changed the subject. "So my big news is this: I did not tell either of you that I was getting an MRI to check the status of the MS and Lord be praised, it is all gone! The doctor was astonished! I told him I was healed by the power of Jesus. He shook my hand and said congratulations. It was one of the best days of my life so far."

"That is amazing news Jose! Your faith has been rewarded. That means you are growing in strength and heading toward the Light. Just keep being diligent with your studies, the Lord will continue to speak to you and bless you."

"Thank you, Grandma Domenica. I wouldn't have gotten healed without you. I am growing in faith and I can feel myself becoming more spiritually aware. The Lord is speaking to me all the time and I now know how to listen."

They continued talking and eating, and Jose could swear he was picking up on small signals the two ladies were giving him, but he attributed the confusion to the pot that he had just smoked or that maybe he was just thinking too hard. The night ended with Jose saying goodbye to the two ladies. He made his way back to his condo, and made his way through the garage to the front desk. As he approached he saw the doorman Earl Johnson laughing with another resident. When they saw Jose approaching the resident quickly left, laughing. Jose thought it was weird and that they may have been talking about him, but he gave Earl the same welcoming smile he always gave him.

"Good evening, Congressman. I hope you had a great night. I hope you don't take offense to my laughing. I was just joking with Aaron about this chick I was with last night."

Jose thought it was weird that Earl would say something that corresponded to what he was thinking a few seconds prior. Suddenly the thought of Earl with an ugly woman flashed across his mind, as Earl was not exactly a lady-killer in physique. Earl continued to smile as Jose turned the corner toward the elevator. "Punk ass pussy," Jose heard it quietly but he could make out the sounds that sounded like punk ass pussy. He immediately turned back to Earl to confront him, but when he turned the corner Earl had already started talking with another resident. Jose went up to him. "Did you say something to me? Did you just call me a pussy?"

Earl was shocked and immediately put his hands up in protest. "No, sir! Never would I say anything bad about you, Hero. You are my friend."

"Yeah that is what I thought too, Earl. I am sorry for getting confused. I must have just had a long week." Jose was confused even more and he retired to his room. The way people were speaking to him was weird but Jose tried not to think much of it as he tried to sleep that night. His thoughts kept ranging back to Jay and his growing love for everything about her.

The Mexican Congress would come back in session at the middle of next month, so Jose was mentally preparing himself to fight his next fight, by getting the Mexican Congress to enact a forced installation of government monitored X-chips to every returned illegal immigrant. Jose was up for the task, and if his recent success in the American Congress showed anything, it was that Jose was on top of the political world in North America.

"Here is where the final launch site will be," one of the UN engineers told Freddy and Lenz as they walked the shuttle site.

"Everything looks spectacular," Freddy said. "You all did a wonderful job of following my specs for the shuttle. This is going to be one of the most exciting days of my life. We finally have the power to reach Mars safely, and we are doing it to benefit all of mankind."

"None of this would be possible without you, sir. From the entire staff, thank you," Lenz said.

"I appreciate your kindness, and you are welcome. Now tell me more about the shuttles. December 11th is so close that I can picture the shuttles flying right now."

"Well we have 15 colony shuttles which will hold the Mars staff, six drill support shuttles, and nine dark matter storage shuttles. All of the staff has been adequately trained and everyone is in final preparations for these last three weeks until the shuttles launch."

"Excellent news, everything is going smoothly and a lot of that is thanks to you. Now Lenz tell me, what is the current news from the Zone Five, Nine, and Ten leaders?"

"Well production has been running smoothly in Zone Five, and Israel is really in a boom. Thousands upon thousands of Palestinians are moving out and they are being replaced by returning Jews from around the world. There is plenty of work in the extraction process now that wealth is spreading to neighboring countries. War is still on the mind of Malik Jabbar, the Zone Five leader. I have been talking to him almost daily about ways to avoid it, but he says he cannot control the actions of an acting Khalifa. He put him in office to rule of the Muslim faith, and that is exactly what he is doing. Malik feels powerless to stop him and upset the ravenous Muslim populations in the Middle East. Zone Nine Leader Nazmi Cutar and Zone Ten Leader Yando Illidasy both have pledged to support Ethiopia's cause.

"The entire continent of Africa that is not mired already in religious violence will send men and arms to the Northern Front. This is turning into a mighty clash of religions and all the men in charge feel powerless to stop it. The Muslims have been on the verge of complete war for decades. They just needed a leader to combine them into one force again. That could have been the worst mistake I have made in my political life, letting Malik create a new Caliphate."

"No one could have seen this coming. Ethiopia has always been a beacon for religious harmony. It should be no surprise the lure of dark matter's power and wealth changed the sympathies of the Muslim minority."

"Freddy, please pray for the world."

"I will."

Chapter 21

"What time are they arriving at my office?" Jose questioned his chief of staff Chester Begg as he was putting on his tie in the back of the limo.

"They should be there in about fifteen minutes. We will beat them there."

They were driving through the streets of D.C. near the Capitol trying to get to the security clearance gate. "This is the final step of my first agenda in Congress. I think I have the political power to get this done. Mexicans have been in love with me ever since I brought the UN manufacturing center to Mexico City."

"Just be careful in how you phrase yourself, sir", Chester said. "No using the term illegals. It is highly offensive to Mexican people. If you want to get them to force install the X-chip on people, you must bow to their Mexican pride. This will help both countries so that is the message you need to sell."

"I think I am ready, Chester."

They pulled up to the curb and Jose and Chester got out. They made their way to the office and made sure everything was set up for their visitors. The top Mexican Congressmen came into the office and went in the back room with Jose. The dashing young Texas Congressman worked his magic on these men for an hour, selling them on the short and long term benefits of X-chip investment in their country. The Mexican Congressmen were already impressed with Jose from afar, but up close and personal he wowed them out of their pants. They left the office promising to get the legislation passed.

By the beginning of the next week the bill was passed through the Mexican government and signed by their president. Jose just secured himself a major ally of the X-chip and the American Protectorate, and further entered into Mexico's heart as their long lost American son.

Freddy and Jennifer were standing with Lenz and his wife on the audience watching platform talking about the future of dark matter as the countdown began. The crowd all turned toward the shuttle field, where each of the shuttles was in launching position from their launching pads. The crew was all set inside of each shuttle and they all gave the go-ahead. "This is it Lenz, the beginning of the colonization of the universe for mankind. The future is in our grasp."

The countdown ended and the first shuttle took off, followed shortly by the next in line until they were all launched and out into space. It was an amazing sight, seeing another one of mankind's great achievements bursting into the empty space of the heavens to settle on a distant planet. "Let's hope that as long as the Mars dark matter extraction stays in UN hands, the countries of the world will not feel the need to fight over it," Freddy said dauntingly. "When there is money involved, anything is possible. Let's just hope and pray for the best."

James and Abal came into the office to pick up Justin after his duties for the day. Dr. Berihun saw them when he came out of his office and called James back with him. "You are just the man I want to see, James."

They walked into his office and the prime minister told James to take a seat. "I really like what you have done with the website, James. I hear we are getting tons of hits and people trying to sign up for the Army on the government website. People are coming in the thousands from all around Africa to protect the black Holy Land. The problem is the Caliphate's army is growing much faster than ours. Reports are that their army is in the tens of millions and they are mobilizing in Jordan. Apparently the Jewish Prime Minister, Adiel Tuchman, has signed an agreement with the Khalifa to allow the Muslim army to march through their borders. This is a setup for a formal non-aggression treaty to be signed after the end of the war. We cannot rely on our Jewish brothers to come to our protection; the entire world has betrayed us. We are on our own James, just us great Naga people against the world of hate and jealousy. We will stand and fight with the Lord on our side."

"Do you have any idea when they are going to attack?"

"All reports from our spies indicate a New Year's day attack on Egypt. Our army will be there to meet them head-on. We may lack the numbers compared to them but we have the Lord Christ fighting for us."

James looked nervously at the prime minister. "I will pray every day for our safety. If the Lord truly desires us to be great again, He will assuredly grant us a great victory in the field."

"Get your rest, James. We mobilize the Army in Egypt over the next few weeks and we will join them for a massive rally to celebrate our Lord and Savior Jesus Christ before the great battle for the reign of the black man to begin."

"Are all the security check points cleared?" James asked as Justin was walking through the security detail of new clerics checking to make sure they were all stationed and checking the crowds appropriately.

"Every person in the staging area has been checked with a metal detector. I can promise you, the only people with weapons in here are the clerics," Justin said. He was talking to James and Abal as they made their way back up to the front of the stage. Justin had grown in importance in the Order over the last few months. His physical skill in combat was impressive, and although his military strategy was slow coming he was gaining confidence. He was sure that Dr. Berihun considered him a valuable asset to the Order. "You two go over into the crowd so I can take my position on the stage."

James and Abal left Justin and went over to Lilly. James was nervous but on this important day he felt it was time to finally make the move on Lilly. He told Abal of his plans. "Hey Abal, I am going to ask Lilly out on a date after the battle is over. We have been getting really close and I just think we really connect on a deeper level."

"Well I cannot blame you, James. She is very beautiful and intelligent. Just be careful, you do not know where the loyalty of her heart lies. She is a heartbreaker that one, and the last thing I want to see is you get hurt. You are my friend and I want to protect you."

"I understand your concern, Abal, but you have to trust me on this. I know she is the right one for me."

"I will support you. Go talk to her, I will distract her friends."

The pair went up to the group of girls and James asked for Lilly to talk to him personally away from the group. "Hey, Lilly, how was your flight up here?"

"It was a terrible flight to a terrible place. War is an awful thing, but Lord willing we will prevail so no one will ever stand to our people again. I am glad to see you though James because your face warms my heart."

"I am glad to see you too. Words cannot express how your face brightens my spirits."

"That is very kind of you, James. What did you bring me over here for? Is there something you wanted to tell me?"

"Well, I have been putting a lot of thought into you Lilly, and I think we have grown really close over the last year. I am interested in getting to know you even more. I would like to take you out on a date after all of this terrible war business is over with."

"Oh my James that sounds wonderful but I just do not think I can do that. It has nothing to do with you. It is all about me. I am marked as an Order Princess. I can only marry a Great Prophet. If you want to spend time getting to know each other better, I am all for it. Unfortunately, we cannot turn it into a romantic situation as much as I would truly enjoy that. I have had feelings for you for a long time now, James. If I could date you I would, but my father and the Order would never approve."

"Well that is an awful shame. As much as it pains me to hear you are interested in me too, I understand if the obligations to the Order prevent you from dating me. I do not want to cross your father the wrong way."

"Thank you for understanding. We can talk more after the speech is over. I think my father is making his way to the stage right now."

Dr. Berihun made his way to the podium and quieted the crowd.

"Today is a great day for God's peoples, my Nagas. The Lord has delivered my message into reality once again. He gave me a great vision this morning, a vision of victory on the battlefield. A victory led by the great Horus that he promised would return to lead our people to greatness. He showed me his face and I immediately recognized him. He is among the crowd right now. He is actually among my very staff. He has done great work for me, growing in physical and mental strength every day since I met him. The man who the Lord revealed to me as Horus is..."

"Wait!" Karlo Staggs, one of the most senior clerics in the Order, came off from the side of the stage and approached the prime minister. "Before you finish I have something to tell the crowd."

"OK come forward my Naga, be in haste though please."

He came up to the mic and spoke to the crowd. "I have not been a Christian my entire life. I converted after I met the good doctor here. He is a great man who has done and said wonderful things about our people. Unfortunately, my real faith had a calling to me last night, and I must do what I can to return to the arms of Allah. It starts by killing this Infidel. Allah Akbar!"

He pulled a gun from his waist and shot Dr. Berihun in the chest and stomach several times before Justin and several other clerics were able to shoot Karlo down. The doctor fell to the ground and Justin and the other clerics came up to him to give him aid.

"Go get a doctor damnit!" Justin yelled as Dr. Berihun lay clutching to life. In his last few breaths of life, he grabbed Justin and pulled him close whispering in his ear. The all- inclusive African crowd watched in horror as the doctor died right in front of them. Justin sat emotionless from the news he heard from the doctor's dying gasp. He stood from their dead leader and approached the microphone. "He said I am Horus."

James and Abal walked into the command center in Cairo. People were running everywhere yelling over each other, giving constant reports from the battle field. The shelling from the Khalifa's Army had begun and Justin was making the final preparations on his battle plans. "Reinforce squadron two with more armor, and ready the reserves because the artillery shelling will be brutal."

Justin was standing strong in his customary cleric black suit. His jacket was sprawled on a nearby table and his sleeves were rolled up. His muscles were pulsating with the fervor of the moment. The shelling continued for an hour before reports of gunfire came through. Skirmishes were breaking out all throughout the warzone. "We must hold them here! If they break out into Africa it will spell doom for us. Muslims from the interior will join their cause and it will be an unbreakable wave. Tell our men to be strong!"

More and more reports were coming in with news of heavy casualties. The generals on the ground were giving orders, but the superior fighting force was breaking the will of the African defenders. The sounds of retreating forces filled the airways as the Muslim fighters broke through the lines with armor and men. "How are things going in the skies? India was kind enough to give up planes and pilots, so are we making the most of them?"

One of his generals spoke up. "We have lost air superiority, Great Prophet."

"Jesus Christ," Justin yelled in anger. "We must bring in all reserves of men and armor, if we don't hold them off here, we never will."

James and Abal were watching from the corner, listening in horror to the reports of death and destruction at the hands of the Black Flag Jihadi army. The reserves all across the front moved into action, but were quickly repelled. As the battle lay lost, Justin sounded the full retreat. "We must retreat back to the Holy Land, and hope that more forces come to our aid and that the Lord will have a miracle for us still." The message went out and the entire military encampment packed up for a speedy retreat to Ethiopia.

Chapter 22

It had already been a special Friday night for Jose and Juanita, but he was ready to top it off with the most important part of the night. They walked through the park on their way back to the car. There was a large rainbow lit fountain in the middle of the park on the way to the car, and Jose knew exactly when it was going to turn on. He walked Jay to the middle of the park and just before the fountain came on, he grabbed her hands and looked deep into her eyes. "Ever since you came up to me at my first American Protectorate meeting, a minute has not gone by where I don't think of you. We have spent all of this time together growing in friendship, but I feel like we have reached our peak in that area. I want us to move on to what I feel like we should have done months ago. I am interested in you as more than a friend and I am not going to hesitate any more to tell you. I want to date you. I want you to be mine. I have done all I can to prove I am a good man, now it is up to you to decide if you want me to be that special person in your life."

The fountain came on and lit up the night with amazing colors and a spectacular water display. "Oh this is so beautiful, my Hero. I didn't know you had it in you to plan all this." Tears exited her eyes and she came in quickly and gave Jose a love-filled kiss. "I know what my heart is telling me, but my head is telling me something different."

"What is the problem? I will do anything to have you."

"Well, I am not comfortable sharing that information with you yet, but let's just say my 'real' dating is very selective. I am only allowed to marry certain people due to my Order obligations. However, my loving Hero, I have faith in you. I believe you are something special, more than just the average man. You are going to do great things for this world Jose, and I would love to be by your side."

They kissed deeply again and after a long embrace, they walked to the car so Jose could take her back to her hotel room in Dallas. "Let me turn on the radio and spark a blunt." She flipped through the station and got to a new song on the radio Jose had not heard before. As she smoked, he began listening to the lyrics. "I come to you and draw you in, fill your world with lust and sin. Now you are finally mine my sweet, your soul is fresh and ripe to eat."

Jose was shaken by these lyrics. "Shake your booty girls, get that man to drool. Make him become the devil's tool."

Jay was smiling at Jose with a menacing look as Jose quickly turned the station. "I didn't like that song," he said as he tried to play it off.

"I could tell, put it on something you like."

He flipped through the stations and put it on a song he had heard before and thought he knew, but never really listened to the lyrics. "Join the movement lost ones, we are what you are searching for. Turn your hearts toward heaven and pray for the Lord." Jose thought to himself, "Oh a nice song about the Lord, this will calm me down." The song continued as a mix of beats, "Heaven is here and the Lord rules over Earth, now is the time to prove what you are worth." The song went into a mix of melodies and beats and left Jose thinking. "The Lord does not rule over Earth, the devil does. Oh no", he exclaimed to himself. "This is the devil's music. It is the devil everywhere."

He opened his eyes wide but tried to stay calm. He looked over at Jay who was already staring at him with a smile on her face. Jose turned off the radio. "No more radio for tonight, let's just focus on me and you for the drive home."

They pulled on the freeway and in a few minutes were in downtown Dallas where the hotel was located. Jose was thinking about if the night would lead to more than kissing when he dropped her off. Just as he was about to turn his mind from the subject and try to remain a gentleman, Jay spoke up, "What are you doing for the rest of the night?"

Jose answered, "Going over some notes for a speech I have to give on the Russia and Ukraine issue in the Foreign Affairs committee on Monday."

"You are more than welcome to come up if you were thinking about it."

Jose did not know what to say. It was exactly what he wanted and exactly what he had been thinking. He hesitated, feeling uneasy about the entire situation because his head was just not in the right place. "My mind has been playing tricks on me all night. I think I am going to head home for the night. We will have plenty of time to spend more nights together getting to know each other. No need to rush a great thing."

Jay looked at him, surprised, disappointed, but willing to concede the fight for another night. "I care a lot about you, Hero. This is one of the happiest days of my life. Please drive home safely."

Jose pulled into the roundabout in the entrance of the hotel and got out and opened Jay's car door. They walked up to the front doors, and they embraced once again with a soft kiss and a goodbye. There weren't any people out there at the time but as Jay walked in and when Jose turned back to his car, an SUV pulled up. Out of the passenger seat, the man got out and instantly recognized Jose. He came up to him and shook his hand, "You are doing great thing for this country, Sir, please keep up the good work."

"I appreciate your support, thank you for the kind words."

He turned and walked away, and Jose heard, "He must be a faggot for not fucking Jay tonight."

He yelled out to the man, "What did you say?"

The man turned around and said, "Nothing, Congressman. Why? Did you hear something? It might have been my brother's car radio."

Jose put his hand on his head and shook it in confusion. He knew what he heard but it didn't appear as if he heard it from the man. "No I am sorry, I just partied too much tonight. Thank you again and have a great night." Jose went home, with the radio off, and tried to get to sleep as fast as possible to forget about all the confusing things happening to him.

"Where are the men that Yando Illidasy promised me?" Justin wanted to know.

"We already sent them in, Great Prophet. Our armies are being soundly defeated."

Just when things could not get any worse for James, in came Lilly to talk to Justin. As she moved her voluptuous body through the room, no one was looking at her, only attending to their tasks. She looked right into James' eyes and mouthed the words, "I love you" and "I'm sorry." She walked up to Justin and interrupted his thoughts. "Great Prophet, I come to you in the memory of my father. He raised me to be a Princess of the Order, and my first obligation is to marry a Great Prophet. Please Great Prophet, do my father one final honor and declare me to be your loving wife. I have trained my entire life to serve you. I must marry the Great Prophet. It is my destiny."

Justin seemed incredibly torn and unsure with this information. He looked at James for some sort of clearance to say OK to Lilly, knowing his deep affection for her. James just nodded his head, knowing he could not change the will of the Lord. His destiny was not to be with Lilly, and sooner or later he would have to get that through his head. Who was he compared to a Great Prophet? James just sighed and looked into Lilly's eyes.

Justin turned back to the woman. "In your father's memory, I will take your hand in marriage. We will retreat back to the next military installment, and there we will be wed," he said.

"Go your way; your father lives. That is what I heard in my dream last night. What do you think it means?" Jose and Jay were out to dinner Saturday night. It had been two weeks since he asked her out at the fountain park.

"The Lord is trying to communicate with you again. You are becoming a seer just like my grandmother said. The déjà vu was a true sign that you are a seer. Now that you are getting closer to the Lord He is trying to give you visions and messages. I do not know the meaning of this dream but I am sure my grandmother can help us."

They continued eating and talking about their respective jobs, when Jose started feeling uncomfortable again. He kept feeling like people were giving him evil looks, piercing into his soul. He was also hearing weird things from the people who were walking by his table. He tried his best to block it out and finish dinner.

When they got to Domenica's house it was very late. The pair had been out eating and drinking and talking at night. Despite the late time, Domenica was at the door waiting for them as they walked up to the house. "Jose, my dear, I have something urgent to tell you. I was reading my Bible and the Holy Spirit cried out to me to give you a message."

"What is it, Grandma Domenica?"

"Go your way; your son lives. Does that passage from John 4:50 mean anything to you?"

"Wow," Jose was left wide-mouthed.

Jay spoke up for him. "He had a dream with almost that exact passage in his head. A voice told him, 'Go your way; your father lives.' What do you think it means?"

"Well the story in the Bible is of a man who begs Jesus to come to his dead child. Jesus, feeling as though the man was doubting His ability to perform miracles under any circumstances, told the man He need not come to his child's aid because his child lived. The man believed the word of the Lord and his faith was rewarded with the revival of his son. What the Lord is telling you is that He will revive the presence of your father in your life, if you only believe his existence to be true. Have faith in the Lord and what He is trying to tell you. As you become the seer you are destined to become, you must learn to trust the Lord regardless of what He tells you. It doesn't matter how amazing or painful the message, you must accept it."

"I do not know where my life would be without you, Domenica."

"We were meant to meet each other, always remember that."

Chapter 23

"The ETA of their arrival on the surface is thirty minutes, Professor," said one of the members of the shuttle management team back in Baghdad. The dramatic increase in flight speed from the dark matter engines held true to Freddy's expectations. This was the day that the entire world had waited for these last two months. Man will have finally conquered its first planet. The countdown neared zero and the reports from the astronauts guiding the thirty shuttles were that all landing mechanisms were deployed. As reports came in from each shuttle with a successful landing update, the crowd of managers and scientists in the Baghdad control center did not celebrate until the last shuttle touched down successfully. "Congratulations men, now is the dawn of the new age of man!"

Everyone came up and shook Freddy's hand and popped champagne bottles. Jennifer celebrated the success of her husband's endeavor, but deep down inside, she knew that the Lord was not happy with him and his science. She only hoped that Jesus could truly find his way inside of his heart for good before it was too late. His faith was not strong enough to fight off an attack on the Lord if that day should come.

"We are on our last leg, Great Prophet. The men are exhausted, beaten, and bruised of body and spirit. We have been waiting for deliverance by our one true Lord Jesus Christ, but we continue to suffer. Men doubt you, men doubt the Lord. We have many deserters who have converted to Islam and left for the Jihadi army. What are we going to do?"

Justin looked to the sky and then looked at James. He closed his eyes and shook his head. "We must fight to the last man., I still have faith that the Lord will restore our cause."

"Well just in case sir, we must prepare plans to put you in hiding. We have been developing a top secret series of safe houses and communications outlets all throughout Africa to hide you if we lose the southern half of Africa. We must not let you leave Africa. People will turn from you in the thousands if you flee. We must keep you safe and in hiding until we can gather the strength to take back what is ours."

Justin looked at Mendeli and thanked him for his kind words, then he looked at James and Abal. "I just hope the Lord sees that in my heart I believe I am doing the right thing. Always remember that everyone, I am only following the feelings the Lord put in my heart. I cannot betray my heart."

"We stand by you, Great Prophet, to the death if need be. You are our great savior!" Mendeli roused up the crowd in the room to begin chanting for Justin. He smiled and accepted their praise, knowing that he had to continue on being strong as the Great Prophet of Africa.

As Jose and Jay were walking through the condo parking lot, they could not keep their hands off each other. They kissed the entire way to the elevator and up to the room. Jose was thinking to himself, "Is this finally it?"

Jay whispered in his ear, "Yes."

Jose did not know what she was saying yes to since he did not say anything. Once again, Jose decided he needed to stay grounded in reality. "People cannot hear what you think, Jose. Get a grip on yourself," Jose shouted in his head. Jay could tell he was distracted from kissing her,

"Is everything OK, my Hero?"

"Everything is fine baby, let's go inside." He unlocked his door and they went inside and sat on the couch. Jay leaned on his shoulder and just enjoyed his warmth. Jose was turning on the cable box so he could find music. Jay sat up and looked at him and smiled. Jose smiled back and turned away to the television to find a station. "Here is a good one," Jose said. It was slow jams, perfect for the mood that was set in the room. The tension of the situation could be cut with a knife. Jose came in for the kill, starting to nibble and suck on her neck. It was her weak spot and she instantly became prepared for the situation. He stood her up and started to undress her and himself while continuing to kiss on her neck. Their bodies were close to each other and they were breathing in unison as the moment heated up. Jose's belt was undone and he stepped out of his pants. Jay took initiative and kissed down his body to pleasure him.

Jose's eyes rolled into the back of his head. This was one of the best moments in his life since he had waited so long to service this woman. She stood up and led him naked through the condo to the bedroom. She laid him on the bed with his manhood reaching for the stars. She climbed aboard his saddle facing the opposite direction. That was when Jose first noticed the birthmark of a star on her right shoulder blade. There was no doubt that it was a star, and it was not a tattoo. Jose could clearly see it in the moon light. His mind turned to other more pressing matters and he focused his mind and body on pleasuring his new girlfriend. The sex went on for several sessions over several hours, a clear release of all the sexual tension that had built up since they first met.

Just after they finished Jose heard a noise like someone was talking through the walls, loud neighbors he guessed. Then he could clearly hear, "So he must not be a faggot."

Jose listened more intently to see where the sound came from, but he could not pinpoint it. He just figured it was the neighbor talking shit. He asked Jay to confirm. "Did you hear someone talking just a second ago?"

"No, my Hero, I only hear our heartbeats and our breathing. Is everything OK? You have been asking that question a lot lately."

"I really cannot tell you if everything is OK. Let me be perfectly honest, I have been hearing a lot of crazy stuff lately. People are looking at me different, I can hear people saying nasty things about me, and sometimes when I ask them to repeat what they said to my face, they say they didn't hear anything. I have been ignoring it for months now. I just attributed it to too much stress or stopping my MS medicine."

"Oh my baby, that is not good at all. We need to keep a close eye on this to make sure it does not get worse. Now stop worrying about things out of your control and give me a kiss. I am dead tired. Let's go to sleep."

Jose gave her a sensual kiss and they embraced naked under the sheets as they slept the passion off.

Chapter 24

All of the reporters were flashing their cameras and yelling out in English to get the professor's attention. He raised his hands and quieted the crowd so he could speak. "Thank you for coming today for my announcement. We have been working very hard here at the dark matter research lab, and our hard work has paid off. I would like to announce to you and the world that we have developed the first personal flying car."

The crowd of reporters erupted into applause at the great news. "It is dark energy powered, and will take the environment destroying automobile off our roads forever. We will produce them cheaply at every manufacturing center around the world, ready for distribution by the end of next month. We found a way to harness the power of dark matter to reverse the gravitational pull of any dark energy powered craft. From large to small, anything can float and be powered to move, all by dark energy."

The flashbulbs flashed and the crowd crowed over the news of the new personal transportation device. The more Freddy hoped his inventions would change the world, the more the world stayed the same. More wars over resources and gods, things would never change unless someone had the courage to try and stop it. Maybe one day Freddy would step in and lead the world to a better place, but he was comfortable where he was and did not want any major changes disrupting his current run of success.

James, Justin, Abal, and Lilly were all on the run through the secret backdoor channels set up by the clerics all throughout Africa. The African Freedom Army had been soundly defeated, and the Order of Horus disbanded. Only a few hundred clerics stayed loyal to the Great Prophet, still believing he would deliver them a great victory one day. One day yes, but it would not be anytime soon. Millions of strong young black men had perished on the battle field and there was no replacing them any time soon. Malik Jabbar ruled over Africa now, and he turned his sights to India and Bua Phan, leader of Zone Seven, South East Asia. He and India had contributed major military aid to the African Freedom Army, and Malik Jabbar and the Khalifa decided that they deserved to be conquered as well for aiding the anti-Muslim Ethiopians. So the Zone Five/Caliphate Army spread through Africa to control the population, and the remaining forces marched toward India with a renewed sense of purpose.

Jay and Jose came into Domenica's house on that mid-April Sunday to try and receive some good spirit into Jose's heart. Ever since he got healed from MS he had been under attack mentally. He had increasingly had trouble getting a grasp on reality. Jay set up this prayer meeting for him to help get his mind and his soul back on track to receiving the Light.

"Welcome my dears, come on in. I am so happy to see you but unfortunately it is for the wrong reasons. We will get you back on the right path my son, just have faith." They came inside and she made everyone a cup of coffee. They gathered around the table and Domenica began the proceedings. "Dear Lord, this man is coming to you in great need of your service. He has done so many great things in your name and you healed him of an ailment, but his mind is under attack by the dark one. Give him healing Lord, and give him freedom, so he may pursue your mighty presence."

They all held hands and prayed their own prayers, asking the Lord to give them healing. Jose closed his eyes and with all his power he prayed to the Lord, crying out for His mercy. He all of a sudden felt another pressure on his eyes, just like he had when he was first coming down with MS. Feeling weird, he opened his eyes to ask Jay if he looked weird when there was a large scream. "Oh my God, your eyes," Jay screamed as Domenica and she looked upon Jose. His eyes had turned bright yellow. Just as soon as the yellow had come it began to fade away into brown, leaving Jose back to looking normal. Jay turned to her grandmother and before she could even ask the question, Domenica answered, "He has received the Light."

"When will Malik's and the Khalifa's quest for blood be satisfied?" Freddy asked, worried.

Lenz tried to calm his nerves. "After they attack India and Zone Seven, the world will be at peace. That is what Malik promised me. He is a good man, Freddy. He just got caught up in this global religious war. Thankfully, it should be over soon. India made a terrible strategic mistake by supporting the African Freedom Army. I understand they were trying to help their ancient ancestors, but there is a time and place for honoring the past."

"I think India thought they would win, hell we all did. No one could have guessed that Malik's military strategy would be so untouchable. He is amazing in the field, which is surprising for a career politician."

"He studied the art of war by himself through absorbing every military journal and strategic book he could. Late at night he would be up studying in the local library from what I hear. All that preparation really paid off. It was like he knew this day of war would be coming."

"I thought he was secular and a good-hearted man? Why was he so quick to jump to war?"

"He claims it was the Khalifa who made him do it. He chose the Khalifa so he could supply another source of control over his volatile region. Now it seems as though the Khalifa has stepped into his place as the most important political leader in the region."

"Does Malik do well with sharing power?"

"He has been doing it so far just fine. We will have to see what moves he makes long term. For now, let's just pray that he will be satisfied with his conquests."

Chapter 25

Jose walked into his D.C. apartment exhausted from the week. All he wanted to do was relax in front of the television and catch some baseball. He turned it to his favorite Texas team as the game was nearing the seventh inning stretch. "Just in time to catch the good part of the game," Jose thought to himself. He decided this would be a good time to light up a blunt to celebrate a good work week. He lit it and melted into his couch. Just as the effects of Jose's blunt were kicking in, so too did his paranoia. "Sure he had sex but I still think he is a faggot," he heard someone scream out during the television broadcast of the baseball game.

"Whoa that was weird. Why would someone scream that out at a baseball game?" Jose questioned himself as he lit up a second blunt. "Pussy," someone screamed at the game, almost directed at Jose on the other side of the screen. "No, people are not screaming at you Jose, get a grip on yourself."

He continued smoking and the voices he was hearing were getting worse. "How could he ever please her with such a little dick?" he clearly heard yelled in the television.

"How is this possible?" Jose asked, extremely confused over the situation. "They cannot be yelling at me. That would make no sense. I don't even have a little dick."

He tried his best to continue watching the game but every few minutes he would hear someone scream out from the crowd seemingly directed at him, watching the game thousands of miles away in D.C. After the torment continued for some time, Jose just decided to turn the television off. The voices stopped when the television went off, so Jose thought that maybe it had something to do with the electronics. "Well maybe now that I have the Light, I can sense people's innermost thoughts without them speaking. Domenica did say something about that."

He kept trying to explain it away because he had no plausible explanation for what was going on. He just lay down on his couch and decided to go to sleep to ease the confusion of what he was hearing. He hoped that what he was hearing was not serious and would go away soon.

It was a dark moonless night in southern Africa where James, Justin, Abal, and Lilly were walking through town keeping a low profile as they made their way to the next safe house. The cleric's hidden network was doing an amazing job of keeping them safe from the Khalifa's police. The police had no idea where the Great Prophet was and they were determined to find and execute him for his crimes against Islam. "Right this way," Justin said and he looked at the address scribbled onto a white piece of paper. They went up to the door and he knocked softly as to not wake up any neighbors. A wide man with a wide smile opened the door.

"Right this way, Great Prophet, right this way." The chubby man led them to the main room in his house where he had dinner already ready for them. "This is the least I can do for our great savior. I am sorry about what happened with the initial attack from the Khalifa, but I have faith, Great Prophet. I know we will rise up and dispel the Muslim invaders from our lands one day."

The four of them sat down to a refreshing meal and talked about important business and the future of Africa. This was their life now, bouncing from safe house to safe house, only moving at night to avoid detection. Until Justin could manage to rile up some serious support for a new army, this would be how they were going to live. The Khalifa destroyed their army but not their wills. They all still believed in the words of the great

357

Dr. Berihun. In his death, they pursued his message of hope and prosperity for the black race. It would take time, but Justin was determined to one day rule Africa again.

Jose held up his left hand and tapped it with his right index finger. He held his hand out in front of him, and a screen popped out giving him options to select. He selected call, went to Carmela and pressed the call button to initiate the process. His X-chip was the newest off the line. Jose wanted to wait to get his installed so they could iron out the initial wave of inevitable bugs. He tried to get his mother to have her X-chip installed but she was low on her eosinophil count.

Jay had hers installed with Jose. Most of the American Protectorate, including the non-member Ron L. Boone, got their X-chips installed. It allowed for seamless and instant communication with anyone throughout the world. It was the technological marvel of the decade.

The phone rang several times before Carmela picked up. "Hello my son, how are you?"

"I am fine, Mother. I just wanted to let you know I am in town and I want to stop by. I have some great news to share with you."

"OK I will unlock the front door so just come on in. I will be watching television in the front."

About twenty minutes went by and Jose came almost running through the front door to see his mother. "Mother, you still watching TV?"

"Yes I am in here, come have a seat." She cleared the pillows and some blankets off the couch. "What is the big news Jose?"

He looked at her with a pulsating smile, and said, "I am going to ask Juanita Mills to marry me."

Carmela, knowing he was going to read her reaction, managed to force a loving smile and a warm face. "Oh son, I am so happy for you. If you are sure she is who you want to be with and you have properly vetted her life, then I am all supportive."

"I do not believe she has anything to hide, do you?"

"I am unsure of any woman who sets her eyes on you son. You are a prized commodity, what woman would not want to be with the dashing young and handsome Hero? I know you have been friends with her for a long time now and you are not rushing into this, but I just want you to be careful."

"I think I am making the right decision. So do I have your blessing?"

"Yes, you do, my Son."

"Do not take your blindfold off yet," Jose said to Jay as he led her by hand out of the car and into the field.

The sun was belting Jay's face. "Please, I am sweating under this thing. We have to be there by now."

"Yes we are here, take it off."

She removed her blindfold and she adjusted her eyes to the light. She saw a giant hot air balloon with a friendly operator waiting inside. He opened the door to the balloon and said, "Right this way, Miss Mills." Jay yelled out with glee and hugged Jose. He must have been listening to her conversations when she told him she had never been on a hot air balloon. "What a special and amazing thing this is, Jose."

She gave him a kiss on the cheek and climbed aboard the balloon, followed closely by Jose. They got on the balloon and off they left. Into the warm June Dallas air, they went. Just as they reached the climax of their trip, Jose told Jay to turn to him. "I have been in love with you from the first time

I saw you in person. You are an amazing soul, Juanita Mills, and I want to spend every moment of the rest of my life with you by my side. I love you, and I want to know…"

He bent down on one knee in the small basket, "Will you marry me?"

"Oh yes, yes, I will marry you, my Hero!"

Jose put the ring on her finger and stood up to kiss her. They tangled their tongues in love for what seemed like an hour before Jay broke away with dread on her face. "I do have some bad news though. I told you before about how I have to seek special permission from my elders of the Order of Rome before I can marry you. I just know that they will see in you what I see in you, and they will allow us to marry."

"What do I have to be in order to marry you, Italian?"

"No it is not a racial thing, it is a spiritual thing. I just have to convince them that you are someone special, and they will grant me permission. We must fly to Rome as soon as we can work it into our busy schedules to meet with them. I am so excited, my Hero! This is the happiest day of my life!"

They kissed again and just stood in loving silence for the remainder of the trip. Jose was still confused by the entire process with her elders, but he trusted that everything would work out. The Lord put this woman into his life for a reason, so everything had to work out.

When they got off the plane and walked through the airport, almost no one recognized them there in Italy. A man was waiting with a sign saying "Mills" as they neared baggage claim. He was their driver who would take them to the Order's headquarters. The Order's driver made Jose wear a blindfold so he would not know where the Order's headquarters would be. After what seemed like over an hour of driving they finally arrived at the sprawling mansion where the Order's elders were located. Jay peeled off Jose's blindfold and they got out and walked to the mansion. As they got to the door it opened for them, and out stepped a well-groomed man about six feet tall.

He had thick Italian hair and spoke with an accent. "Right this way, Sir and Madam, the Elders have been expecting you."

He led them through the door and through the house into a large dark room. After the guide left them in the dark room the lights came on and revealed a panel of what seemed like judges in long golden and purple robes. "What brings you here, young Princess?" asked the main Elder sitting in the middle chair.

"I have come to ask your permission to marry this man, United States Congressman Jose Valdez of Mexico and Guatemala. "

There was a loud rumble of grumbling coming from the Order's Elders as the main Elder once again spoke up. "By your birthright, you are only allowed to marry a Great Prophet. Why do you bring this man to us as if he is one? We already have an idea who the Great Prophets will be, and this man is not on that list."

"I have studied with him and given him much guidance. I have prayed to the Lord and He delivered me Jose at the exact right time. I know he must be a Great Prophet."

"Which Great Prophet do you suggest that he is?"

"He is the great Quetzalcoatl reborn, the Great Prophet of Mexico. I have prayed on it, and I know it is him. I believe it with all of my heart and I know it must be true. You must allow us to marry dear Elders, it is my destiny."

The Elders grumbled again in the dim light as they discussed what they should do. The main Elder spoke, "We will deliberate to our great

Oracle, and she will tell us if this man is the Great Prophet of Mexico. Wait here and we shall return shortly."

So Jose and Jay waited for thirty minutes in the dimly lit room for the Elders to come back. As they filed back into their chairs, Jose and Jay looked upon them optimistically. The main Elder spoke up one last time. "We have deliberated with the great Oracle and she has told us that this man is not the Great Prophet you expected him to be. Therefore, you are not allowed to marry him under any circumstances. We are sorry that you flew all the way out here to hear bad news, but that is the judgment of your Elders and you must accept our ruling."

Jay immediately burst into tears as she saw the Elders stand up and begin to leave the chambers. "No! Please," Jay screamed out but it was no use and she knew it. If the Elders did not believe he was the Great Prophet of Mexico, then the marriage would not be allowed. She fought off her tears and looked at Jose. "I don't care what they say. I still love you and we are going to get married."

They left the mansion with Jose in a blindfold and they made their way back to the airport. It was a rough flight home but Jose was not as worried as he should be regarding the situation. He did not know who these Elders were or anything about her Order, so he had no reason to fear. All he knew was that the woman he wanted to marry was going to marry him, and it was as simple as that.

There was about a week left in July on their marriage day. They kept the ceremony quiet and secret, as to not alert the Elders. Only Carmela and Domenica were there to witness the proceedings. Jose stood nervously with his mother as he waited for his soon-to-be-wife to come down the aisle. As she came down the aisle the beauty of Jay and the beauty of the moment almost made Jose tear up. She came down to him and the ceremony began. After the end of the Pastor's lines the two kissed and became wed as one.

Chapter 26

"What is the news from the war front, Lenz?" Freddy walked into the council meeting eager to hear updates from the Indian front.

Lenz answered, "Attacks started early this morning, heavy casualties on both sides but the Jihadi army is pushing through. They never stood a chance, not with the rest of the world just watching. We have done all we could here at the UN to try and quell the situation but it is beyond the power of words. Bullets and blood were the only solution to this problem."

"What do you expect from Malik after he is done conquering Zone Seven?"

"I have spoken with him several times and in order to stop further military conquests I had to make a concession."

"No, Lenz don't tell me…"

"Yes, I am stepping down as Secretary-General and suggesting to the UN to elect Malik Jabbar of Southern Iraq. It just makes sense, Professor. He is from here and good with the people. He is young and very smart. He will do great things in the world. You will have nothing to worry about."

"Where are you going to go?"

"I am going to run Zone One from my homeland in Germany. I will do what I can to promote your will, Professor. I fear that one day the Western world will have to protect itself from outside aggressors, so I must do what I can to prepare my people over these next few years should violence break out."

"Well, thank you Lenz for all you have done in my life. I hope this is not the last time I see you. We will keep in touch via the new X-chip we just had installed. I will keep you briefed on the new secretary-general's actions."

"Thank you, Professor, and good luck, because you are going to need it."

Chapter 27

"Abal, please translate this to the president of Angola: We are at war for the survival of the black race, the independence of the black race, the future of the black race. We cannot afford to turn away from our goal of black supremacy, we are the chosen people, and we are the first sons of God. We are destined to reign so we only need to give the Lord a chance to work a miracle. It starts with you, President. I ask, as your Great Prophet, to secure military personnel and supplies for the African Freedom Army when the time is right for an attack."

The president responded and Abal translated for Justin, "We are living comfortably under our new master. He protects us from the rebels as long as we enact Muslim laws and bow to his rule. It is much better to have a strong central ruler than a soft ruler over a broken Africa. As long as Islam is on this planet, it will reign supreme. Even the power of the Great Prophet cannot stop the power of Allah. You must understand my position. You have no leverage. Hell, even the men on the street grumble that you were no Great Prophet. They grumble that the doctor really told you another name and you took the credit for yourself."

"Where did you hear these lies!"

"Do not get mad at me, Great Prophet. I am simply delivering you the reality of the situation. You lost your cause when you lost your army. You are defeated, now go run away back to the United States and leave the big boy problems to the men."

"You son of a bitch…" Justin took a run at the president but was quickly stopped by James and Abal. The president's guards stepped in front of the trio and demanded them to leave. The visit was another unsuccessful bid for military aid for Justin. He would not give up the cause though. As long as he was alive he would fight in Dr. Berihun's memory. He would not let his death be in vain.

"Malik Jabbar wants to sign the capitulation and be sworn into office in Jerusalem? I do not get it Freddy baby, what is he trying to gain?" Jennifer was putting out Freddy's shoes for him as he got ready to go to the laboratory for work.

"With the fast advancement of dark matter production and dark energy machinery, the need for oil is greatly diminishing. He wants to secure both the sources of dark matter so he can control the wealth of the world. It is brilliant politics if you ask me. Israel has become his most important ally. As long as he can keep the religious harmony between the Jews and Muslims, he has landed himself into a goldmine. Militarily, no one can touch him, politically, no one can touch him. He has fast become the most powerful man on Earth. With India due to surrender within the next several days, he has to reassure the world that his conquering days are over and that peace will come to the earth under his reign. Do I believe him? To be honest I do not know what to believe about this man. I think he was forced into a bad situation with these wars. I will hold out hope that the man taking over control of the UN is just as fair as he is strong."

It was another beautiful night for the young newlyweds. Jose wanted to celebrate their love by going back to the park where he first asked her to be his girlfriend. "It is so nice out tonight, the stars are shining so bright with the dark moon," Jay said as she gripped Jose's hand a little tighter with love.

"Every day with you is a perfect day in my eyes, Jay."

They casually strolled through the park to the fountains, watching them as their water and light display lit up the sky. After they were done they took their time as they walked out of the park. As they left the park they saw that two elderly people were having some car issues. Jose, in the mood to help, walked over to them with Jay at hand.

"Hello friends, can I be of any help?"

The elderly white man said, "Oh yes, can you take a look, Congressman?"

He left Jay to stand with the elderly woman as he walked over to look under the hood. As he scanned the engine, he could see nothing wrong. When he looked up, he was instantly startled when he saw the elderly woman with a white cloth in her hand covering Jay's mouth and nose. Jay was struggling but quickly succumbed to the toxins. Jose, enraged, got up from the hood to run over to her aid but just as he lifted his head a loud thud of a tire iron against his head was the last thing he heard as he fell into blackness.

Chapter 28

All of the world's top leaders were there in Jerusalem for the swearing-in ceremony. Freddy and Jennifer were honored guests, sitting in the front row as the commencement for Malik Jabbar to become UN Secretary-General was coming to a close. The ceremony was complete and Malik was the new ruler of the world's great international body. As he walked to the microphone he had the confidence and swagger of a young emperor. "Please everyone remain standing for my announcement. In honor of the aid Israel gave the Zone Five Army, and for all of their generosity with the Palestinian's migration, I have decided to perform my first task as Secretary-General. Prime Minister Adiel Tuchman, please come forward."

The proud leader of Israel came out of the crowd amid cheers and screams from the crowd in his support. He walked up to the Secretary-General and he began speaking again. "For all Israel has done to aid us, I stand here today to announce the UN-Israel Defensive Pact. I promise the world that Israel with have the military backing of the UN in any endeavor for one hundred years from this day. Israel is the Holy Land for all Christians, Muslims, and Jews, so it is time to heal her and let her grow and prosper. World scholars will look back on this day a century from now with accolades and great affair. Rejoice O' Israel, your safety is in my hands."

The crowd rejoiced as Adiel came to the mic. "I would also like to announce the reconstruction of the Holy Temple beginning on this joyous day. Israel will no longer live in fear!"

"Baby, my Hero, Jose." Jay kept whispering to Jose to get him to wake up. "Jose!" She screamed a little louder and that seemed to do the trick. Jose woke up to almost complete blackness. In the dimly lit room he could make out his wife tied up to a steel chair, just like he was as he was soon to discover as he collected his bearings.

"My dearest wife, can you tell me what the hell is going on?"

"I think one of my biggest fears came true, my Hero. This has all the makings of the Order of Rome trying to punish us for getting married. I am scared because I do not know to what extent they will go to punish us for what we did. I lied to you before about my parents. They did not die in a car accident. They were killed by the Order of Rome after my birth for trying to leave the Order and go into hiding with me..."

The conversation was halted by the sounds of an opening door. A line of lights came on thirty feet away from the pair that showed several chairs lined up beneath them. The light shone on the men entering and sitting down in their seats. "The Elders," Jay whispered to Jose nervously.

As they took their seats the door opened again and in walked a monstrous man with rippling muscles and jagged chin who towered over all the people in the room. The head Elder spoke to him in Italian as he slowly walked toward Jose and Jay. Jose spoke up first. "What the hell is going on here? I am a sitting United States Congressman. I demand to know where I am and what is going on."

The head Elder just nodded his head to the bruiser as he came over to Jose and punched him hard in the side of the face, and then in the stomach. Jose coughed out a response, "What the fuck! Get your fucking hands off me!"

The bruiser took instruction from the head Elder and hit him several more times. Jay began to protest and the bruiser went over to her and hit her several times to shut her up. Jose was staggering in and out of reality as the pain and the screams of his wife made him question if he was just having a bad dream. He snapped out of it and demanded the Elders tell him what was going on. The head one answered, "You have gone against an explicit command we gave you. She was not yours to marry. She was born into her place in this world and that place is not with a simple man like you. We warned you clearly and fairly that there would be consequences for going against our command. Now you must pay the toll. Our ruling is as follows: Beating and flogging for the Princess, Death for the Congressman."

Jay screamed out no and started pleading for a second judgment on the issue, but the Elders turned a blind eye. The bruiser took hold of the back of her chair and dragged her out of the room to her cell in the other chamber amid screams for her husband and pleas for help. Jose tried to talk calmly and reasonably to the men, "You cannot do this to me, I am a powerful Congressman. People will be looking for me. Release me and my wife at once."

The head Elder responded, "Our ruling is final. Your execution will commence shortly."

Jose, powerless and out of options, did the only thing he felt like he could do to save his life. He prayed, and he prayed with all his might and all his soul. He prayed loud for Jesus to deliver him from this situation. His eyes were closed tight as he prayed and when he looked up, his eyes were bright yellow. A gasp came out from the group of Elders as the bruiser came back into the room to finish off Jose. The head Elder spoke up, "So my Son, you have the Light? I wish you would have told us this before. There is a small chance that you could indeed be a Prophet if you have the power to attain the Light. Let us reconvene and reconsider the issue later tonight. Your execution will be postponed until tomorrow morning. By then we will find out what we need to know about you to make a proper decision."

With that the Elders left the room and the bruiser took the back of the steel chair and dragged Jose to his cell in another chamber. Jose could feel the Spirit coursing through his body as his eyes faded from yellow back into brown. He did not know what to make of it, but he could feel that that Lord was listening to him.

After Jose was put into his cell he did his best to try and get out of the restraints on his body. After hours of sobbing and praying, he had just about given up. He prayed one last time for the Lord to come save him and he gave up. It was impossible for the Lord to get him out of this cell, he thought. There was no hope for him. Just as his last ounce of faith was leaving his soul, there was loud sound that shook the very foundations of the building. Astonished, Jose looked up and saw that the ceiling had disappeared from the roof, leaving an opening. Confused and scared, Jose watched as a bright light came floating out of the sky. It floated right into the room a few feet away from Jose. When the bright light wore down, it revealed an incredible sight: A beautiful blue creature with stunning white wings that stood ten feet tall. He had a sharp angled chin and jaw structure and his eyes were soft and yellow. He took a step toward Jose who cowered in its presence, terrified of what was going on.

The creature spoke to him. "How can you be afraid of me, you silly man? I am exactly who you called for."

Jose looked up at him, "God?"

The creature laughed and unrolled the roll of paper he was carrying in his right hand and wrote down some notes. "You never cease to amaze me, Jose Valdez."

"Then who or what are you? Are you here to help me?"

"You cannot recognize an angel when you see one?"

"I have never seen an angel before. Now that I have, I cannot stop the tears of joy that are coming from my eyes. What an amazingly beautiful angel you are. Thank the Lord that He sent you to save me."

"Yes the Lord allowed me to come save you. I have been watching over you since you were conceived, young Jose. I have watched over thousands of men before you. My task in heaven is to be a guardian angel, and I am yours, Jose. I have watched over you once before, when your spirit was born into this world thousands of years ago. One time, I used to call you Elijah the Prophet."

"Elijah? I am having a hard time understanding."

"You simple man… You are one of the Greatest Prophets of our time, the Great Prophet Elijah reborn, and one of the Two Witnesses. In a few years you must take your place on the Wailing Wall and speak out the message of the Lord to the world in these dark times. You are the final beacon of hope for the nonbelievers, and the final warning to all Christians that the end times are finally upon us. The Anti-Christ is here among us now. It is time for you to begin your training to become one of the Two Witnesses, one of the two Lamp stands."

"I remember reading something about them. They have great powers and speak the final message of the Lord to the unbelieving world."

"Good, I am glad you have an idea of what you are to become. The choice is still yours on who you want to be though. You will be offered the land of your ancestors, to rule over them as the reincarnation of the Great Quetzalcoatl. You must choose whether to serve men, or to serve the Lord. The decision is yours. For now, though, I will release you from this prison and you must find your father."

"My father is alive?"

"Yes, and your mother has been hiding you from him to protect you. She knows what your father will bring to your life. He has been telling her since before you were born that you were to become a Great Prophet. She still holds out hope that her only son will grow old and raise a beautiful family. She prays every day that the end times are not coming like your father told her so long ago. She, along with every other true Christian who survives the Great Deception, will need you Jose to guide them and protect them in the Holy Land of Jerusalem.

"Go see your father and he will take care of everything else that you need to worry about."

The shackles and restraints fell off of his body and Jose stood up. "Take my hand and close your eyes tight."

Jose took the angel's free hand and closed his eyes. He could feel the rush of cold over his body as he felt his body floating out into the fresh air. They stayed moving for a while before Jose felt the hard ground on his feet. The angel said, "You are now safe, open your eyes."

Jose opened and saw that they were in a vacant lot in the dark of night. The angel spoke, "You must find the second Witness. He will be the Great Prophet Moses, otherwise known as the Great Prophet Horus. He, just like you, must make a choice on whether or not to serve the Lord in these dark days. Your father will take you to him when the time is right. For now, you must focus on your own journey to the Lord. Take these keys and drive this car to your mother's house. Tell her everything you saw and she will reveal to you how to contact your father."

"Thank you again, my angel. I hope to see you again one day."

"Indeed you shall!" A bright light encompassed the angel's body and he floated off into the air. Jose was torn on whether or not he should drive off and save himself or try to look for his wife. The angel made no mention of her. The angel only said to go home. Jose was distraught with fear over the safety of his wife as he got into the car and started to drive.

The road markers said he was in New York. The silence of the empty road was bothering him so he decided to turn on the radio as he drove. The first song came on, "Go East to your Love, your Love, your Love, Go East to your Love my Hero." He could feel the sensation in his head coming back to him as each new station he turned to kept telling him to go back to his love. Something was trying to tell him not to go back home but to find his wife. He did not know what to do as he drove and kept switching stations. Finally, he found a Christian radio station and heard a familiar soothing voice. It was Pastor Rich Urban, his new and favorite pastor from just outside of Dallas that he experienced the Holy Spirit with when he went to his church with Jay. Jose settled in and listened to Pastor speak almost directly to him. "Do not be afraid of the coming challenges, my friends. The Lord has a purpose for each and every one of us. We must take the message He is sending us and apply it to our lives. Do not listen to the devil in your secular friends, or the devil on television or the radio, telling you to do things you know you should not do. Listen to your heart and listen to the Lord, not the world.

"The world is nothing but the devil's playground. He rules this planet in the hearts of evil men. Only trust the Lord and He will deliver you."

The pastor's words calmed Jose down tremendously. It was exactly what he needed to hear at the exact right time. The remainder of the drive from New York to Dallas, he listened to this Christian station. The Lord spoke to him the entire way home, giving him words of encouragement and love. He knew it was the devil in his head and on the radio trying to influence him and he managed to block it all out and take it out of his system. After driving all night to get there, he finally arrived at his mother's house early in the morning.

He parked his car abruptly and ran up to the door and banged on it loudly. "Mother, are you here? Mom!"

He yelled out and rang the doorbell to get her up. He saw the lights come on in the house as she made her way to the front door. She said, "Who is it?" Jose answered back that it was him and she opened the door.

"What is wrong Jose? What are you doing here? You didn't call or anything."

Jose proceeded to tell her the entire story of what happened with the Order of Rome and the angel. She had to take a seat to gather herself before she spoke. "Yes Jose, your father is alive," she said.

"I wanted to protect you from the kind of life he wanted us to live. You would never have been a Congressman nor done anything successful if you were raised by that crazy man. All he talked about were his visions and the end of the world. He wanted to raise you in secret away from the world where he was going, but I would not let him take you or me with him. So instead of letting you find out about who your father really was, I kept it a secret. I have been feeling guilty your entire life about the decision I made. Now I can see it was not the best of choices. No amount of protection can keep you from fulfilling your duty to the Lord. All I have is a phone number for your father that he left for me to give you to call him when you were ready."

She went upstairs and came back quickly with a piece of paper. He called the number on the phone with his mother nervously by his side. After a tense few rings someone answered, "Hello", the man on the other end said.

"My name is Jose Valdez. I am looking for my father, Francisco Basurto."

There was a long pause on the phone and then he spoke. "I have been waiting so long for this phone call, Jose. We have much to discuss, but I cannot talk to you over the phone. Come to 7652 Nae Road, Showton, Montana. I will be waiting for you there."

Jose hurried and wrote down the address, before he could even say anything else there was a dial tone.

"Looks like I am off to Montana. I want you to stay at CC's house to stay safe while I am gone."

"OK, I will go over there right now. Have a safe trip my son and tell your father that I said hello and that I still love him."

"I will, Mother. I love you and I am not mad about you withholding my father from me. You were only doing what you thought was best. I will contact you as soon as I can after I get there."

They hugged and Jose left for the airport. He called and got a flight to the Great Falls International Airport where he would then drive to Showton. He was nervous but he was ready to finally meet his father. Since the angel said he had to see him, he knew that it was in God's plan to meet him. He took more time off from Congress, and prepared himself to take another important step in his life.

Chapter 29

"Well that went well, Justin," James said as they made their way to the car. The trio had just left an elder tribal leader's house. Justin, the Great Prophet, had been traveling through Africa looking for support for an uprising against Malik and the Zone Five Army.

"The lovely couple who took us in at the safe house made the most amazing breakfast. Lilly is lucky to have had a chance to stay back and get some more of their cooking."

They all climbed in the car and Abal drove them back to the safe house. As they pulled up to the road that led to the house they could see smoke billowing into the sky and a large crowd gathered outside of the safe house. "Something bad has happened. Justin, stay back here with Abal while I go look." James got out of the car and ran up to the safe house in a frantic panic as he saw that there had been an attack that took place.

"Oh my God, is Lilly still alive?" is all he could think about as he raced through the front door past the crowd. "Lilly, where are you?" he screamed as he tore through the house which was left in shambles. He turned a corner and saw the old lady who took them in dead in the kitchen. As he made his way into the hallway he saw the loyal old man shot in the head. James was starting to lose it. The woman he loved, and his cousin's wife, could have been killed by the Zone Five forces.

He went upstairs through the smoke to Lilly's room. He opened the door and saw nothing. He then noticed on the bed was a note. It read, "We trade the prime minister's daughter for the Great Prophet Horus. You have until November 3rd to turn yourself in, Prophet. On the 3rd, we execute your wife."

James ran out of the house to where Justin and Abal were hiding, and shared with them the news and the note. None of the three knew what to do with the situation. Justin was the last great hope for the black race, but Lilly was his wife and the daughter of the man who put him in this position of power. They did not have the resources to execute a rescue mission, so their only option was negotiation. For the next several weeks, Justin would try bargaining for her release. Malik wanted nothing from Justin except for his head, so as November 3rd slowly approached, Justin's nerves grew tighter and tighter.

"What the hell is this place?" Jose pulled up the dark street to the broken down and decrepit house his GPS was telling him was the house he was looking for. "This must be the place, but who the hell could live in a house like this?"

He shook off his confusion and his nerves and walked up to the house. Not a soul was outside in any direction. He went up to the door and rang the doorbell. It did not seem to be working because it did not make a sound. So Jose knocked firmly on the door. When he did, it creaked open. It was left unlocked, so Jose poked his head in and yelled out, "Father, it is Jose? Is anybody here?"

He walked through the front door into the main entryway and still saw no signs of life. He walked to the kitchen and into the main room and still no one. He gave up and started to walk toward the front door when he felt several pairs of hands jump onto him and throw a brown bag over his head. "Get your hands off me," Jose yelled as he fought against his attackers.

One of them spoke up. "We are your friends. We are taking you to your father but we cannot let you see where we are going or who we are until we know you are safe."

Jose stopped struggling. "OK I will calm down. Just get your hands off me and let me walk."

Jose unclenched his fists and allowed the men to take him to a car where they drove off somewhere in the darkness to go meet his father.

"Ah, Professor Slater, I am so glad you were able to make it with your busy schedule," Malik said as he stood above the other seated councilmen.

"It has been a slow day in the command center so I decided to come up here and contribute to the council meeting. Thank you for continuing to have me on this council, Secretary-General. I hope I can add some valuable wisdom to this already established council you have assembled."

Freddy took his seat as Malik continued, "News from the African front is that we have captured the Great Prophet Horus' wife and the daughter of the late Doctor Berihun. She will be a valuable asset to our pursuit of getting rid of all African resistance."

Freddy was concerned with this news. "What do you plan on doing with her?"

Malik, sensing his compassion, wanted to stomp out the feelings of guilt the professor was having over this news. "We plan on executing the traitor in about a month's time, unless her husband turns himself in."

"Are you really going to go through with the execution if he doesn't come forward?"

"Yes, Professor, it is very important that we establish a rule of law in this dangerous world. If you speak out or act out against me, you will be crushed. All of my enemies will know my name and fear it. I am the greatest man on Earth and those who follow me will find great wealth and power, while those who oppose me will be food for the carrion."

"No sane man would ever step to your gracious rule, Secretary-General. It is clear that this man is tainted by his religion. He does not know that his God is no match for the holy power of your spirit, Secretary-General," said one of the other councilmen.

Freddy agreed. "Yes, the Prophet Horus is another example of religion poisoning the minds of men. However, the girl should not be punished for the sins of the men who raised her or wed her. She has not fired a weapon at our soldiers. She is a harmless pawn in this entire endeavor. Please consider letting her go, especially if Horus in fact does come and turn himself in."

"For you, Professor, I will consider it. I have urgent business to attend to in the United States, so Professor I am leaving the council in your control. You are a man of science and knowledge, and I trust your judgment. Please do not disappoint. I will return shortly, in time for the execution."

"I will be honored to run the council in your stead, Secretary-General." The meeting adjourned and Freddy went off to the command center to check on the Mars mining project. He really admired Malik. Even though he enjoyed him, he was worried that perhaps one day he might take his views on religion and try to push them onto the world. Freddy himself would not mind terribly much as his faith was waning, but what would come of his wife? He loved her, but her Christian faith was becoming an increasing burden and liability. Hopefully he would not have to make a choice between serving her and her faith and serving the world.

Chapter 30

"Please, Congressman, put this metal bag over your hand so we can scramble the X-chip surveillance system. We know you are being monitored and watched by the enemy, so we must take extra special precaution before you are cleaned up."

Jose complied with the unknown men as the road changed from smooth to bumpy and rough. Jose could tell they were going up into the mountains somewhere. After a long time of driving they finally stopped. Jose got out of the car and they removed the bag from his head. The men who captured him varied in size and race, but they all seemed to have a giant smile on their faces when they finally could meet the Congressman face-to-face.

"Right this way, Great Prophet," said the tall husky man who had been talking to him this entire time. He had a dark red beard and warm friendly eyes. "My name is Denard," he said. "This chubby black guy here is Yolon, and the computer nerd here is Sam. We all work for your father producing his end times magazine called, 'The Hour Glass.' Please come this way, the opening to the sanctuary is right here."

He walked around a set of trees and there in the grass was a hatch. Denard walked up to the hatch, entered a pass code, and the hatch opened up. Down the stairs they went into the white painted underground compound. Through several rooms they walked until they got to the main room, where there was an older Hispanic man with dark black hair and gray streaks with a wide smile and open arms. "My son... I have imagined this day in my head from the day that I left Texas."

They both came in for a warm embrace. Jose fought back the tears of happiness when his father continued, "We have much to discuss, but first we must cleanse you of the tools of the devil. This compound is signal proof, so we can remove the X-chip and the demon in your head without compromising our situation. Come sit down so we can begin the exorcism."

He took a seat, a little confused but willing to cooperate. "What do you mean a demon in my head?"

"Haven't you been wondering how it felt like everyone around you was reading your mind? The radio has been speaking to you, and you are getting spiritual messages from everyone you get in contact with."

"Yes that has been happening, but my wife Juanita and I were thinking that it was the onset of schizophrenia. I wanted to get checked out but I was just nervous."

"Yes, in the medical world they call it schizophrenia or psychosis, but in the spiritual realm, it is a demonic possession. It can only be removed by reciting a special prayer that the Apostle Paul was given in a dream which can remove the evil spirit from a person's soul. Just close your eyes and try to stay in the Spirit."

He placed his hand on Jose's forehead and began to pray. The prayer took several minutes, which he recited from memory. As he got toward the end Jose could feel this pressure in his head, and then he began to hear a voice in the room yelling out at him and his father. "The day of our lord is coming, your Lord is weak and men are ripe for the holy one's great harvest."

"Get back to hell in Jesus' name, you foul beast!" his father yelled. There was a loud painful scream as the voice faded away into non-existence. Next they took Jose to the operating room where Denard removed the X-chip. Now that Jose was cleansed of the devil's tools, his father began talking to him.

"Son, we are in the middle of a great war. The Light and the Dark are fighting for the souls of all men, and control of this world. We all must soon decide who we are going to serve, the Lord, or the devil. Your entire life has been a huge lie, Jose. The government you work for, the woman you married, the television you watch, the music you listen to, everything of this world is controlled by the devil and the Order of the Illuminatus. The Illuminati have been a part of this country since its first discovery by Europeans. They saw a land of milk and honey where they would be free to pursue their dark plots without judgment or suspicion.

"The Capitol, where you work, is an architectural beacon for the spirit of evil. The very foundation and location of its buildings signals an allegiance to the Dark One. You are a great Prophet, my son. I have seen this in a dream after you were conceived. I had to wait until you were ready, and I believe you now are."

"So what you are telling me is that everything I stand for, everything I have worked my entire life for, has been for the devil?"

"That is exactly what I am telling you. Unfortunately, I feel as though you need to see the devil for yourself before you are truly ready to assume your position as one of the two Greatest Prophets. Mexico and Central America have been watching and waiting for your arrival son, now that they know you are the Great Prophet Quetzalcoatl, they will do everything in their power to get you on their side. They have already infiltrated your mind through your wife."

"How does she have a part to play in this? She believes in Christ."

"Yes my son, she believes in Christ, but she is no Christian. She is part of the Illuminati, an Illuminati Princess in fact. She may be a Princess for the Order of Rome, but that is only a cover for her true intentions. She was raised by her family to serve the Dark One and only him."

"But she loved me father, I know she did. She would not want to do anything to hurt me."

"Yes she may have fallen in love with you over time, but her initial purpose in befriending you was to see if you were the Great Prophet. The Order of the Illuminatus sent agents out to all prospective candidates who they felt could one day be a Great Prophet."

"This is all so much to take in, I do not know what to say or do. I do not want to give up my career and my life just yet. There is so much I can do from my position of power and there is no way they can force me out. I can serve as an agent for the Lord in the Congress. I would be much more effective there."

His father Francisco sighed, "You do not understand yet my son, and I do not blame you. This is a lot for you to take in. I want you to begin your training for the Prophesying, but I do not think you are quite ready. I feel as though it will be best for you to go back to your life and see how long you can last before you are forced to make a decision to serve the Lord or Satan. When that day comes, and if you decide to serve the Lord, you come back here to me in these mountains and we will begin your training. My men will take you to the airport and you can see how to get back here on your own. We will also leave you the password to get in the hatch. I love you Son, and I want you to be careful in the next few weeks."

"I will be careful, Father. I must go back to Dallas and D.C. to continue my mission. If the Lord wants me back here He will let me know."

With that, they hugged again and parted ways. The trip back to the airport was not as long with the bag off his head. Jose had to find out what to do about his wife and his career. He was not ready to give up just yet.

James and Abal had left Justin in the next cleric safe house to get a bite to eat. When they returned they could not find him anywhere in the house. When they questioned the clerics who were hosting them, they answered, "He said he had something very important to do and he left you this note."

James took the note and read it inside of his head, "Dear James, firstly, I want you to know that everything I did was to protect you. I did not think you were ready to be who you were supposed to be. I wanted to protect you from harm, so I took your position away from you. I have been lying to you and the world this entire time. I am not the Great Prophet Horus, you are. Dr. Berihun's dying words were that he saw you, James, in his dream and that you were the Great Prophet. Call it a mix of fear for your life and jealousy, but I did not think it would be good for you to be in charge.

"You had no military training and you are not a soldier or a fighter. I did not think it would be safe for you to assume your role as the Great Prophet. I can now see that it was a mistake this entire time thinking I could change the will of the Lord. He desired you to be the Great Prophet and to lead our people. I have decided to go to Jerusalem for Lilly's execution to turn myself in and get her released. I want you to know that I never touched her, Cousin! I knew you loved her and that she was destined to be your woman, but I had to marry her to keep up the appearance that I was the Great Prophet.

"I never kissed her or even held her hand. I wanted to keep her pure for you for when I told you that you were in fact the Great Prophet Horus. Do not fear my death, Cousin. I will gladly give my life for the cause. Use my death as fuel for your fire, and use the distraction of my death to recruit a real resistance army to defeat Malik and his Army. Forgive me, Cousin! I hope to see you soon in the afterlife. I love you."

Chapter 31

It was Monday and things were busy at the Capitol for Jose's first day back in weeks. He was making his way back from a vote when he got a call from a very special friend. "Hello, Ron, what do I owe the pleasure of this call?"

"I am in town with a very dear friend who would like to speak with you. I just got to your office. Do you have some time to stop in and talk to us?"

It was Ron L. Boone, the man who had supported Jose since he was in college. "I will be there in five minutes, go into my office and relax."

Jose hurried to his office and walked in. There were several security guards in the hallway and in the office, so he knew it must be someone important. He opened the door and saw the familiar face of Boone; the other man heard the door open and turned around. It was Malik Jabbar, secretary-general.

"Congressman Valdez, it is an honor to finally get a chance to meet you." He walked over to Jose and shook his hand. Jose, surprised by the visit from the most powerful man in the world, said, "No Secretary-General, the pleasure is all mine. What is the meaning behind a visit from such a respected man?"

Jose took a seat in his chair and invited the two men to do the same. "I am here because I want to acknowledge a great talent when I see one. I have been doing a lot of research on you, Congressman. I feel like you still have a ton of untapped potential for greatness. I want to be the man to harness that power."

"What do you have in mind, Secretary-General?"

"The production of my Zone Three leader has been incredibly lacking. I want to bring in someone who can really control the region and give me some security at night that the most lucrative part of the world is in good hands. I want to offer you the position of leader of Zone Three. You are destined to be a great leader for the Mexican and Central American people, Congressman. They look up to you and respect you. Where else could I find a man with energy and passion who can lead such an expansive and diverse group of people? I know your constituents would not feel slighted for you taking one of the most powerful positions in the world. This assignment would be for life, or as long as you would want it. You would be the most powerful man in the Americas, free to shape what legislation and policy you desire."

Jose was stunned by the proposition. He would have all the power in the world to do what he wanted. "The offer sounds extremely enticing," Jose then thought back to his father's warning. "But I have to sadly turn it down. I have been through some very traumatic experiences lately and I just would not feel comfortable taking such an offer with my current state of mind."

Ron spoke up, "But Jose, this is all you could ever ask for! Do not be a fool and turn this down. Men who turn down the great secretary-general do not last long politically in this world. Do not turn what could be a great ally into a great enemy."

"I understand the ramifications of my decision and I will live with it. I am not the man for the job, Secretary-General. Thank you for coming all of this way to see me but, but I must decline."

Malik was enraged at this obvious slight, and stormed out of the room with Ron quickly in tow. Jose knew this would be bad news for his career, but he was thinking a lot about what his father said about making a choice. He stood up to the most powerful man in the world and told him no, so saying no to Congress did not sound like too big of a step. He would wait to officially make up his mind though. First he wanted to find out what happened to his wife before he made any drastic moves. He tried calling her over and over again but her X-chip was off. He had all but given up hope.

Jose had a long couple of days and really wanted to get some sleep, so he put his X-chip on silent. When he woke up, he casually checked his X-chip and saw twenty missed calls and several text messages from his staff and friends. As he started reading through the texts he turned on the television and saw Jay on the screen having a press conference. He looked upon the screen, confused, and turned on the sound to his television.

"We are going live to New York where singer and actress Juanita Mills has an urgent press conference."

Jay had bruises all over her face and arms, undoubtedly from the beating she took at the hands of the Order of Rome. Jay began, "First off, I want to reiterate that I am not here to press charges against anyone. I just think the public should be informed about one of their most popular politicians. The camera panned out and to Jose's astonishment, Malik Jabbar was standing in the background behind her with a smug look on his face. Jose was confused as to what Jay was about to say, but he was glad to see that she was OK.

"My husband, Jose Valdez, is not fit for office in the United States Congress. He put his hands on me two weeks ago in a fit of rage. He has been having schizophrenic episodes all the time lately, thinking that people can read his mind and are talking about him negatively. He was so paranoid and crazy that I just did not know what to do. He refused to go to the doctor and he kept telling me that everything was going to be OK, but things were not OK. He came home one night over two weeks ago in a rage that he thought I was reading his mind just along with everyone else. When I could not give him the answers he was looking for he started hitting me. I kept telling him that none of it was real but he did not believe me and he kept hitting me."

She started crying to add to the effect. "He is a sick and crazy man and I do not think he is fit to stay a Congressman. I am not going to file charges against my husband. I just want him to get the help he needs outside of a position of power. Any man who puts their hands on their woman should not be respected. That is all I have to say."

The crowd in front of her erupted into questions but she was quickly hurried away by her staff. Jose knew that Malik somehow got to her and convinced her to lie to get him out of office. Hurt to his core, Jose decided right then and there that living a life with people doubting his credibility would be too much to bear. He knew he did not harm his wife, but there was no way he could prove it.

If he started talking about the Order of Rome and the Illuminati they would really run him out of town for being crazy. He felt it was best for himself to take his father's advice and step out of the public spotlight to begin his training to become one of the two Great Witnesses. He held a press conference as soon as he got to the Capitol to resign. He did not admit to hurting Jay, but he did confess that he was having schizophrenic episodes. He left office in disgrace. People laughed and heckled him wherever he went in the city. All those fears of people talking about him negatively came into reality. He was shamed and shunned in every direction. He knew that the Lord was helping make his decision to serve Him an easy one. Jose, the Great Prophet Elijah reborn, now officially started his service in the Lord's army.

They quickly checked in to their Jerusalem hotel and put their stuff down in the room. James and Abal were in a rush to beat Justin to the execution site. "OK, we have everything, let's go try and save them."

Just as James turned to rush out of the door, Abal halted him. "Wait James, I have something to tell you."

He turned to Abal and said, "OK but please hurry."

Abal sighed and drew a deep breath. "It is my fault we are in this situation."

James, confused, asked his longtime friend what he meant.

Abal replied, "I saw what harm Lilly did to you and I hated her for it. I wanted her to pay with her life for breaking your heart. So I called the Zone Five Army and told them where she was as we were leaving the safe house. You see James, I am in love with you. I have been in love with you ever since I first laid eyes on you. I had never felt this way about another man before. I just did not know what to do to get your attention. I felt like punishing Lilly would have made you happy. I felt like without her in the way we could be together.

"Please James I beg you, forget about Justin and Lilly and return with me to Africa where you can begin your rule as the rightful Great Prophet Horus. We can recruit a massive army with my help. Once Africa knows you are the true Prophet, they will flock to you. Let me be by your side as your closest confidant and your lover."

James lost all words temporarily as the anger in his heart began to burn bright. "So you want me to leave the woman I love and my blood cousin, to spend my life running around Africa with you in sin? What the fuck were you thinking Abal?"

"But James I…"

"No Abal! You did everything wrong in this situation. You are an enemy to me. I will forever hate you and curse your name Abal. You are nothing to me. I am leaving to go save my wife and my cousin. I never want to see you again."

James left in a hurry to get to the execution site while Abal, crushed, lost all hope for life. There was a field adjacent to the hotel. Abal bought a hangman's noose and went to the tree in the field. He stood on a chair and slipped the rope over a sturdy branch. "I do not deserve to live," he screamed out as he plunged a sharp knife into his stomach and jumped off the chair. His entrails busted open over the field and he swung dead in the breeze for all to see.

James frantically ran to the execution site, but just as he arrived he saw Justin walking up the stairs toward the stage where Malik was talking to the crowd. James turned and saw Justin as his bodyguards swarmed and held Justin's arms. Malik said to his guards, "Release him and let him take his place on the executioner's block."

Justin went over and grabbed Lilly and threw her into the crowd where James was waiting to grab her. As Justin approached Malik, he stopped and reached in his back waistband. He pulled out a plastic green one-shot pistol that escaped the metal detection of the event's security. Malik froze and Justin took aim and fired, hitting him squarely in the chest. Malik hit the ground as the crowd screamed and his guards quickly grabbed Justin again. James forced Lilly to move toward the exit but they both still watched in horror as Justin was held on the stage.

The entire world was watching as Adiel Tuchman, the Israeli prime minister, hovered over Malik crying out, "In Malik's holy name and in the name of his holy spirit, revive yourself and stand for the world to see. You cannot die. You have the power of a god, Malik Jabbar, and the world needs you too much."

The world was in silence as they watched as Adiel prayed as hard as he could in Malik's name for him to rise from the dead. Just when the crowd was losing hope, Malik opened his eyes and stood to their gasps. The wound in his chest stopped bleeding and when he ripped open his shirt he showed the crowd that the wound had been miraculously healed. He turned to Justin and yelled to his guards, "Get him on the block! I will swing the ax myself."

His guards forced Justin to the block and onto his knees. They forced his head onto the block and tied it down. They held his body amid his struggles as Malik took the ax from the executioner. "A Great Prophet dies today as a great god lives." He swung the ax and Justin's head fell from his body and rolled a few feet down the stage. In horror, James grabbed Lilly and quickly exited the event area. The crowd erupted into a ferocious cheer, and Malik's supporters around the world had reinvigorated reason to call him a god among men and not only serve him, but worship him.

It had been two weeks since the Great Prophet Horus died and the world was beaming with anticipation for a great future with Malik as their ruler. He held a press conference regarding the severe drought that was hitting China. Freddy was there in the wings with Jennifer watching the worldwide press conference place. "On my great spirit, China will see rain. I have prayed and it shall be so because I deem it necessary."

The crowd was astonished by these bold words, but quickly people's phones began to ring with reports of rain in China mere minutes after Malik announced his promise. "To all those who continue to doubt me, watch and wonder." He held his hands up and slowly began to levitate off the ground. Everyone in attendance and around the world could no longer doubt that this man Malik had supernatural powers beyond that of any other man. Jennifer, feeling incredibly uncomfortable, asked Freddy if they could leave. He said yes to her but could not understand why she continued to fight the idea of Malik being somebody special. Freddy was getting increasingly annoyed and impatient with her Christian sentiments on the new world. He still loved her, but he had the worst feeling in the world that her religion may lead to a separation.

"Twenty more pushups and you will be done for the day," Francisco told Jose as he was working up a serious sweat in the compound gym. "We will begin Bible study in thirty minutes so I suggest you get something to eat after you are done."

He finished his pushups and then looked at his father. "So what did you think when you saw that I was elected into Congress?"

"I was worried that the enemy would get to you. The United States Government is run by the Illuminati. My magazine details all of my theories on the demonic actions of our government. They killed JFK, they began every war the United States has ever fought in, and they never landed on the moon. Ninety percent of all government conspiracy theories are actually true. The public is just too dumb to realize how smart they actually are."

"I am so overwhelmed by all of this. I need a smoke. Do you have any weed in here, Dad?"

"Marijuana? Did you not learn your lesson? Marijuana is a tool of the devil. Sure it is harmless if intentions are pure, but weed brings out the innermost sins of a person. It is a gateway to communication with other dimensions. Didn't you wonder why the voices came so strong after you started smoking? It opened up a gateway in your soul. When God put marijuana in the Garden of Eden he intended it for only spiritual use. But the influence of the devil corrupted man's relationship with the holy plant. Only a few can attain the original spiritual benefits of smoking weed. No Jose, you are no longer allowed to smoke the devil's plant. Try to focus on the Lord only, not quenching your physical body."

"OK, Father, I understand."

James and Lilly had left Jerusalem for Ethiopia and The Garden compound outside of the village of Aboto. There they hoped to find any remaining clerics who could help them in their quest for vengeance. When they got to the compound they found a handful of loyal clerics who swore their allegiance to the true and proper Prophet Horus. James and Lilly also decided to wed. Their ceremony was small and fast, but true love had survived that day. After the marriage and days of planning, they set off for South Africa where they would start the recruitment process. James used social media to announce that the true Prophet Horus had arrived to lead Africa to its freedom. The continent-wide interest in James was growing and he only had to tap into it to succeed at his mission.

Freddy and Jennifer were having a lovely Christmas dinner, to celebrate the birth of Jennifer's Savior. Freddy did not care much for it, but he wanted to try and make her happy. She was increasingly growing uncomfortable with the rhetoric of Malik and the Khalifa who ruled the land they lived on. Malik was completely turning away from God, cursing all religions, even Islam in private. Jennifer figured that she could at least enjoy this holy day in peace with her husband when there was a knock at the door. Freddy got up from the table and walked over to answer it, "Hello, who is it?"

"Secretary-General Jabbar has called an emergency council meeting. You must come at once, Professor."

"OK, let me get ready. I will be right there."

Freddy was frustrated. He had told Malik that he wanted the day off to enjoy Christmas with his wife. Nonetheless Malik was in charge and Freddy had to obey, so he told his quickly angered wife the news and got ready and left. When he got to the meeting the entire council was there waiting for him. "Please take a seat, Professor, so we can begin," said Malik.

Freddy took his seat and Malik started his announcement, "We are having growing reports of terrorist plots and subversion all over the world. Our UN forces have been attacked on every continent by those who are not willing to accept my rightful position. So in response to these threats, I want to implement a policy that will better allow us to control and subdue the population. Starting at the end of next month, we will enact a mandatory installation of the X-chip on all world citizens who are medically able to have the device. All currency and passports will be located on the X-chip, so no one can buy or sell or travel internationally without special permission to not have the X-chip. Not only will it diminish the technological gap between countries, it will also unify and connect the world on a seamless communication device. This is part of my plan to create a world without borders, a great new world where we can communicate and teach each other across boundaries and languages. This will be an important part of that plan."

He had finished talking and the council blasted him with applause and approval. They showered him with praise and positive remarks. Freddy approved the measure as well. He loved his own X-chip and he could see the wonderful possibilities this technology could bring to the world. He knew Jennifer could not have the chip because of her low eosinophil white blood cell count, so he hoped his installation would keep the Secretary-General satisfied. Freddy was seeing that Malik wanted to turn the world into a world of science and reason, not gods and superstitions. His appreciation for the secretary-general was growing by the day.

Chapter 32

James had been traveling through South Africa for weeks gathering fighters for his raiding army. He had a group of about 300 men in his fighting force, and he wanted to put them to the test to show his growing strength and ferocity in the field of battle. The first target they chose was a UN military barracks. They attacked at dawn, surprising the UN soldiers and catching them off guard. Within the hour they had dispatched all resistance and taken over the barracks. They took valuable documents and information, along with a large cache of weapons. After they were done they burned the barracks to the ground. News quickly spread throughout South Africa that Horus' Army had returned. Thousands upon thousands of men arrived to join the African Freedom Army over the few weeks. More military success and James' skillful promotion of himself led to thousands, even millions of men coming to his side.

After multiple successes on the battlefield, James decided it was time to launch a full scale attack on all UN forces in South Africa. The attack lasted three days, but in the end the Great Prophet Horus' Army prevailed and drove the UN forces across the border fleeing north. More men came to James and more weapons collected from barracks and local leaders were growing his army at a tremendous rate. He continued his march north with his millions of black fighting men, driving the UN forces farther north each day.

"I am glad the angel told you who the other Witness would be," Francisco said. "I had always thought Horus and Ethiopia would provide the other Witness. They had Jesus and the Lord in their hearts. Even though the Great Prophet Horus would most definitely be fighting for his own people, I think the Lord will help us sway him from war to join the Holy cause in these end times. Great Prophets are popping up everywhere from orders around the world. The Order of Rome has found their Great Prophet, the new Pope that was just elected. The Order of the Buddha has a sixteen-year-old monk who was born with special powers. He has been meditating for three straight years. Men and women from all of Asia have travelled to see him in person. Millions are flocking to the Buddhist faith. Former Secretary-General and now Zone One leader Lenz Krause has led Germany into a golden age of wealth and prosperity. He is the Great Prophet of the Fourth Reich. The Order of the Mahdi believes that the great Khalifa is their holy Prophet sent to take over the world for Islam. The Order of the Illuminatus believes that Malik is their Great Prophet, sent to place control over the entire world for their unholy cause.

"The age of the Great Prophets has arrived, my son, and we are running out of time. We must go to Africa to find and speak with the Great Prophet Horus and tell him that he must assume his position on your side as the other Great Witness of Revelation. He may not be dissuaded from his pursuit of vengeance on our visit, but we must at least put the idea in his head, give him our contact information, and let the Lord do the rest."

"When are we leaving?"

"We leave in two weeks. I have a loyal Christian who will smuggle us in his plane to Africa. We must take your mother and all Christians who are close to you. I know the Great Deception is coming soon and we must be in the Holy Land for your ministry. We cannot afford to try and come back to the United States when Israel is so close to Africa. I will meet you in Dallas in two weeks because that is where my friend Randall will pick us up."

Jose left the underground installation to urgently go home. He told his mother the plans and she readily accepted. Freddy wanted to bring both his friend's Cylan "CC" Chiap and Lorenzo Daugherty but Lorenzo wanted no part of it. Lorenzo did not believe in any of the story that Jose was telling him. He did all he could to save him, so he would have to leave it up to Jesus to turn his heart in time. CC was very receptive to the amazing story Jose had told him, and had faith that Jose was indeed a Great Prophet sent by God to warn the world of impending judgment. So Jose recruited his mother Carmela and his friend CC.

His father Francisco brought his end times crew of himself, Denard, Yolon, and Sam the tech geek. The seven of them gathered in Dallas and flew off for Africa together on a great mission of the Lord. Francisco already had Christian loyalists who were working underground in Jerusalem who would house them and keep them safe. Francisco's entire life had been preparing for this moment when he would lead his son to be one of the last Holy Messengers of God.

It took a month to get to Africa and find James on his warpath, but Jose and his father Francisco did through his Christian connections. They requested a meeting with James saying that the Great Prophet Elijah had come to talk with him. Meeting another Great Prophet piqued James' interest and he arranged for the meeting on the 20th of March, 2019.

When Jose and Francisco came into the encampment they saw a swarm of activity. The African Freedom Army was growing at a tremendous rate, faster than James had expected. The AFA was marching soundly through Africa, conquering the lands of their people. Jose and Francisco walked into the command center and introduced themselves to James and Lilly. "It is a pleasure to meet you, Great Prophet Elijah. Whatever do I owe this pleasure of your visit?"

"I have come to meet you, Great Prophet Horus, to beg you to give up your war effort and join me in Jerusalem to begin our Holy Testimony. You are the other Witness of Revelation, the Great Prophet Moses reborn. I know the Lord has been speaking to you as He has been speaking to me. I have had visions of our joining together just as I am sure you have too."

"Yes I have had visions of oil and a Hispanic man such as yourself, but you have come at the wrong time. We are conquering the lands of our people, taking them from the brutal and foreign hands of the UN and the Zone Five Army. God has been on our side, guiding us to victory every day. Why would He want his Great Black Prophet to abandon his Holy cause for justice?"

"He wants you to do it because Jesus did not sacrifice himself on the cross for men to go to war over pride, vengeance, and power. He sacrificed himself to have peace and love in the world in His Holy name. Please, disband your army and tell them to all begin preparing for the end times which are already upon us. We are running out of time. The Anti-Christ is among us and he is set to enact the ending of our world. You must trust me, Great Prophet. I have travelled all of this way to plead with you to join me at my side as the second Great Witness of Revelation."

"I am sorry, but my answer is no."

Jose looked at his father, who gave him a nod and a look that everything was going to be OK. Now was the time to trust that the Lord would make things right. "OK, we will leave you our contact information in Jerusalem. We will pray for you, James."

They gathered themselves and left back to the crew that was waiting at the underground Christian safe house. Jose had faith that the Lord would save James from himself and deliver him to the Holy Land where he would begin his rightful mission.

Malik's Great Muslim and UN Army had gathered on the border of Ethiopia to push back the AFA army. It was going to be a massive battle with millions of men fighting, and millions more dead. It took all night for James to get to sleep. He was tossing and turning with horrible feelings in his soul. In his deep sleep he had a vision. He saw all the men on the battlefield, on both sides, dying and spilling their blood for their race or religion. The horror of the battle was shown to him in full during his dream. Just when James thought it couldn't get any worse, he saw a glowing vision of a man in white. He came close to James and closer, until James could make out who he was. He appeared to be his Lord and Savior Jesus Christ. He told James, "Seek me, not yourself."

He said it over and over again until James woke up in a cold sweat. He was disappointed in himself that he let things get this far. This was not what he wanted with himself. He did not want to conquer and rule, he wanted to serve. The only way he knew how to serve God was to give up the war and join Jose, the Great Prophet Elijah, in Jerusalem. He immediately called for a press conference where he said he was giving up the war. He told his men to return home and pray and go to church, because the end times were among them. He pleaded for the end to war and suffering and gave a prayer to the Lord Christ to close. Lilly came up to him and gave him a warm embrace and kiss. She knew he was doing the right thing. His soldiers, disappointed in him, called him a coward and spit when he walked by. The entire world would call James a coward for running from the battlefield. He knew better than to listen to the world in these dark times. He made arrangements to be smuggled into Jerusalem with Lilly. Per Jose's instructions, he also arranged to have their families come out to Jerusalem for protection. The end times were here, and Christians must flock to the Holy Land for protection against the inevitable might of the Antichrist.

James and Lilly arrived in Jerusalem a few days after their respective families did. Their families and Lilly went into hiding while James stayed above ground with Jose and Francisco to begin their intense physical and spiritual training.

Chapter 33

Freddy came home after another long night at the Mars command center. Jennifer had been at church praying all day for many things, but most importantly her husband. The Christians at the local church, along with Jennifer herself, have been extremely worried about the direction the new secretary-general was taking the world. They felt as though his miracles and speech against the Lord were all demonic. They feared that he may be the Antichrist. Jennifer told Freddy these things when he came home but he wanted nothing of it.

He was growing tired of her Christian ramblings and verbalized that to her. Jennifer was stunned and hurt by his words. She left the room in tears as Freddy stood there sturdy in his convictions and refusing to give in to her delusional ramblings about his friend Malik. Freddy enjoyed his anti-religious stance, and he felt as though his miracles were a gift from the universe to help show people that man has the power and not some invisible being in the sky. Their relationship was still sturdy, but things were slowly beginning to unravel.

It had been two years since Jose and James started their training. They were in peak physical condition and their mental sharpness was at an all-time high. Through tedious studying of the Word they had become novice biblical scholars. They knew the time of their service was nearing when Jose had a vision. He envisioned a great lie that took many members of the faith away from Jesus. He saw that it was coming soon and he warned all of their company to beware and be prepared.

Freddy and Jennifer's marriage had been rocky these past two years but they had managed through it. The Mars project was running smoothly and all dark matter production was humming at a steady pace. Freddy was in the Mars command center as they were digging deeper into the Martian crust for more dark matter. Suddenly they got a report from the front lines of the mining expedition that they had discovered something. They took a camera down there to show Freddy and the command center what they saw. It was a large metal door buried in the Martian red soil. They brushed it back with their tools and revealed a door handle. With Freddy's permission they entered the building. After they entered and turned on their bright lights to illuminate the room, they discovered that the building was a lavish temple with pictures and drawings over smooth beautiful metallic walls. The pictures all depicted Earth in catastrophe.

Men were running from great balls of fire falling from the sky. It was all so beautiful yet daunting to all who witnessed it. As they entered the next room, they saw that this was the main room of the temple. Here what they saw astonished everyone involved. They saw a giant statue of a man who undoubtedly resembled Malik Jabbar, secretary-general. Freddy told them to stop and examine the statue, which had some sort of foreign alien writing on it. One of the scientists checked his reader and saw that the air had plenty of oxygen to breathe. The technology needed to power such an elaborate temple must be highly advanced. Just when they could not expect any more surprises, a side door opened and out walked three nine-foot-tall gray-skinned lizard humanoid creatures. They had yellow eyes with jet black lines that seemed to move independently of one another. They spoke to the men in English, shocking the crew and the command center further.

"Greetings humans, we have been waiting for your arrival. The time is short and you must take us back to Earth. Great misery and pain are coming to Earth unless you heed our warning. A great god of a man was born to you. His appearance is carved into the great statue. We call him, Yasua, the savior of the solar system. We are the Leedite race of Mars, and we have been spared by our great god to try and help the human race, which our people started on Earth. Our lives have been prepared for this great day when the Leedites and humans rejoin each other in harmony.

"Our planet was destroyed much in the same fashion your planet will be as well soon. We were destroyed under judgment from the great god. In order to satisfy the hunger of the gods, all mankind must pray to the Yasua and give him their spiritual energy. Only he, with the power of all mankind, will be strong enough to repel the attack from the heavens. Please take us with you back to Earth so we can spread this message to all in time to save your planet."

Freddy immediately gave the OK for the Leedites to join a shuttle back to Earth.

Thirty days later came the day of the Leedites' arrival. There was much fanfare around the world for the alien visitors. World leaders from every country came to welcome the visitors to Earth. As the shuttle landed and the bay opened up, the crowd oohed and ahhed at the size and look of our distant relatives. The Leedites came to the podium with Malik and Adiel and said hello in every human language. Then they began speaking in the most common tongue, which was English. "We have been studying your race for thousands of years. We have seen all and know all about your people. Believe us when we say that your beliefs and gods are all manifestations of what we brought to you. There was no Buddha, there was no Jesus, there is no one God. We are a universe of many gods. Each god has his sphere of influence over different galaxies and solar systems.

"The god of this galaxy is called J'huan, the great unknown. He birthed a great savior to our people, but we would not heed his holy warning of the judgment of J'huan. We come to you now, people of Earth, to tell you that the judgment Mars received will soon come to Earth if you do not drop your folly religions and worship the savior Yasua, Malik Jabbar the Great. Witness his power now in front of the whole world. Watch as his servant Adiel prays on him and transforms us into an earthen animal."

Adiel took his position and prayed out to the god J'huan and prayed out to Malik's spirit. He shot out his arms and yelled and a plume of smoke arose around the Leedite. In an instant the Leedite was transformed into a baby bear. He growled and stood up. The crowd, initially astonished by yet another miracle from Adiel, broke out into applause. Adiel rose his hands again and then shot them out, and the smoke came back, transforming the Leedite back into itself. The international delegation was thrilled, but the Jewish inhabitants of Israel were beginning to sour on Adiel and his antics. They believed him to be the Mashiach, the soon-to-be restorer of the Holy Temple and restorer of the Jewish law in the land. They dealt with his blasphemies for now, but further provocation could lead to altercation.

"We got the website up and running guys," Sam said while punching away at the keyboard. "The encryption I put on here would take a supercomputer years to figure out. This baby will be safe for the duration of the end times. Make sure you two both get more practice with the video camera. I am going to give you enough batteries to last for five years so it will be plenty good. The video will be up streaming on the website with commentary from our staff."

James was very pleased. "Excellent news, Sam. I have our first article written and ready to go. It deals with how these Leedites are actually shape-shifting Nephilim, as described in Genesis 6:4 where it states, 'There were giants on Earth in those days and also afterward (the flood), when the sons of God came in to the daughters of men and they bore children to them.' These Leedite lizard men are the offspring of demonic fallen angels and women from thousands of years ago.

"The Illuminati have been in contact with them for thousands of years, planning for the conquest of Earth in their lord Satan's holy name. We must spread this news far and wide. We will be hated. We will be targets of negativity, but the message must go out. This is the Great Deception, men must not turn to the devil."

Sam took the article off the flash drive and posted it. Traffic was slow at first, but over the next two weeks it was reaching hundreds of thousands of visits per day. True Christians worldwide were ready for the message of the Witnesses in these dark times.

Lilly tried her best to force her husband to eat. "James, you need to eat something. It has been three days."

James shrugged off her suggestion. "I am just not hungry. I cannot explain it but I feel full all the time. It is like I am being nourished already."

Francisco came into the room and heard the tail end of what he said. "Yes James, you are beginning to transform into the Witness. Your body will not require sustenance, as you will be totally sustained by the power of the Lord. Your Holy powers will come soon as well. The time is near, James. I just got back from telling Jose to prepare to say goodbye to everyone. Once the abomination that causes desolation takes place, the prophecy shall begin. Get your rest and please your wife as much as you can these next few days. The Lord will be calling for you soon."

Chapter 34

The media trucks were lining the street and hundreds of thousands of people packed the alleyways. Large television screens were set up outside to show what was happening inside of the Jewish Holy Temple. Malik had a major global announcement to share with the world. Freddy walked inside of the Holy Temple with his wife Jennifer, proudly displaying her cross necklace her father gave her before she left. There were two large boxes on both sides of the temple, and Freddy was definitely curious to see what was under them.

The world and especially the Jewish people, watched and listened as Malik took the stage. "Welcome, my people, to the Holy Temple of Solomon and David. We are gathered here today for a very special announcement. I have considered the words and council of the Leedites, and I have decided to place a ban on all religious worship that does not involve my holy name. I am your god now, and for all time. All religious symbols and temples worldwide will be changed to a golden Y for Yasua, the great savior of mankind. You all must worship me or face imprisonment or certain death. The Great Khalifa has agreed to establish me as god, as well as the Pope. The Great Buddha will acknowledge me as lord as well. The time to save Earth is now. Follow me so I can save all of our lives and souls."

The crowd was in shock by his words, but when they lifted the boxes and showed two golden statues of Malik, the murmur of disapproval from the Jewish people turned from a murmur to an uproar. They screamed insults and threats to Malik inside and outside of the temple. His guards had to quickly usher him away to the motorcade. The crowd started attacking the cars with rocks and bottles, the guards inside the cars opened fire on the crowd, killing many.

The cars took off running over people making their way to the exits to flee the city. They made their escape, leaving hundreds dead in their wake. The abomination that causes desolation had occurred, and the Jewish people started a war against Malik and his UN forces. Malik was lucky he escaped with his life, and Adiel was crushed that his people turned on him. Israel, with the huge influx of dark matter wealth, had built a massive army.

Unfortunately, the wealth of Malik and the UN was even greater. Even with the help of the United States and Western allies, the Jewish people could not stand a chance. Russia, China, Africa, and Southeast Asia all declared their allegiance to Malik. The great war of the end times had begun.

Freddy pleaded with his wife to take off her cross and adhere to the ban but she refused. She laid down an ultimatum. "You either leave your job and come with me into hiding in Jerusalem, or you leave me and continue your quest for power and science alongside your blasphemous false savior."

Freddy finally gave up on trying to fix his wife and make her believe in Malik. "I cannot save you now, Jennifer. If you leave me to be by myself, you are on your own."

Tears welled up in her eyes and she ran away. Freddy did not know where she was going or if she knew anyone in Jerusalem. He did not care. She was already dead to him.

Both James and Jose put on the sack cloths they were told to wear in Scripture as they prepared to leave the hiding spot for one last time. They kissed their loved ones goodbye and headed off for the Wailing Wall. They heard about the abomination that causes desolation and they knew this was their time. The Holy Spirit came upon them and they knew they had the spirit of the Lord in them. They took the video equipment and the supplies with them on their trek to the Wailing Wall. When they got there, the Jewish people were in a frenzy because the time of war had come upon them. Nobody put much care into the two men as they set up the video equipment. They turned on the lights and begin their prophesying.

"Listen to the words of the Holy Scripture," Jose screamed.

James continued, "Blessed is he who reads and those who hear the words of this prophecy, and keep those things which are written in it; for the time is near."

Jose yelled with a booming voice that miraculously filled the sky. "The first of the Seven Seals has been broken, and the abomination that causes desolation has already come upon us. Your time to repent and save yourself is growing smaller by the day. Take heed to our warning. We are the Two Witnesses as described in Revelation Chapter Eleven. Hear the words of our Lord as He describes us, 'And I will give power to my two witnesses and they will prophesy one thousand two hundred and sixty days, clothed in sackcloth. These are the two olive trees and the two lamp stands standing before the God of the earth. And if anyone wants to harm them, fire proceeds from their mouth and devours their enemies. And if anyone wants to harm them, he must be killed in this manner. These have power to shut heaven, so that no rain falls in the days of their prophecy.' We are the Two Witnesses, and we are here to warn you, sinful world, of your impending doom. We now begin our Holy Testimony. Many of you Christians will die in the coming years, leaving only 144,000 of you to join us in the end. However, know that you will be draped in white in heaven as God's Holy children. Now, listen to scripture, 'And I looked, and behold, a white horse. He who sat on it had a bow; and a crown was given to him, and he went out conquering and to conquer.' That is the first seal which was broken. The rider on the white horse is the Antichrist, your false savior Yasua, Malik Jabbar.

"He has been given permission from the Holy Lord of lords to conquer as he sees fit. Beware the rider on the white horse and his unholy lies. The Nephilim were here, spawned by the unholy angels, to trick your world. Do not let the evil of Satan into your hearts. Take the mark of the beast out of your foreheads and hands and cry out to the Lord, 'You are my Lord and Savior Jesus, through your blood I am eternally saved.' Beware the dark times that are coming."

They continued preaching the message of God all through the days and nights with no break. Crowds were gathering and news cameras were coming to watch them. As their message against Malik began to spread, anger and frustration over their lack of punishment from the great Yasua was beginning to grow. Adiel sent a special team of loyal Jews to take out the Two Witnesses in the middle of the night. A small crowd was around them as they were yelling out their warnings and preaching the scripture. The team went in guns blazing, to dispatch the two men.

But as they approached and shot at them, their bullets were swallowed up with fire from their mouths. As the men approached to attack them by hand, they were swallowed up by a stream of fire and turned to ash. The remaining men fled the scene. The crowd who witnessed this attack and the people watching on the news at home were speechless. How could these men have these special powers? Where did they get it? The wise heeded the Witnesses' warning and fled to Jerusalem for protection, while the hardheaded and the wicked thought that the Witnesses were sent by their devil to trick them and guide them away from the holy Yasua.

The next day, the two Witnesses announced the coming of the second rider as battles and skirmishes broke out between the West and

Jerusalem against the forces of the world and the international UN. James yelled out, "Listen to Scripture, 'He opened the second seal, and I heard a second living creature saying, 'Come and see.' Another horse, fiery red, went out. And it was granted to the one who sat on it to take peace from the earth, and that people should kill one another; and there was given to him a great sword.' The red horse and its rider are upon us world, O' weep for the dead on the battlefield, O' weep for all mankind."

Millions died over the next month in battles all across the world. Malik had much success on the battlefield globally, conquering large chunks of land. His forces were struggling against a rabid and powerful Jewish army, but Malik knew the Jews could not sustain it.

The global wars destroyed crop fields worldwide, and millions of men and women in the workforce were forced on the battle field. This caused a great shortage of food and supplies for people of all wealth statuses. The world was starving. The Witnesses announced the coming of the next horseman and the breaking of the third seal. Jose began, "O' woe to the world and what is to come. The third seal and the third horseman have come to the world. Listen to scripture, 'So I looked, and behold, a black horse, and he who sat on it had a pair of scales in his hand. And I heard a voice in the midst of the four living creatures saying, 'A quart of wheat for a denarius, and three quarts of barley for a denarius, and do not harm the oil and the wine."

"A denarius is pay for a day's work. As you have been seeing at the market, food for a night of dinner is beginning to cost a day's wages. These were all foretold to John by the Holy Lord. Listen to the Scripture, read the Scripture, save yourselves O' world, save yourselves."

Freddy was in the council room for the meeting, eager to hear more news from the front line. Reports were coming in that Jerusalem was surrounded by the UN army. Malik had been waiting for word from the attack all day when the phone rang during the meeting. He answered, "Yes this is Yasua. Yes, uh huh, what!? How could that happen? Retreat our men back across the border until our doctors can figure this out."

He slammed the phone down on the table. Enraged, he told the council what happened, "Our army was stricken by an infectious skin eating disease seemingly overnight. Millions have been hospitalized and died. Half of our army has been incapacitated. We are forced to retreat and leave the blasphemers to themselves for now. We are running out of time though, global disaster is here upon us and I am the only man who can save us. Why are these rebel Jews and Christians so stupid?"

Freddy spoke up, "We must deal with these men and women of ill faith harshly. Public execution and killing of young ones should all be acceptable in these urgent times. We must stress the importance of all men worshipping you, Great Yasua."

"Yes that is a very good idea. Let's increase our violence against the nonbelievers. They do not need to be spared. Their death will only increase the power of those left on Earth to worship me."

The Witnesses announced the coming of the fourth horseman, the pale horse rider. It says in Revelation 6:8, "So I looked, and behold, a pale horse. And the name of him who sat on it was Death, and Hades followed with him. And power was given to them over a fourth of the earth, to kill with sword, with hunger, with death, and by the beasts of the earth."

As Jose and James were prophesying the Scripture, they stopped when they noticed a glow starting to emerge on their foreheads. They saw the glow slowly form into a cross on their foreheads. They knew the time of the fifth seal had come. Jose announced the coming of the fifth seal, and as he was getting to the end of his speaking it was interrupted by a woman in the crowd with a hood over her forehead. Jose looked closely and saw that it was his estranged wife Juanita Mills. She whispered loud enough for them to hear, "My Love, my Hero, I have come back to you. I am sorry for the things I said and did to you. I was forced to do it all, I swear it. I was scared they would kill me if I ever tried to leave and I have been afraid in my house all these years. But when I saw you here on the wall I knew I had to come see you.

"I have been praying every day for my own salvation, but I knew I would not reach heaven until I came back to my husband and made things right."

Jose was slow to believe her. "How do I know you are not lying again?"

She looked at him and pealed back the hood on her sweater, to reveal a bright cross implanted on her forehead. "Oh my love you are saved!"

The pair ran up to each other and kissed with a long embrace. "It is not safe for you here, though. Malik and Adiel have agents all around watching us. Here, call this number and my father will be able to connect with you and take you underground. I love you, Jay. I always have. Stay safe until these dark days are over. I will see you in Heaven."

"I love you too, my Hero," she said with tears in her eyes as she left to go call his father.

Malik stood up violently from the council chamber and slammed his hands on the desk. "These Christians from around the world need to die for their blasphemies. The man I assigned to the task has a weak heart. He is not producing the numbers of dead that I want to see."

Freddy, zealous with faith in the Yasua and eager to make him happy, spoke up. "I am eager to take over the position as non-believer commissioner. I will do all that I can to punish and kill the non-believers."

"Thank you for your volunteering, Professor. I think you would be the perfect man for the job. Adiel is still trying to find ways to kill the Two Witnesses without sacrificing any more of his men. He is pouring over the Christian Bible to get any clues on how to kill them. I hope one day he comes up with a solution because I want to see them dead!"

"I will pray for a fast resolution, my Yasua."

It was time for the Christian faithful to begin their migration to Jerusalem. Christians were being murdered all over the world and the only place where they could truly be kept safe was in Jerusalem. The Witness announced the migration of the 144,000, spiritual Israel, the last true church of Christ and the last Christians on Earth.

James yelled out, "Beware the coming of the six trumpets, which will be man's final warning to repent and call on the Savior before the Harvest. I have great sorrow for those men of folly who are left behind after the Harvest and have to suffer through the bowls of judgment."

The final seal before the trumpets was near and the witnesses announced it to the world before it happened. "'O' woe to the world for what is about to come, I say listen to what the Scripture says: 'I looked when He opened the sixth seal, and behold, there was a great earthquake; and the sun became black as sackcloth of hair, and the moon became like blood. And the stars of heaven fell to the earth as a fig tree drops its late figs when it is shaken by a mighty wind. Every mountain and island was moved out of its place. And the kings of the earth, the great men, the rich men, the commanders, the mighty men, every slave and every free man hid themselves in the caves and in the rocks of the mountains.' This will soon come to you, O' world of unbelievers. Repent, the hour of the Lord is at hand!"

When he was done saying his warning the earth gave a mighty shake and his words came into truth by the will of the Lord. Flaming rocks fell from the sky and the earth moved violently. Every man and woman in the world who was not Christian fled to the mountains and hills during this mighty rumble. The sun became black as night and the moon blood red.

Two weeks later the Witnesses announced the next catastrophe. "The seventh seal has been broken. A great angel will throw his fiery censar to the earth, causing great thundering, lightning, and an earthquake." Shortly these things came to pass in the world, as another mighty earthquake shook the world and killed many.

Jose yelled out, "Beware O' wicked world, the first of the trumpets is about to sound! Listen to Scripture and beware, 'The first angel sounded: And hail and fire followed, mingled with blood, and they were thrown to the earth. And a third of the trees were burned up, and all the green grass was burned up.' These horrible things will soon come to pass." Shortly after Jose's message the hail and fire came.

Malik prayed all he could to pass the Holy storm but his efforts were futile. Just as Jose said, a third of the trees were gone and all the green grass was burned up. Many people died in vain to hide from the attack.

Scientists in the space command center picked up the mighty space rock months before it arrived. Malik and the world prayed for deliverance from its impact but there was no use. The two Witnesses saw this coming and foretold the outcome over the six months since the first trumpet sounded. James spoke, "Listen to scripture and beware, 'The second angel sounded: And something like a great mountain burning with fire was thrown into the sea, and a third of the sea became blood. And a third the living creatures in the sea died, and a third the ships destroyed.' Listen to these words foretold in the book of Revelation. Heed our warning and repent for your sins before it is too late!"

Shortly thereafter the massive rock fell from the sky and hit the ocean. True to His holy word, a third of the creatures in the sea perished, and a third of the sea became like blood, and a third of the ships of the ocean fell to the bottom of the sea.

Adiel came to the council meeting that day to announce his plans for the Two Witnesses. "They are bringing destruction and doom to our planet and it has to stop. I have calculated the radiation coming from that site, and if my calculations are correct, in two years they will lose their power and will be allowed to die."

Malik was frustrated with the amount of time he had to wait, but he appreciated the good news. "The Coward and the Crazy need to die, those Two Witnesses are sucking essential prayer power away from me. I will never be able to stop this destruction without them two dead!"

"Beware the warning of the third trumpet," James yelled out. "Listen to scripture and take heed of its warning, 'The third angel sounded: And a great star fell from heaven, burning like a torch, and it fell on a third of the rivers and on the springs of water. The name of the star is Wormwood. A third of the waters became wormwood, and many men died from the water, because it was bitter.' The mighty star Wormwood is on its way now. You can see it burning in the sky. Before it is too late and you perish, you must turn to the Lord Jesus Christ for salvation."

A few days later the great flaming star fell onto Earth and performed the tasks foretold by the Holy Lord.

"Here comes the sounding of the fourth trumpet, all those nonbelievers listen to our words. Listen to Scripture! 'Then the fourth angel sounded: A third of the sun was struck, a third of the moon, and a third of the stars, so that a third of them were darkened. A third of the day did not shine and likewise the night.' These things will shortly come to pass, and you will know it is the work of the Lord because I told you they would happen." Shortly thereafter the things that they said came to pass, and the sun and moon and stars were struck of their brightness, and the day and night were shortened.

"O' woe to the world for the wrath of the Lord is coming upon you. Beware the pain and punishment of the fifth trumpet! Listen to Scripture and beware! 'Then the fifth angel sounded: And I saw a star fallen from heaven to the earth. To him was given the key to the bottomless pit. And he opened the bottomless pit, and smoke arose out of the pit like the smoke of a great furnace. So the sun and the air were darkened because of the smoke of the pit. Then out of the smoke locusts came upon the earth. And to them was given power, as the scorpions of the earth have power. They were commanded not to harm the grass of the earth or any green thing, or any tree, but only those men who do not have the seal of God on their foreheads. And they were not given authority to kill them, but to torment them for five months. Their torment was like the torment of a scorpion when it strikes of man. In those days men will seek death and will not find it; they will desire to die, and the death will flee from them.' Beware these unholy creatures which will soon come upon you. They are coming to bring you to your knees in the sight of the Lord. Beware!" Soon after they spoke these words the air and the sky filled with smoke from the bottomless pit and locusts went out to torment the world.

Freddy had been under attack by the evil locusts for weeks. The pain was insufferable! He was driving in his hover car to a dinner meeting with Malik about the continued pursuit of non-believers when the car suddenly died. He pulled over to the side of the road and kicked his car in frustration. The locusts were burning his skin and he screamed out in pain for help, any kind of help. Just then he saw a tall man in a white robe walk up to him slowly from the distance. As the man got closer the locusts began to flee. He arrived to Freddy, and asked him what was the problem?

Freddy said, "My damn car broke down and these locusts were killing me. I am late for a meeting and nothing is going right."

The soft-faced man spoke to him sweetly. "If you want peace in your heart, stop seeking my people."

"My people?" Freddy looked again into the man's eyes and warmth came into his heart, and for the first time in his life, he had peace. "I know you! I know you!" Freddy's eyes began to water and he fell on his knees in the face of Holiness. "Oh Lord I am sorry for all I have done! Please have forgiveness on me. What must I do to wash the filth of my actions from my soul? I want to be with you Lord. You are my Savior."

"My son, you have done enough already. Look into the reflection on the car window." He looked at the window and saw a glowing cross on his forehead. He had the mark! He had heard what the Witnesses had said about the seal of God. Excited beyond words, he looked up to thank Jesus but He had already disappeared. Freddy knew what he had to do! He had to join the other believers and find his wife. The first place he would look would be at the Wailing Wall with the Two Witnesses.

Freddy got to the wall as the Witnesses were announcing the sixth trumpet. Jose yelled out, "Beware O' wicked world, the judgment of the sixth trumpet is coming to you. Repent now and save your souls in the eyes of the Lord. Listen to Scripture! 'The sixth angel sounded: And I heard a voice from the four horns of the golden altar which is before God, saying to the sixth angel who had the trumpet, 'Release the four angels who are bound at the great river Euphrates.' So the four angels, who had prepared for the hour and day and month and year, were released to kill a third of mankind."

Jose finished his message and looked out into the crowd and saw Freddy, with the mark on his forehead that only Christians could see. He went to the crowd and ushered him close to him, away from other ears. "Oh Professor Slater I am glad to see you. What a great sight to my eyes to see you are saved. I take it you came here to find fellow Christians and your lovely wife?"

"My wife is alive!?"

"Yes, she is safe in hiding, where you must go also. Here take this number and call my father. He will meet up with you in the city and take you to the underground."

He turned back to the crowd and warned them again, "Repent O' sinners of this world. Repent!"

Freddy left and called the number. Francisco told him where to meet and after a few hours he came to get him. They went down several streets and dark alleyways before they came to a secret entrance to an underground compound. When they opened the door and went inside, there were thousands of Christians inside talking of the things to shortly come. He did not see his wife, but she immediately saw him.

"Oh my baby! I can't believe you are here right now! How did this happen?"

Freddy told her the story of meeting Jesus on the road like the Apostle Paul. She could not believe he had met Jesus and spoken with Him. The entire congregation was asking him questions about his visit from the Lord. After he satisfied their curiosity, he retired to a back room with his wife.

"What is going to happen to the Witnesses?" he asked Jennifer as he rubbed her legs.

"They will be dead very soon, and we will see the glory of the Lord when He raises them back up from the dead in three days."

They talked more about everything they had been through over the last few years without each other and thoroughly enjoyed each other's company in the privacy of their room.

The Witnesses were out prophesying the final trumpet when they saw Adiel in disguise holding a special gold rifle. They knew their time had come, as the days of their prophecy had reached twelve thousand and seventy-seven days. "Our last warning before our time has come," James said. "Soon after our death the final trumpet will sound. Listen to Scripture! 'Then the seventh trumpet sounded; and there were loud voices in heaven, saying, 'The kingdoms of this world have become the kingdoms of our Lord and of His Christ, and He shall reign forever and ever! Then the temple of God was opened in heaven, and the ark of His covenant was seen in His temple. And there were lightnings, noises, thundering, an earthquake, and great hail.' Beware these things as they come to pass, because soon after will be the harvest and thereafter the seven bowls of judgment!"

Jose and James joined hands and prayed out, "We come into your Holy service O' Lord, make our path to your heaven straight!" With that, Adiel took aim and shot them both in the chest, spilling their blood for the world to see. He quickly fled the scene with his loyal henchmen to go back to the UN side of the battlefield just outside of Jerusalem. The Crazy and the Coward were dead and the world rejoiced.

They exchanged gifts and threw massive parties. The men of the world left the bodies there to rot for they were too afraid to touch them.

In three and a half days, the world was astonished when the camera caught live the Two Witnesses rising from their death. The whole world gasped at this miracle, and all the eyes of the world saw them enter into a cloud from the heavens and whisk away to God's land in the sky. There was a great earthquake and seven thousand people died, just as it was foretold in the Holy Scripture.

The underground compound was vivacious with commotion. The UN Army had breached the Israeli defenses and they were coming straight for the city. Sensing this was their time, Francisco sent out the word to all the safe houses for the marked Christians to flee to the Mount of Olives, where the Lord would be taking them into Heaven. All 144,000 came to the mountain, in white robes and holding hands. They sang a song together that none of them knew the words to, only inspired by the Holy Spirit. They all sang out to the Lord as the UN Army came into the city and surrounded them. Malik spoke out to them, "Give up and surrender now or face certain death."

He gave this warning three times and none of the Christians moved from their spot. Freddy and Jennifer were nervous but they had faith. Freddy looked deep into her eyes and said, "I love you," as the cracking sound of gunfire fell upon the crowd. As soon as the firing had started it suddenly stopped. Freddy's vision went from darkness to all white, as his body was being lifted from the ground with the other believers into the air in a cloud where they met Jesus in the sky.

All Freddy could see was white for what seemed like hours, or days, or months, or years. He could not tell. Just when the sensation of all white was too much to bear, he suddenly found himself waking up in a ditch outside of the Temple of Solomon. He stood up and brushed himself off. He was still wearing his white robe. He looked out and saw multitudes of other Christians in white robes walking to the Temple. He looked desperately for his wife, and when he had given up hope, she found him. "We are here Freddy! We are here! Isn't this beautiful?"

She guided him to the temple and when he went inside the statues of Malik had been replaced by statues of Jesus on a donkey. "The Holy City of Jerusalem has been returned to us! This is the beginning of the thousand-year reign of Christ on Earth."

Up on the stage in the Temple Freddy saw a welcoming sight. He saw James with his wife Lilly, Jose with his wife Jay, and all of their families surrounding them singing hymns to the Lord. It was a beautiful day, a day none of them would ever forget for all of eternity.

All signs of the UN and unbelievers were wiped from the earth. The world was theirs to lift up the Holy word of God and Jesus our Savior. Freddy and Jennifer kissed and they made their way to their designated house to begin creating a family line which would last a thousand years.

Bibliography

"Ancient African Writing Systems and Knowledge." *Blogspot.com.*
  Accessed 2012.
  http://bafsudralam.blogspot.com/2009/06/naga.html.

"Bible Prophecy: Two Witnesses." *googk.com.* Accessed 2012.
  http://www.googk.com/Documents/Bible_Prophecy/Two_witnesse
  s.htm.

"CERN." Wikipedia. Accessed 2012.
  https://en.wikipedia.org/wiki/CERN.

"Dark Matter." *CERN.* Accessed 2012.
  http://home.cern/about/physics/dark-matter.

"Ethiopia." *Link Ethiopia.* Accessed 2012.
  https://www.linkethiopia.org/ethiopia/.

"Intersecting Storage Rings." Wikipedia. Accessed 2012.
  https://en.wikipedia.org/wiki/Intersecting_Storage_Rings.

"Large Hadron Collider." Wikipedia. Accessed 2012.
  https://en.wikipedia.org/wiki/Large_Hadron_Collider.

"Mashiach: The Messiah." *Jewfaq.org.* Accessed 2012.
  http://www.jewfaq.org/mashiach.htm.

"Muslim, Jewish, and Christian End-Times Prophecy Comparison."
  Contender Ministries. Accessed 2012.
  http://www.contenderministries.org/prophecy/eschatology.php.

"Nagas: The Ancient Warriors and Rulers of India." *Histhink.* Accessed

2012. https://histhink.wordpress.com/2011/02/12/nagas-the-ancient-warriors-rulers-of-india-dalits-dravidian/.

Pease, Allen and Barbara. *The Definitive Book of Body Language*. New York: Bantam Dell, 2004.

Perry, Richard H. "Last Days - Timeline." *Lastdaysmystery.info*. Accessed 2012. http://www.lastdaysmystery.info/revelation_timeline.htm/.

Perry, Richard H. *Of the Last Days: Listen, I Tell You a Mystery*. Ontario, Canada: Guardian Books, 2003.

"Quetzalcoatl." *Wikipedia*. Accessed 2012. https://en.wikipedia.org/wiki/Quetzalcoatl.

Ready, Romilla and Kate Burton. *Neuro-linguistic Programming for Dummies*. Chichester, England: John Wiley & Sons, 2004.

"Revelation Timeline." *Popular Issues*. Accessed 2012. http://www.allaboutpopularissues.org/revelation-timeline-faq.htm.

"Rome-Arno 1944." *history.army.mil*. Accessed 2012. http://www.history.army.mil/brochures/romar/72-20.htm.

"Texas's 30th Congressional District." *Wikipedia*. Accessed 2012. https://en.wikipedia.org/wiki/Texas's_30th_congressional_district.

"Texas Senate, District 23." *Wikipedia*. Accessed 2012. https://en.wikipedia.org/wiki/Texas_Senate,_District_23.

"The Arrivals part 1." *Youtube.com*. Accessed 2012. https://www.youtube.com/watch?v=YaqybvymYIE&list=PLCB70

4045F6979F23.

"The Black African Foundation of China: The First Chinese." *Rasta Livewire*. Accessed 2012. http://www.africaresource.com/rasta/sesostris-the-great-the-egyptian-hercules/the-black-african-foundation-of-china-the-first-chinese/.

"The Black Shogun: An Assessment of the African Presence in Early Japan." *Destee.com* Accessed 2012. https://destee.com/threads/the-black-shogun-an-assessment-of-the-african-presence-in-early-japan.69846/.

"The Temple, the Two Witnesses, and the Seventh Trumpet (Rev 11:1-19)." *Bible.org*. Accessed 2012. https://bible.org/seriespage/temple-two-witnesses-and-seventh-trumpet-rev-111-19 .

"The Two Witnesses of Revelation 11." *Thetwowitnesses.com*. Accessed 2012. http://www.thetwowitnesses.com/.

"Timeline for Revelation." *Rapturechrist.com*. Accessed 2012. http://www.rapturechrist.com/timeline.htm/.

"When Blacks Ruled the World." *Youtube.com*. Accessed 2012. https://www.youtube.com/watch?v=WKGRSkVvzqk.

"White blood cell." *Wikipedia*. Accessed 2012. https://en.wikipedia.org/wiki/White_blood_cell#Overview_table.